Praise for *Jimmy Bluefeather*

"[A] splendid, unique gem of a novel." —LIBRARY JOURNAL (Starred)

"What makes this story so appealing is the character Old Keb. He is as finely wrought and memorable as any character in contemporary literature and energizes the tale with a humor and warmth that will keep you reading well into the night." —THE NATIONAL OUTDOOR BOOK AWARD

"This is not just a well-crafted picture of an elder; it is unforgettable, in the direct lineage of *The Old Man and the Sea*." —DOUG PEACOCK, author of *In the Shadow of the Sabertooth*

"Heacox does a superb job of transcending his characters' unique geography to create a heartwarming, all-American story." —BOOKLIST

"Librarians, if you missed this book, order a few copies for your collection and be sure to promote it to anyone who loves beautifully written fiction driven by a strong sense of place and character." —WILDA WILLIAMS, *Library Journal*

"Kim Heacox's love for the land and people of Alaska shines forth in this character-driven saga, brimming with craft, humor, and deft turn of phrase." —NICK JANS, author of *A Wolf Called Romeo*

"A convergence of ocean, land, and spirit as only Kim Heacox can tell it, with wisdom, humor, and grace. A welcome new novel of relationships, forgiveness, and reinventing oneself." —DEB VANASSE, author of *Cold Spell*

"Every page glistens with authentic genius born from Kim Heacox's wise and deep-rooted sense of place. . . . The characters seem like people we've known; they ring true, and feel vivid." —CARL SAFINA, author of *Beyond Words: What Animals Think and Feel*

"With humor, passion, and respect, Kim Heacox brings us a voyage of discovery like no other. . . .You'll be torn between packing your bags for Crystal Bay and living more fully in your own storied place." —MARIA MUDD RUTH, author of *Rare Bird*

"Heacox, a writer and explorer of renown, offe
portrait that is rare in the literature of the forty-
—ANDROMEDA ROMANO-LAX, author of *Th*

T0164001

ave

Jimmy Bluefeather

A NOVEL

KIM HEACOX

ALASKA
NORTHWEST
BOOKS®

Library of Congress Cataloging-in-Publication Data
Heacox, Kim.
  Jimmy Bluefeather : a novel / Kim Heacox.
    pages ; cm
  ISBN 978-1-943328-71-0 (softbound)
  ISBN 978-1-941821-68-8 (hardcover)
  ISBN 978-1-941821-87-9 (e-book)
  I. Title.
  PS3608.E226J56 2015
  813'.6—dc23
                        2015007906

Edited by Tina Morgan and Kathy Howard
Designed by Vicki Knapton

Published by Alaska Northwest Books®
An imprint of Turner Publishing Company
4507 Charlotte Avenue, Suite 100
Nashville, TN 37209
(615) 255-2665
www.turnerbookstore.com

For the wild inhabitants of Icy Strait

"The canoes of these people are made of light wood, called *chaha* [red cedar], which grows to the southward. A canoe is formed out of a single trunk, and is, in some instances, large enough to carry sixty men. I saw several that were forty-five feet long; but the common ones do not exceed thirty feet. When paddled, they go fast in smooth water. The largest are used for war, or for transporting whole families from place to place. The smallest serve for fishing, or other purposes that require but few hands. They are ingeniously constructed."

CAPTAIN UREY LISIANSKI, 1814
A Voyage Round the World in the Years 1803–06
[journal entry from Sitka, Alaska, 1805]

PART ONE

the weight of air

USED TO BE it was hard to live and easy to die. Not anymore. Nowadays it was the other way around. Old Keb shook his head as he shuffled down the forest trail, thinking that he thought too much.

"Oyye . . ." he muttered, his voice a moan from afar.

He prodded the rain-soaked earth with his alder walking cane. For a moment his own weathered hand caught his attention—the way his bones fitted to the wood, the wilderness between his fingers, the space where Bessie's hand used to be.

Wet ferns brushed his pants in a familiar way. He turned his head to get his bearings, as only his one eye worked. The other was about as useful as a marble and not so pretty to look at. It had quit working long ago and sat there hitching a ride in his wrinkled face. The doctors had offered to patch it or plug it or toss it out the last time Old Keb was in Seattle, but he said no. Someday it might start working again and he didn't want to do all his seeing out of one side of his head. He was a man, for God's sake, not a halibut.

A wind corkscrewed through the tall hemlocks. Old Keb stopped to listen but had problems here too. He could stand next to a hot chain saw and think it was an eggbeater. All his ears did now was collect dirt and wax and grow crooked hairs of such girth and length as to make people think they were the only vigorous parts of his anatomy. He always fell asleep with his glasses on, halfway down his nose. He said he could see his dreams better that way, the dreams of bears when he remembered—when his bones remembered—waking up in the winter of his life.

Nobody knew how old he was. Not even Old Keb. He might have known once but couldn't remember. Somewhere around ninety-five was his guess, a guess he didn't share with any of his children, grandchildren, great-grand-children, great-great grandchildren, or the legions of cousins, nephews, nieces, friends, and doctors, who figured he was close to one hundred and were on a holy crusade to keep him alive.

All his old friends were dead, the ones he'd grown up with and made stories with. He'd outlived them all. He'd outlived himself.

He was born in a salmon cannery in Dundas Bay to a mother and father who managed to die before Keb had any memories of them. His mom was a beautiful woman (he'd been told), a Tlingit Indian with some Filipino and Portuguese thrown in, who got crushed by a tree that a good-for-nothing logger said would fall the other way. His dad was a Norwegian seine skipper who got drunk and walked off a pier and drowned. His Uncle Austin, his mother's brother, *du káak,* a *kaa sháade háni* clan leader, raised Keb and his brothers and sisters on the other side of Icy Strait from Crystal Bay, the memory place where long ago his people hunted and fished and picked berries and made the stories that held them together. All this before a great glacier got the crazy idea to come down from its mountain and swallow the entire bay like a whale swallows herring. Gone, every living thing buried in ice, the earth pounded silent beneath a cold carved moon. The hungry glacier evicted Old Keb's Tlingit ancestors and forced them to paddle their canoes south across big water where they built a new village—Jinkaat, Keb's home.

It's written in the rocks, Uncle Austin used to say. Nature doesn't lie. It might not tell you what you want to hear. It might be a brutal truth. But it is the truth.

Keb reached the outhouse and fumbled through the door and sat as he always sat, folded into himself. He thought he heard a *woolnáx wooshkák,* a winter wren, a walnut with wings, and so believing sketched in the missing notes with his imagination. Notes like water over stones. He thumbed through the catalogs and magazines on the bench next to him. Eddie Bauer, whoever he was. Cabela's. Good fishing stuff in there. L.L. Bean. Why so many catalogs? Why so many magazines? Why so many of so much? He found a big glossy report from the Coca-Cola Company. What the hell? Yes, he remembered now. He'd been to California a few years back to see Ruby's son, Robert, the sugar water man who worked sixty hours a week for Coca-Cola Company and was hoping to move to the big office in Albuquerque, Albany, Atlanta, Atlantis, something like that, some place far to the east. Robert was married to a white woman named Lorraine who had expensive hair, a poodle on Prozac, and a cat named Infinity. Boy could she talk. Talk all day, talk all night. Talk, talk, talk. She had a little phone attached to her ear and even talked in her sleep. The only thing she let interrupt her from talking to one person was the chance to talk to somebody else. She spent all her time at the mall shopping for time-saving devices and lived with Robert in a big house next to a million other big houses all different but all the same. Big houses on big streets with names like Shadowhawk Drive and Peace Pipe Lane. Big houses Keb remembered with sadness and fatigue, how the hot sun burned its way across thirsty country and stirred everybody up. Got them speeding in their shiny cars and eating so much fast food that—what? What happened? Keb didn't know. So many cars and people, all chasing the sun. A beautiful madness, California. Could they still slow dance after eating all that fast food? Slow dance the way he and Bessie used to?

"Eyelids," Lorraine told him. "People can tell you're getting old when your eyelids sag." She was scheduled to have hers lifted, along with everything else.

Robert the Sugar Water Man would spend all day Saturday in his driveway washing and cleaning his Mercedes. That's how it is in California, he said. Your car is half of your personality. He'd wax the cleaner and clean the wax and buff the wax and clean the buffer until Old Keb got tired just watching him.

Keb never did own a car. Just trucks. Fords, Dodges, GMs, every one a rolling box of rust that died and was stripped for parts at Mitch's Greasy Sleeves Garage. Come to think of it, he never did take comfort in a car or a truck like he did in a boat, out on the water, under the pull of the moon and tides. Skiffs, trollers, seiners, gillnetters, even the old gray punt he traveled in with Uncle Austin. All of his best memories were in boats, memories shaped like the boats themselves. Graceful, curving, and languid; exotic and erotic as a woman, the feeling of falling in love and falling beyond that.

Rowing with your heart.

And don't forget canoes. *Yakwt lénx'*, large canoes. And *yakwyádi*, small canoes. And *yáxwch'i yaakw*, canoes with high, carved prows, and *seet*, a small, nimble canoe with a pointed prow. Canoes with flat bottoms, like *ch'iyaash*, from the up-north town of Yakutat, good for moving up a shallow river, and *xáatl kaltságaa*, the toughest canoes of all, with twin prows to push aside solid ice. Keb's best boats were the ones he learned to carve with Uncle Austin, and later, the ones he carved himself and gave away. The ones he built for friends, long ago.

Nobody traveled by canoe anymore. They didn't have the time.

Lorraine would keep Keb on the sofa talking all afternoon, talking until she gave him a headache. She told him that she wanted a pet bird, a parrot or a cockatoo or some damn thing in a cage. Pity the poor parrot that tried to mimic her. He'd be dead in a day. God loved the birds and invented man. Man loved the birds and invented cages. Best of all was little Christopher, Robert and Lorraine's delicate son, the boy with Down's syndrome and a defective heart, the sweetest human being Keb knew, the child whose smile could fill a valley. They would drive down to Malibu for ice cream. Keb tried rum raisin and found too little rum, too much raisin. He tried "death by chocolate" and an hour later was still alive. Next time he'd have a double scoop. Christopher ate "Killer Vaniller" and wore most of it on his chin. Lorraine stuck with "Sensible Strawberry." They sat on a bench, facing a sidewalk, and beyond that, a fine sand beach and the sea. Kids zipped by on skateboards and rollerblades. Lorraine held little Christopher and sang, "Puff the Magic Dragon." She said it was peaceful, the sea. "It's so tranquil and still, it makes you believe that everything will be okay."

"I don't dream here," Keb told her.

"What?"

"Here, in this California leaf-blower place, I don't dream here."

"Oh, Keb, maybe you do and you just don't remember. You have trouble remembering, remember?"

Back at her big house, Lorraine gave him the annual Coca-Cola report. On its cover, in large, bold print, large enough that Keb could read it without effort, it said, "A billion years ago intelligent life appeared on earth. A billion minutes ago Christianity emerged. A billion Coca-Colas ago was yesterday morning."

"Oyyee . . ."

Lorraine had insisted that Keb bring it back with him to Alaska; that he show it to Robert's mom, Ruby, Keb's older daughter. How proud she'd be.

Like all great literature, the annual report ended up in the outhouse.

Keb stood, or attempted to stand. His knees creaked. A sharp pain shot through his whole being. Next thing he knew he was leaning against the outhouse door, heavy on the rough wood, the sound of his own breathing ragged to him, his hips too cold, not right, made of plastic or fiberglass or Kevlar or some damn thing other than old Tlingit Norwegian bones. At least no pain cursed him when he pissed. Not this time. Sometimes things down there felt like they were on fire. Whichever one he was supposed to have two of—kidney or liver—the other one had been cut out and Old Keb couldn't remember why. Doctors had gotten in there, digging around for a swollen this or a funky that, and decided to take out the kidney because it got in the way or it didn't look right and that was that.

It began to rain. Keb stepped outside to inhale the wet earth, the May aromas of skunk cabbage, blueberry, alder, spruce. His nose still worked pretty well. In this regard he considered himself an old bear, a hunter with wild strawberries in his eyes, on good days at least. He had fewer good days all the time. Most days he was a pocket of a man, parceling out his vitamins and pills, staring into his own receding face. Awhile back he had caught himself in a mirror and thought, *When did I stop being me?*

A gust of wind caught his white hair and stirred the ferns. Back on the trail, he stopped to taste the cool salt mist blowing in from the sea, the fragrance of rocks. He tightened his arthritic hand around his walking cane and was about to go on when he froze. There at his feet, apparently dead, was *Yéil*. A raven.

A shiver ran through him, deep as a shiver can go. His heart jumped in his throat. For a minute he didn't move; he would say later that he didn't breathe then either. In all his years in Alaska, Old Keb could count on one hand the number of times he had found a dead raven. No other bird or animal was more storied to him and his Tlingit people.

He lowered himself to one knee, slowly, mindful in some ancient way of the rain falling harder, the storm filling its lungs. He bent forward to better see the sightless glare of the obsidian eye, the blue iridescence that shone and was gone. Minutes ago it had not been there, this bird that spilled nightfall off its wings, this bird that created the world and stole the sun. Keb looked into the sky and continued to look, unblinking, his face turned to the rain and the great somber trees. The wind stood and listened. Keb gasped. He could see now, see in a way new to him. Every branch and needle and raindrop falling with ten thousand other raindrops had extreme clarity. The sky cleaved open. The earth, wild on its axis, shot through space and pressed upon him the entire weight of its spinning. The stars, cold and conscious on the other side of the world, suspended themselves in the blackness where Raven got its shape and voice. Something had happened. Something bad. A small whining sound grew louder. A presence brushed his face, soft yet strong, the weight of air taking flight. The whining was big and getting bigger—shrill, serrated, sputtering. An engine? Yes, a motorcycle.

Old Keb didn't move.

The motorcycle skidded to a stop. A young man killed the engine and climbed off. He walked toward Old Keb, wearing a baseball cap backward over his long hair. His baggy jeans scuffed the ground. His loose-fitting jersey said, "L.A. Lakers, World Champions." He had the manner of a *jánwu*, this kid, a mountain goat grown mostly in the limbs, lanky, quick, unafraid of heights. He had cool, arctic eyes.

"There's been an accident," he said.

Old Keb nodded, "Yes, I know."

a face like the surface of water

IT WAS JAMES. The accident belonged to James, the crack shot with Old Keb's Remington 30.06 and a pair of Michael Jordan's Nike Air Specials; the boy who practiced a thousand days and nights to float over his chosen court with the weighted dreams of every basketball kid in Jinkaat. James, the younger first cousin of Robert, who drank Coca-Cola like water and ate cheeseburgers like seal meat, who smoked cigarettes behind the school gym and played video games with toned muscles tight over his shoulders. James Hunter Wisting, half Arapaho by blood, all Tlingit by heart, made from the rain, Tlaxaneis' Kingfisher Clan, Héen Wát River Mouth House, the youngest son of Old Keb's younger daughter, Gracie, who found happiness in all things except marriage, and so raised her children alone and brought them to where they belonged, salmonlike.

"What happened?" Old Keb asked.

"Logging on Pepper Mountain," the kid said. "He's banged up bad."

"Bad? How bad?"

"Bad, I guess. Charlie Gant says he's got a smashed leg and a concussion and maybe a punctured lung because he's breathing funny and he doesn't look right. They flew him to Juneau."

Old Keb reminded himself to breathe.

The kid said, "His mom thought you should know."

Gracie. Old Keb could stand in a mountain gale unbowed, but Gracie, his flower, Ruby's younger sister, could bend him with a smile. Every man should have a daughter with a face like her mother's, a history of affection. Teacup eyes. Soft hands like *yán*, like hemlock, easy to hold. Keb got to his feet and winced with pain.

"You want a ride?" the kid asked.

Old Keb climbed on and locked his arms around the kid's lean frame.

The ride was mercifully short. The kid drove like hell. Keb thought: If there's another accident, we'll be the first ones there.

He tapped the kid on the shoulder to stop at the carving shed where Keb lived, on the edge of the clearing under the big spruce. It was a small shed, perfect for an old man who once carved great cedar canoes and now shuffled through shavings on the planked wooden floor while the lanky kid leaned in the doorway, lit a cigarette, and let the blue smoke rise off his fingers. On a stool in the far corner sat Kevin Pallen, a simple boy, sag-shouldered, a mop of hair in his face, a carving tool in one hand, a block of yellow cedar in the other. To know him by his smile was to know the moon by its reflection. But he wasn't smiling. Kevin looked at Keb with wet eyes, wanting to hear that James was okay and still bound for Duke University and the NBA—something like that, anything like that.

Wanting too much.

The kid with arctic eyes and blue fingers motioned Kevin outside.

Old Keb stuffed two shirts into a pillowcase. What else? Socks, he could hear Bessie tell him. Don't forget socks, and extra underwear. He wanted to lie down with her just then, down under the weight of it all. Lie down and take a nap and never get up. Lie down like an old bear too tired to hunt, right there, right now; sleep against the kitchenette that Ruby's husband, Günter, had built for him all those years ago. Lie down with the peeled logs and milled timber he'd known all his life—*seet, yán, xáay, shéix'w, duk*, Sitka spruce, western hemlock, yellow cedar, red alder, black cottonwood. Uncle Austin had taught him to read the grains with his eyes closed, to smell the fresh cuts and the smoke, to know the wood as you know a living thing. Even when it's dead it's alive.

Old Keb wrapped his arthritic hands around his carving tools. They didn't fit. They weren't his tools anymore. They weren't his hands anymore. Even his adz was a stranger, its shape a distant past. How long since he carved his last canoe? How long since he shaped something and felt it shape him? He looked around the shed, grabbed his clothes and pills and made for the door. The kid had fetched Ruby's Dodge one-ton truck from her empty house next to the shed. He had Kevin in the cab with him.

They shot down the road and swerved past Steve, the barking mongrel dog that belonged to Keb's neighbors, Ty and Ronnie Morris. Nobody called him Steve. Given his big head and predatory nature, they called him Rex, short for Tyronniemorris Rex: the king of the road, the fang-endowed Doberman-Rottweiler-Rototiller that dug up flowerbeds, peed on people's legs, stuck his nose in other dogs' butts, and shared his bark and growl with anybody who passed by.

Not exactly Lassie. "That's a smart dog," the kid said. "He hunts by scent."

Keb thought, *What else is he going to hunt by, a map?*

The kid said, "Remember that old rat-haired collie that used to lie in the middle of the road all day? We called him Speedbump. I always thought he'd get run over, but he never did. He just died of old age." As if it were a disgrace, a bad way to go. That was the kid's tone. Better to explode in a burst of glory, go down with guns blazing.

The kid hit nearly every pothole but reached the airstrip in good time. Keb was tempted to tell him to go back and hit the few potholes he missed. Make it a perfect run.

A crowd stood at the bush plane counter, knots of people casting light and shadow on each other. Keb came through the door and Mackenzie Chen flew into his arms and nearly knocked him over. Once enfolded into him though, she felt weightless, forceless. People called her Little Mac. On most days she was a bee in the sun, undiminished by events around her. Not today. She was James's girl, off and on, and today was a bad day. Truman Stein put a hand on Keb's shoulder and asked if he could get him a cup of coffee. Keb would have preferred lemonade, mixed just right, the way Little Mac made it on warm summer days. But coffee would do. Keb saw the Nystad brothers, Oddmund and Dag, who must have closed things down at Nystad's If We Ain't Got It You Don't Need It Mercantile and General Supply. They were talking to Vic Lehan, the town barber who always had something to say. Even when he fell asleep, Vic awoke with an instant comment. Each acknowledged Keb in a quiet way; in a small town you're never far from a friend. Was Father Mikal in the crowd? So many people, some who only seemed to show themselves during a crisis. Neighbors, relatives, the old and the young, rich and poor, ambitious and lazy, Tlingits and Norwegians mostly, but also Swedish, Russian and Ukrainian, German, Filipino, Portuguese and Chinese, plus half a dozen California hippies who'd moved north to find themselves or lose themselves or lose somebody who was out to find them, and several big-city hoity-toity types whose lives were knotted in neckties before they came to Alaska. Most stood still and frozen-faced, not knowing what to say, or saying little as they fed on the news, bad as it was, just as they would feed on a miracle, the profound events that sustain small towns. Keb could see that many had eyes made of unshed tears, trying and failing with hands in their pockets to express the inexpressible, heads low and postures bent by the inadequacy of words. Could it be? James Wisting, the best Native high school basketball player in Alaska . . . in Juneau with a crushed leg?

The fancy-pants magazine *Sports Illustrated* had mentioned him as a "high school standout." Duke University had sent an e-mail and talked to Coach Nicks.

Old Keb never did understand basketball until one night, years ago, in the school gym. He sat on those hard wooden bleachers with three hundred people going crazy in the fourth quarter, his back aching and the score tied. He listened as Truman, a writer who used to live in Manhattan, told him to think of men long ago hunting mammoths and mastodons, working as a team. You see? A kid charges down the court dribbling the ball. He passes to another kid, equally fast, who flips the ball into the air. Not into the basket, but near it, where a third kid, graceful as a gazelle, catches it and banks it off the glass. He misses. But the first kid, always alert, makes the rebound and bounces it to the third kid who flips it to a fourth kid who fakes a shot and passes to a fifth kid who floats a jumper that swishes through. Backpedaling now, those same five kids must defend their end of the court from five others who have just as much heart. "It's more than just sport," Truman said. "It's something difficult and beautiful and all the more beautiful because it is so difficult. It's what you do in Alaska these days. It's basketball, the new hunt."

"Hey, Keb," the air-taxi office manager yelled across the crowded office. "There's a NMRS plane coming over from Bartlett Cove that'll be here in ten minutes and take you and Little Mac into Juneau. Gracie's already there with James and Coach Nicks and some of the kids from the team."

Keb nodded his appreciation as his one good eye continued to survey the room. Seated against the far wall were half a dozen Greentop boys, loggers tipped back in their chairs and eating pizza from Shelikof's, the local takeout. Idaho rednecks, hard-bitten timber men with wood chips on their pants and frowns on their faces, cigarettes in their fingers. Oil-stained gloves tucked under their belts. Silver metal hats upside down on the floor, spinning when they kicked them with their steel-toed boots. Old Keb shuffled over.

Charlie Gant got to his feet and wiped pizza sauce off his lips with an oily sleeve. A disk of pepperoni fell on the floor. Steve the Lizard Dog snarfed it up. Charlie offered a hand. "Hey, Keb, we're all really sorry. Damn, I mean—it just happened and like, I don't know. . . ."

Sitting next to his older brother, his face opaque, Tommy Gant had his eyes on Mackenzie Chen.

The crowd moved in behind Old Keb. He could feel their weight, their hunger for an explanation. Truman handed Keb a cup of coffee.

Keb asked, "What happened, Charlie?"

"It just happened, it was an accident."

Keb studied him hard.

Charlie said, "James was a choker-setter and . . . I don't know." He shrugged. "I can't say." Tommy and Pete and the others nodded, thumbs hooked in their suspenders. Yep, can't say.

AIRSICKNESS NEVER BOTHERED Old Keb until he started flying in these little planes that shouldered their way into dour clouds. Rain pelted the windows. Keb closed his eyes over the clear-cuts of Chichagof Island and Port Thomas, mountains and valleys stripped of their trees. Streams brown with sediment. A ravaged land. The timber industry had never bothered him until it all went wrong. Until chain saws brought out the worst in boys and corporations the worst in men and his own people lost their way.

The affable pilot pushed his headset mouthpiece away and said over his shoulder, "Hang on, Keb. I'll make this ride as smooth as possible. There's a headset in the seat pocket in front of you if you want to use it. I got Buddy Tabor on channel one and Emmylou Harris on channel two."

Keb didn't move. Opposite him was a woman in a NMRS uniform, and behind him were two other uniformed federal officers who worked for the National Marine Reserve Service, a new federal agency that Truman had said was established to protect America's threatened oceans, though exactly how the oceans were threatened Keb didn't know. He wasn't sure he *wanted* to know. Everything was threatened these days.

"I'm sorry about your grandson," the pilot added.

A nod from Keb. He was going to barf any minute unless this buckaroo got his plane to calm down.

When the pilot did find smoother air, Keb leaned forward and asked him, "Do I know you?"

"Terry . . . Terry McNamee." Big smile. Crooked teeth. "I contract out to the National Marine Reserve Service. My mom works at PacAlaska with your daughter, Ruby Bauer. She's your daughter, right?"

Keb nodded. No matter how much she irritated him, she would always be his daughter. Chichagof Island receded off their tail.

"It's been a bad spring," Terry said, as Keb studied whitecaps below on Chatham Strait. "Crappy weather. And now this, you know . . . the accident. . . ."

Old Keb nodded again.

"Remember that basketball game last year against Unalakleet, when he scored thirty points and had two defenders on him all night? Damn . . . I sure hope he's okay."

Old Keb shrunk into his big coat. He stuffed his hands into his pockets and found, to his surprise, a feather. He pulled it out, stared at it. Raven black. How did it get there? Holding it by the shaft, he twisted it slowly between his thumb and forefinger. Had he put it there? The hand that held it felt more agile. The feather flashed with rare light, not black but blue, a stormy sky over indigo water. Keb trembled and dropped the feather. For an instant he was a boy again with Uncle Austin in Crystal Bay, ninety years ago, watching golden leaves fall off tall cottonwood trees, spiraling down, laughing as they tried to catch them.

"We're over Admiralty Island," Terry said to him. "How are you doing?"

"Fine," Keb lied.

Admiralty Island, what kind of name was that? A square-rigged British name. Keb's people called the island *Kootsnahoo*, Fortress of the Bears. A little to the north, off the plane's left wing, was Point Retreat, so named by Lieutenant Joseph Whidbey of His Majesty's Ship *Discovery*, when a warrior band of Auke Tlingit pursued Whidbey and his sallow-faced sailors, those scurvy-wracked, black-gummed, homesick men who rowed facing backward while the Tlingit paddled facing forward. According to Uncle Austin, who knew everything, Whidbey served under the bloated Captain George Vancouver, a man without imagination. "Captain Van," his men called him, but never to his face. Now the chase off Point Retreat, the Tlingit warriors stabbing the sea with each stroke, each man fixed with a *niyaháat* and a *shak'áts'*, a breastplate and a double-ended dagger. The cedar canoe running true. The *x'igaa káa* in his *shadaa*, a wooden helmet, fiercely beckoning his men forward. Not far ahead, Whidbey's men rowed for their lives, muskets ready. A rising wind filled their sails and gave them a close escape. Five years later the Russians arrived with Aleut slaves and powerful cannon and a lust for furs. The Tlingit fought bravely, where Sitka stands today, and lost. Evicted from their home, they lived apart from the Russians. Then came the missionaries and whalers. In time, the shamans died, and so did the Tlingit language—almost—and the world was never the same. "You see, little man," Uncle Austin would say to young Keb, "when you're rich, it can all be taken away."

The plane buffeted. The NMRS woman seated next to Keb handed him his raven feather. Blue uniform. Shipwrecked eyes. A face like *héen xuka hinxuka*—the surface of water. "Do you remember me?" she asked.

Just then Terry butted in, "Whoa, Keb, sorry about the turbulence. We'll have you there in a minute. Remember that game against Skagway, the state championship? James was in rare form that night, I'll tell you. . . ."

a real cliff dweller

RUBY WAS AT the airport. "Hi, Pops," she said as she looped her arm through Old Keb's. "Thanks for coming."

How was it she managed to be taller than him? Everybody was taller than him these days. At the rate he was shrinking, they could bury him in a shoebox. It was one thing to be a *shaan,* an old person, but another to be a *shannák'w,* a little old person.

Gray-streaked hair framed Ruby's brown face, her eyebrows tipped in black. A kittiwake among gulls, she was a cliff-nester, a risk-taker, a big shot Princeton graduate and university professor and president of the PacAlaska Heritage Foundation.

Keb watched her ignore Little Mac.

He sucked in air. The airport was too crowded, too hot; the lights too bright. Where was the blue uniform woman with the shipwrecked eyes? Did he remember her? Why should he remember her? He heard voices, the cut of sharp words and questions. He fumbled with his buttons, trying to remove his heavy coat. He could hear Ruby above the others, speaking . . . to him? No . . . about him. About James, too. Then he understood . . . the heat and light were television cameras. Oyyee . . . He raised his hand to shield his face.

A man yelled from the back, "Ruby, Ruby! Allen Jenkins here with the *Juneau Empire.* Do you know the exact nature of James's injury? Have you heard anything from Duke or the NBA?"

Old Keb staggered and nearly fell and somebody caught him. "I got you, Gramps." It was Josh, Ruby's eldest. Faithful Josh holding him and walking him away, and Little Mac helping, walking him to a row of seats and sitting him down and treating him like a breakable thing, a piece of pottery. Dear God. How many times since Bessie's death had he sat alone with the silence, with only the sound of time? How many times had he thought about dying without dying himself?

"I'm hot," Keb told Josh.

"I'll bet you are."

"When do we go to the hospital?"

Josh didn't answer. Ruby appeared, kneeling, her thin, bony hand strangely talonlike on Old Keb's arm. "When do we go to the hospital?" he asked again.

"They sent him down to Seattle, Pops. It's a head injury. He needed to go right away. There's another flight in a couple hours. I've booked you on it with a first-class upgrade. Robert and Lorraine are coming up from L.A. You want something to eat?"

"What?"

"Food, Pops. You hungry?"

"I have to go to the bathroom."

"All right, all right, let me finish this interview, okay?"

"Don't talk to those people."

"I'll handle it, Pops."

The minute Ruby left, Josh and Little Mac got the old man to his feet and walked him to the restroom. Shuffling along, Keb looked down to see two angels beside him, two little girls with open faces, smiling their missing-tooth smiles, red ribbons in their hair, lips moving, making birdlike voices. Josh's kids? Yes . . . but their names? What were their names? Would they grow up to resent each another, like Ruby and Gracie?

A sadness came over him. He was tired. Tired of himself and everyone else. Tired of forgetting. Tired of eating pills. Tired of being tired. He wanted to lie down and never get up; fall over dead—dead before he hit the floor—as the doctors said would happen when the aneurysm burst near his heart. It could happen any day, they said. Keb's family had listened with long faces as the doctors explained that the aneurysm was inoperable. That was five years ago and here he was, still on his feet, dying by degrees. And the strokes? At last count he'd had twenty or more, the doctors said. Little pieces of scar tissue dotted his brain where memories used to be. He didn't know the names of his great grand-daughters, but his mind like a fist held on to the names that brightened his own childhood, the ones he learned when traveling with Uncle Austin on the water— the name of the hunter who could outsmart a seal, the name of the island with big wild strawberries, the name of the woman who could clean a salmon with her one hand (a wolf took the other one, she said), the name of the inlet where mountain goats came down to shore to eat algae, the cove that offered protection from a north wind, the sandy shore where a family of river otters played.

These he remembered, but so much he did not.

Standing at the urinal with his forearm against the wall, his head against his arm, he peed an old man's dribble. Damn, he had known discomfort before, but nothing like this. His cousin Johnny once used a pistol to shoot a halibut in a skiff and put the bullet through Keb's foot instead. That didn't feel so good. Falling off a cliff on Jonas Island and shish kebabbing himself on a spruce branch ranked up there too. A chain saw ripped into his thigh once. He did his best to forget that. There was the time he went berry picking in Dundas Bay and fell asleep barefoot in the sunshine and awoke to find a bear licking the berry juice off his toes. He yelled and the startled bear took a bite and ran off, leaving Keb with five toes on one foot and four and a half on the other. And of course, the war, the shrapnel in his hip, the artillery thunder, he and the others pinned down by machine guns, the gut-shot men moaning through the night, crying for their mothers. That was pain too, a scar. Why did he live when so many others did not? He never talked about it, or tried to make others understand. He wasn't sure he understood himself.

He grabbed a paper towel and dabbed the sweat off his brow and thought about all the old farts in the rest home who sit around killing time until time kills them. Everybody wants to go to heaven but nobody wants to die. What to do? Keb straightened up and sealed his mind. He'd go south to the city by the sea, the city named for the great chief who said all men were children of the Earth, the city of coffee and computers. He'd visit his grandson and tell him Raven doesn't care about fame or fortune. Raven doesn't care about diplomas or degrees. Raven looks for scars, the signs of suffering that give a man his depth. Add this wound to the others no strangers see. Add it and move on because it's the only thing to do. There are two tragedies in life: Not getting what you want, and getting it. That's what he would tell his gifted, tormented grandson. After that, Old Keb Wisting would return to Alaska and walk into the woods and lie down and die.

THE FLIGHT TO Seattle put Old Keb right to sleep. First class, lots of room, recliner seat. He awoke with a sense of suffocation; had to get his shoes off. No easy task. Socks too. Ruby sat next to him and helped. How good it felt to let his toes breathe. He wiggled them and drank bottled water; she drank two Bloody Marys, then four, six. Little vodka bottles everywhere. She buried herself in her work, fingers pounding her small computer, PacAlaska papers and three-ringed binders spilling out of her seat and into Keb's. His eyes fluttered open and closed, heavy from the weight of so much change. What would Uncle

Austin say? It had been more than forty years since Congress passed the Alaska Native ClaimsSettlement Act that gave Alaska Natives land and money—nearly a billion dollars—to invest in their future. No reservations. No Trail of Tears. No Wounded Knee but no Custer either. Things would be different in Alaska. The meetings lasted forever. To manage their land with all its oil, minerals, timber, fish, and tourism potential, the Natives created thirteen regional corporations and more than two hundred village corporations, with each Native a shareholder. They hired attorneys to set things up and protect their interests. It was all so daring and new. Keb remembered it clearly, too clearly—all that money, all those lawyers in Fords and Chevys instead of canoes. On the day the act passed and celebrations erupted across the state, Uncle Austin, sick at home with cancer, said, "I hope we did the right thing." That night he died.

According to Gracie, corporations around the world had become cultures: General Motors, Toyota, Apple, Nike. But never had indigenous cultures become instant corporations. It was an experiment, like splitting atoms.

The regional Native corporation in Southeast Alaska was PacAlaska, one of the state's largest and most profitable. As far as Keb could see, the more it grew the more it wanted to grow.

"Pops," Ruby said, "we need to talk."

"Oh?" His eyes fluttered.

"Remember the jurisdiction case I told you about?"

"The what?"

"The jurisdiction case in Crystal Bay? The Ninth Circuit Court case coming up this fall, remember?"

"I don't want to talk about that."

Ruby took a deep breath.

"No," Keb said. Of course he knew about it. Everybody knew about it and talked, talked, talked about it like Lorraine and her parrots. It went like this: The State of Alaska, backed by PacAlaska, was challenging the federal government for jurisdiction over the waters of Crystal Bay to develop twenty Native inholdings that showed strong mineral and tourism potential. The heart of the matter was that Crystal Bay, ancient homeland of the Jinkaat Tlingits, was now a national marine reserve, and PacAlaska wanted it back. Yes, the glacier had evicted the Tlingits hundreds of years ago, advancing as it did. When it retreated, the feds moved in and claimed the new bay as a great scientific laboratory for the study of plants and animals on land and in the sea. First they made it a national monument, then a national park, then a biosphere reserve, then a world heritage site and finally, just a year ago, a national marine reserve. So many names and titles.

Ruby was back on her computer, pounding away.

"Gracie opposes PacAlaska in Crystal Bay," Keb said.

"Gracie opposes everything about PacAlaska, but she cashes her dividend checks, doesn't she?"

"She needs the money."

"She needs the money because she has four children by four husbands, after four divorces, with two girls in rehab, and now a boy with a crushed leg."

"She never divorced James's dad. He's Apache."

"He's Arapaho."

"Oh right. Arapaho."

"She's going to have to live with this, you know, what's happened to James. He shouldn't have been logging on Pepper Mountain. I feel sorry for her. I do. But Gracie's going to have a heavy burden if this costs him his career."

His career? "He's only seventeen."

"Exactly."

"When I was seventeen I fell and hit my head and broke my collarbone hunting deer with Uncle Austin on Lemesurier Island. He carried me down the mountain and rowed me to Juneau in a punt. Took five days in bad weather. Long time. His fingers almost froze off. It was cold like a knife wound, k'eik'w litaa eeti."

Ruby stared at him.

"It was November. Uncle Austin caught a halibut using—"

"Pops, this is different. When you have the chance to go to Duke University and get into the NBA and be a millionaire athlete, you don't go into the woods with a chain saw and heavy machinery."

"Charlie Gant's been a foreman for many years. They say he's the best."

"I know. I also know that loggers have a code of silence, especially when things go wrong. I've asked the troopers to investigate. Remember when James tried out for varsity basketball as a freshman and took Tommy Gant's point guard position when Tommy was a senior? Tommy sat on the bench most of the season that year. Then last summer, Tommy's girl, Little Mac, hooks up with James. It's a recipe for bad blood, don't you think?"

Keb shrugged. "Don't argue with Gracie. Not this time. Not in the hospital."

"I won't. But if she starts—"

Keb raised a hand. "Don't argue."

THEY FOUND GRACIE, Coach Nicks, and the others at a table in the hospital cafeteria, a knot of people sitting solemnly beneath sterile white lights. Old

Keb shuffled up behind his youngest girl and touched her. She turned to bury her face in his tattered coat. He held her shaking head with his bent fingers and didn't tell her it was going to be okay. He just hummed the way he used to when she was impossibly small, hummed until he could feel her mind close around the sad truth of it.

Without a word, Ruby grabbed a meal tray and got in line for something to eat. Coach Nicks stood and thanked Old Keb for coming. Three basketball boys who had flown down with Ruby, Keb, and Little Mac joined their teammates at the table, grabbed the last of the French fries and wiped greasy fingers on their baggy pants. Built like rails, they had no hips that Keb could see. Shunned by Ruby, Little Mac stood in reserved silence, her dark eyes without reflection. Coach Nicks said the surgery had taken two hours. James was in post-op. The doctors would see him and Gracie in ten minutes or so to "give a prognosis."

Prognosis. Old Keb remembered the word. He remembered the hospital too, the shiny floors and bright lights, the clattering of metal gurneys and the strange, sweet smell of antiseptic, the green Jell-O and purple potato salad, the absence of wood smoke and birdsong and children playing and the sky leaping to every horizon. Nurses who woke you up to feed you a sleeping pill.

Keb had to pee. He had to pee so often he reckoned his bladder was the size of a thimble. Big ears, small bladder, bad teeth. These were his rewards for achieving old age and outliving his wife, his friends, his brothers and sisters, and hardest of all, his three sons. Only Ruby and Gracie were left, tested by God to see beyond their differences.

Keb followed the others as they made their way up to intensive care, and waited. So much waiting, people holding each other, staring into the distance, turning the pages of glossy magazines but seeing nothing. An hour later Coach Nicks broke the news. None of James's injuries was life threatening. The MRI—whatever that was—showed no brain damage. The punctured lung would heal. No sign of infection. But the knee was gone. Old Keb watched the color drain from Coach Nicks's face as he heard Coach say, "James will never play basketball again."

One of James's teammates let out a wail, his voice so hurt-filled that it nearly knocked Old Keb off his feet. Another boy reached for him but Coach Nicks said, "Let him go," as the grief-stricken boy bolted and ran down the hall. The others stood firm, fighting back tears. Coach Nicks pulled them into a huddle, football style, and said things Keb couldn't hear.

Nearby, Gracie and Little Mac held each other and cried.

The old man shuffled to the window where Ruby stood facing outside, away from him, her elbow on the wall, one hand running through her long gray-streaked hair, the other gripping one of those little phones. "It's not good," he heard her say, probably to Günter, her husband.

Günter was talking now, the good German engineer who tried to fix everything. Ruby had met him at Princeton, dated him for one month, and married him.

"You're not hearing me," Keb heard Ruby say, as if she were arguing with the window. "Beyond basketball, James's dreams end, his life will be over now, as far as he sees it. . . . He's going to be lucky if he ever walks again without a limp or a cane. . . ."

Keb felt the world spin. He wanted to reach for Ruby and find her through the distance of years, through the thousand things that made them different to the one or two things that still made them the same. He turned and caught Coach Nicks looking at him. "Keb," he said, "you want to join us?" One step at a time, the old carver approached the huddle. It opened to take him in. The boys kept their heads down and shoulders low. Keb didn't have to bend down like them. They were at his height now. "Is there anything you'd like to say?" Coach Nicks asked.

It's damn hot in here. That's what first came to Keb's mind. He wasn't a sports philosopher like Coach Nicks. He didn't have a leadership award from the governor. He didn't study games on TV. He thought March Madness was cabin fever until Truman told him it was a college basketball tournament. During games in the school gym, with the bright lights and everybody shouting and pounding their feet, Keb would get a headache. He attended on Gracie's insistence, and sat next to Truman, who had a way of making one thing into another: basketball players into mammoth hunters, cheerleaders into princesses, referees into cops, the court into a battlefield.

"It's a real cliff dweller," Keb would say during a tight game.

"Cliffhanger," Truman would correct him.

So what to say now to these broken-hearted young men?

everything closed over him

"TELL A STORY," Uncle Austin used to say. "We are a story people." Old Keb said into the huddle, "My sister Dot, she died of cancer in a hospital in Juneau. She was the youngest of us all, and the happiest, and she was the first to die."

The boys listened hard. Keb could feel it. They listened hard because the old man's tongue didn't work like it used to. Half his teeth were gone. He spoke in a soft and syncopated manner. Hearing him required effort, but he had wisdom, a great heart. The oldest man in Jinkaat, he was a respected Tlax̱aneis' elder, part Norwegian Viking berserker and part Tlingit Raven trickster, as the Raven rattle had the tail of the Kingfisher. Austin Skredsvig, a clan leader, had raised him in the ways of the long ago time. One of Austin's cousins had been the last shaman in Sitka, a great man who knew the language from a thousand years ago. Most everybody in Jinkaat knew stories of Old Keb and his Uncle Austin walking over mountains. How they traded blankets up north with the Ice People, carved canoes down south with the Haida, and hunted seals in Crystal Bay.

Gracie and Little Mac joined the circle while Ruby stayed at the window, facing away and talking on her little phone.

"She had an operation, my sister Dot," Keb said. "She liked to draw with pencil and paper. She got good at it. So one day in the hospital she made a picture of a black vase, and she put a crack in it. One crack, right down the middle. That was Dot; she did things like that. A woman visiting her dying daughter in the next bed asked Dot why. Dot said it was her scar, the one she got from the operation. You know what that other woman did? She took that drawing in the middle of the night and colored a yellow line over the scar. Just like that. She told Dot it was the light coming in. 'That's what cracks do,' she said. 'They let in the light.'"

AFTER THREE DAYS, Old Keb found time alone with his grandson. Visiting hours had ended and Gracie was down the hall, asleep. Robert and Lorraine were back in their hotel room with little Christopher. Many people had come to visit. Near as Old Keb could tell, James saw none of them. Anger and self-pity blinded him. How dark and brooding he looked in the starched white bed, his head bandaged, the TV channel-changer captive in his hand. Little Mac sat nearby with her knees pulled to her chest, reading a book. She wore a black beret and a sad face. Old Keb could see that she too had failed to console James.

Ruby came in with her little phone, gave it to Old Keb and said, "It's your friends in Jinkaat. They want to talk with you." Keb pulled it to his mouth. "Put it by your ear, Pops, like this," Ruby showed him. "Talk. They'll hear you."

"Hullo."

"Hey, Keb, you still alive?" It was Oddmund, or maybe his brother, Dag.

"I think so."

"How's Seattle?"

"Busy."

"How's the coffee? Everybody down there drinks coffee."

"Good, I guess."

"How's James?"

"Not so good."

"Keb?" It was Helen Pasternak, who, together with Myrtle Applewhite, a chicken wrangler, owned the Rumor Mill Café. "Keb, we've got hermit thrushes singing up here."

"Oyyee . . ." Keb loved thrushes. He loved Helen Pasternak too, her cooking anyway, and the way she looked in an apron and might look in only an apron. But she was too young for him, in her sixties. He had never had a woman since Bessie. Never would.

Helen said, "Hang on, Keb. Truman wants to say something."

"Hey, Keb, you staying out of trouble down there?"

"I guess."

"I finished another chapter in my war novel." Truman was always writing a war novel, what he called "a John Steinbeck–Joseph Heller kind of story," a sequel to *Catch-22*. *Catch-23* maybe, or a prequel, *Catch-11*, only half as good but still damn good. "You know what I mean?" he would ask.

Keb had no idea what he meant. But he liked Truman, and listened, and imagined eating the "death by chocolate" ice cream that Helen ordered special from Sitka. It never tasted as good as the stuff he had with little Christopher in

California, but he would eat it all the same and thank Helen, and maybe put off dying for a while. Maybe get out of bed each morning to move his bones and live another day. Maybe hear another story down at the Rumor Mill, or Vic's Barbershop, or Nystad's Mercantile, or Mitch's Garage, or Albert Bestow's Measure Twice Cut Once Fine Carpentry and Cabinetry, another story from another friend that made him laugh and helped the sun rise in his eyes.

"Hey, Keb," said Dag (maybe it was Oddmund), "Daisy's kicking our butts in cribbage. You'd better get back up here and put her in her place."

"I'll do that," Keb said, suddenly tired.

Dag told him that Steve the Lizard Dog had eaten one of Truman's books. Truman wasn't so mad about it because the dog had literary taste. "Get it? Literary taste, eating a book?" Keb didn't get it.

"Give James our best," Helen said. "And Gracie and Little Mac too."

They hung up. Ruby had gone out. Where was Little Mac? Keb tried to turn off the phone. Too many buttons. He put it in his pocket and pulled out the feather. Standing, he felt dizzy; he'd forgotten to eat and drink. He saw James glance his way and turn back to the TV. They were alone now, grandfather and grandson. But the advertising man on TV did all the talking: "You can't get by without it. The new Resolve, the aftershave you've always been waiting for. It's everything you need."

Everything you need? Wasn't it enough, Keb wondered, to feel the wind in your face, to drink the rain and pet a friendly dog and know the softness of a woman's thigh? Wasn't it enough to hear a wolf howl, to build a morning fire in the kitchen cookstove, to taste the first nagoonberry pie of summer, to carve a spoon from alder? Wasn't it enough to feel the tide run beneath your boat, a boat you built with hand tools and great heart? Keb put the feather on his grandson's bed, and made for the door. "What's this?" James asked, his voice flinty.

"It's for you, to help you get well. It's from Raven."

"I know it's from a raven."

"No, not *a* raven. It's from Raven, Yéil."

James turned back to the TV.

"What color is it?" Keb asked.

"It's black."

"Look closer."

"It's black, Gramps. I'm not stupid."

"Look closer."

"What? What am I supposed to see?"

"Something to help you get better."

"Get better? How am I supposed to get better? My life is ruined. It's over. I might as well be dead."

His words broke bones. Keb's hand went heavy on his cane. Part of him faltered, another part straightened. A seventeen-year-old boy? His life over? Keb wanted to thump him over the head. No need. Little Mac did it for him. She came into the room and said, "Shut up, James. I'm sick of your bad attitude. We all are."

James's mouth fell open.

Little Mac began to cry. "We all feel bad for you, we do. But you've got to get it together. There are a lot of people way worse off than you."

Keb flashed back to the foxholes in Italy where he'd seen a thousand boys dead in the cold morning mud. He'd almost been one himself. He could hear James and Little Mac exchanging sharp words, but didn't catch them, torn as he was between his devotion and contempt for this fatherless kid. A few years back, when he was new at being a teenager, James seemed to take cold satisfaction in tormenting his mother and saying the old Tlingit ways were corny, that nothing could stop the future or preserve the past. He'd been cruel and unattractive then, a shadow of his father. Later, his hidden goodness required less digging. His basketball game soared. He found his smile, and seemed to take new pride in being Tlingit.

And now this.

Keb wobbled.

"Are you okay?" he heard Little Mac ask, as she braced to hold him up.

"Gramps?" James said with alarm. "You need to sit down."

"No," Keb said. "*You* need to stand up. You need to be stronger than you've ever been. Stronger than you can imagine. You need to give your mother something to believe in. Do you hear me?"

James stared.

"You are not dead. You are not broken. You still have those." Keb pointed.

"What?" James asked, bewildered, alarmed.

"Your hands. You still have your hands."

James stared at his hands. He turned the feather slowly. "What am I supposed to see?"

Sometimes the only thing we see is the thing we're most afraid of. Still leaning into Little Mac, Keb tried to focus. Did he see a hint of amnesty in his grandson's eyes? A kindness, a hope? Oyyee. . . . He took a ragged breath and heard himself say, "A light. Turn the feather just right and you'll see a light, a little daylight in the night, a little blue in the black." Suddenly he was more tired than he'd been in a long time. His legs turned to water and everything closed over him, as Old Keb Wisting, the last canoe carver of his kind, collapsed.

the raven, it was nothing

FAR TO THE north, in Crystal Bay National Marine Reserve, a soft rain fell as a woman named Anne moved about her government research boat. She decided the rain was more mist than rain, more patient than the downpours she had known in Hawaii. A rain taking its time. She let her boat drift and watched it swing to starboard, pushed by the tide; eager fingers of foaming water on the white hull. Green, gauzy trees formed a rain-forest veil on the distant shore, as much a rendering of another place as the place itself. Beyond that, Anne imagined mountains that elbowed into the clouds.

She glassed in every direction with her binoculars. Where were the whales?

The channel narrowed. The waters swirled and eddied over a shallow bottom. She looked for rocks, signs of broken water that would betray their presence just below the surface. The boat continued to spin, slowly. Her nautical chart said that no navigation hazards existed in this channel. But in Crystal Bay, where channels and coves quickly filled with glacial silt, it was different. The land—the actual crust of the earth—depressed by a massive glacier that filled the bay only a few hundred years ago, now rebounded an inch each year. Shorelines shifted. Reefs played tricks. Nautical charts became obsolete; they deceived. A Tlingit legend said a dark spirit reached out and capsized boats. What to do? Take nothing for granted.

The channel widened. The waters sighed. The current slowed and the boat eased into it. A bowl of pink light, cradled in morning clouds, spilled against the snowy flanks of weathered mountains. Anne caught herself breathing. Thousands of birds chattered and splashed about: ducks, geese, gulls. A flock of sandpipers zipped by, flaunting their aerial supremacy: restless, northbound, so many miraculous beings fixed on stars and arcs of magnetism, wild and vast yet intimate and near.

"Hello, Alaska," Anne heard herself say. "It's good to see you again."

Twelve years ago, fresh out of Juneau-Douglas High School, she couldn't wait to get away. Now she was back, and near tears. She had Nancy's ashes. Her sister's ashes.

She hoped to find humpback whales moving with the moon and storms, flooding into Crystal Bay on the first strong tides of June, hunting for the fat-rich forage fish—herring, capelin, sandlance—they needed to replenish themselves after months of fasting and a long swim from Hawaii. She gave herself ten minutes, and with that gone, another five. Another two. Nothing. She pulled out her journal and wrote:

> The sister had no suitcase
> No way to say good-bye
> She packed a duffel with long underwear,
> An old hippie vest, a tie
> She took the ashes too
> Wouldn't you?
> The urn heavy and cold
> Was she ever, truly ever bold?
> Maybe now, somehow
> Maybe here.

ANNE LISTENED, AND in her listening she forgot her deepest sadness and regrets. Her radio was off. Her National Marine Reserve supervisor, a by-the-book man she called Ranger Ron, would not approve. He had called her yesterday to remind her about the mandatory all-employee safety meeting at reserve headquarters in Bartlett Cove.

Yes, well, the whales came first.

She closed her journal, climbed onto the foredeck, and sat against the metal railing in her Helly Hansen rain pants and sou'wester slicker. She dangled her legs over the side, her feet snug in XtraTuf Neoprene boots. The double-tined Danforth anchor rested at her side on the scrubbed white deck. From her daypack she pulled out a small tin and opened it. She dried her fingers on a red cotton bandana and drew a thin line of marijuana into a square of cigarette paper. She rolled a joint, licked it shut, and held it. "Maui Wowie," she said. "They'd fire my ass if they saw me doing this."

Still holding the joint, she opened the *Capital City Weekly* and read about the Crystal Bay jurisdiction case. "We simply want the federal government to have some perspective and wisdom and let us have our lands back," the paper quoted Ruby Bauer, "so we can pursue our dreams and maintain our cultural heritage. . . ." And make a ton of money in mining and zip-line tourism, Anne thought.

She didn't buy it. What bothered Anne most was that Ruby was the daughter of Old Keb Wisting. How did that happen? Why did some girls get the good fathers, and others the bad? And why did some girls die young, like Nancy?

Deeper into the *Capital City Weekly*, Ruby appeared again, this time talking about an investigation into the Pepper Mountain accident that ended the basketball career of her "infinitely talented" nephew. "To see a God-given gift like that taken away at the beginning of a person's life is a crime," Ruby said. "That's why we want to make sure we know exactly what happened. We want to know the truth. Nothing more, just the truth."

The truth, Anne thought, there's a slippery fish.

"Do you remember me?" she had asked Old Keb in the NMRS plane as she handed him his raven feather five weeks ago. Of course he didn't. Yet she remembered him and was astounded by how little he'd changed. The open face, white hair, ancient hands, and kind eyes. What struck her most was how small he was, and how he seemed to regard everything around him as a breathing universe of water, earth, and air that flowed one into the other, and he with it. He had magic; he *was* magic, the grandfather she never had, the man who gave her a vision.

THE ROUND EARTH rolled. The rain stopped. The tide percolated softly against the hull. A bald eagle called through the wet air and Anne snapped from her reverie. Her hand, still holding the joint, began to shake. Must everything desirable be forbidden?

She stood and looked around. No whales.

For eight years she had studied humpback whales in Hawaii, their acoustics and courting and mating, their migrations and energetics, their complex social structure and language. Now here she was, back in Alaska where the magic began for her as a little girl, where she first fell in love with boats, whales, and wilderness; where hungry humpbacks from Hawaii spent their summers eating nearly half a ton of fish per day, and sometimes sang.

Alaska, yes, where Nancy died, and part of me died too. Dear God.

She put the Maui Wowie in the pocket of her blue uniform shirt, under the gold badge, and made her way back to the wheelhouse, still thinking about Old Keb. That's when she stopped, breathless. Perched on the transom was a raven. It cocked its head at her but otherwise didn't move. Neither did Anne. Her hand gripped the rail. Her heart fluttered. What speed and stealth had brought the bird here that she hadn't seen it or heard it? She could feel it looking at her, looking *into* her, measuring her with its dark intelligence. It walked the rail with a shaman's authority, black talons clicking on the white fiberglass, tapping out an ancient beat. Had it stolen the moon? Invented the night? Come as an echo of the Ice Age?

Whooosh . . . It lifted away on broad wings, circled once, and flew north into the mountains and glaciers until she could see it no more, until it became part of everything distant and abstract. Slowly, her heart calmed and her mind became rational again and she remembered the mandatory safety meeting in Bartlett Cove, and convinced herself wrongly that it was nothing. The raven, it was nothing.

Just a bird.

a soul on fire

SOME DAYS, THE pain never left.

When you lived on the ragged edge of North America, a thousand miles north of Seattle, where the Pacific was not pacific and storms slammed into high mountains and glaciers skulked in valleys and silent bears made tracks up your spine, you knew as Keb knew that dying was an art when done right, and no final act should be without mystery and grace. More and more though, men died in the wreckage of their own lives, shadowed by false prophets, lost in the thumping, grinding world those same men created for reasons that didn't seem reasonable anymore. Remember Reggie Plant? His brain soft with whiskey, he walked in front of a loaded gravel truck and let all ten tons roll right over him. People said he wasn't too recognizable after that, not that recognition gets you into heaven. And Gil Johovic? Stubborn old goose, he took off in his skiff in an Icy Strait gale; said he wanted to catch a fish. They found his body washed ashore a week later. Never did find the skiff. A shame. It had a fine four-stroke outboard on it. Billy Mills got too confident in his Cessna and surprised nobody when he disappeared over Lynn Canal. George Bethany overfilled a backhoe tire and blew himself into the rafters of Mitch's Garage where he hung on a lag bolt until the volunteer fire department pulled him down. Gus Talzic got frostbite when he went winter deer hunting with a hole in his boot. A patient man, he waited until the gangrene marched up his leg and into his crotch before he went to see Miss Byers, the nurse practitioner. He was never the same after that. Neither was Miss Byers.

Old Keb missed his cribbage games with Gus and George, the three of them planted in Keb's carving shed, eating cornbread and venison stew. He could work long and hard and never tally all the ways his friends had died. Not one had lain down on a bed of moss to let the country swallow him. Not one had paddled away in a canoe. It seemed a fine way to go, one that appealed to Old Keb, a lot more than courting cancer, ending it all in a hospital, kept alive until your wilting was complete. Uncle Austin got so sick and frail that all he did was sleep. So did Samson Ehlme, a good carver in his day. He lost so much weight that his coat hung on him like laundry on a tree. He had a disease named for a famous baseball player back in the 1930s. It messed up Samson in the legs first, then climbed into his lungs and filled them with water. But it kept his mind sharp, a dirty trick and a tough end for the big Swede, a cold, windswept man. Two of Keb's brothers died of cancer, and his sister Dot, and his wife, Bessie, twenty years ago. Even in her final days, surrounded by family, she did more giving than all of them, dying as she did without complaint. "I am grateful," she said. Those were her last words. Keb had lived too long without her. So much cancer these days, it was a cancer of cancers. And if cancer didn't get you, Parkinson's or Alzheimer's would, your body loaded with mercury and other bad stuff, your brain turning to oatmeal. Remember Rita Killbear? She said what bothered her wasn't that life was so short, but that we're dead for so long.

They were gone, all his dearest friends, his deepest love. He had no more illusions of turning full-faced to the sun. Everything was more alive than he'd ever be; every day harder than the one before. He felt as if he were cheating, breathing air that belonged to others. He could remember the names of friends who'd died seventy years ago but not the names of his great-granddaughters who walked at his knees, chirping like birds. He had to find strength in surrender. If a messiah can be born in a manger, can't an old man die in the forest, on a bed of moss? Or better, in a boat? A canoe?

RUBY'S TRUCK ROARED up the hog-backed road and stopped at the carving shed, its windows filmed with summer dust after three weeks without rain. It sat there running, a living thing, doglike, panting in the heat. Nobody got out. From his rocking chair inside the window, Old Keb watched that truck catch its breath, sitting on its blue tail of hot exhaust. It turned off, and for a moment the quiet was big again, the way Keb liked it. James got out the passenger side and slammed the door. Using a metal cane—his knee in a brace—he hop-stepped across the clearing to his Aunt Ruby's house, where she hadn't lived since she moved to Juneau. He went inside and slammed that door, too. He was the best door slammer in town these days. Gracie got out on the driver's side and stood there wearing the weight every mother wears who gets more than she bargained for. She leaned her broad frame against the truck and looked up, as if hoping some clarity might fall out of the sky.

When she was little, about three or four, Gracie loved to play hide-and-seek with the bigger kids. She'd stand in the middle of the meadow with her hands over her eyes, hiding from the entire world, invisible in a child's logic. If she couldn't see them, they couldn't see her. Ruby, eleven years older, would yell, "Gracie, you're standing in broad daylight. We all see you. You have to hide behind a tree or something." Unyielding, Gracie would hold her hands over her eyes until the seeker pegged her. Each time she'd drop her hands, her face alight, her laughter filling the sky, her little mind oblivious to rules and the importance of winning. It was the happiest Keb had ever seen her.

Keb considered going out to visit her, at the truck, but that required standing up and moving and was no small task when his joints worked like rusted oarlocks. She came in and walked across the creaky wooden floor; flipped on the single bare lightbulb that hung over the kitchen table. Her eyes adjusted to the evidence of frugal living.

"Hi, Pops."

"Hullo."

"You hungry?"

"No."

"How about I make you some waffles?"

"Okay."

She lit a cigarette, pulled butter and syrup from the fridge, and said heavily, "Did you hear? James got into an argument with some of the Greentop boys at Shelikof's. I wasn't there but everybody's telling me about it. I guess he accused Charlie of skidding the logs up on Pepper Mountain and making things more dangerous than they needed to be." She blew out smoke, sucked in another deep drag, blew out again.

Keb shifted. "Skidding the logs?"

"Yep."

"That's not good."

"I know, Pops. That's why I'm telling you. I guess the troopers have been talking to everybody who was up there."

Poor Gracie. Every kindness the years had shown Ruby had been cruel to her. Ruby the elegant kittiwake, Gracie the honker goose with flat feet and a pear-shaped figure in baggy pants and teardrop glasses, her uncombed hair piled on her head. Keb could see she wasn't well, her color wasn't right. He struggled with his feet. He had to get his shoes off. An old Norwegian Tlingit can only absorb so much bad news with his toes bottled up. Uncle Austin used to say, "Never trust a man who takes away your language or makes you wear tight shoes. You want to understand the world and where you came from? You want to know who you are? Free your toes." Let them breathe.

"Nobody should make trouble with the Greentop boys," Keb said.

Gracie dabbed cigarette ashes into an empty Dinty Moore can. "I told James that. He got mad at me. I can't tell him anything anymore. Nobody can."

Keb said nothing.

"What's he supposed to do, now that he can't play basketball?"

"I'll handle that," Keb said, too softly for Gracie to hear.

"You know, he started dating Little Mac when Tommy was sweet on her. There are hard feelings there, too."

Keb warmed at the mention of Little Mac. Part Chinese and part Scottish, with a little Tlingit and Filipino thrown in, she was a one-girl melting pot. "Chop Suey," the other girls called her, fighting off envy and losing every time. As a kid, Little Mac would pop wheelies on her bike, eat apple cores, and skip rocks. She could outrun and out-spit most boys her age, and she grew into a beauty made all the more beautiful by the way she moved, a young confident woman who never learned to fear the future. Keb loved her questioning intelligence, the fact that she was incapable of holding a grudge in a town built on them. Now sixteen, she had breezed through her junior year at a Seattle high school and returned north to spend another summer with her family in Jinkaat, where every logger and stevedore hit on her without success. Nearly a century ago, her great-grandfather, Milo Chen, had worked the salmon cannery in Dundas Bay with Keb's pregnant mother, Nora. When Nora's water broke and the cannery foreman told her to keep working or she'd lose her job, Milo, the hardest worker of them all, got onto his knees and delivered the baby—little Keb—while a dozen salmon-packers did double-time to cover for him. Milo cut the umbilical cord with a bone-handled filet knife, held Keb over his head, and sang a Mandarin blessing as pure as rain over rocks. He put little Keb on his mother's chest and finished sixteen hours of packing salmon to make rich men richer down in Puget Sound.

After Keb's mother and father died, the salmon industry collapsed and the Dundas Bay cannery closed down. Keb was about twenty by this time, back when Uncle Austin found Milo back-bowed on a construction job in Juneau, pouring concrete for two dollars a day. What exactly had Milo said when he held little Keb over his head? Uncle Austin wanted to know. "We are not human beings on a spiritual journey," Milo told him. "We are spiritual beings on a human journey, born into our lives for one reason only: to seek the road that makes death a fulfillment."

"Keb Zen Raven," Milo called the boy. "The philosopher bird."

All these years later, people in Jinkaat made a sport of watching Little Mac, Milo's great-granddaughter, the way she moved on coltish legs and wore her beret and tied patterned scarves in her faded jeans; how she kicked rusty beer cans down the road and waved at passersby, no matter that they didn't wave back. What suspicion they must have felt, watching her commit the sin of being different in that breezy way of hers, with that look in her eyes that said she was a continent away.

"I SWEAR," GRACIE said, "we are hard on each other in this town. A lot of people say they wanted my James to get into Duke. Maybe they did and maybe they didn't. We're like a bucketful of crabs. Any time any one of us tries to crawl out to be somebody, the others pull him right back down. That's what happened to my James. He's talented. He's a good student. He's a Tlingit crab trying to get out with everybody pulling him right back down. It's sick."

Just then James angled his way through the door, a wide-shouldered silhouette, heavy on his cane. Old Keb couldn't see his face. He didn't need to. Eyes like chestnuts, downcast, vulnerable, one slightly higher than the other. Flat mouth, set jaw. Contours hardening in the cold journey of consequences that turns a boy into a man.

Gracie said, "I'm making your grandpa waffles. You want some?"

No reply. Keb could see the boy assessing his place, the wood shavings on the floor, the faint oily smell of yellow cedar, the hand tools on the wall and on the corner workbench where Kevin Pallen had been carving a block of hemlock.

"You need to beat on something?" Keb asked him.

"What?" James answered distantly.

"You need to beat on something?"

James turned. A motorcycle crested the hill, coming fast. It blasted up to the truck and skidded to a halt. Riding it was the kid, the same feral boy who delivered news of the accident to Old Keb six weeks ago. He wore the same baggy pants and ball cap and Lakers jersey like winter fur on his weasel back. He had a lean and hungry look, fed on conflict more than food, as though no part of him would go unused in a fight. As he loped to the door, Keb heard Gracie say something but didn't get the words. Dust veiled things. Sunlight slanted through thirsty boughs in the trees. Keb couldn't see a whole lot, but one thing he did see rattled him. Standing in the doorway, the kid was a soul on fire. "Charlie Gant's coming," he said. "He's got the Greentop boys with him."

removed and strangely dispassionate

E VERY FAMILY FACES moments when the world rises up to bury it, that's what Uncle Austin used to say. Be ready. They're little moments that get big fast, each one different for a thousand different families, each one made of truths and lies woven into patterns or woven not at all. Some approach with naked teeth, others you can't see until they drag you into darkness. They change everything and nothing. Wounded Knee, Trail of Tears, Pequot Wars, all big moments. Little moments have no telling in the history books. Still, lives end. Tribes and clans disappear, and the hurt comes from how easily others forget. This could be one of those moments, Keb knew. He had to get his shoes off. Gracie passed him and was out the door when he heard the ATVs—five big-wheeled machines that roared up the narrow rutted road into the clearing past Ruby's house. They stopped a short distance away and rumbled beneath their rebel riders who flanked Charlie Gant two to a side. Old Keb recognized Pete Brickman behind silver mirrored sunglasses, true as any shadow. Next to him was Charlie's brother, Tommy, his eyes the color of ice in a pan. The two riders to his other side added nothing to the descriptions of the first. All were short-haired and grizzly-bearded except Charlie, who was clean-shaven with dishwater blond hair down to his shoulders. All five wore T-shirts except Tommy, who wore no shirt at all. Keb watched one rider roll a toothpick between his teeth. "Stihl Crazy After All These Years" read a sticker on Tommy's ATV, Stihl being a chain saw favored by loggers who rendered forests into slash. After clear-cutting Idaho, these gentlemen had come to Alaska for the last big slice of American pie. Keb wondered what they would do when all the ancient trees were gone. Cut grass? Mow the big boss's front lawn?

James stood next to the truck and faced them, his hand on his walking cane. His mother, standing behind him, appeared snake-bit. Old Keb rolled his tongue and clenched his hand thinking it's a young man's nature to have an adversary.

Charlie turned off his machine and motioned the others to do the same. "Hey, James," he said. "You got time to talk?"

James shifted his weight but said nothing.

"The troopers are asking a lot of questions and I've been answering them," Charlie said. "We've all been answering them, haven't we, fellas?" He looked at his buddies, who nodded. Tommy's nod lacked enthusiasm, Keb thought. But it was a good beginning. Charlie added, "I'm sorry about what happened. We all are. It's a bum deal for you, and it was an accident. It really was."

Again, no comment from James.

"It would have been cool to see you make it in the NBA," Charlie said. He sounded so sincere, looked sincere too, with his open face and expressive eyes and winning smile. Remember Custer? Uncle Austin used to say. He had a winning smile and long golden hair and didn't smoke or cuss or drink; he loved the opera and classical music, adored his wife, spoke sincerely, and shot Indians.

"Anyway," Charlie said, "my brother Tommy has something to say to you."

By now Tommy had dismounted his machine and was standing next to it, but didn't look at all comfortable. Keb thought he might catch on fire from the friction eating away at him. A wounded moment limped by. Keb had to get his shoes off. He tried to swallow. Everything was too hot and dry. How long since it had rained? Keb loved the rain. From his position behind James, near the truck, he watched the Lakers jersey kid circle to his left. The kid was lean and small, but something in the way he moved said it didn't matter.

Tommy said to James, "Just before the logs rolled, I heard something break, a D-ring, I think."

James stared at him.

"You might have set the choker wrong," Tommy added.

"I set it right," James said, his hand shaking on his cane. "You were the crew boss, Charlie. You made the decision to skid the logs and not high-lead them."

"That has nothing to do with it."

"That has everything to do with it."

"Read the Alaska Forest Practices Act. Skid logging and cutting in the buffer strip are completely legal."

"I don't think so."

"I know so."

The Lakers jersey kid kept circling, aiming to outflank Charlie and Tommy and the others.

"Stop right there," Charlie yelled, pointing a finger at him. The kid stopped.

A hot wind blew up then, like a breath, crazy as it sounds, but that's how Old Keb felt it, as a parched, dry sigh that whipped up dust and grit, and brought people's hands to their eyes. It funneled through the open cab of the truck where a raven feather lifted off the seat and sailed out the cab window and onto the ground. Keb alone saw it, from where he stood behind James. As quickly as the wind arose, it died.

Keb reached down and picked it up.

"Hey, Keb," Charlie said, "I didn't see you back there."

Keb nodded. He had nothing to say.

"It's time for you to leave, all of you," Gracie said as she wiped the dust from her eyes.

Charlie had more to say, Keb could tell, but Sheriff Stuart Ewing roared up in his Jeep Grand Cherokee and parked next to the only puddle that three weeks of sunny weather had failed to vanquish. Coated with pollen and dust, it lay concealed until Stuart opened the door and stepped right into it. Kaploosh. "Everybody stay where you are," he said in his best sheriff voice. He kicked his feet dry and strode forward on skinny legs.

A train of vehicles followed, the rusty, dented cars and trucks of coastal Alaska, ATVs too, bringing a small-town theater of eager onlookers keen on any conflict. Coach Nicks was there, and Dag Nystad, and Truman, Helen, Myrtle, Little Mac, and several of James's friends from the high school basketball team. Coach Nicks said, "Go home, Charlie. All of you, go home."

Sheriff Ewing said, "I'll handle this, Coach." Problem was, he wasn't a sheriff. He was the former Jinkaat village public safety officer and now deputy sheriff-in-training, the wheat-haired son of a retired Alaska state trooper who Truman said got the other end of the male chromosome. Instead of doing what he should have done—sell kitchenware in a Seattle Sears—he became a cop. His shoulders sufficed for little more than a coat hanger. Still, you had to admire his fearlessness and determination, even though they would probably get him killed one day. With arms extended referee-style, as if breaking up a fight, he stepped between Tommy and James and said, "All right, what's going on here?"

Nobody spoke. Charlie started up his machine.

Tommy looked wistfully at Little Mac.

A RAVEN FLEW overhead just then, northbound. Not any raven. Imagine an oracle rising from the dead, a bird with one feather missing, cutting the sky. Imagine the feather in Keb's hand lifting too. Not a downy feather from the bird's neck or breast, but a primary feather, broad and black as a January sky. Made for lift and speed. What happened then Keb couldn't say. It seemed as if hours passed, but in truth only seconds went by. He saw himself on the bird's back, everything visible from Raven's eye. Icy Strait appeared below. Up ahead, approaching fast, a vast wall of ice commanded the entrance to Crystal Bay. Keb recognized it as the great glacier that long ago marched down from the mountains and forced his ancestors from their home, the glacier that locked the bay in cold storage for hundreds of years before it melted back. Had it returned? Was yesterday tomorrow and tomorrow today? Raven seemed to float, the shadow of his wings patterned onto the glacier's deep blue crevasses. Reflected in one wing-shadow, above the ice, Keb saw his own face. In the other wing-shadow, James's face. Between them, the glacier climbed in fractured towers of ice—the colors separate yet one. The sky was an untended grave, rolling back on itself. Keb forgot to breathe. Then a movement, far below. Approaching the ice was a small canoe, hewn from wood, sharp-prow, *seet*, the most beautiful boat in the world. Keb watched as two men paddled that canoe right through the glacier as if ice were water. Then a voice: "Pops? Pops . . . are you okay?"

He gasped.

"Talk to me, Dad." Keb was flat on the ground, pressed to the earth. He blinked through dusty shafts of sunshine. Hovered over him were Gracie, Coach Nicks, Little Mac, and Deputy Sheriff-in-Training Stuart Ewing, their faces half in shadow, half in bright light. Tyronniemorris Rex was there too, Steve the Lizard Dog, his head cocked in bewilderment. Gracie stroked Keb's hair. "Say something, Pops. Can you hear me?"

"I hear you."

"Can you sit up?"

He was lying on his back. He sat up and saw James not kneeling beside him like the others, but removed and strangely dispassionate, still on his feet.

"You stopped breathing," Coach Nicks said. "You feel okay, Keb?"

"Am I breathing now?"

"Yep."

"I feel fine." Keb got to his feet so quickly that he startled everybody. "Where are Charlie and Tommy?"

"They left."

Keb looked around. His stomach rumbled. "I'm hungry. Let's make waffles."

the death of too many dreams

THE CONFRONTATION HAD unsettled Gracie, Keb could see. She was more fragile these days. "We'll eat in Ruby's place," Keb said. "It has a big kitchen table."

"Ruby won't like it," Gracie said in a weak voice.

Keb shrugged. Ruby was in Juneau or Anchorage or Washington. He couldn't keep track of her anymore. "We need waffles, Gracie. Make them like you used to."

"Little Mac will help me," Gracie said.

Little Mac smiled, her way of saying yes.

Old Keb watched James, the radius of his heat, his hands working in and out of fists.

Coach Nicks and his boys set the table. Truman made orange juice. Gracie pulled out the sourdough starter, added cinnamon, whipped it up, and gave each waffle a minute in the waffle iron. Little Mac opened a couple rashers of bacon. Out came the butter with maple syrup tinged with spruce tips and nagoonberry jam. Best waffles in Alaska. Keb tried to remember if James had ever turned them down. Wounded and confused, James probably wanted to get away with Little Mac. That's why Gracie recruited her, and Truman and Coach Nicks and the ballplayers, James's best friends, hoping as hopeless people do that things could be as they once had been, back when her son had two good legs and lived in an ocean of light. Back when she made waffles after every home game victory—there had been many—and the lanky-legged boys ate and laughed and told stories with such bravado you'd have thought they'd just slain a mammoth.

The Lakers jersey kid zoomed off on his motorcycle to follow the Gant brothers down the hog-backed road to make sure they didn't double back. Who was this kid? Keb was beginning to like him. Coach Nicks said his name was Hugh; he lived alone in a rat-hole trailer down at the boat harbor and worked as a carpenter and heavy equipment operator. He looked about fifteen, but according to Deputy Sheriff-in-Training Stuart Ewing, he had a driver's license that said he was twenty-three. He came from up north and never got cold and smoked cigarettes and sometimes wore wire-rim glasses that made him look like Johnny Depp, though his manner was all dispossessed Indian. Stuart had run a criminal check on him and come up clean. Beyond that, nobody knew much.

Ten minutes later the kid motored back up the road, parked his motorcycle, and stood at the door until James waved him in. The waffle iron was hot, the bacon browning.

"Smells good," Kid Hugh said.

"Did you see the Gant brothers?" Coach Nicks asked him.

"Nope."

He sat down with a polite nod to Gracie and Little Mac. Everybody listened as Stuart's Jeep rumbled up the road. He came through the door with Carmen Kelly and Daisy Robinson, Carmen with her book of horoscopes, Daisy with her cribbage board.

"Where'd they go?" Coach Nicks asked Stuart.

"Up the Pepper Mountain Road."

"You going to talk to them?"

"I already did."

"What'd you say?"

"I said they need to stay civil and calm. So do you, James."

James shrugged. Kid Hugh opened a small knife, cut a callus off the palm of his hand, and said to James, "You should probably get a gun."

"No," Gracie snapped.

"For protection," Kid Hugh added.

"No guns," Stuart said.

"Everybody in America has a right to bear arms," Carmen said.

"And arm bears," added Daisy, a flaming environmentalist who like Carmen had a crush on Truman.

"Charlie's a Gemini," Carmen announced. "That's why he's witty and adaptable and clever but also devious and superficial. With Jupiter in ascension the way it is right now, and with Mars totally in Virgo, he's not the one to worry about." Keb watched Coach Nicks roll his eyes. "Tommy's the one to worry about. He's an Aries. So is Pete Brickman. That's why they're friends. That's why Tommy has a bad temper. He's going to be even more unstable with Mercury in retrograde and with Venus as a morning star."

"I thought Venus was a planet," Daisy said.

"It is."

Keb ate his third waffle and did his best to follow Carmen, talking the way she did: like, oh my God, everything so totally like something else. Truman called it simile shock, whatever that meant. He said her horoscope was actually a horrorscope, since most of what she predicted was doom and gloom. But she did it with a fetching smile, and since Truman's heart was as big as a pumpkin, he treated Carmen like a scholar and she loved him for it. Others thought she was a fruitcake. Carmen and Daisy were good friends, and that went a long way. In fact, as Keb looked around the table and saw so many people knitted together by friendship, it warmed him and reminded him that when he grew up as a kid in Jinkaat he had good friends too. The best friends. He didn't know Mercury from Venus back then, or Leo from Virgo, or a bagel from a burrito, but he knew who he was, and where he belonged.

WAFFLES LANDED ON plates and disappeared as if slam-dunked. Coach Nicks called for a full court press. The table became a free-for-all. Gracie and Little Mac kept it coming like short-order cooks. Daisy and Carmen pitched in, Keb watched one of the basketball boys connect a gadgetgizmo to speakers above the stove. Music soon thundered through the kitchen and everybody sang along in words Keb couldn't follow. But the beat thrilled him. When Gracie went to the pantry to get canola oil, Little Mac flipped a waffle Frisbee-style at James. He caught it one-handed to the gleeful hoots of his teammates. Everybody laughed and cheered. It was the first time Keb had seen James smile in weeks. Gracie returned. "What happened?"

"You have to stick around if you want to see the action, Gracie." Coach Nicks said something about major league baseball and the "crazy big salaries."

One of James's teammates responded, "The Rockies paid a hundred million dollars for that pitcher dude from Japan."

Keb tried to imagine what he could buy with a hundred million dollars.

"If money is so important," Truman asked, "why do some of the best basketball players come from the poorest inner cities?"

"It takes heart first," said Stuart. "You have to have great heart."

"And natural talent," somebody said, Old Keb didn't catch who; the conversation was too fast among a dozen people who sat at the table eating and talking like a pack of wolves, making a big mess. Ruby would have freaked out.

"You're either born with talent or you're not," somebody else said.

"It's all in the planets and the stars," Carmen announced. "I know you don't believe me, but it's true."

The boys chuckled. One said sarcastically, "You mean when the planet Pluto is aligned with the planet Mars?"

"Pluto's not a planet anymore."

"It's not?"

"Who's got the maple syrup?"

"It's a funny thing, how talent improves the more you practice."

Underwear, Keb thought. Bessie would want me to have new underwear, and new socks. If I had a hundred million dollars that's what I'd buy.

"In team sports it's not the best player who wins," said Coach Nicks. "It's the best team, the team that thinks and moves as one, and puts the *we* before the *me*. The guy with supreme talent has to surrender his self-interest for the greater good."

"*Sacred Hoops* and The Zen of Basketball," Truman replied.

"That's right."

"When did Pluto stop being a planet?" Keb asked. Nobody heard him.

"You're talking about Phil Jackson," Kid Hugh said.

"Who's Phil Jackson?" Daisy asked.

"The winningest coach in the NBA. He led the Bulls and the Lakers to three consecutive championships each."

"Jack Nicholson's a Lakers fan."

"Who's Jack Nicholson?"

"A movie star."

"Is Neptune still a planet?" Keb asked, louder this time.

"Phil Jackson had incredible talent to work with: Michael Jordan, Kobe Bryant, Shaquille O'Neal."

"But none of those guys were on a champion team until Jackson came along."

"Is there any more butter?"

"Wasn't Jack Nicholson in *One Flew Over the Cuckoo's Nest*?"

"There's more butter in the fridge."

"Phil Jackson used to play with Bill Bradley."

"He's taller than he looks."

"Phil Jackson?"

"No, Jack Nicholson."

"Phil Jackson is six eight, at least."

"Jack Nicholson was awesome in *A Few Good Men*."

"The whole sports and money thing is out of control," Truman said. "In the last thirty years the salaries for major university professors have increased by 30 percent while the salaries for head football coaches at the big universities have increased 750 percent."

Old Keb scratched his head. How much was 750 percent? And what about Neptune?

Gracie pointed a spatula at Truman. "Did you know that student debt is now more than total credit card debt in this country, almost a trillion dollars? How insane is that?"

Keb thought: There's my Gracie, the firebrand she used to be. He watched James squirm to see his mother become a little strident.

"I did know that," Truman said.

"I didn't," Carmen said. "That's terrible, students going into debt while coaches get superrich. Neptune is still a planet by the way, Keb. But it doesn't have the cosmic influence that Jupiter or Mars or Mercury or Venus have."

"I can't believe you buy into that astrology crap," James said.

"I can't believe you buy into basketball," Daisy fired back. "What does it matter what team wins? Does it feed the hungry or comfort the weak or shelter the homeless? All it does is entertain people who should be out doing something better with their lives."

"Basketball was charming once," Stuart said. "Today it's big business."

"Welcome to the United States of Money," Truman announced. "That's why PacAlaska wants to get into Crystal Bay. It's all about money."

"Mining, timber, and tourism," Gracie said. "What better way to screw over a people's homeland."

Again, James squirmed.

"What's so wrong with money?" Coach Nicks asked. Old Keb could see him chewing on Truman's comments, wiping his plate with waffle number six. He had blue eyes and butch-cut blond hair, and came from Kansas, where basketball, according to Gracie, was a religion. He taught history at Jinkaat High School and volunteered at the local library and read books the size of concrete cinder blocks and never missed church and was considered the most learned man in Jinkaat until Truman showed up with his dark ponytail and goatee, the coach's mirror opposite. Truman was from New York. He said that his hippie parents conceived him at Woodstock while Jimi

Hendrix played "The Star-Spangled Banner" left-handed and upside down. He was born eight months, three weeks, one day, and fourteen hours later, at the exact moment the Ohio National Guard opened fire and killed four students at Kent State University. It was destiny, Carmen said, that Truman should become a writer and antiwar activist, and make cosmic babies with her or Daisy, which he had yet to do, but both women remained hopeful. Truman Stein was a genius in their eyes, an almost-Einstein, given his name, a partial visionary, a thinker of almost-great thoughts, which for Carmen and Daisy, was enough. He never went to church, and once told Coach Nicks that imagination was more important than knowledge, and knowledge more important than faith, but Keb could tell the coach had a hard time imagining it. The Kansas conservative said, "You reward excellence with money. A good professional athlete deserves a good income."

The New York liberal replied, "What's the dollar limit?"

"As much as somebody's willing to pay," James said. He sat aslant of the table, his body turned so his braced leg could extend from his chair, his eyebrows stitched together as the discussion spiraled onto sports and money. Not good topics, Keb thought, for a wounded warrior feeling trapped by the bland inevitability of the rest of his life. So much heart and heartache over a game. *He needs to beat on a log,* Keb thought. *He needs to work with his hands. Build a boat.*

Gracie said, "Who wants another waffle?"

Hands went up. Little Mac dumped more bacon onto the table and it disappeared. She said, "How'd everybody get so hungry?"

Stuart said, "I think Tommy and Charlie are up on Pepper Mountain looking for something."

"What, exactly?" Carmen asked.

"Probably whatever it is they said broke that day, when the logs came loose on the skid trail."

James huffed.

The table went quiet.

"Tommy's the dangerous one," James said.

"He's not a bad person," Little Mac said. "He can be kind. He taught me to play the guitar and to sing harmony."

"Then why not run back to him, if you like him so much? Start a band, go on tour, have a baby."

Little Mac froze. Was it pain or anger Keb saw in her eyes? He sometimes wished she wouldn't be so stoic. She was Milo Chen's great-granddaughter all right, a little thing and a big thing all in one.

Gracie wiped her hands on an apron, and James said he'd take a couple more waffles, "Not overdone like those last ones."

"You've had enough," Gracie told him.

"Just make 'em, Mom."

"You've had enough."

"I don't fucking believe this."

Old Keb was on his feet in seconds, shame filling his heart. The boy looked at him with shock; Old Keb took his stare and turned it back on him. "Apologize," he said.

"What? What's the big deal?" James blushed.

Keb thought: *Better a red face than a black heart.* "Apologize to your mother."

"Jesus, Gramps. All I said was that I wanted a couple more waffles. What's the big deal?"

"Apologize."

James got to his feet and shoved his way past everybody and hobbled stiff-legged to the door. He turned flint-eyed to face them, tormented by anger and fear and the death of too many dreams.

"Oh, James," Gracie said, beginning to cry.

He burst outside and slammed the door so hard it snapped a hinge.

first you need to learn the language

AWEEK LATER, Keb found James holed up in Brad Freer's windowless basement playing shoot-'em-up video games. The boys sat at computer monitors, each with a mouse in one hand and a beer in the other, eating Doritos, eyes rimmed red. Hip-hop pounded out the big speakers. The place reeked of marijuana. Beer cans everywhere. Computers plugged into the wall, and these guys plugged into the computers. Keb tried to focus. Brad looked as though he hadn't been outside since the Ice Age. An Iraq War veteran, he was the worst commercial fisherman in Jinkaat, the guy who ate tuna from a can while his rust bucket troller, *Call Me Fishmael*, sat in the harbor leaking diesel. Near as Keb could tell, the sky was a dead thing to Brad. His jaw seemed to unhinge when Keb walked in with Little Mac and Kid Hugh. "What are you doing here?" Brad said.

For days nobody had known James's whereabouts. Gracie worried herself sick. The night before he showed up at Shelikof's Pizza, where people said he and Tommy Gant got into a shouting match and nearly went at it before Stuart Ewing intervened.

To give James a break and get him out of harm's way, Robert the Coca-Cola man and his jabbermouth wife, Lorraine, had offered to take him on their cross-country drive to Atlanta. He could sit in the back with the poodle on Prozac and Infinity the cat, and play games with their son, Christopher. They planned to leave next week, and drink Coke all the way. Stay in four-star hotels. Maybe hit a roadside motel and have a big adventure, since Lorraine's idea of wilderness camping was to go one night without cable TV. Their first stop would be Las Vegas, where they planned to attend the World Pet Expo. Dogs and cats on parade. Very exciting.

Old Keb had another idea. He asked Brad to turn off the music. Brad ignored him, so Kid Hugh unplugged it. Still engrossed in his computer combat, James worked the mouse hard. "I need your help," Keb said to him.

James ignored him.

Kid Hugh pushed Brad aside and unplugged the computer. Just like that, the make-believe world vanished. Only then did James look up, his face hangdog.

"I need your help," Keb said again.

James took a long draw of beer. "What kind of help?"

"You need to beat on something."

"What?"

"You need to beat on something, work with your hands. But first we have some heavy lifting to do. I need you to put that beer away and come help me."

"Did Mom put you up to this?"

"She told me you apologized to her. That's good."

James brought the can to his lips. "No," Keb said, surprised by his own sudden ferocity. "You can finish that beer, or you can put it down right now and come help us. I won't ask you again."

Little Mac said, "James, it's a canoe. It's the last canoe."

He regarded her as if through a thick cloud, where beneath all the bluster and confusion and loss was a quiet plea to be rescued. Keb could see it and figured Little Mac could, too, by the way she took James's hand and said, "C'mon, we need you."

THEY DROVE TO the carving shed and walked to the back, following Keb, whose gait was surprisingly nimble. A recent rain had been received by such thirsty ground that little evidence of it remained. Under a carport, Kevin Pallen sat on a massive, twenty-five-foot red cedar log, carving an alder spoon and smoking a cigarette. The log was on the ground, and deeply notched near both ends. Between the two notches, the upper one-third of the log's midsection had been removed—planked away along the clear grain—while the ends retained their full diameter. Next to the log stood six sturdy sawhorses, each built at one-quarter height and double strength.

"That's not a canoe," James said. "That's a log."

"Not for long," Old Keb said. "We need to roll it over and get it on the sawhorses. Loop that line around the end."

Keb and Kid Hugh had devised a pulley system using a chain-saw winch and a come-along tied off to a big spruce. After several attempts the log didn't budge. Keb sat down, breathless. Little Mac stirred up some lemonade.

Kid Hugh zipped away on his motorcycle and half an hour later rumbled up the hog-backed road driving a front-end loader. He lifted one end of the log, then the other, and soon had it where Keb wanted it, saddled on the saw-horses, bottomside up, with the keel line right down the middle. Little Mac served more lemonade, and Keb drank. He hurt everywhere but felt more alive and purposeful than he had in a long time. After a good rest, he picked up his adz and swung it with surprising agility. Thwack! It sunk into the log. Gasping for air, he said, "The adz marks need to be the same size and depth, parallel to each other for the whole length of the canoe. We add the bow piece later, secure it with pegging. Put a hogback in the middle that will level out when we steam it open and increase the beam-width and fit in the crosspieces. Flaring sides, rounded bottom, buoyancy, speed. Vertical cutwater to throw off high waves in a storm wind, *k'eeljáa*." Keb took another breath, rolling now, coming alive. "Oyyee . . . carve out the interior to where the hull reaches even thickness . . . two fingerwidths on the sides, three on the bottom. Drive in pegs, maybe—guides for even thickness. Nathan Red Otter didn't need pegs. He gauged perfect thickness by running his hands over the hull. His hands carry knowledge you cannot explain in books. Perfect symmetry, the wood is lighter on the south side of the tree, the ground needs to be dry; it's important we split it and chisel it out east to west . . . use wedges and hand mauls for that. Use the chips for fire scoring, wet moss to keep the heat not too hot." Keb lifted the adz for another strike.

"Gramps, what are you doing?" James said, alarmed. "You can't do that. You're almost a hundred years old."

Keb struck the log again with an artful blow. Anybody watching him could see he had once done this with accuracy and grace. He took another swing, his arms like withered twigs on the sturdy handle, hands shaking.

"Gramps, you're going to kill yourself."

"If I'm lucky."

James put a hand on his shoulder. "Take it easy, okay?"

Old Keb sat down and accepted more lemonade as Little Mac stroked the white hair off his forehead. James and Kid Hugh stared, half expecting him to have a heart attack. Kevin sat apart, still carving his alder spoon, a tidy puddle of shavings in his lap, his lower lip trapped between his teeth. For a moment Old Keb envied his dull mind, the gift of quiet that must come with it. Ruby's Dodge one-ton rumbled up the road just then, not with Gracie driving, but Ruby herself, eaten up with urgency. She had her son Josh with her, and his two daughters with ribbons in their hair. The door opened and the little girls ran to Keb and threw their arms around him. Ruby strode over, long hair on her shoulders, eyebrows black yet the eyes themselves unchanged, marooned on the wrong side of history. How different things would have been had Keb's kittiwake daughter greeted the rapacious Russians when they arrived in Alaska hungry for sea otter pelts. She would have seduced them, slit their throats, burned their ships, and freed their Aleut slaves. Even as a little girl she carried the biggest banner, the deepest wounds, as if she alone would right every wrong since Columbus, that arrogant Spaniard who left Europe not knowing where he was going, arrived in America not knowing where he was, and returned home not knowing where he'd been. Alone if necessary, using canny politics and the tinted prism of her pride, Ruby would reclaim the sovereignty of the Tlingit Nation. Never mind that she was only part Tlingit, her mom Bessie having been half Filipino, a real beauty. Keb shook his head. Watching her was like watching his own life reflected and distorted at the same time. Did he love her? Yes. Did he like her? Well, we like someone *because*; we love someone *although*. Keb rose to greet her. She embraced him, then moved to James. "Hello, nephew, how are you?" She made slight acknowledgment of Kid Hugh and Kevin Pallen, while Little Mac she ignored altogether. "Pops," Ruby said, "we need to talk about the lawsuit against the feds in Crystal Bay. It's heating up."

"Oh?"

"I'll make you dinner tonight, white king salmon. I'd like you to join us, James. You need to be made aware of this issue."

Need to be made aware? Old Keb's ears hurt. Why couldn't Ruby talk like a normal person?

"Can I bring Little Mac?" James asked her.

Ruby ignored the request, and patted the log. "What's this?"

"It's a canoe," James said as he picked up the adz and turned it in his hands. Little Mac moved in and put her arm around his waist.

"Dáax," Keb said quietly. Nobody heard him.

"A canoe?" Ruby frowned. "Why not a totem pole?" Totem poles were memory columns to the Tlingit people. They were heraldry and social standing, written in wood. "I think it should be a totem pole."

"A totem pole tells a story," Keb said, "a canoe makes a story."

"Yes but—"

"Ruby, this is a canoe."

THAT NIGHT OLD Keb skipped dinner with Ruby and ate instead with

Oddmund and Dag, and with Daisy, who brought her cribbage board. He drank too much red wine and dreamed crazy dreams. A raven spoke to him, a salmon too, *nóosh*, a spawned-out dead drifting sockeye with its hooked jaw, muttering Tlingit and laughing. Milo Chen appeared on a wet cannery floor, gesturing as if to fly, then pounding the boards with his swollen hands. The next thing Old Keb knew, his bedding was knotted around him and early daylight spilled through his dusty, cobwebbed windows. He heard a loud thwack, the sound of sharp metal striking wood. Another thwack. He sat up and winced as he planted his feet and willed himself to stand. His heart jackhammered. He asked himself who he was. Keb Zen Raven, Nine and a Half Toes of the Berry Patch, son of a Norwegian seine fisherman and a coho woman from Crystal Bay, sign of the north wind. That's who I am, or used to be. Forgetting his morning pills and dietary supplements, he entered the carport barefoot, wearing only jockey shorts, and found James swinging his adz. Cedar chips flying. "Stop," he yelled.

James looked up, hair in his eyes. Something about him seemed older and more mature. Keb rolled his tongue to find his voice. "What are you doing?"

"Making a canoe."

"You want breakfast?"

"Already ate."

"That the gunwale sweep you're working on?"

"I guess."

"You working toward the front or the back?"

"Front, I guess."

"You better decide. Get it wrong and it'll go through the water like a salmon in a gillnet. It'll fight you every stroke."

James took another swing, another dig.

"That's good," Keb said. Truth be told, he feared James. It hurt and was no easy thing to admit that the boy rubbed him wrong. James's father had been a dog-whipped, smoky-eyed son-of-a-bitch who treated Gracie like a mule until one day she gave him what she got and whacked him back. He whacked her and she buckled to the floor, mouth bleeding, and told him to get the hell out. This time he did. He grabbed the stashed cash, got into the Ford Bronco they had just paid off, drove onto the ferry and left her with the mortgage and credit card debt and four kids. He moved back to Denver and nobody saw him after that. His son wore his shadow, though. In ways more apparent each year—his walk and talk—James echoed the man who beat his mother. For that, Old Keb had a mountain to climb. It's no easy thing to see a man you despise in your grandson's face. "You're beating on something, that's good," Keb said to the boy, thinking: better a piece of wood than somebody's head.

James looked at him with eyes gleaned of expression. "You're not going to tell me what everybody else tells me?"

"What's that?"

"That it could be worse? My leg, my career, me, I'm lucky to be alive?"

"No."

"Good. I hate it when people tell me that."

"The Haida, *Deikeenaa*, they chose this tree, long ago." Keb patted the log. "You have to treat it with respect. You have to be quiet, and at peace, and purify yourself."

James ran his thumb over the cutting edge of the adz.

"You have to get rid of your bitterness, your anger. Throw it away before you work on a canoe. Or else it won't be right. You have to meditate and give thanks."

"I thought you—"

"Shhh . . ." Keb said. "We're meditating now."

James leaned against the log, put down the adz, and picked at his knee brace. After awhile he said, "Are we done yet?"

"No."

"When then?"

"Soon."

"How soon."

"Later."

"Later than when?"

"Later than now."

"How much—"

"Shhh—we're meditating."

Keb sat still while James picked at the knee brace.

Remember Gavin Timmerman, the hoity-toity lawyer with the syrupy eyes of a dreamer? He came to Alaska to make something new of himself. A painter, he told Keb that the best art pieces are the ones that continue to have a conversation with you long after you create them. He had a painting in his home that showed a group of people staring at the sea beneath the stars. A caption on the frame said, "The people stared at the sea and the stars, and forgot themselves." This canoe could be that, an art piece. The sea and the stars, a place to forget some things but to remember other things. How many minutes passed by then? Keb lost track. He took a deep breath and said to James, "You got the right tools?"

"What?"

"That adz, _xút'aa_. You want it?"

"Sure."

"You have to hold it just right. Two-handed, near the blade, like this, and get low, on your knees." Keb grabbed it cross-handed, made a cutting motion, and took a bite into the canoe. "This position gives you better consistency when cutting along the hull. You ever watch a crossbill eat seeds from a spruce cone?"

"No."

"Watch sometime. Same technique." Keb handed the adz back to James, who made a couple cross-handed practice swings. "You can have it," Keb said, "but first you need to learn the language."

"The language?"

"Tlingit."

James looked away. Keb knew what he was thinking. It was an old people's language. The boy turned back and said, "Why?"

"Words are tools too. They shape everything."

Keb could see that James was sick of rules and tradition. He could go with Robert and Lorraine and the poodle on Prozac, visit Las Vegas, the geography of nowhere. Cruise the casinos. Pick up girls. Play blackjack and the silver slots. Eat at the all-you-can-eat Sunday brunch buffet beneath big signs that said, "You Deserve It." Watch sports on the big screen. Maybe stay. Get a casino job, a fast car, a swimming pool. But Keb could also see that James was not who he had been a few weeks ago. He had apologized to his mother. Not an easy thing to do. He no longer looked at the red cedar log with cold, indifferent eyes. One day he might stumble into somebody he could be. What happened on Pepper Mountain, well . . . the world was supposed to end after that, right? After the crushed leg? But here it was just beginning. And so Keb found in his heart the most unexpected of sentiments—hope—and gave his grandson his adz.

"If I learn Tlingit," James asked, "what then?"

"You'll find out."

a sharp sea breeze

WHAT ARE WE listening for, exactly?" Ranger Ron asked as he rocked back and forth, foot to foot.

"A summoning call," Anne said, as she lowered the hydrophone cable over the side of her boat. She explained how humpback whales sometimes dive together under their prey and release bubbles that act like a net to corral the fish. "Near as we can tell, several whales spiral up and exhale slowly to release the bubbles, while a single whale summons the others with a high-pitched call. The whales join together and rise quickly inside the net, forcing the fish upwards until they run out of water. That's when the whales lunge to the surface through the tightly packed fish and eat dozens at a time."

Anne watched the two men standing next to Ron shake the city dust from their eyes. They too were fish out of water, Department of Interior lawyers from the gray federal landscape of Washington, D.C., here to research and prepare arguments in the Crystal Bay jurisdiction issue.

"So, the fish don't swim through the bubbles?" asked Matt, the lawyer who reminded Anne of her genetics professor in Hawaii.

"No," Anne replied.

"Why not?"

"I don't know. I'm not a fish."

"I'm being serious."

"So am I. I really don't know. Nobody knows. The whales do it probably because the fish respond in a predictable manner. The bubbles are an impenetrable wall for them."

"That's amazing. I've never heard of such a thing."

"And get this," Anne added, "only a select few humpbacks do it, and they're not a family group. They're not related. It's one of the few cooperative non-family feeding strategies found in the entire natural world."

"And they teach it to other whales?"

"We think so, yes."

Matt looked at his colleague, a huge, stern-faced man named Victor. He was something of a whale himself, Anne thought, a three-hundred pounder, a walking heart attack who smoked a pipe and pawed an iPhone. They were here to talk legal matters, not natural history, to strengthen their case and take a boat ride. The fourth man was Paul Beals, reserve superintendent at Crystal Bay, a tall, sandy-haired career ranger who, unlike Ron, wore no sidearm. Anne had warmed to Paul these past few weeks, the way he let a "by golly" slip through the cold acronyms of his profession. He worried her, though, how he seemed to sidestep conflict. The final guest, who the four men fawned over like schoolboys, was Kate Johnson, the first director of the National Marine Reserve Service, a former NASA astronaut and big celebrity, though Anne had never heard of her. She sat cross-legged on the engine cowling with her sharp-featured face turned to the shining mountains. "A summoning call," she said. "I like that."

The four men nodded. A summoning call, yes, very interesting. Now that Director Johnson liked it, they did too, by golly.

ANNE NEGLECTED TO tell her visitors that bubble netting was extremely rare among humpbacks in Crystal Bay. "Dazzle them if you can," Paul Beals had told her by radio before the four men and Director Johnson arrived by floatplane an hour ago. Anne maneuvered the boat and worked the hydrophone and talked whales and kept the Maui Wowie squirreled away in her breast pocket. At least one person on board might one day smoke it with her—Taylor de la Croix, her boatmate since the Safety Committee had announced: "No NMRS employee will work on the water alone." Of all the employees Anne could have assigned to her, Taylor was her favorite, a friend from Juneau, where they had attended Juneau-Douglas High School and studied marine biology, made field trips to Crystal Bay, and fell in love with wild Alaska and humpback whales. They still laughed like schoolgirls, even when things weren't funny. Right now, though, Taylor was on her best behavior in her blue uniform, looking trim and poised.

Seven people on a twenty-three-foot boat.

Anne thought, Is this safe?

"So, the name of your boat," Matt asked her. "What's it mean?"

"*Firn*? It's a glaciology term for an intermediate stage between snow and dense glacial ice. Many of the NMRS boats in Crystal Bay are named for glacial features: *Arete, Serac, Esker II, Drumlin*."

"So you guys are the ones who'll argue this case?" Taylor asked Matt.

"On the federal government side, yes," answered Victor in a superior tone, turning as if noticing Taylor for the first time.

Paul and Director Kate asked about the case, and Victor answered by quoting Samuel Johnson and Alexis de Tocqueville. Anne pointed out a cruise ship at a distance that was traveling down bay after visiting the tidewater glaciers. Matt said, "I've heard that people will save up their entire lives to make one trip to Alaska."

Paul pulled out maps and spread them on deck. The maps showed twenty Native inholdings in Crystal Bay. Paul pointed. "Here's where PacAlaska wants to mine for gold and copper. Here's where they'd probably build sportfishing lodges and tourist resorts, all in an environmentally sensitive manner, they say."

"Sportfishing in a marine reserve?" Taylor asked.

"Probably not a reserve anymore, if PacAlaska wins," Matt said.

"Can they win?" Anne asked, feeling a kernel of fear harden in her chest.

"In the Ninth Circuit, probably not," Victor said. "It's a liberal court. But if they appeal it up to the Supreme Court, which is more conservative, and the Supreme Court takes it, I think they could win. They'll play the role of the displaced and disenfranchised to appeal to sentiments cultural and capitalistic. They'll say they've unfairly lost their ancient homeland and their best business opportunities by not having access to Crystal Bay, and that the federal bureaucracy, in keeping them out, is just as cold as the glaciers that originally displaced them. Have you heard about the canoe in Jinkaat?"

"No," Paul said.

"It's a red cedar dugout canoe being carved by a Tlingit elder named Keb Wisting, the oldest man in town, father of Ruby Bauer. You certainly know who she is."

"Yes," Paul said, "everybody knows who she is."

Anne felt her heart skip at the mention of Old Keb.

Victor said, "It's a clever stunt to gain sympathy and downplay corporate motives. The canoe represents the old ways they can't have anymore because the callous federal government kicked them out of Crystal Bay. This is the argument they'll use. One of many, actually."

What? Anne thought. "I don't think so," she said, as she pulled up the wet hydrophone cable, seawater dripping off her hands. They turned to look at her. She swallowed hard. "I know Keb Wisting. I doubt he has those intentions at all. Ethnically, he's more Norwegian than he is Tlingit, and he's not at all political. He's a sweet old man."

"But culturally he's Tlingit," Victor said. "Maybe not everybody in Jinkaat prefers comfortable illusions to actual fact, I can't be sure. And it's wrong to paint an entire people with a single brushstroke, I know. But I also know that once a culture becomes a corporation, or a corporation a culture, it falls prey to industry capture and two cognitive tricks: self perception and subjective perception."

"Meaning what, exactly?" Kate asked.

"Meaning the culture ignores valuable information that's at odds with its worldview. It couples uncomfortable information with reaffirming facts in order to make itself feel better. That's how the assailant sees himself as the victim, or the aggressor as the oppressed. That's how PacAlaska sees itself in a way different from the way other people see it." Victor paused and looked at everybody, as if waiting for them to catch up. Anne's mind pinwheeled back to her own history of discomfort, her last day with Nancy all those years ago, the storm off Shelter Island, the boat capsizing . . . *Dear God.*

"The trick is to make the court see it our way," Kate said.

"Yes," Victor said.

"Tell me more about this canoe," Paul asked.

"You can find it on YouTube. There's lots of video shot by people in Jinkaat."

"Has the press gotten hold of it?" Kate asked.

"Not yet."

Ron said, "We could send undercover rangers to Jinkaat."

Never one to make a big decision, Paul turned to Kate. "No," she said. "No rangers in Jinkaat. Maybe later, but not now. And never undercover."

As Ron rocked nervously from foot to foot, Anne caught herself feeling sorry for him, even though he had a permanent job with full medical benefits and she did not. Ron had served in Iraq and inhaled so many toxins that he got that not-so-rare sickness the Pentagon said didn't exist until one hundred thousand other guys got it. No Purple Heart or Silver Star, but he did qualify as a ten-point disabled vet who could get one federal job after another and milk that advantage for the rest of his life, much to the chagrin of applicants twice as qualified and three times more educated. He chose the National Marine Reserve Service, a new agency, because he liked boats, he said. He could be what he'd been in the army, a ranger. A "danger ranger," Taylor called him, well-meaning and eager to please, but the kind of guy whose compass was half a bubble off-level. Spend a day with him and you knew all there was to know, Taylor said, and that was too much. Poor Ron, he wanted to be admired, and in this he would be forever disappointed. Anne thought her sister, Nancy, would have liked Ron, were she still alive. Nancy liked everybody.

Nancy, her lifeless, ragdoll body lifted from the sea all those years ago by Keb Wisting. . . . The water stinging cold, his powerful hands. *Does he remember? Does anybody remember? I lived and she died. Why?*

Ron said, "Ruby Bauer had a nephew in Jinkaat who was a basketball star until he ruined his knee in a logging accident. He might have made it to the NBA; now he'll end up flipping burgers at McDonald's in Juneau."

"His name is James Wisting and he's not flipping burgers in Juneau," Victor announced. "He's in Jinkaat helping his grandfather carve the canoe, along with a lot of other people."

"I think we're too preoccupied with this canoe," Paul said.

"I don't," Kate said, rising to her feet, sunlight dancing off her graying golden hair. "If this basketball kid has charisma, and he and his grandfather and his clever aunt make a statement with this canoe, if anything related to this legal case pulls on heartstrings and weakens our position, we'll have a public relations problem and I won't be happy. But right now I'm hungry. I'm always hungry in Alaska. I propose that Ron and Taylor make lunch while Anne drives us up the bay and you gentlemen talk legal strategy so we can win this thing. We're not going to lose the first major legal challenge to this important new agency. The oceans are turning acidic, and only six percent of the world's marine fisheries are healthy. And now radiation from Fukushima could end up in Pacific salmon. On top of that, the North Pacific Garbage Patch, a miasma of floating plastics north of Hawaii, is twice the size of Texas. I've seen it and had nightmares about it."

"I've seen it too," Anne said. "It's horrible."

"Highly regarded scientists see the natural world failing everywhere, and at nobody's peril more than our own," Kate said. "If we pass any single tipping point beyond all mitigating strategies, we'll never again have the bountiful world we once did. When I was a little girl watching TV, I rooted for the Indians, not the cowboys. I never liked Scarlett O'Hara on her big plantation, or Clint Eastwood with his big gun. This legal case isn't anti-Native. It's about big business buying whatever it wants, including our own government, and destroying the natural world. Well, guess what? We're part of that natural world. And now big business wants Crystal Bay, the only national marine reserve in Alaska, home to salmon, sea otters, and humpback whales. Well, I have news for them—they can't have it."

Kate's pronouncement hit Anne like a sharp sea breeze. She looked at Taylor, who grinned. She was catching her breath when Kate asked, "There's a tidewater glacier north of here, right?"

"Yes."

"Well, let's go."

cold metal burning

I T WAS A canoe, or the shadow of one. No denying it, Old Keb told himself. This wood was going to sea, and so was he. He rubbed his hands over it every day, many times a day. Dreamed about it at night, many times a night. He tried to remember how many years ago he had floated the log with the Haida, and gathered stories and blessings when they shot the gunwale lines. Were the lines still true? It's no easy thing to make a dugout canoe. Your hands turn to leather, arms to pistons. Trees are living things and if done right, canoes are too. They grow with the rain, and run with rivers, and like all rivers, return to the sea. You had to get the cedar just right, on your side; know the grain as you know the rain, make it work with you. Bless the tree. Tell more stories. Give thanks and sharpen your adz. Plank it down, shape the hull, and from the planks make paddles, some for gifts. Hollow it out just right. Then firescore it and steam it open. That would draw a big crowd. Add the raised bow and stern pieces, the thwarts and gunwale rails, maybe a mast or two, and simple cloth sails. Work with old tools in the old ways. They slow you down and make you think. Never mind outboard motors and aluminum boats and the empty faces of people who sit stone-still at the tillers and see little of what sees them.

Every man should take an epic journey, Uncle Austin used to say. Paddle into his terror, the secret language of storms, back to a time before television and the chaos of too much stuff, too many things, too many gadgetgizmos, back before basketball, when we slept on the ground and the full moon needled us awake, when wintertime was story time and even the sky listened, when we belonged to no banner or monarch or team, only the kingdom of trees, a kingdom without a king. Remember *yakwtlénx'*? Big red cedar canoes. You could travel blue water in them. Steer by the stars until the stars made no sense and the senses made new maps and the maps made a new you, a you that feared to forget until you forgot to fear. Follow gray whales to the Arctic.

Bring back stories of *hintak xóodzi*, the polar bear, and *kooléix'waa*, the underwater brown bear, or walrus. You could define yourself by your canoe; see it as a living thing, a steady companion.

Remember those first couple swings of the adz? For days afterward Old Keb couldn't lift his arms over his head. His elbows hurt day and night. He couldn't sleep or feel his thumbs. "Bursitis," Nurse Byers told him. "Why are you building this canoe?"

"For my grandson . . . to make him believe."

"Believe in what?"

"Himself." *And in me, the journey I need to take.*

Keb could have used the raven feather, but James had taken it with him to Seattle for more surgery. Such darkness filled the boy these days, his mother, too, her health failing. Twenty years of Coke, and now diabetes. Keb worried that no matter how old he got, Gracie would still be his daughter, and James his grandson, their pain seeping into him like January rain. For long days James would disappear. Ask him where he'd been and he'd give you a look like the flat edge of a knife. How is it that young people most need our love when they least deserve it?

It was now late July, nearly three months since the accident on Pepper Mountain. These last couple weeks, James had worked on the canoe with great inconsistency, some days handling the adz well, other days swinging it with such brute indiscretion that Old Keb had to send him away.

It brought to mind a word from Old Keb's Norwegian side, one he had learned at fifteen when he moved to Petersburg, a fishing town south of Juneau, and lived there for two years with his cousins. Uncle Austin had told Keb it would be good to leave Jinkaat and taste the Scandinavian side of himself, catch fish as Petersburg boys do, by troller, seiner, gillnetter, and grit, back in the heyday of salmon, before the big crash and any fancy talk of sustainability. Men would get angry, their tempers afire over the dying bounty. They always blamed the other guy. But there was another kind of anger, one described by the Norse word *angr*, that described not a short temper but a deeply felt grief at what had gone wrong with the world.

That was James. A prisoner of *angr*.

AGAIN, OLD KEB heard the motorcycle before he saw it. It caught air coming up the hog-backed road and skidded to a stop near the carving shed. Kid Hugh climbed off and came loping over, wearing that same Lakers jersey and ball cap backwards on his long-haired head, a tool belt on his waist, hammer tapping his thigh. He nodded at Kevin, who sat on a stump, carving another alder spoon. "I got news," he said. "Taff Neumayer fired Charlie Gant this morning."

Oyyee . . . that was news. Charlie had been Taff's foreman for years. He'd done a good job by all accounts. But everybody said he was in trouble for what he did on Pepper Mountain, skidding the logs upslope instead of high-leading them. Had this contributed to James getting hurt? The trooper investigation was ongoing.

"That's not all," Kid Hugh said. "Tommy Gant got mad and went into Taff's office and cut his big hemlock desk in half with a chain saw."

Keb got his mouth working and said, "Where's Tommy now?"

"Nobody knows. He took off with Pete Brickman and could be anywhere." A million miles of old logging roads ran out of Jinkaat all over the place. Roads to nowhere. Hundreds of hideouts. "Stuart is out looking for them. Coach Nicks says two troopers are flying out from Juneau. Do you know where James is?"

"No."

Kid Hugh had just come from Helen's Rumor Mill Café where he heard Daisy say that Truman said that Taff must have decided it was no accident that James got hurt with Charlie on the yarder. "So he fired Charlie, and Tommy got pissed, and Tommy's saying that James lied to Taff in his report, for revenge."

Revenge. Not a pretty word. Keb felt a chill. Kid Hugh was talking so fast that he made a train wreck of his words and left Old Keb lying on the tracks feeling run over.

"Anyway," Kid Hugh said, "I think James is in danger."

Danger. Did that word have a Norse root too? Old Keb put his weathered hands on the canoe. He thought about his time as a boy hunting deer with Uncle Austin, holding so still he had to remind himself to breathe. Now again, he reminded himself. . . . If James died, Gracie would too. Die in a way that left her walking around but seeing nothing. Keb reached into his lungs. Drawing on his fine command of language, he said nothing. He ached and felt small, pinned to the ground by the knowing of it all. He saw Kevin watching him, lower lip between his teeth; Kid Hugh watching him too, those arctic eyes. He remembered how Uncle Austin talked about bears having hands, not paws, and how to catch a coho you had to put a smile on the face of the herring, the baitfish. Not the same as hunting and gathering at Fred Meyer and Costco, stalking the crafty canned vegetable or the fleet-footed packaged hamburger. He could pray, but he wasn't good at it, not like other people who spent all their time angling in this life for a better deal in the next life. Damn, he missed so much. Too much. He thought: the Russians killed us and the Americans incorporated us, but we are still here. After all you've done to us, we are still here.

After a minute he picked up the heavy adz and was about to strike the canoe when Kid Hugh raised an arm and took the adz. "Let me," he said.

Everybody used those words: "Let me."

No one person would carve this canoe. No single master carver and his young spirit helper in time-honored Tlingit tradition. Keb was too old to do it himself, too brittle and bent over. Everybody knew it. So they arrived in their oil-stained work gloves and boots, and followed his instructions, a dozen hands swinging the adz. No ordinary adz either, but the one Keb gave to James, made from a leaf spring from one of Mitch's old junkyard trucks, some forty years ago. First Coach Nicks, then Big Terry McNamee, the air-taxi pilot and chief of the Jinkaat Volunteer Fire Department. What they lacked in precision they made up for in power. Soon other carvers brought more adzes, and the canoe began to take shape. Watching Big Terry bite into it you'd have thought he was made from parts of Mitch's truck, too—pistons for forearms, exhaust manifold for a face, hot sweat dripping off his nose. He would have blown a gasket had Little Mac not rescued him with lemonade. Oddmund skipped a day of fishing to help. Dag too. And Truman. The basketball team showed up. Even Deputy Sheriff-in-Training Stuart Ewing managed a few good swings. Now Kid Hugh removed his tool belt, pulled on his gloves, set his feet apart, and lit into the red cedar with strike after strike, all accurate.

Keb sat down, certain of the coming conflict. Charlie and Tommy unemployed. People talking. Angr rising. Uncle Austin used to say that when men set out to destroy each other, the first victim was always the same: truth.

THIRTY MILES TO the northwest, in the heart of Icy Strait, James Hunter Wisting hobbled down a mountain, hauling a head-shot Sitka black-tailed deer, a small buck with a rope around its neck. Before dragging it down through mosses, sedges, and small twin flowers—plants the deer had eaten all its life—he'd taken a sharp knife to the belly, opened it and found a fragrance, the moist smell of Earth, something Gramps had spoken of. He had said that when it happens, when the deer gives itself to you this way, it's a gift the hunter must accept with gratitude. That was asking a lot these days. James was sick of thankfulness and the same old pep talks from his mother and from Coach Nicks and his everything-will-work-out-for-the-best bullshit on what's right and wrong and what lies in between. Sick of himself. Mostly himself, and the boneheaded idea that one day he'd stumble into somebody he could be. James liked Ruby because she said none of this. "You got robbed, nephew," she'd said instead. "You shouldn't have gone logging up on Pepper Mountain. You know that now. Pull yourself together and land on your feet because it's better than landing on your head."

James had laughed when she said that, and she laughed too. Then they hugged.

The day had begun early for James, before dawn, when he went down to the Jinkaat Boat Harbor and stole the *Lumpsucker*, Oddmund Nystad's aluminum skiff. Oddmund always kept the skiff tied abeam of his forty-foot Bayliner, the *Norway*, where the *r* kept falling off. Every time Oddmund replaced the *r*, it'd fall off again, or a raven would take it. So the *Norway* became the *No Way*. James figured that he hadn't really stolen the *Lumpsucker*; he'd just borrowed it, since Oddmund had said he could use it anytime he wanted, so long as he asked.

He just forgot to ask.

Yes, he could have taken the *No Way* and made a nice meal in the big galley, taken a hot shower, and lived like a king. But the *No Way* had a top speed of eleven knots. That might be fine for Oddmund and Dag. But James wanted something fast, a rocket, a skiff fast enough to outrun any NMRS ranger boat.

He had told Taff Neumayer the truth about the Gants, how Charlie had skidded the logs that day, and Tommy was jealous of him dating Little Mac.

"Tommy and Little Mac don't concern me," Taff said. "I want to know about the skidding operation. Write down everything you remember, then sign this statement."

James hung the deer from a sturdy spruce just inside the alder fringe, a good place, as Lemesurier Island had no bears or wolves. Gramps had explained that the island had no large predators because of strong currents in Icy Strait. Mainland bears and wolves couldn't make the swim. But how did the deer get here? Long ago, when the glacier filled Crystal Bay and reached across Icy Strait, ice might have bridged the mainland to the island. Hungry deer could have crossed over the ice, looking for food, and found a new home. When the great glacier retreated far back into Crystal Bay, a small population of deer would have remained on Lemesurier Island.

What would it have been like to live back then, when stories colored the world and even the sky listened? When Tlingit people stood thigh-deep in cold rivers, naked; caught wild salmon with handmade nets and spears, and ate with the people they loved, and everybody pitched in, and nobody complained? When people spent so much time on the water, in the water, they became water themselves, liquid people. They didn't bemoan their way of life or say it was hard. It was the only life they knew. They didn't say, "We're going hunting." It sounded arrogant. According to Gramps, they said, "We're just going out to have a look around." That way, the animals came to them.

Awhile back, Gramps had told James to start bathing in the ocean, to get ready, get tough.

"To become a warrior?" James asked.

"No, the world has too many warriors. You'll be a peacekeeper, a healer."

JAMES MADE QUICK work of skinning the deer. When he finished, he felt calm. Gramps was right, working with your hands was a good thing. He sat on the cobble beach and pulled out his sharpening stone. He missed Little Mac and considered that he liked himself best in her company. She sometimes got upset with him, and when she did he knew she was right. She had told him to stop feeling sorry for himself, to start looking beyond his accident.

"It wasn't an accident," he had said.

"You don't know that."

"You don't know what I don't know." What a stupid thing to say. Why did words always get in the way? He could always think more clearly out here, outside, as if he could hear himself better and arrive at conclusions he couldn't otherwise find.

Aunt Ruby had high expectations of him, as she had of her own sons: Josh the investment banker, and Robert the Coca-Cola executive. Their dad, Günter, a German engineer and businessman, had opened the first Audi dealership in Juneau. Everybody said he would lose his shirt, but the dealership boomed, and Uncle Günter and Aunt Ruby took expensive vacations to Europe.

Meanwhile, his mom worked as a teacher's aide and lived like a pauper. Looking back, James couldn't remember one tender moment between his mom and father. Eight years ago, when he was only ten, James flew down to Denver to surprise him. "You're such a little guy and the plane is so big," Mom had said in the Juneau Airport departure lounge. "I'll be okay," James told her, trying to be a man. Mom said, "He's going to disappoint you, but you need to learn that for yourself." James came home early, his face wet with tears, and never talked about his father after that.

THE TIDE WAS rising. James hobbled down the beach, pushed off the skiff, and started the outboard. He pulled out his iPod, plugged himself in, and opened the throttle. It was like flying: the boat skimming over a flat sea, music drumming in his ears, wind sweeping back his long hair. He motored north to Point Carolus, just inside Crystal Bay. By doing this, he added a second violation to his first: he shot a deer out of season, and entered a national marine reserve in a motorized vessel without a permit. The rangers would ticket him if they caught him.

Let them try.

He bow-landed on the flooding tide and ran his anchor line up the beach. It was late afternoon. He could not stay long. He sat on the rocks and ate and worried about his mom, how she looked lately—not well. He reached into his big coat pocket for a cigarette and found the raven feather. Had he put it there? He pulled it out and watched it catch the sun, the blue iridescence. He saw a vision of a woman in a boat; no, a woman in rough seas next to a boat, her face stricken, her hand reaching for his. It startled him. The rifle suddenly felt heavy across his lap. He tore his eyes away and looked north to the distant mountains dressed in snow, wintry despite the July sun. Would those mountains gather enough ice one day to rebuild the glaciers and reclaim the entire bay? Gramps had Tlingit names for those mountains and glaciers. Names for every cove, river, and meadow, every plant and animal, and stories behind the names.

A bald eagle landed in a nearby spruce and made a piercing cry. Eagles mate for life. If one dies, do they mourn for life? James caught himself wanting to cry or scream. What was it Gramps said? It takes a while to understand that there is something out there bigger than you, something greater than what you've designed for yourself.

Aunt Ruby had spoken to him about his "new future." Yes, he would never play for the NBA, but he could make a big difference in a more important game, help her one day take back what was hers, his, theirs.

The feather stirred.

James looked about for the wind, as if it had a face. A whale surfaced nearby, its blow so percussive it startled him. Another whale surfaced, then two. Humpbacks. A minute ago there were none. Now there were—what? Four . . . five . . . six? Where had they come from? They blew again and showed their flukes. Minutes passed. In the absence of his own breathing, James heard the strangest thing. Again, his rifle felt heavy, and warmer than before. Cold metal burning. He set it on the ground and got to his feet, certain his ears were playing tricks. He listened with fierce intensity, trying to purge all noise from his mind. He opened his mouth, thinking it would help, but thinking itself was a kind of noise. A low melody arose, and for a moment James was the only human alive. What he heard was singing.

Whales singing.

the rounded shore the same

SIXTY MILES TO the north, Anne dropped anchor and Kate Johnson announced that the two of them, she and Anne, would row ashore in a small punt while everybody else stayed on the *Firn*. Paul Beals frowned.

"It's okay, Paul," Kate said with a rueful grin, "we'll send up smoke if we get lost or attacked."

Anne pulled on the oars and watched Paul watch them as a father would watch his daughters going off on their first date with their hemlines too high and their necklines too low. A Mormon, he had a passel of kids, six or seven, most of them grown and making kids of their own, a sea of all-American faces with striking blue eyes and gossamer hair, a tribute to Genesis from the Old Testament that we humans be fruit flies and multiply. Near as Anne could tell, Paul differed from many Mormons. He had read Aldo Leopold and concluded that nature wasn't a commodity humans owned, it was a community we belonged to. Anne liked and respected him, and felt sorry to see him looking so forlorn as she rowed away with the former astronaut and first director of the National Marine Reserve Service.

"He'll be fine," Kate said. "He's the one who needs to talk to those lawyers, not me. Besides, your friend Taylor looks like she can handle those four."

The oars dipped in and out of quiet water. Small icebergs tapped the hull. Black-legged kittiwakes called from their cliff nests near the tidewater face of Margerie Glacier, a blue-white river of ice flowing into the sea. "Their eggs are elliptical," Anne said of the kittiwakes. "That way they roll in tight circles and not off the ledges."

Kate acknowledged this with rich, liquid eyes. She leaned back, elbows on the gunwale. The punt had less than a foot of freeboard, yet she showed no concern. Small in size only, she seemed to embrace the day in a way that made everything else large. She reached over to trail her fingers in the cold water. Her golden gray hair, previously pulled back in a tight knot, fell across her face. She picked up a piece of ice, studied it and let it go. Anne kept pulling. "You said you knew this old man canoe carver in Jinkaat," Kate said. "How well?"

The sun had come out. The air felt kind.

"Not well. He saved my life when he pulled me out of the ocean twenty years ago. A storm capsized my boat, off Shelter Island, near Auke Bay."

"Are you serious?"

"Yes . . . my sister, Nancy, was with me. She didn't make it; she hit her head and drowned. I remember him pulling her out of the water with incredible strength, trying to save her, revive her, get her to breathe again. I remember his hands, his amazing hands."

"Oh my—"

"I doubt he remembers me."

"You've not reconnected with him?"

"No."

"He might not remember *you*, but I'm sure he'd remember the incident, and he'd be happy to see you again, see how you're doing."

"I've lived in Hawaii for the last twelve years. I got my master's degree there in marine biology at the Manoa Campus in Honolulu, with a focus on whale acoustics. I did my fieldwork in the Pailolo and Auau channels between the islands of Maui, Lanai, and Molokai. This is my first summer back home, in Alaska."

"So Alaska is home?"

"I think so."

"How's it feel?"

"Cold."

"I'm sorry about your sister."

"Yes . . . me too, thank you."

"Whale acoustics, what's that?"

"Whales vocalizing, singing. They do it in Hawaii, during courtship, males mostly, and we think they do it here, too, in Alaska, but not as often."

"You do seem at home here, I have to say."

"Is that a compliment?"

"Take it as you wish. It warms my heart to see young, skilled, dedicated women like you and your friend Taylor in the NMRS."

"We're not that young." *Or dedicated. Maui Wowie.*

"You know what I mean."

"Yes, I know what you mean."

THE LITTLE PUNT slid onto shore and Anne rested the oars. Kate asked, "How well do you know the Tlingit people in Jinkaat?"

"Not well."

Kate's expression said this wasn't the answer she wanted.

"I know their culture is matrilineal," Anne added.

"Meaning?"

"In the past, every Tlingit was born into the moiety of his mother, but had to marry into another moiety. A raven married an eagle, an eagle married a raven. But I'm not sure it's still that way, since Jinkaat has a lot of Norwegians and Germans."

Kate shook her head. "I want to know how the Jinkaat Tlingits see their relationship to Crystal Bay."

"From what I've heard, many feel displaced, and want more time in the bay to collect gull eggs and hunt seals and live like their ancestors did, when Crystal Bay was their homeland, their grocery store."

"But PacAlaska is a corporate approach."

"Yes, and I think that worries many Jinkaat Tlingits."

"So while many want a greater presence in the bay, only some support the PacAlaska lawsuit?"

"I think so, yes. They're relieved that Crystal Bay is a marine reserve, and protected."

"Are they willing to say so publicly?"

"You're asking the wrong person. This is my first summer back here. I've only been to Jinkaat a couple times to land at the airport, the last time in a single-engine Piper Cherokee before going on to Juneau. That's when I last saw Old Keb Wisting, in May, when he got on our Marine Reserve Service plane after his grandson hurt his leg."

"The Marine Reserve Service gave him a ride into Juneau?"

"Yes. It was Paul's idea."

Anne could see Kate processing this, figuring out how to make it work to her advantage. Kate said, "Paul tells me you spend a lot of time on the water."

"Looking for whales."

"Looking. Seeing. Developing your vision."

It was true. Anne had sharp eyes.

"Do you plan on making a career in the federal government?"

"I don't know. I'm still figuring it out. I've thought about starting a nonprofit someday, for community development. I also love whale research."

"I ask because you're a seasonal employee with no retirement or benefits. You have little to lose by telling me the hard honesty of what you see and think and know."

"About what?"

"Anything. Your job, your boss, the PacAlaska jurisdiction case, the people of Jinkaat who consider Crystal Bay their homeland. Whatever you feel free to tell me, I'll hold in strict confidence. You have my word."

Paul Beals is a nice guy but has the courage of a rabbit. I hate safety meetings and love mango salsa. . . . "Other than Keb Wisting, who's mostly Norwegian, I've never spent much time with a Tlingit from Jinkaat."

"Here's my concern: as this PacAlaska case heats up, Tlingits in Jinkaat could get excited and start staging press events in the bay, bring media attention that could affect the final court ruling. However this lawsuit goes, it could set case law for other marine reserves and ocean conservation policy. It could weaken our jurisdiction everywhere."

Everywhere? The last time Anne checked, the US had seven marine reserves: two in Florida, two in Hawaii, and one each in California, Maine, and Alaska. No more. The US Marine Reserve System was young and small, with Kate Johnson handpicked by the president, like an apple. "They want their ancient homeland back," Anne said. "Every summer the NMRS brings the Jinkaat schoolkids into Crystal Bay on a tour boat, so they can see and learn and develop their own relationship with the bay."

"Yes, I support it 100 percent. But the Jinkaat Tlingits are part of a large corporation now. They've made their choice. They can't have it both ways."

Can't they? Anne decided she liked Kate Johnson better back on the *Firn* eating lunch, when she had pita bread in her mouth and hummus on her hands and laughed at Taylor's wit.

Kate climbed out of the punt, stood on her toes, and stretched. Anne could hear distant streams tumbling off mountains, a thousand voices speaking of ice melting into water, rock pulverized into silt, habitats coming alive, rebirth and change, everything on its way to becoming something else.

Kate said softly, almost to herself, "I became a grandmother two months ago. It changes everything, you know, motherhood. Are you—"

"No. I was engaged once, but he loved sports more than he loved me."

"When I was in the space shuttle, my own hand was larger than the world we call home. I was traveling at five miles per second, and could cover Africa with my finger." She studied the mountains with her steady eyes. "It changed my life."

"I think the sea is the same," Anne said. "Go deep enough and the blue turns to black, right? It's not outer space, it's inner space."

"Like the human heart," Kate said with a rueful smile.

Yes, well, the human heart, forever inexperienced. Anne remembered her stepfather, a plum-faced man who mocked her mom and fished off the pier and pitched cigarette butts into the sea. "You, a scientist?" he had said to Anne when she came home from first grade after learning about Rachel Carson and announcing what she'd be one day. "Where'd you get a crazy idea like that?" It's a brutal thing to discover that some men should never be fathers, and yours is one. She thought about Nancy, beautiful Nancy, who could get people to tell her the truth even when they lied to themselves.

"I hate him," Anne had whispered late one night in their bedroom.

Nancy, three years older than Anne, whispered back, "Just because his dreams didn't come true doesn't mean yours don't have to."

KATE REACHED INTO her pocket and extended a hand. "This is my card. Do you have a cell phone?"

"Yes, but it doesn't always work in parts of the bay."

"Do you have a satellite phone?"

"No."

"Get one. Paul tells me you're working the lower bay this summer, out into Icy Strait, off Point Adolphus."

"If that's where the whales are, I'm there too."

"That's where the Jinkaat boats will be. If you see anything suspicious, I want you to call Paul. If you can't reach him, call me. Don't worry about waking me, with the four-hour time difference between here and Washington. I'd like to hear from you."

"I've got VHF radio contact with Ron at reserve headquarters, in Bartlett Cove. He's my immediate supervisor."

"I know. Feel free to call me as well."

Anne stared at her.

"Are you comfortable with that?"

"I'm a whale biologist, not a patrol ranger."

"You're an employee of the US National Marine Reserve Service. Paul tells me you have a law enforcement commission."

"I do. Point Adolphus isn't in the reserve, you know?"

"But the waters around it are administered by the National Marine Fisheries Service, our sister agency. You've got jurisdiction there."

Was this true?

"We need you to be our eyes and ears, Anne. That's all I'm asking. Be our eyes. Report everything you see. You can still do your whale work."

Anne told Kate what she wanted to hear. She would be her eyes and ears and call by VHF radio, cell phone, or satellite phone. What she didn't tell her was that long ago native Hawaiians used a member of their tribe—a wise old woman called a *wahanui*—to protect their identity by divining the biases of outsiders who came looking for knowledge and telling them exactly what they wanted to hear. She would confirm their prejudices and make them think they knew everything, while in fact they knew nothing, and send them packing as ill-informed as when they arrived. Another thing Anne didn't tell Kate was a story she'd heard years ago about an astronaut and an anthropologist who visited a remote island tribe. When the anthropologist told the tribe that his colleague had been to the moon, an old shaman was brought forward, who said that she too had been to the moon, many times.

Anne was thinking that no science is so complete or poem so perfect that one cannot benefit from the other. A cold wind brushed her neck, a breath off the glacier. She heard Kate announce that she was going to take a short walk. Would Anne be so good as to wait with the punt? A crazy impulse hit Anne, to pull out the Maui Wowie and smoke it in front of the Grandmother Astronaut. Kiss it all good-bye. No retirement. No benefits. Little to lose. She pulled out her journal instead, and sat with her back against a rock.

Remember when we talked all night
and rounded the rounded shore?
the sky was cold, and old
and young, too
Did I say that,
or did you?
Frozen stars, melting sun
Watching the rivers run
We finally slept
when morning came
everything new, ancient, patient,
the rounded shore the same.

KATE RETURNED, BREATHLESS with an idea. "Paul is scheduled to speak in Jinkaat next week. It could be challenging. I'm going to change my plans and join him. My celebrity status can be a plus in times like these. I'll have Victor join us. That way we can be a triumvirate of sorts, a team, to explain our case in Crystal Bay. What do you think?"

"Great," Anne said.

Wahanui strikes again.

a cornbread crime

OLD KEB FIGURED that if a greedy man could put his money where his mouth is, stuff it all in there, then he couldn't talk anymore and that would be a good thing.

This particular man was Harald Halmerjan, chairman of the board, looking mighty smart up there in his suit and tie. Important, too. Most people with money are, or imagine themselves to be. There's nothing more powerful than the imagination, as Truman said. So they make their reputations by the acre, as Harald did now, on stage in the Jinkaat High School gymnasium, at one end of the basketball court, talking about a hundred high-minded things, so many things and so high-minded that Old Keb heard his voice as a sticky, wet, bubble-gum hum. Harald had a lot to say and was saying it to a packed audience. He gripped the podium with his big ham hands. Never mind that he used other people's time. Seated next to him and waiting her turn was Ruby.

Keb felt his heart break.

He set his mind on pies. Strawberry, nagoonberry, or rhubarb pie, any pie. Cherry pie from Juneau Safeway. Apple pie from Fred Meyer. Cow pie from Trinidad Salazar's lupine field and horseshoe pitch with his inflatable puffin. Shoe-fly-pie from Peter Becker's Boot Shop. Any pie to erase Harald Halmerjan, the Great H. H., often wrong but never in doubt. Gracie once said that H. H. treated Big Oil like a good neighbor, or an ATM, whatever that meant.

H. H. blathered on.

Keb sat in the back row in a small metal chair that cut off blood to everywhere. His toes were numb. His ass felt like lead. His back ached. He had to pee. He was hot. His heart raced. He had no pills. He had to get outside and breathe the earth, if it was still there. The gym smelled like paint thinner or a lacquer of some kind. He wondered: Why do we sit in here to decide how to do things *out there*?

His leg twitched. He moaned.

"Okay, Pops, get up," Gracie said, sitting next to him. She helped him. As bad as he felt, she looked worse. It wasn't just her size anymore. Gracie had always been big. Other people ate and she gained weight. It wasn't her fretting over James either, or her diabetes. Something else was going on. Gracie wasn't well.

Now Ruby was speaking, saying all the same things H. H. had said. Keb heard a lawyer cut her off from across the stage, a big guy who quoted a Frenchman named Alex Cokeville. That's how Keb heard it, *Cokeville*, a sugar water man with a lot to say about how runaway enterprise and industry built America but also threatened to destroy it. Apparently this Cokeville knew more about America than Americans knew about America, which didn't sound very American. It sounded French.

Gracie said the tall man next to the lawyer was Crystal Bay Superintendent Paul Beals, a nice guy by most accounts. Keb had met him once. The woman next to Paul was the famous astronaut who'd walked in space. That's what they called it, walking in space. Keb wasn't fooled. All they did was float along, tied to the mothership like a baby on an umbilical cord. He'd watched movies with Mitch, Vic, Oddmund, and Dag. Anybody could do it, Mitch said.

It was Oddmund's turn to testify. He approached the microphone, hunched forward like a human question mark, rolling up on his toes with each step.

Keb had to pee. He shuffled off toward the men's room at the back of the gym, a long and perilous journey on a waxed basketball court. He made it and did what he had to do. More peril. He washed his hands, gently soaping his new calluses from the adzes, wedges, and mauls that shaped the canoe. When he reentered the gym he was surprised to see Charlie Gant and a couple sidekicks standing nearby in a defiant knot. Charlie waved, and Keb waved back. That's what you do in a small town, you wave. Charlie walked Keb's way, open-faced, wearing an easy smile. As he did, Stuart Ewing called from nearby, "Hey, Charlie, got a minute?"

The smile fell off Charlie's face.

"Where you been?" Stuart asked.

"Around," Charlie said.

"You seen Tommy?"

"No." Charlie wore a dungeon face, a chin full of stubble under bloodshot eyes. His long hair was matted and unclean and sprinkled with spruce needles. Keb wondered if he'd been out sleeping under a tree.

"You know he's in trouble for cutting up Taff's desk," Stuart said. "The sooner he turns himself in, the better."

Charlie shrugged.

"People are wondering, who were the choker-setters that day, up on Pepper Mountain, and why you had the crew skidding the logs."

"Bugger off, Stuart. I made my statement to Taff."

"Where was Pete?"

"Pete?"

"Yes, Pete."

"He was cutting, I think. Felling trees further to the west, down the line."

Keb walked into the discussion. More of a shuffle than a walk.

"Hey, Keb," Charlie said, his face brightening. "How ya doing?"

"Fine."

Keb noticed that Stuart had the good sense to step aside. Charlie reached out and shook Keb's hand gently, allowing for the old man's bent, arthritic fingers. Coach Nicks walked up with Mitch and Vic and several boys from the high school basketball team.

Important things were being said back on stage. Oddmund had finished and Superintendent Beals was wrapping up. "You good people always make us feel welcome here in Jinkaat, by golly. Thank you for your attention, and your thoughtful questions."

Charlie said something that Old Keb missed.

"What?" Keb said.

"The canoe," Charlie said. "My buddies and me, we were wondering if we could take a couple swings at the canoe, when you work on it next. We heard it's kind of a community thing."

"Any time," Keb said.

"James won't mind?"

"No. He won't mind."

The shadow of a wolf crossed Charlie's face. "Look Keb, I have no argument with you or James. But you should know that what he did was wrong, telling Taff what he did about Pepper Mountain. It cost me my job."

"What is it you're saying, exactly?" Vic asked Charlie.

"I'm saying James is looking for somebody to blame and there isn't anybody to blame."

Coach Nicks stepped forward to project his full coachness.

Keb fidgeted. There was too much going on . . . too many people.

Charlie snapped his head back and forth as a crowd gathered. Keb tried to spread his arms, to give Charlie room; Charlie appeared to do the same for Keb. The crowd thickened and pressed in, moving toward the gym doors. Somebody stepped on Keb's foot as he felt himself jostled to and fro. Is this what Coach Nicks meant about a full-court press? Then, as quickly as it began, it ended. Keb could breathe again; the bulk of the crowd had passed by and was out the doors.

Keb looked over in time to see Stuart reach for Charlie and Charlie flick his arm away with terrible speed. Stuart's face turned the color of paper ashes in a cold stove. Charlie burst through the doors. Keb watched him, hoping he'd turn back for a final friendly gesture of some kind, but he did not.

BY NOW, TWO dozen people milled about the waxed gym floor like pebbles that wash up and down a beach, rubbing each other. No sooner had Charlie left than a new rubbing began, this one between Ruby and Gracie. By the time Keb got his foot to stop throbbing and his head tuned in, they were well into it. "So what then?" Ruby said, "you think we should live on government handouts? Live on welfare, buy cigarettes and booze with food stamps?"

"No," Gracie replied.

"What then? Move to a reservation? Build a casino?"

"No."

"What then? What's your solution?"

"I don't have a simple solution, okay? Nobody does. Not even you."

Ruby was going to win this argument like she won everything else. Keb knew what she was thinking: Wake up, Gracie. You're still standing in the middle of the meadow with your hands over your eyes. You're fooling nobody but yourself. It's the modern world.

But Ruby said none of this, bless her heart.

Gracie looked at him with a face full of apology.

At times Keb felt he could better govern a kingdom than a family. "Our children will be beautiful," Bessie had told Keb sixty years ago when they were expecting their first, Ruby. Yes, they were beautiful, and pigheaded and poor. The bills never stopped coming. Neither did the kids. Money was always tight. Work was toil, one odd job after another. What Keb loved most was his carving. It never earned him a cent, but it made him happy. So much risk and imagination, it set him free. That's it, isn't it? We are most free when we are most at risk. He gave it all away, the dozens of cedar masks and ornate paddles, the spoons, crests, and canoes. His family had a few happy years until the first son drowned, and Bessie died, and his two other boys had affairs with Jack Daniels. That left Ruby and Gracie divided in a new kind of poverty. "We are each other," Keb would tell them. "Like it or not, we are each other."

He heard a commotion and turned to see the famous woman astronaut working her way through the crowd, the biggest celebrity to hit Jinkaat since TV star Walker Texas Ranger bought licorice in Nystad's Mercantile and did some Kung Fu fighting with the local kids out in the street. Next to her was the big lawyer, bantering with Truman about Cokeville the French philosopher and other important things. Tall Paul Beals was in the mix too. Tall as a tree and taller still, the closer he got. Reaching down to shake the old man's hand, he said, "Keb, it's good to see you again. I've heard about your canoe and would love to see it."

Keb had no time to respond.

Harald Halmerjan swept into the crowd and got busy telling Paul how Crystal Bay National Marine Reserve, with help from PacAlaska, could better serve all Alaskans. Others piped in. Did one of the voices belong to the famous woman astronaut? Did she know Kung Fu like Walker Texas Ranger? Keb turned his mind to his canoe. Was the float line still straight and true? The next thing he knew, Paul was introducing him to the woman astronaut who walked in space and maybe did Kung Fu, and Harald was blathering on to anybody who would listen or not, raising his voice louder and louder until the famous astronaut winced and walked away, taking Paul with her. Where was Gracie? And Little Mac? And James? Keb needed fresh air. He needed Little Mac's fingers light on his forehead, brushing away his hair, playing sad songs on her guitar. Happy songs. Sappy songs. A glass of lemonade. The smell of cedar. The cut of the adz. Salty dreams, that's what he needed. The sounds of the sea. But all Keb heard was Harald Halmerjan, the great H. H., talk, talk, talking.

THE LAST TIME Harald came calling was on a cold, rainy October night a couple years back. Keb was pulling hot cornbread from the oven. While some people make their cornbread round, Keb made his square, and took no small satisfaction when it came out piping hot, lightly browned, ready for butter.

Of course he offered some to Harald.

Picture a man not fat but not thin, built-to-last, barrel-chested, balding. What little hair he had he combed over the crown of his condo-sized head in poor compensation for the cards Mother Nature dealt him. So much room up there, you could rent it. That was Harald, the former mayor of Jinkaat, a fine tenor with money in his pocket and gold in his teeth. Truman said he slept every night with a lawyer under his pillow. So what did Harald do that rainy October night? He grabbed a plate—no crime so far—and took a corner piece of Keb's cornbread.

Everybody liked the corners.

As Keb saw it, a perfect geometry defines square cornbread, cut four-by-four into sixteen pieces, equal in size but not texture. The best pieces are the corners. Harald took one. Could you blame him? But he didn't stop there. He went on to take three more, all corners, lathered in butter and stuffed down with hot venison stew and a bottle of cold Alaskan Amber, all while Keb watched in stunned silence.

"That's fine cornbread," Harald clucked.

Keb nodded.

To make matters worse, Ruby sat there and said nothing. She had arrived with Harald, dripping wet from the rain. "You know, Keb," Harald said (Keb remembered every word, his mind sharp in the presence of a cornbread crime), "you're the oldest man in Jinkaat. You're a knowledge-keeper."

"A what?"

"A knowledge-keeper, Pops." Ruby explained that a knowledge-keeper was an elder with great wisdom who never drew attention to himself, who kept his own wise counsel, avoided politics, had little interest in money, never stopped learning or teaching, knew a great deal about the land and sea, and had the respect of many people, young and old. He hardly ever spoke in public, but when he did (only for the most important causes) his words were unassailable. "It's a conundrum, you see. By staying out of the spotlight—out of the fray, you might say—a knowledge-keeper maintains his purity of heart and mind and soul. By entering the spotlight he enriches others with his wisdom, but he also taints himself with their attention and admiration."

Conundrum? Keb was thinking, what's a conundrum?

"We want you to know that we appreciate you," Harald said.

"Me? Why?"

"For everything you stand for, all the ways you enrich our lives."

"What do you want from me?"

Ruby touched his hand. "We don't want anything from you, Pops. We just want to thank you for all the support you give us."

"Support?"

"Yes, you know, in all the ways we want to make life better for the

Tlingits of Jinkaat and Icy Strait and Crystal Bay."

"Nobody lives in Crystal Bay."

"Not anymore, but they used to," Harald said.

"Long ago," Keb said, "when people traveled by canoe and had summer fish camps and knew all the right places to get food. Oyyee . . . good times but hard times too."

"Not that long ago," Ruby added.

It was then that Keb remembered looking down at his hands, the fingers bent, the nails warped and split, the skin deep brown, almost black around the knuckles. Uncle Austin's hands had looked the same when he was old. The October rain came down hard that night, but not a single drop got through the roof of the carving shed, Keb's home. The floor was bone dry. It's funny how we build things small, then big, then bigger. Everything was bigger these days, except open space. Uncle Austin used to say that the Tlingit never did build anything you'd find in the history books. Don't look for a Machu Picchu or Great Pyramid in Alaska. The greatest gift we can leave this world is the forest and the sea the way we found it, separate and the same, the oldest home of all, older and more beautiful than all the things industrious people pride themselves in building.

It was time to ask Ruby and Harald to leave. Keb dreaded it. It turned out he didn't have to. Gracie came through the door with James and Little Mac. Gracie took one look at Ruby and said, "I know what you're up to."

"He's my father, too."

"Leave him alone, Ruby." This was the old Gracie, back before her health turned bad, when she still had salt and vinegar in her. Keb had to hand it to Ruby. She didn't argue. She and Harald got to their feet and moved to the door and put on their raincoats. There'd be hell to pay later.

James and Little Mac watched with saucer eyes. He was a high school sophomore then, she a freshman. They didn't hold hands, but their shadows did.

"How's practice?" Ruby asked James as she pulled on her boots.

"Good."

"You going to play in the NBA someday?"

"I'd like to."

She tousled his hair. "You will." Without looking at Little Mac or her own sister, Ruby turned to Keb, "Thanks, Pops. I'll check in on you next week. It's nice to see this place so warm and dry. I guess Günter and Josh did a good job on the roof. Call if you need anything, okay?" She went out the door with Harald.

After a long silence, Gracie said to Keb, "She wants you to be a spokesman for PacAlaska. You know that, right?"

The old man looked at his hands.

"She's using you, Pops. I can't believe it. No, in fact—I can believe it. She's shameless. She wants you to help her get into Crystal Bay, so PacAlaska can make a ton of money. Do you know she makes two hundred grand a year in salary and bonuses for being on the board? It's obscene. Nobody needs that much money."

James said, "She bought me my last pair of basketball shoes, you know? Really good ones."

"I know, honey. She believes in you. I appreciate that."

"Do you?"

"Of course I do."

"She bought me other nice stuff, too."

"I know."

"Then why treat her the way you do?"

"James," Little Mac said softly, touching his arm.

He pulled away but didn't take his eyes off his mother. "How come every time I tell Aunt Ruby I'm going to play for the NBA, she says I will. But when I tell you the same thing all you ever say is 'Do your homework, do your homework.' That's all you ever say."

"James, I want you— "

"You want, want, want. Why can't you be more like Aunt Ruby and think about what other people want? Why can't you believe in me the way she believes in me?"

"I've always believed in you."

"Not like Aunt Ruby."

"I want your dreams to be realistic; I want your dreams to come true. I don't want you to be disappointed."

"Disappointed? Are you serious?"

"Yes, I'm serious."

"You're too late for that, Mom. Can't you see? You're way too late."

He grabbed Little Mac by the hand and stormed out the door.

KEB WOULD NEVER forget how Gracie turned to the wall and trembled, how he felt nailed to the chair, thinking: we build a perfect picture of what we want our children to be. And when that picture falls and shatters, what do we do? His sister Dot once told him: we get on our hands and knees and put the pieces back together, and call it parenting.

every sound drowned

IS THIS WHERE I'm supposed to be?
Anne poured herself a cup of coffee and drifted in the fog. August had blown in as if it were October: cold, wet, determined, dour. June seemed years away, May a distant memory. Come September, new snow would whiten the mountains and signal the end of summer. "Termination dust," Alaskans called it. Anne would be back at reserve headquarters, in Bartlett Cove, shackled to a computer, buried in data. Strange, how she had looked forward to office time earlier in summer, when the air was too cold, the water too deep, the distances too far. But now, after living day and night aboard the *Firn*, things had changed. She had changed. She loved the iron clouds and watchful trees, the million daily miracles seen and unseen. She loved anchoring up in quiet coves, fixing simple meals, using her polar fleece jacket for a pillow, sleeping without dark dreams. A while back she had awoken and realized the entire previous day had come and gone without her once thinking of Nancy.

Was it okay to forget?

The sea offered a calm reflection, a portrait, a mirror. On some days she could live above her sorrow, other days below. And what of the fog? *Am I off Point Adolphus?* She could have used her GPS, or radar. But what fun would that be? She could have stayed in Hawaii too.

She sipped her coffee and studied her map.

Immediately south of Crystal Bay, Point Adolphus was the northernmost landfall on Chichagof Island, where strong tides collided in a vortex of upwelling. Nutrient-rich bottom waters circulated up to mix with sun-bright surface waters in a rich seafood buffet of kelp, herring, sandlance, capelin, salmon, and krill that attracted eagles, seals, sea lions, orcas, and humpback whales. Only one percent of one percent of the world's ocean waters upwelled like this. Humpbacks could feast on huge numbers of krill and forage fish, mostly herring. "Great balls of herring," Taylor called it.

Okay, where are they?

A deep quiet had settled down with the fog. Anne was tempted to write of a silence that stretched all the way to Asia. But it wasn't so. A million birds were up early with a million things to say. Murrelets trilling and gulls chattering, silk-screened on a painted sea—mew gulls, Bonaparte's gulls, glaucous-winged gulls, even black-legged kittiwakes seventy miles from their cliff nests near Margerie Glacier, at the north end of Crystal Bay. Anne heard another call: plaintive, lyrical, leaking through the fog in a way unfamiliar to her. A loon? She drifted east with an incoming tide. The chart showed no offshore rocks, a good thing, unless she found an uncharted one at great expense to her boat and career, if she had a career.

Kate Johnson's words kept coming back to her: "You're a seasonal employee with no retirement or benefits." Ranger Ron had told her a dozen stories about luckless mariners who'd fetched up hard on rocks, some of them charted, others not. Be safe. Travel in twos.

Well, she'd take her chances. She liked being alone with her radio off, at least for a while, not lost but not found either, the business card from Director Kate and the satellite phone from Superintendent Paul deep in her pack with the stale crackers and smelly socks. Her patrol partner, Taylor, had found a sexy summertime boyfriend in Strawberry Flats, the small town next to Crystal Bay, and had asked Anne to patrol solo for a while. Find those whales, said Taylor. Make them sing. Bribe them if you have to. Taylor would join her on the next patrol, or the one after that. And safety? "Can't have too much safety," Taylor would say with sarcasm. "One day we'll seal ourselves in our homes and bubble-wrap our kids."

Folded over her map, Anne traced the north shore of Chichagof Island from its western extreme where it opened into the Gulf of Alaska, past the little fishing village of Elfin Cove to Point Adolphus, and east to Port Thomas and the town of Jinkaat. The map's creased and worn texture gave her comfort.

She had always loved maps.

She lowered the hydrophone, switched it on, and heard nothing but soft static. After half an hour she turned it off. A foghorn sounded at a distance, probably a cruise ship entering Crystal Bay, all those passengers wanting a sunny day. Even the wealthy can't bribe the weather. This fog had attitude, a low-pressure tenacity that would keep planes down for days, strand hundreds of travelers, force locals to ask why they lived here, and show no interest in their answer. Not many people went out in fog like this.

"HEY," a gruff voice yelled from nowhere, "watch your drift there."

Anne jumped to her feet. Dead ahead a skiff emerged from the fog with two young men, fishing poles in their hands, floating as if in a dream. Their boat pulled hard on an anchor line and was about to get smacked by a larger boat—her boat, a white, gleaming Bertram. A federal government boat. She turned the ignition and the *Firn* rumbled to life. She put the twin engines in reverse and backed away, swinging her stern to starboard. She could see them now, shaking their heads and talking as she wheeled the *Firn* around and approached them from their downside-drift. She needed to apologize.

"You got radar on that boat?" one man yelled as she drew near.

"Yep."

"Then use it. You almost ran us down."

"Ran you down? I was adrift at one knot."

"More like three or four knots if you ask me." He turned to the other guy. "What do you think?"

"Five knots, I'd say."

"Maybe ten knots," the first man said.

Yeah, right. Forget the apology. Anne throttled forward to hold her bow in the current, beam-to-beam with these two yahoos in their skiff, their anchor line played out with lots of scope. She had a good view of them now. Men? No, boys pretending to be men, thinking they were funny. Untouched by the wet and cold, the bigger one wore a T-shirt and jeans and a ball cap backwards over thick black hair. He had a darkness about his mouth and eyes. He wore a brace on one knee, and moved as if determined that his bum leg wouldn't slow him down. The other guy was spider-thin but tough, made of sinew and scars. He wore a Lakers jersey and looked young and old at the same time. What caught her most about the boy with the bum leg were his offset eyes, one a little higher than the other. Searching eyes. *Just goes to show, everybody is looking for something.*

"Pretty quiet out here," she said, as they reeled in their fishing lines.

"It was," answered the boy with the bum leg.

She could have asked what they were fishing for, and how it was going, but she didn't. Fishermen liked their secrets. She knew this from a summer on the Oregon Coast where she'd worked in a marine research lab. Ask any troller, gillnetter, or seine skipper "How's fishing?" and he'll likely say, "It's okay," or, "Getting by," or, "Could be better." Even if it's the best year he's ever had, he'll say, "Could be better." Anne knew. Don't ask. Find something else to talk about. "You a Lakers fan?" she said to the smaller guy.

"Yep."

"Not the Supersonics?"

"The Supersonics moved to Oklahoma."

"When did that happen?"

"Five years ago or so."

"Maybe ten," said Bum Leg. "Or twenty."

"The Oklahoma Supersonics," Anne said contemplatively. "That doesn't sound right."

"It's the Oklahoma City Thunder," said the smaller guy.

"So, you a Thunder fan?"

"Nope."

"Ah," Anne nodded and wondered, are these guys Tlingit? "Are you guys from around here?"

"I guess," Bum Leg answered. He asked his friend, "We from around here?"

"I guess."

He looked back at her. "I guess we're from around here. How about you?" Anne was thinking of a response when he added, "You know you've got a line over the side?"

Shit. The hydrophone cable. To avoid hitting the skiff Anne had steered a tight turn and forgotten the cable over the side. She put the *Firn* in neutral and left the controls. The minute she did, she began to drift. She hauled in the cable and coiled it on the deck. "It's a hydrophone," she said, as she powered forward and came back alongside.

"A hydrophone," Bum Leg said. "What for?"

"To listen to whales."

"You from Crystal Bay, the marine reserve?"

"Yep."

"What are you doing here at Point Adolphus, if you're Marine Reserve?"

"Looking for whales."

"You're not a ranger?"

"Some days I'm a ranger, other days I'm not. Do I look like a ranger?"

"A little."

"How?"

"You got a fancy-pants government boat."

"Lots of people have fancy boats and they're not rangers. I'm a biologist."

"You got a uniform?"

"Yeah, but I don't always wear it."

"How come?"

"Because I'm a biologist first, a ranger second. I don't like uniforms."

"You carry a gun?"

"Sometimes. How about you?"

"All the time. There are sea monsters out here, you know." He grinned.

"I didn't know that."

"You will."

"I'm just looking for humpback whales."

"But you work for the reserve. The reserve is over there." He pointed north.

"But the whales are here," she said. "They don't recognize reserve boundaries."

NEITHER DO WE, James thought.

This woman was a spark plug, a real lynx. No little flute of a voice. No makeup or neatly combed hair. She covered her deck with swiftness and ease, a can-do gal who'd come out of the fog like a vapor but then got behind the wheel to handle her boat better than most men, a nice touch. And she didn't ask, "How's fishing?" James tried to look at her without staring. No easy thing; she sat with her arm out the window, like what's-her-face in *Thelma and Louise*, the chick who didn't take shit from any man. "Where'd you learn to drive a boat like that?" James asked her.

"On the water."

"On the ocean, I'll bet."

"Same ocean as you got here."

"Yeah? Where?"

"Hawaii."

"They got lots of ocean there?"

"Enough."

"Any glaciers?"

"Just volcanoes."

"Any wolves?"

"Just dogs. Lots of dogs."

"How about bears?"

"Just whales."

"We got whales here, too."

"I know. That's why I'm here."

"What's a firn?" Hugh asked. He was studying the name on the bow. Studying everything.

"It's snow that's partly hardened into glacial ice."

"Any snow in Hawaii?" James asked.

"Nope, just lava."

"So you chase whales in Hawaii?"

"I don't chase them. I study them. I listen."

"And now you're chasing them here?"

She looked away from James, and said to Hugh, "Actually, there is snow in Hawaii, on the tallest volcanoes on the Big Island and Maui."

"And you listen to the whales with that thingamajig of yours?" James asked.

"It's a hydrophone."

"You record them?"

"I try."

"You ever heard them sing?"

She sat up like a watered flower. "Here in Icy Strait? No. Have you?"

"Yeah, once, in Crystal Bay."

By now Hugh was standing at the bow and pulling on the anchor line. He said to James, "Put it in gear and give me some slack. We have to go." It was time to get the cohos back to Old Keb for the big celebration. Lots of food. Lots of people. Lots to do.

"No, wait," the whale woman said. "You guys want some coffee?"

"No, thanks."

"It's Kona coffee, good stuff."

"No, thanks." James motored into the current as Hugh pulled up the anchor with cold water dripping off his hands.

"Where in Crystal Bay did you hear them sing?" the woman asked.

"See you later, lady ranger." James waved as he turned the skiff toward Jinkaat.

"I'm not a ranger," she yelled, "I'm a biologist."

James looked back to see her recede into the fog, suddenly distant in the roar of the outboard, every sound drowned.

against the wind

TOMMY GANT WAS supposed to be in jail, wasn't he?

Old Keb couldn't remember. He tried to focus. Tried to think. Days like this he felt as if he'd been old since he was young. His mind slowly closed around the vague notion that Tommy was supposed to be in jail, or on the run from state troopers and Stuart Ewing and everybody else, hiding somewhere, hunkered down wet and cold in a culvert under a logging road, eating slugs and shrews and toads.

But here he was, Tommy Gant, standing over Old Keb on the front step of Keb's carving shed, free as a wolverine, sodden and scruffy, arms fish-belly white, a guitar in one hand, a big baseball bat in the other. How strange was that? Louisville Slugger. Breakfast of Champions. Oyyee . . .

"Hey, Keb," Tommy said, "you got Little Mac in there?"

"What?" Keb looked up from his porch chair.

"Mackenzie Chen. Little Mac. I need to talk to her."

Keb blinked. Everything seemed to fall away into the distance. The fog, that was it. Tommy had come out of the woods and the fog. Keb's carving shed was in a clearing on the edge of town, far away from everything else, exactly where somebody could emerge unseen. A desperado and his sidekick. Tommy's buddy stood with him. Keb couldn't remember his name. When you deal with guys like this, you remember faces more than names. Brickman, that was it. Pete Brickman. More brick than man. Gracie and Little Mac were in the shed all right, whipping up a big feast for the noon potluck when lots of people would arrive from everywhere to steam open the canoe. Helen had opened up the Rumor Mill Café and enlisted half a dozen women to help her bake pies.

James and Kid Hugh were out catching *l'ook* for the grill. Coho salmon. Just thinking about it made Keb's mouth water, though right now his mouth had gone dry. Blame it on Tommy, who handed the Louisville Slugger to Pete, pulled the guitar over his shoulder, and stood there like a minstrel tuning it up. He began to play. Keb had to admit it sounded good; Tommy's hands moved like hummingbirds. People said he was the best musician in town, even after he clipped a finger on a table saw.

"Hey, Mackenzie," Tommy yelled. "I learned a new song I want to show you. Come on out. I know you're in there."

"Go away, Tommy," came Little Mac's voice.

"C'mon."

"Go away. I'm busy."

Tommy kept playing. Keb had questions for Tommy about what happened on Pepper Mountain, questions he wanted to ask and didn't want to ask, answers he wanted to hear and didn't want to hear. Pete took a couple swings with the Louisville Slugger, whiffing the air. His arms were bigger than most people's legs. Was he drunk? Yes, he was drunk. Tommy too, by Keb's estimation. Keb watched Pete walk over to Gracie's truck and swing the bat with great ferocity, missing the sideview mirror by inches.

Facing the front porch of the shed, his back to Pete, Tommy began to sing in a beautiful tenor voice.

Keb climbed to his feet. He had to think. Gracie had no more fight in her. She was sick and refused to go to the clinic. Little Mac had spunk, but in physical strength amounted to a *kaatoowú*, a chickadee. Tommy and Pete must know about the canoe, the steaming, the big feast. Pete took another crazy swing. Not good. Keb had a shotgun inside, an old one, like him, but couldn't remember where. He had a pellet gun, too, somewhere near the bed, a real zinger when you hit your mark. Worked good for shooing bears out of the garden.

He hesitated at the door.

Tommy stopped singing and yelled, "C'mon, Mackenzie, you gotta hear this. I wrote it just for you."

Pete leaned against the truck and lit a cigarette.

Keb went inside and let the door slam behind him. It took a minute for his one good eye to adjust. He saw Kevin in the corner, whittling knife in his hands, fear on his face. The two women stood near the kitchen table, under the bare light. Little Mac had the pellet gun, a Crosman Pumpmaster.

"Pops," Gracie said quietly, "where's the shotgun?"

"I don't know."

"What's happening out there?"

"They're drunk. Pete's got a big baseball bat."

"Is this thing loaded?" Little Mac asked.

"I think so. You have to pump it."

"Mackenzie!" Tommy yelled.

"Go away," she yelled back.

"Pete and I are coming in there."

"Go away."

Somebody laughed—not Tommy. Must have been Pete, Keb guessed. But the laugh died quickly, the voice changed. "Hey boy, back off—"

Keb opened the door to see Tommy and Pete backed against the truck by the menacing approach of Steve the Lizard Dog stalking them with forty sharp teeth and a menacing growl. Pete raised the Louisville Slugger. "Tell this damn dog to back off."

"He's not my dog," Keb said.

"Tell him to back off or I'll beat the pulp out of him," Pete said. "I swear I will." The cigarette, tight in his mouth, bobbed up and down as he spoke.

At that, Little Mac stepped onto the porch, pumped the pellet gun, and aimed it square at Pete's head. Keb could see the bat sweaty in his hands.

Steve held his ground, ratty hair and all, a stubby tail that he'd chewed off himself. Mitch said he must have chased his own butt until one day he caught it. His owners worked at Greentop and often forgot to chain him up. So Steve roamed about town like he owned the place, and got into nasty fights with other stray dogs. It fell to Old Keb, who made a project out of petting a dog, to discover Steve's soft side and take him in. One day each year any stray dog in Jinkaat could be shot on sight, by town ordinance. Imagine the betting pools that rode on the demise of Steve the Lizard Dog. Were it not for Old Keb, he would have been shot dead years ago.

Tommy looked at Little Mac forlornly. "I just wanted to show you a new song."

"Some other time," Little Mac said, her aim true.

"Let's go," Tommy said to Pete.

Gracie pulled out her little phone. Deputy Sheriff-in-Training Stuart Ewing would arrive in minutes. Keb found himself feeling sorry for Tommy, who eyed the dog, Little Mac, and the dog again.

Pete took a threatening step toward Steve, the bat held high. Steve erupted into barking more ferocious than before. Keb pulled his hands to his ears.

"C'mon, Pete," Tommy yelled.

Pete didn't move.

"What happened on Pepper Mountain?" Keb heard Gracie yell at Tommy.

Tommy shook his head. "I don't know. I've told everybody . . . I DON'T KNOW. Something broke."

Pete laughed a crazy laugh.

Little Mac shot a BB past his ear.

"Jesus Christ, woman, you almost hit me."

"Go," she said. She quickly pumped the gun.

Slowly the two men backed away, stalked by Steve. At the far edge of the clearing they hesitated, then slipped into the forest. The dog let them go but stayed put, ears up, listening.

"I think my James is in danger," Gracie said. "I have to figure out a way to get him out of town."

"I already have," Keb said.

A MILLION PEOPLE showed up for the steaming and potluck. That's how it seemed to Old Keb. Maybe two million, two hundred anyway, all in the clearing between the carving shed and Ruby's house. When he saw all the food—salmon, halibut, black cod, crab, venison, moose, dozens of pies and cakes and ten large plates of brownies—Keb's one good eye nearly fell out of his head. He had expected two dozen people, maybe three. But now it seemed as if the whole town was here, and more: the whole nation, universe, old friends and clan members from near and far, lots of people he knew and didn't know and others he didn't know if he knew and still others he didn't know if they knew he didn't know. But they all seemed to know him. So many handshakes and hugs and gestures of deep appreciation, people admiring the canoe, running their hands down its gunwales and flanks, a twenty-five-footer, not half as big as a great Tlingit war canoe but impressive still, a real beauty, pitched and smoothed with dogfish oil from Nathan Red Otter. Keb imagined his canoe culture as it once had been, reaching far back to when canoes made his people who they were, a liquid people with means to travel and trade and fish and hunt, before white men arrived with machines and words and poverty and wealth and tight shoes and quarterly earnings and Jesus on the cross. The canoe culture died, like Jesus. But could also be resurrected, like Jesus. Keb grinned. So many people happy to see each other and saying so. *Ax tòowoo sigóo ee xwsatèenee.* It felt like a potlatch from the long-ago time that Uncle Austin used to talk about, a heritage community—family, clan, nation, earth—when places had spirits, and those spirits adopted humans as newcomers and showed them how to hunt seal and catch salmon, and humans belonged to the land instead of the land belonging to humans; when canoes arrived from far away to mark a wedding, a birth, a passing into the great beyond.

James and Kid Hugh got the bonfire going and raked aside a large bed of coals for grilling salmon, halibut, black cod, venison ribs, and the four large moose flanks contributed by Oddmund and Dag. Floyd Bonner brought more than a thousand pounds of lava rocks from Mount Edgecumbe, a volcano near Sitka, to use in steaming open the canoe. He brought his mother, too, Galley Sally, an unsuccessful seafood chef who had no sense of smell and no clientele. Mitch said her peanut butter cookies made good roofing tiles. With her restaurant closed, Sally had time to help Floyd load the rocks into his seiner and make the two-day run up the outside coasts of Baranof and Chichagof Islands, a risky affair in bad weather.

Coach Nicks and the ballplayers met them in the boat harbor, loaded the rocks into trucks, and hauled them up to the festival. Everybody stacked the rocks around the fire to get them hot. Next, they poured seawater into the canoe. The parking area filled so quickly that people had to leave their rigs on the hog-backed road and walk into the clearing as if into a dream. Bonfire blazing. Dancers beating drums and moving about in their colorful regalia, wooden raven hats on their heads, *naaxein* about their shoulders. Chilkat blankets. Laughter and song and storytelling.

Keb loved it, and moved through the crowd in a happy daze, forgetting about Tommy and Pete as he licked pie juice off his fingers. He received warm greetings from people who said how good it was to have a beautiful new cedar canoe in Jinkaat. How long had it been? Nobody could remember. Daisy Robinson shed tears of joy and wasn't even Tlingit. She was Irish-Polish, from Boston. The whole thing was so wonderful, she said. She gave Keb a sloppy kiss that put cherry-red lipstick on his cheek. Carmen told him his horror-scope was looking good, then burst out, "My God, Keb, this is like so frickin' cool. All these people and that canoe, because of you. You rock. You totally rock. I love you so much." She kissed him too. Little kids ran around the clearing, and in and out of Keb's shed; bigger kids played Frisbee. Ty and Ronnie Morris thanked Keb for being so good to their dog, Steve. Looking back, Keb didn't remember when he didn't like dogs. Besides, things went both ways between him and Steve, as they did now, the old man slipping Steve bits of smoked coho and nagoonberry pie. Truman congratulated Keb and told him he was working on his screenplay, remember? The one he'd written years ago, the comedy mystery that his literary agent said was missing two key ingredients: comedy and mystery. He didn't stop talking until Brad Freer came by, green-gilled and lantern-jawed, looking for James. Not far away, Porter Danes, a Catholic, cruised the buffet table to pocket barbecued ribs and brownies. Reverend Billings watched him, straight-backed and judgmental, until he drank too much boxed wine and could be heard saying, "Praise the Lord and pass the potato salad." A dark-featured Latvian seine fisherman—Keb couldn't remember his name—came up to Keb and said, "If a thousand beliefs are destroyed in our march to the truth, we must still march on."

MITCH ARRIVED WITH his flatbed truck and front-end loader, ready to haul the canoe down to shore after the steaming. Keb saw him talking with James, Brad Freer, and Kid Hugh, all four sucking down cigarettes. Kid Hugh had that same lean and hungry look, as if he hadn't eaten in a while.

Too tired to work anymore, Gracie handed off her kitchen duties to Little Mac and Galley Sally and a hundred other women who chattered and laughed into the night.

When it came time for the steaming, a large crowd gathered. Nathan Red Otter, an old Haida from the Queen Charlotte Islands, a dear friend of Keb's from the time of Uncle Austin, was supposed to direct things. But Nathan was late or not coming or maybe dead, and Old Keb anguished. Only Nathan could tell the proper story—the history—of this canoe. The red cedar tree with its beautiful straight grain had come from his home, long ago, and been gifted to Keb. Nathan's uncle had selected it. Now the going-to-sea blessing belonged to Nathan, who was an old carver like Keb. Where was he? He was traveling with a granddaughter who had one of those little phones but wasn't answering.

A Tlingit master carver named Warren talked it over with Keb and James and Keb's good friend, Father Mikal, a Russian Orthodox priest. Warren came from Haines, north of Crystal Bay, and was the eldest son of Giff Taylor, the best friend of Keb's eldest son, both deceased. After a big discussion, Keb gave Warren a nod and directed him to climb high onto Mitch's front-end loader.

The crowd quieted.

"Sh tugáa haa ditee yagéiyi át kaax," Warren announced. "We have much to be thankful for." With a deep, strong voice he thanked everybody who helped to carve the canoe and otherwise showed their support, on behalf of Keb, who was honored by this outpouring of love and tradition.

"Gunalchéesh yá haa t'éit' yeeynaagi."

"Gunalchéesh," came a soft rainlike chorus of reply. Thank you. "Gunalchéesh."

"Gunalchéesh áyá yáa yee tula,aaní."

"Aaá. Gunalchéesh."

Warren explained that by putting hot rocks into the water-filled canoe, the steam would make the cedar pliable. Teams of men and boys would then use clamps and ribs to coax the canoe into greater capacity.

James had devoted hundreds of hours—more time than anybody else— to the carving, and become something of an artist, contouring the inside of the canoe with smaller bladed adzes. He no longer scowled, but he still limped, and probably always would. He stood now at the beam with his hand on the hog-backed gunwale, shoulder to shoulder with other men. The entire basketball team was there. When Warren finished the blessing and ceremoniously asked the name of the canoe, he looked at Keb.

The old man didn't answer.

James did: "*Óoxjaa Yaadéi,*" he said. "*Against the Wind.*"

a time singular and different

THE CROWD CHEERED as the first hot rocks hissed and dropped into the water. The steaming would take eight hours or more, with teams rotating through the work. Everybody got back to eating, storytelling, laughing, drinking, playing. Lots of storytelling. Keb was sorry to see Alaska State Senator Elrod Dufek glad-handing his way through the crowd, always campaigning, and a young man following him with a big camera, and a woman with a microphone. Mitch said she was with Channel Four News in Juneau. They listened to Elrod talk big words. Then watched the camera turn onto Harald Halmerjan. How did he get here? Keb felt the marrow drain from his bones. Ruby's son Josh appeared with his twin girls, who hugged Keb about the legs. "Popsi," they called. "Hello, Popsi."

Their names?

Was Ruby here?

The camera was on him now, Old Keb. The woman reporter said, "I'm now speaking with the oldest man in Jinkaat, Keb Wisting, who organized the carving of this important canoe. Keb, how does it feel to see your work receive this much attention?"

For some reason—it must have been the nagoonberry juice on his fingers—Old Keb was thinking of pies. How Florence Wilson used just the right amount of sugar. It's easy to oversweeten a pie. The trick is to leave the right amount of tartness. Nobody did it better than Florence.

"Again, this is Tanya Pantaletto reporting from Jinkaat, where people have gathered to steam open the first dugout canoe hand-carved here in a long time. We're in a large clearing on the edge of the forest, on the edge of town, and I daresay on the edge of time. There's lots of music and good food. Here with me is the mastermind of it all, Keb Wisting, who lives in the carving shed behind me, near the house that belongs to his daughter Ruby Bauer, president of the PacAlaska Heritage Trust."

Mastermind?

"Keb, is this canoe event related in any way to the PacAlaska lawsuit to gain more access into Crystal Bay?"

Helen Cornelius was a mastermind at making pies, but her husband worked for the Forest Service and transferred to Montana, and took Helen with him. Too bad.

"Keb, could you please share with our viewers . . ."

The crust was important. Don't over-knead the dough. It knocks out all the air. Makes it tough.

"Popsi," a little girl said with a tug on his pants, "the lady is asking you a question."

"He's not a mastermind," James said. "He's a canoe carver. He's my grandfather. These are his two great-granddaughters." James picked up one. Josh had the other.

"And you're James Wisting?" the reporter asked. "You're the basketball star?"

"Not anymore."

"Did you have anything to do with the making of this canoe?"

"A little."

"Don't be modest, James," a voice boomed from the crowd. Harald Halmerjan, he of the condo-sized head and cornbread crime, stepping into the camera. Everybody knew who he was. Why bother with introductions? "This is a special day," Harald said as he devoured the scene. "For thousands of years our people have traveled by canoe through the uncharted waters of Alaska. At the end of the last great Ice Age . . ." You'd have thought he was a scholar, a professor with a degree, what Mitch called a "duh-gree."

"How does all of this make you feel?" the reporter asked him.

"How does this make me feel? I feel great. This is a great day." H. H. extended his arms. "Look at the friends and kids having fun, the good food from the land and the sea, the old and young, the giving and sharing. Twenty, thirty, and fifty years ago our young people weren't interested in our old ways. We've changed that with our heritage programs, and events like this that make us proud again, that enable us to rediscover who we are and where we belong, and how we can take better care of what belongs to us."

Tanya What's-Her-Toes was about to ask another question when Harald raised his hand. "We can't abandon our old ways. We can't live exclusively in them either. We need to be part of the modern world before it steamrolls over us. That's why we formed our own corporation. To protect our interests."

"Isn't it true," Tanya asked, "that more than a few Tlingits are uneasy about the corporate approach to the natural world?"

Harald shook his big head. "Look at the improvements. We have better schools, better computers, better business opportunities for our young people."

An image came to Keb just then, not of a raven, kingfisher, or bear, or his dear wife, Bessie, or Uncle Austin, his voice carved from an ancient riverbed, or his sister Dot, bless their souls, makers of beautiful memories. It was an image of the most accepting, guileless creature he knew, his great-grandson Christopher, the Down's syndrome son of Robert the Coca-Cola sugar water man and Lorraine who talked a lot, warm in his home with the poodle on Prozac and the cat named Infinity and the bird in a cage. He wanted little Christopher to see the canoe, see who his people used to be. *Why must we be so far away from each other?*

He walked to the canoe and helped affix clamps and ribs as the water steamed and the wood softened and the canoe slowly gained beam-width and dimension.

HOURS LATER, LONG after nightfall, Deputy Sheriff-in-Training Stuart Ewing leaned against his Jeep in the middle of the festivities where he'd just arrived. He told Keb what he knew and didn't know. He didn't know where Tommy and Pete were, or Charlie. But he knew the Alaska State Trooper Pepper Mountain Report was just out. Among other things, it said Pete had not been cutting the day of James's accident. He was a choker-setter working ahead of James. Stuart wondered if Pete might have improperly bundled the logs so that once Charlie and Tommy jerked them from up on the yarder, the logs came loose down the skid line. This was speculation, of course. There was no physical proof. But still . . .

A crowd gathered to hear what Stuart had say. Mitch said something about finding the Gants and Pete Brickman and getting to the bottom of things.

"Deputize us all," Dag said.

"No," Stuart said.

"A deputy can't make new deputies," somebody said.

"Sure he can."

"No, he can't."

"Stop it!" Stuart yelled. "I don't want anybody going off and pretending to be a posse and making things worse. There's no immediate danger."

"Yes, there is," Little Mac said. Everybody turned to see her on the edge of the bonfire, more in shadow than light, sweat on her brow from the steaming, the smallest and biggest among them.

James and Kid Hugh joined the crowd, sweat-soaked like Little Mac. When Kid Hugh took off his T-shirt and pulled on his Lakers jersey, Old Keb caught a killer whale tattoo on his chest, and below that a large diagonal scar across his iron flat stomach.

James wrapped his arm around Little Mac as she folded herself into him.

Mitch invited Keb, Gracie, James, and Little Mac to stay with him and Irene that night, should they all want to be together, since Little Mac's mom was visiting her two brothers at the big university. Keb nodded in appreciation.

"Might not be a bad idea," Stuart said. "Now, if it's okay with everybody, I'm going to get something to eat." He sauntered over to the buffet tables with a big gun dangling off his needle butt. He might have moseyed or ambled or sashayed. Keb couldn't tell.

Never one for the sidelines, Harald stepped in and reminded James that his Aunt Ruby was busy in Seattle and wanted to hear from him.

"She's left me messages," James said.

"You should be down there with her," Harald said.

"She should be up here with us," James shot back.

WARREN THE MASTER carver climbed onto his perch above the canoe and announced the steaming was finished. The beam measured five inches wider than when they began, with the hogback gone. The gunwale line sighted level and true. The bow was nine inches higher with the bow piece pegged in. A cheer went up. Drummers pounded; dancers spiraled about. Old Keb saw James wearing a smile, talking with everybody around him, caressing the canoe. He recalled a couple months ago, when James's face was so empty Keb had closed his eyes to keep from having to see it. Not anymore.

Keb had no idea what hour it was. Hours didn't exist anymore. People gathered at the fire to do more talking and eating; talking about the way things used to be and might be again. Who knew? Anything seemed possible with a new canoe.

A couple hours later, things were winding down when Kevin Pallen emerged from the carving shed where he'd been all night. He walked over to Old Keb carrying a yellow cedar box about five feet long, one foot wide, and one foot deep. He set the box at Keb's feet, backed away, and sat down on the opposite side of the fire. "It's for you," Kid Hugh said to the old man. "It's a gift."

Keb stared at the box. On its lid, carved in relief, was a kingfisher, *tlaxaneis'*, Keb's clan crest.

"Open it, Gramps," James said. Little Mac sat next to him with her guitar in her lap. By the light of the fire Keb lifted the lid and removed four paddles hand-carved from *xáay*, yellow cedar, each with a thin rib down the blade for stability and strength. Warren took one of the paddles from the box, admired it, and passed it on with Keb's permission. Soon the four paddles were making the rounds. More people walked into the firelight to see them and touch them, to run their fingers over the elegant lines and smooth surfaces. They spoke in whispered admiration, if they spoke at all.

Keb climbed to his feet and shuffled over to Kevin. All the boy could do was sit there, head down, eyes behind a mop of hair. Often the master carver made the paddles himself and gave one or two away as part of the canoe blessing. This time was singular and different, like so much else. "Do these paddles belong with this canoe?" Keb asked the boy. Kevin nodded. Keb asked him to stand, then turned to everyone and said in Tlingit, then English, "This is Kevin Pallen of the Auke Bay Clan, Small Lake Tribe. He is one of the best carvers I know." Turning to Kevin, he said, "Gunalchéesh, Gunalchéesh, ax tòowoo kligéi ee kàa-x. I'm proud of you."

For the first time in a long time—longer than anybody could remember—Kevin raised his head and smiled.

our finest decorations

RAVEN DESCENDED THROUGH a heavy sky, its shadow rising. It landed on a bed of snow, a seer, a rascal, a maker of all things that made the earth, sun, moon, and stars. People, too. Yes, Raven made people, first from rock, which made them too strong, and later from dust so they would be mortal. Walking now. Raven was walking on the snow in a funny dance, a messenger bird trying to keep his feet dry, lifting one, then the other. A comical bird, if you had a sense of humor. A battleground bird, if you believed the Vikings. The bird Noah released to find land, if you believed the Bible. The bird that flew into the night and showed us another way, if you believed in another way. Old Keb stirred in his dream. Raven came nearer, dancing still. Was it snow he walked on? No. It was fire. White-hot fire. He wasn't trying to keep his feet dry, he was trying to keep them cool, keep them from burning. "Follow me," he said with a loud croak. "Follow me."

Keb inhaled sharply.

You had to talk to Raven. Make prayers to it. Watch and listen. Remember, before Raven made the world as it is today, he made it easy, where fat grew on trees and rivers flowed uphill and down, and everything was convenient. But humans got lazy. Life isn't supposed to be easy. It's supposed to be difficult and perilous to help sharpen our wits. Quiet servitude is easy. Is that what you want? If that's what you want, go find another bird. A pigeon. A barnyard chicken. A bathtub duck. Fall prey to the hawks and falcons around you.

So Raven made the fat into fungus. He made the rivers flow downhill only. He flew higher than any hawk. He somersaulted over clouds and turned water to ice, and ice into blue glacial rivers that buried a bay and shaped the land and shaped the people, too. He said it was better to die on your feet than to live on your knees. Better to go to sea than go to bed. Sleep on the ocean. Get up. Get up now. He was jumping up and down, this raven, cawing, croaking. "Follow me. Follow me. Get up. Get up."

Keb opened his eyes. His heart pounded. He was in a strange bed, wet with sweat, his head on a soft pillow, too soft, his one good eye registering light through a window, not the bright light of death, but the muted light of a cloudy dawn. He remembered, then. He was in Mitch and Irene's house. With no small effort he pulled his sleep-stiffened body upright. He found himself still dressed in his shirt and pants, redolent with wood smoke. Barefoot, he walked to the bedroom door, opened it, and moved down the hall. In the living room he found James asleep on a sofa, flat on his back, forearm across his brow, snoring softly. Gracie and Little Mac must be in the house, too . . . yes, that's right, all asleep under the same roof.

"James," Keb said with a shake to his shoulder. "James, wake up. There's something wrong."

The boy startled awake and sat up. "What?"

"There's something wrong."

"What, Gramps?"

On the table next to the sofa Old Keb saw James's beaded necklace with the raven feather. He hadn't touched it in weeks. James had needed it more than him. Picking it up, he said, "We have to go."

"Go? Go where?"

"We have to go. Go now."

"Okay, okay." James pulled on his shirt and pants while Keb moved across the living room. He struggled with the front door lock. Raven was jumping up and down in his mind, flapping its wings. "Hurry, hurry," it said, "follow me, hurry. . . ."

The lock opened and Keb shuffled out onto the front deck and worked his way down the wooden stairs. The lights of the boat harbor shone across mirror water. Beyond, he could see the faint outline of Chichagof Island against the dawn. In the distance, a dog barked. No traffic. No sign of anybody up and about. James appeared at his side. "What is it, Gramps?"

They stood in the road for a minute. "Listen," Keb said, "that's Steve barking."

He began to walk down the harbor road toward his end of town, past Mitch's Garage and Nystad's Mercantile. Not his usual shuffle. He walked with such vigor and determination that his grandson had to hop-step to keep up, his knee in a brace. Again, Keb stopped and listened. The barking was more distinct.

"Gramps, look," James said, pointing. On the skyline, a yellow-orange glow threw itself against heavy clouds. Large spruce and hemlock stood silhouetted, as if last night's bonfire were still ablaze. But this was something else.

"You got one of those little phones?" Keb asked James.

"Not with me."

"Go back to Mitch's. Get help. Call emergency. Tell them my shed is on fire."

James stared at him.

"Go," Keb said.

"What about you?"

"I'm okay. Go."

James turned and hop-stepped as fast as he could back to Mitch's house.

Keb walked on, striding on adrenaline that he would have thought his body stopped producing a thousand years ago. He hadn't felt this strong in centuries. He reached the hog-backed road and put his legs into low gear, the feather firm in his grasp. A couple minutes into the climb he heard a motorcycle approaching from behind. The beam of the small headlight danced against trees that flanked the road. Keb stopped and watched it come at him as if it would run him down. He didn't move. It skidded at his feet.

"Get on," Kid Hugh said.

Keb wrapped his arms around the kid's skinny waist, just as he had more than three months before, when the kid told him about the accident. Up the road they charged to the clearing and the shed—what used to be the shed, bright as a newborn sun now, the youngest star in the sky, hotter than hell, a fever fire feeding on death and dying.

"Oyyee . . ."

THE FIRE HAD a mighty appetite all right. Keb and Kid Hugh watched it consume the carving shed in minutes, flames high over the roof, a hungry incandescence biting the sky, sucking the atmosphere dry. Such heat, Keb could feel it pull the moisture from his eyes. He and Kid Hugh stood next to the canoe, across the clearing from the shed.

"It's gone," Keb said. "There's nothing to save."

"It's your home," Kid Hugh said.

The canoe is my home now.

Within minutes, Mitch arrived in his truck with Gracie, James, and Little Mac.

"No, no, no!" Gracie screamed as she climbed out and began walking toward the burning shed, arms up to shield herself from the oppressive heat. James grabbed her and pulled her back. She buckled into him. "Oh God, no, no, no."

Her anguish did more to rip out Old Keb's heart than seeing his home burn. He joined James in comforting her.

About the time they heard the first siren, they found Kevin sitting on the ground near the canoe, his face wet with tears.

"Kevin," James asked, "what happened?"

The boy shook his head.

"What happened?"

No response.

"Did you do this?"

He shook his head.

"Do you know how this happened?"

Using a small carving knife, Kevin wrote in the dirt: TOMMY AND PETE.

"Tommy and Pete were here?"

Kevin nodded, yes.

"They started this fire?"

Another nod.

"This is arson," Kid Hugh said.

Keb wondered: Where's Steve? He'd been barking up a storm twenty minutes ago.

Kevin showed Keb a burlap bag filled with carving tools. He'd managed to get into the shed and save all of Keb's best tools, but burned both hands and his leg.

Little Mac knelt at his side and began attending to him.

"I've got a first aid kit in my truck," Mitch said. He went to get it.

"Those tools belong to you now," Keb told Kevin.

Gracie was still distraught, staring at the burning shed, breathing funny.

Two fire trucks arrived, and three pumper trucks kept the hoses going. So many lights, sirens, and engines, men shouting and running around in red helmets and yellow coats, others tugging on turgid hoses that shot fountains onto Keb's shed, what was left of it, and Ruby's house, where embers landed on the metal roof. "We'll save what we can," Big Terry McNamee told Old Keb.

They saved Ruby's house, and tended to Kevin's burns.

Keb sat on the ground and watched numbly as the fire died and all light seemed to empty into the dawn. A light rain began to fall. Steve walked into the clearing badly winded, as if he'd run twenty miles. If only he could talk. Had he seen Tommy and Pete? Chased them away? Followed them as far as possible? Why would Tommy and Pete do this? Get the right man drunk and he'll do the wrong thing.

Kid Hugh wrapped his arms around Steve and got him a pan of water. Keb rubbed the dog's head and neck and ears. Steve accepted the affection with a modest wag of his stubby tail.

Keb worried about Gracie. She was already in poor condition. Now this. Stuart Ewing asked Mitch to drive her back to his house and maybe have Irene knock her out with a sedative.

"Sorry, Keb," Big Terry said. "We all feel really bad about this. Can I get you anything? Food, water?"

"Water."

Terry yelled, "Somebody get Keb water."

Ten firemen came running with bottles and canteens.

STUART EWING GOT off his little phone and said, "The state troopers are headed out in a chopper. They'll be here in an hour. Once the fire cools, we'll need to tape off the area as a crime scene." He knelt down. "Keb, the firemen secured your propane tank. We need to know if there are any explosives in your place."

"What?"

"Explosives. Are there any explosives or loaded firearms in your place?"

"A shotgun and a hunting rifle, a Remington .270 that Uncle Austin gave me a long time ago."

"What about ammunition?"

"Not much."

"Could you draw me a map of the shed and show me where, exactly, the guns and ammunition are?"

Keb nodded.

A crowd had gathered, extra hands wanting to pitch in. Keb heard somebody say, "Give him some time, Stuart. He just lost his home."

Keb was petting Steve under his chin, the way he liked it. "If only you could talk," Keb said to him.

As the morning brightened it revealed the faces of many of Keb's friends, distraught to see his shed in smoldering ruins. It was the biggest fire since the Fire of '62, when so many baskets and blankets were lost. Keb remembered how that fire made Uncle Austin cry. Now other people were teary-eyed: Carmen and Daisy, Galley Sally and Myrtle, and of course Gracie, back with

Irene in her house, drugged and falling asleep, Keb hoped. More people arrived, a steady stream of cars, trucks, and ATVs.

Squeezing her way through the crowd was Tanya What's-Her-Toes from Channel Four. Speaking of toes, the first thing she saw when she got to Keb was his bare feet. It set her back to see this old man, white-haired in the rain, his one weathered hand petting a dog, the other holding a feather. Nothing on his feet. "Keb Wisting," she said, "this was your home that just burned to the ground. Is there anything you'd like to say?"

Keb watched Big Terry pull her away and walk her and her cameraman back to their rented van, or maybe to the nearest cliff. James, Kid Hugh, and Little Mac were busy talking with Stuart. About what Keb could only imagine.

"We need to find Tommy and Pete," Dag said.

That got everybody talking. Old Keb sat there petting Steve, listening.

"Let's hunt 'em down."

No, Keb thought.

"They burned down Keb's shed."

"We don't know that for sure."

"C'mon—"

"And what do we do when we find them?"

"We arrest them. Citizens arrest."

No . . .

"We can't just stand here."

"We're doing that now."

"That's what I mean. Let's do something."

No . . .

"Shoot 'em with burning arrows."

"Not funny."

"They might be up on Pepper Mountain. We could track them up there."

"Not in this rain."

"We need a good tracker, like the guy who chased Butch Cassidy and the Sundance Kid over bare rock."

"That was in the desert. This is a rain forest."

"We'll need lots of coffee."

"And pizza from Shelikof's."

"No anchovies."

"We should look for Charlie, too."

No . . .

"He went deer hunting up Port Thomas."

"I don't think so."

"And no veggies on the pizza. Just sausage and pepperoni."

"And olives."

"I'll bet they're at a secret hideaway, an old cabin somewhere filled with Snickers bars and Doritos and beer."

"Or a tent camp deep in the woods, surrounded by trip wires."

"With M-16s on tripods, like in *Rambo*."

"Don't get green olives, Gene. Get the little black ones."

"And mushrooms."

"And whole wheat crust."

"C'mon, guys. We need to track these guys down, arrest them, and bring them in."

"No," Keb said forcefully.

Everybody fell silent.

"No posse," Keb said.

"But your shed, Keb. Your home. It's lost."

Keb got to his feet and faced them. "It's not lost." He brought his hand to his chest, palm flat against his beating heart. "It's here."

They stared.

Dag was near tears. "But Keb, your shed—where are you going to live?"

"I'm leaving."

"Leaving? Where are you going?"

"Back."

"Back? Back to where?"

"Just back."

AN HOUR BEFORE midnight, Keb found time alone with James. "I need you to listen. There will be no revenge. You're not going after Tommy and Pete. That's Stuart's job."

"Jesus, Gramps, they burned down your shed, your home. They ruined my basketball career. What are we supposed to do?"

What are we supposed to do?

Father Mikal used to say that the hardest thing when you're digging yourself into a hole is to stop digging. It's one thing to be bold, another to be wise. One thing to be resolute, another to be judicious. Who could James and his friends trust? Who could they model themselves after? The elder who sees blue where they see black? Why is it so easy to disregard the old man? When Keb was young, a man lived alone on the edge of town, past a crude sign that said "NO TRESPASSING." Keb could still see the lines around his eyes, the sad mouth and slumped shoulders. Live in a small town and you learn the simple act of dropping by, and discover there's an art to it, that it's made to look casual while in fact it's deliberate; it involves great caring and compassion. So it was odd to have a guy who wanted none of it. Nobody dropping by. Nobody in his world but himself. Yes, people in Jinkaat watched each other. They watched *out for* each other. But not this guy. He lived out the road and came into town once a month for groceries and nothing more. Spoke hardly a word. His name was Mercer, first initial T. Nobody knew his first name, the one his parents gave him. He never did take that "NO TRESPASSING" sign down. He even fixed it up, painted it. When he died, he died alone; dragged himself out onto the front porch, sat in a rocking chair, and gave up. Simple as that. He died after he took his last breath and said nothing about it. Abigail Tyler, out picking blueberries, came by and saw him covered in crows. No family claimed him or his things. A dozen townspeople cleaned out his house. In a drawer they found stacks of unsent letters written to a woman who probably never knew he loved her, and never loved him back. Somebody said those letters were the most tender and lyrical they'd ever read. After that, the kids called him Mercy. Tender Mercy. Ironic, to name a man after the very thing he needed most but never received. Uncle Austin used to say that ravens build their nests out of twigs, grasses, deer hair, even their own breast feathers. Are we any different? We make our homes from parts of ourselves—the laughter of our kids, the friends who drop by. They become our finest decorations, our best memories, the things no fire can burn.

Keb gripped James hard by the arm and said, "Look at me."

James gave him an earnest look.

Keb handed him the feather. "You have to see blue where there's black."

"I know, Gramps, but—"

"Go pack for an open boat journey. Tell nobody. Bring good foul weather gear and camping gear, some halibut hooks, salmon lures, baitfish and line, two knives, a sharpening stone, a berry basket, matches, dry kindling, and your deer rifle. Invite Little Mac and Kid Hugh."

James's eyes brightened. "The canoe? We're leaving in the canoe?"

"Be at Portage Cove tomorrow night at eight, high tide."

"What about Steve? Can we bring Steve?"

Keb grinned. *He got invited before you did.*

you only have to master yourself

WARREN HAD SAID the canoe would be ready, and it was, thanks to Mitch and Vic, who hauled it down to Portage Cove on the flatbed. And to Albert at his carpentry shop, and Oddmund and Dag, who applied every shipwright skill they learned as youngsters in Norway: the bow and stern pieces affixed, plugs set, false bottom and cubby fo'c'sle laid in, foredeck canvassed, small main mast and mizzenmast bolted in tight. "We put a kroner under each mast," Dag said, "for luck, you know." A coin, like a penny. Nordic shipwrights had been setting them under masts since the Viking days.

A red cedar dugout canoe should not be retrofitted and put to sea so soon after the steaming, Keb knew. It normally needed weeks to cure. But these were not normal times. Warren had no objections. He said this was Keb's canoe, not his.

Both sides of Old Keb's soul told him everything had been in preparation for this journey, this moment. It was James's life to live, Keb's death to die. The rainy mist had become a misty rain, counting time. Irene brought Keb three good blankets and a pillow.

"I put Gracie on the plane to Juneau," she told him, "to go see a doctor. You shouldn't be going off in this canoe when she's feeling so poorly. You know that?" Yes, Keb knew that. He knew that Irene guilt-tripped everybody. She sent Mitch on so many guilt trips that Truman said he qualified for frequent flyer miles. "You know I'm right," Irene said. Irene was always right. Live in Jinkaat long enough and you'd know it too, or pretend to, or pay the price if the pretense wasn't perfect. Irene went around town with curlers in her hair telling everybody how to raise their kids and grow their gardens. Dag said she got those curlers too hot one day and fried her brains, several times. Refried brains.

Galley Sally handed Keb a box and said, "It's mostly fish and vegetables cooked in lemon, and peanut butter cookies. Some sweets and morsels for the dog, too."

"The dog?" Irene said to Keb. "You're taking the dog?"

Steve wagged his chewed-off tail.

The box had a strange fruity smell, as if Sally had squeezed in a kiwi instead of a lemon. Keb thanked her and handed it to Oddmund, who put it in the canoe.

For months Keb had imagined this as a covert launching. He and James pushing away while the town slept; paddling into storms and autumn's darker nights, all the way to Crystal Bay and another blue that's true, a glacier blue. Paddling through time and into another place, another existence: the rib of the raven, the wrist of the whale, the defiance of the kingfisher, the patience of the heron. These past few years, when facing what he'd become, the husk of the man he used to be, Keb had wished he were dead without having to die. It frightened him, though he couldn't say it.

Death is not so bad as dying, Dot had told him in her last shallow breath; if only death came first. But right now, this very minute, Keb was more alive than he'd been in a long time. He felt defiant—was that it? Yes, defiant. And stunned too, that such defiance could still arise in him.

Twenty people stood on shore, and every minute more arrived. People on the edge of the moment, moving with the rain, helping to load the canoe, proof that no secrets survive in a small town. No sign of Stuart or the troopers or James or Kid Hugh. What about Little Mac? Would she make it?

It was dark, a little past high tide. Late August. Time to go.

Keb fidgeted. He heard once that death is like the sun. You can't look straight into it. Die at night then. Close your eyes. Live half your life making stories and the other half telling them. Be grateful. People used to die of toothaches. Wolves still do, but you never hear them complain. Where was Nathan Red Otter? The canoe needed his Haida blessing. Keb was uncertain how it would behave at sea without a proper blessing. He felt his stomach turn, more from excitement than fear. Where was Father Mikal? The second oldest man in town, Keb's friend for fifty years. Father Mikal was almost dead, like Keb, and often bedridden with a million things wrong. He refused to go to Seattle, knowing as Keb did, that if you're sick and go down there to get well, you don't get well. You get sicker and never come home. You die among strangers, and once you die you're dead and have nothing to say about it. Death is the general condition. Life is the exception: a beautiful, love-filled exception. Keb hoped Father Mikal was okay. He hoped the old priest would forgive him for leaving like this, without a final good-bye. As a boy, Father Mikal had known Uncle Austin and hunted with him. That meant a lot to Keb. Father Mikal was a good cribbage and poker player, too, a man of mischief and deep conviction and long robes with hearts and jacks up his sleeves, who once said God must have had a sense of humor to create us.

Keb heard ATVs cutting the night. He saw a motorcycle out in front, going like hell, headlights bouncing along the beachfront road as the machines hit potholes but refused to slow down. The motorcycle roared up first. No mistaking the rider. Kid Hugh climbed off and came loping over. No Lakers jersey or old tennis shoes this time. He wore an oil-stained rain slicker, XtraTuf Neoprene boots, and a duct-taped sou'wester. Over one shoulder he carried a small duffel, over the other, a rifle in a soft case.

James followed on an ATV with Little Mac on the back. She was dressed like Kid Hugh, except for a black beret aslant on her head, and her XtraTufs rolled down to her ankles. They pulled a small cart loaded with half a dozen plastic totes, each filled with clothing, food, and other supplies. They dismounted and got to work hauling. Others helped, and formed a line from the ATV to the canoe. Little Mac hugged Keb hard. For all the chatter of a minute before, the beach was silent. No wind. No waves lapping on shore. Nobody said a word. No voices carried across still water from the boat harbor half a mile away. No geese called out their southbound journey. No loons or ravens or gulls. No soft breathing of porpoises or seals. Only the rain. The strumming, thrumming rain. The canoe sat abeam a floating dock that nobody used anymore. It floated true, near as Keb could tell, and was nicely trimmed out with strong thwarts and ample freeboard. James and Kid Hugh packed it well, watching the trim as they did. Without a word, Little Mac grabbed her pack and guitar and a blanket from Irene and walked down the dock, climbed into the canoe, and positioned her things near the fo'c'sle.

Stuart Ewing drove up in his Jeep.

Keb looked at him, the rain running off the rim of his hat.

"I'm not going to ask you not to do this, Keb," Stuart said.

"Good."

"It's your life."

"Yes."

"You know there's a small craft advisory for Icy Strait?"

"Yes."

Stuart walked onto the dock, past James and Kid Hugh. He shone a small light down the length of the canoe, knelt beside it, ran his hand along the gunwale. "She looks good, Keb." Everybody watched. Nobody spoke. Little Mac was at the far end; Keb noticed that Stuart avoided shining the light directly on her. He could hear Oddmund and Dag whispering behind him, and many others. Stuart stood and asked Kid Hugh, "Are you the registered owner of that rifle?"

"Yes?"

"What about you, James?"

"What about me?"

"I'm supposed to pass along a message from Ruby."

"Oh?"

"She told me she's left several messages for you."

"I've been busy."

"She asked me to stop you from going out in this canoe, in worsening weather. She'll be in Juneau tomorrow morning and plans to fly out here first thing. She said she wants to talk to you about your future."

"Let him go," Oddmund said from the crowd.

"You can't stop him," Dag added. "He's done nothing wrong. You have no authority in this."

James said to Stuart, "This is my future."

Stuart nodded, "I know that."

"But my aunt doesn't."

Stuart shrugged. "She gave me her cell number to make sure you have it." He extended his hand, holding a little piece of paper.

Keb noticed James's posture, the way he stood, not favoring his bad leg like before.

Stuart's hand remained extended.

"I know her number," James said softly, his voice deeper than before.

"The tide's turning," Oddmund said.

Kid Hugh walked past Stuart and climbed into the canoe. Steve bounded in after him.

James said to Stuart, "Have you heard anything about my mom?"

"Only that she's in Juneau. I'll check in with her daily if you'd like."

"I'd like that."

"Take good care of your grandfather."

"I will."

"Pace yourself."

"I will."

"What do you think, Keb?" Oddmund asked, apparently concerned that the tide or rain or building wind would change his mind. "What's it going to be? Stay or go?"

Old Keb reached up and felt the rain in his hair. Nobody carves canoes anymore. He looked at James.

"*Óoxjaa Yaadéi*," James said. "Against the wind. We go."

ANNE FOLDED HER laundry in the large common room apartment in Bartlett Cove, while Ranger Ron and two other men shot pool and drank Alaskan Amber next to a small chattering television. The Juneau eleven o'clock news came on. The anchorman said, "We now take you to Jinkaat, a live report, where Tanya Pantaletto has more breaking news about Keb and James Wisting. Tanya, what can you tell us?"

Anne put down her laundry. Ron put down his pool cue.

"Good evening, Bill. Yes, this is a rapidly unfolding story. About two hours ago, high school basketball star James Wisting and his grandfather Keb Wisting, the oldest man in Jinkaat, pushed off in a newly carved red cedar dugout canoe that was dedicated last night in a big ceremony. Very early this morning Keb Wisting's house burned to the ground, the result of suspected arson. I'm now on the beach in Portage Cove, just outside Jinkaat, where townspeople witnessed the canoe's departure." The camera swept left and right to show many faces behind Tanya, and beyond the faces, the dark of the night.

The anchorman asked, "Where are they going in the canoe?"

"Nobody knows. They initially headed north, toward Icy Strait. From there they might continue north to Crystal Bay, the ancient homeland of the Jinkaat Tlingit."

"What are the sea conditions?"

"It's pretty calm here, with a light rain. But the marine forecast is calling for a small craft advisory, with winds up to twenty-five knots and seas up to six feet. I have with me a friend of the Wisting family, Oddmund Nystad." Next to Tanya stood a lanky man who was no stranger to the rain, slightly hunched with wispy hair across his wet brow, water dripping off his angular face. "I understand, Mr. Nystad, that you witnessed the launching of this canoe."

"Sure did. We all did." His voice whispered through his nose. "They took a dog, too, in the canoe, named Steve."

"The canoe is named Steve?"

"No, the dog is Steve. The canoe is *Against the Wind*."

"Are you worried about them?"

"Not at all. The canoe runs straight and has good freeboard, and a kroner under each mast."

"A kroner?"

"A Norwegian coin, for luck. That's how the Vikings found Greenland a thousand years ago."

"With kroners under their masts?"

"Yep."

"Did they take an outboard?"

"Nope, they didn't have outboards a thousand years ago."

"Not the Vikings. Keb Wisting and his party, did *they* take an outboard?"

"Oh no, Keb don't like outboards. Too noisy. Besides, there's no transom on this canoe, no place to mount a motor of any kind."

"Do you know where they're going?"

"Don't tell her, Oddmund," a voice yelled from off camera. A goofy look came over Oddmund's face, a small accomplishment, Anne thought, given what he had to begin with, all eyebrows and nose. Tanya the reporter made the mistake of swinging her microphone into the crowd to pick up more comments.

"Hey, Oddmund," came another voice, "show her what a real kroner looks like, the one under your mast."

A rueful smile came over Tanya's face.

"They're going to Crystal Bay," shouted another voice.

"Shut up, Roger."

"You shut up, Mitch."

"Nobody's going to find him as long as he's got that magic feather."

The camera swung its light onto more wet faces. A few people waved.

"Crystal Bay," Tanya said, as the camera turned back to her, "is the Native homeland of the Jinkaat Tlingit. It's where they came from long ago, and where, if you ask around, you'll find they want to return again, some to fish and hunt and gather as they did long ago, others to open up industrial economic opportunities through PacAlaska, the regional Native corporation created more than forty years ago, long before Crystal Bay became a national marine reserve."

The anchorman asked, "Is it possible that Old Keb Wisting would try to take his canoe all the way to the glaciers?"

"It's possible. The glaciers are more than one hundred miles from here. They no doubt have special significance for him; they carved and shaped his homeland."

And he's a carver too, Anne thought.

"Old Keb trusts no land that has no glaciers," somebody shouted from off camera.

Anne smiled. *Let the old man go. Just let him go.*

Tanya said, "The glaciers in Crystal Bay today are small remnants of the great glacier that occupied all of Crystal Bay just two hundred and fifty years ago, a glacier that was one hundred miles long, ten to twenty miles wide, and in some places, more than four thousand feet thick. It's the glacier that forced the Tlingit out of the bay, and has since retreated to unveil a new land, a new bay where Keb Wisting hunted and fished as a boy."

"And picked berries," came a voice from the crowd.

The anchorman said, "Keb Wisting is the father of Ruby Bauer, the Pac-Alaska advocate for challenging federal jurisdiction in Crystal Bay. How might this canoe journey affect that lawsuit?"

"Hard to say, Bill. I'll have continuing news on this story in the morning, exclusive here on Channel Four."

The anchorman thanked Tanya and moved on to the next story.

Ron put down his beer and headed for the door. Turning, he said to Anne, "This is the exact thing Director Johnson was afraid of. A publicity stunt to help PacAlaska get into Crystal Bay."

Anne said, "I don't think that's Keb Wisting's intention at all."

"It doesn't matter what his intention is, Anne. It matters what the rest of the world makes it out to be. It matters what the media and PacAlaska turn it into. We're going to need total control on this, with an incident command team and trained law enforcement personnel from Washington. I'm calling Paul." Ron seemed thrilled, as if he fed on conflict. Anne wondered: Did the last flower of summer just die?

It was no time for poetry. She didn't even finish her laundry.

ALL NIGHT LONG, Old Keb dreamed to the rhythm of water, enchantments on the canoe, liquid voices he hadn't heard in a thousand years, voices learned and forgotten and learned again as one life ends and another begins. He could write his story in water: *t'éex', ḵugóos', naadaayi heen, séew*: ice, cloud, river, rain. Begin with his Tlingit name. From there describe his first hunt with Uncle Austin, his mother's brother, *du káak*, how the great man taught him to see, but more important, to observe. "Each animal knows way more than you do," Uncle Austin used to say, as if it summarized everything he knew and believed. Keb remembered how Bessie taught him to waltz, with his eyes closed. "You're thinking too much," she would say. "You're counting your steps, one-two-three . . . one-two-three. . . . Let go. Close your eyes and let go." And with that, she moved him across the floor as the wind moves a fireweed seed.

James and Kid Hugh paddled for hours while Old Keb slept fitfully in the fo'c'sle next to Little Mac. If she moved that night he knew nothing of it. She was little more than a bundle under a blanket.

At one point Keb awoke to feel the canoe at ease. He heard James and Kid Hugh speaking in low voices as they huddled over one of those small, satellite-linked direction-finders. Forget dead reckoning and celestial navigation, the taste of salt, the smell of kelp, the voices of birds or the sound of breaking water, the waves like words slapping the hull and speaking of weather yet to come. Forget the maps and dreams of your ancestors. These boys were setting their course by a gadgetgizmo they got at Fred Meyer, on sale. Great Raven. Someday the future will sell us our instincts wrapped in a little box.

Keb once heard of an old Yup'ik Eskimo who rode a snowmachine all night long through minus-forty to get back home. When he made it, he was too frozen to move. He sat stiff as a board on his machine until his family came out and lifted him off and carried him in to thaw him out. That would be Old Keb after one night in the canoe, stiff as the boat itself, wooden, his bones like cedar. He might die there, dreaming of water.

One day, many years ago, soon after he and Bessie were married, a letter arrived from a cousin in Petersburg. Written in a tight hand, it told Keb that a famous distant relative had died in Norway. Oscar Wisting, champion skier. Not just any champion. Oscar had been one of four men to ski to the South Pole with Roald Amundsen, the legendary explorer. So perfect was their deed that they beat the Englishman Robert Falcon Scott by five weeks and made it look easy. Too easy. "These rough notes and our dead bodies must tell the tale," Scott wrote to the people of Great Britain as he lay dying in his tent, freezing to death. Better to fail flamboyantly than to succeed quietly. Amundsen was first to the pole, but Scott became the hero. The cousin in Petersburg told Keb that the world saw it through Scott's eyes, not Amundsen's. Scott left a widow and an infant son. Amundsen never married. Scott was the better writer, the better actor. Amundsen had no patience for the crowd, no witty responses to reporters' questions. Scott came from the British Empire, Amundsen from a tiny, newly independent country, Norway. Scott's journals were edited by his friend, James Barrie, the author of *Peter*

Pan, who wrote, "Surely it must be an awful adventure to die." Amundsen grew disillusioned, bitter. Years later, he disappeared in a small plane over the Arctic. It broke Oscar Wisting's heart. One night, in a nautical museum in Oslo, while nobody was looking, old Oscar climbed aboard the little wooden ship that he and Amundsen and the others had taken to Antarctica. It had a rounded hull to lift it above the Antarctic pack ice as winter squeezed in from all sides. That way it wouldn't be crushed. The ship's name, *Fram*, meant "forward." Oscar climbed in and bedded down in his old bunk, surrounded by his best memories, his time with friends in an icy world more wild, pure, and white than anything he'd seen before or since. What comfort he must have felt as he closed his eyes, fell asleep, and never woke up.

A damn good way to die. In a boat.

BY THE GRAY light of dawn they could see the opening to Flynn Cove. James and Kid Hugh had raised the small main sail, and reefed it when necessary, and paddled twenty-some miles through the night, without sleep or food, across Port Thomas on an ebbing tide. "It's still raining, Gramps," James said, "and it's beginning to blow pretty hard."

"Kuti kanigi," Keb heard himself say. Tlingit weather watchers. They would sit back-to-back in the big canoes to study the clouds and waves and give good advice. Big canoes rounded Cape Spencer this way, long ago. All these years later, you could still see their tracks through the kelp beds. Forward, Uncle Austin would say. Always forward.

You don't have to master nature. You only have to master yourself.

PART TWO

timeless yet out of time

SUPERINTENDENT PAUL BEALS folded one lanky leg over the other and read the *Juneau Empire* on his iPad. Seated around him, a dozen rangers and administrators spoke softly at a conference table in reserve headquarters in Bartlett Cove. Ron closed his cell phone and said, "Kate Johnson will join us by conference call in a few minutes. We'll run incident command from here, with coordinated public affairs and a clear search and rescue objective before this old guy paddles his canoe into the bay and dies and everybody gets excited."

Anne thought, If words were water he could turn turbines. She listened from out in the corridor, through the open conference room door, where she sat with her back against the wall, near a large notice board filled with memoranda, evidence of a thriving bureaucracy.

"And Ruby Bauer?" Paul asked Ron.

"She wants to be in on the conference call."

"Tell her no."

"She insists."

"Tell her no. And no incident command team until we ask Kate about it."

Ron got to his feet. "Do I make the call to Ruby?"

"Yes."

It must have been a slow news day, Anne thought. "The Old Man and the Bay" story as reported by the *Juneau Empire* had caught the attention of bloggers and media outlets around the state, including an online feature in the *Alaska Dispatch News,* which she pulled up on her MacBook Pro:

All his life, Old Keb Wisting, part-Norwegian, part-Tlingit Indian, has wanted to go home, back to Crystal Bay. Nobody ever expected him to do it in his nineties, in a canoe, in Alaskan waters patrolled by killer whales, icebergs, and federal government rangers.

In the last hour, three Anchorage-based news networks had called Crystal Bay National Marine Reserve looking for an angle. Was Old Keb deaf? Disabled somehow? Libertarian? Leatherstocking? Little Big Man? A Tea Partier? Occupy Wall Streeter? Undaunted by danger? Tough as nails? A shaman? Medicine man? Chief?

"We're just trying to find an angle here, something to work with," said a producer. Is he in a war canoe? Will rangers arrest him if he enters Crystal Bay without a permit? Does he have a death wish? A magical feather? A dog in the canoe that nobody else likes but he does? A dog that will defend him to the death? And the two young men, James Wisting and this Kid Hugh, do they have hunting rifles and shotguns? And this Little Mac, this Mackenzie Chen? What's her story? And the Gant brothers? Where are they?

Jinkaat Deputy Sheriff Stuart Ewing was quoted as saying, "Keb Wisting has done nothing wrong. He's a good man who's wanted for no crimes or questioning. The media is making too much of this. People need to calm down and leave him alone and take it easy."

Anne thought: I like this Stuart Ewing. *Take It Easy.* A great Jackson Browne song made famous by the Eagles. She'd been a Jackson Browne fan ever since she'd seen him sing at a "Save the Oceans" festival in Honolulu, ten years ago. Did Stuart Ewing listen to Jackson Browne?

She pressed herself deeper into the wall and tried to think about whales, think *like* a whale. No easy thing. She pushed the door farther open to see the rangers and senior staff all talking quietly, waiting for Kate's call. There were chiefs of various divisions—law enforcement, resource management, interpretation, administration, and maintenance—plus a cultural anthropologist from Anchorage, and Ron's pool buddies, who happened to be rangers from Seattle, decked out in their National Marine Reserve Service uniforms, the black-and-white orca patch on the shoulder, gold badge over the heart, small NMRS pin on the lapel, long creases down the sleeves. It intrigued Anne to see all these so-called "division chiefs" assembled to discuss what to do with a real Indian. An old man in a canoe. Paul kept reading the same article that had appeared on everybody's iPad that morning:

He grew up in the small town of Jinkaat, near Crystal Bay, where his uncle taught him to hunt seal, moose and deer. Where he picked wild strawberries with his grandmother, who made them into pies. And where, as a boy, he fell asleep in the sunshine, and a bear bit off part of one of his toes, and he came to be known, affectionately by his Norwegian friends and others, as "Keb Zen Raven, Nine and a Half Toes of the Berry Patch."

FLANKING ANNE IN the corridor were half a dozen seasonal scientists and field technicians like herself, all licensed boat operators who would be pressed into action. It was Ron's idea. Use everybody. "O.F.," he called it. "Overwhelming Force, the kind of thing we should have used in Vietnam and Iraq." *Dear God,* Anne thought.

Next to Anne sat her friend, Taylor, texting her boyfriend in Strawberry Flats.

Kate Johnson called in and said by speakerphone, "Where are we, Paul?"

"We'll contain it."

"If this canoe enters Crystal Bay and causes a big fuss, PacAlaska will almost certainly use it to strengthen their jurisdiction case for industrial development. Not good, Paul. Not good."

"We'll contain it."

"The *Juneau Empire* already makes Keb Wisting sound like Hemingway's Santiago and he hasn't even been out there for a full day. Have you heard from Ruby Bauer?"

"She wanted to be a part of this conference call."

"Handle her carefully; contain her but also invite her to Bartlett Cove and mollify her. Tell her that at all costs we will ensure the safety of her father and nephew."

"Kate, this is Ranger Ron Ambrose. We met in June."

"Yes, Ron."

"Can I tell you what I told Paul earlier?"

"Yes."

"At Basic, at Fort Benning, we had a video game called *An Unusually Quiet Day* that taught us that you make decisions by your actions and your inaction. You choose which way things go. We need to keep things safe by being on high alert at all times. We need to accept the inevitability of the unexpected, and be chronic noticers of anything out of the ordinary. We need total control. That's why I propose we have an incident command team and a command leader."

Nobody said a thing.

Anne felt herself go rigid. Taylor leaned over and whispered, "Ridiculous."

"Let me think about that, Ron," Kate said.

Ron's cell phone rang. "I have to take this. It's Ruby Bauer." He stepped out of the conference room and walked past Anne and Taylor down to a private office.

The atmosphere changed. "Kate, this is Clive Dickinson, a cultural anthropologist from Anchorage."

"Yes, Clive."

"Do I have permission to speak freely?"

"Please do."

"This isn't Iraq. This old man and the kids with him aren't insurgents or terrorists. This isn't a video game. These people are—"

"Armed and potentially dangerous," interrupted a ranger from Seattle. "Ron's right. The only way you achieve absolute safety is through a serious mind-set."

Somebody out of Anne's view said, "Keb Wisting isn't our problem until he's in marine reserve waters. Even then, he's in a canoe, and there's no restrictions on the number of nonmotorized vessels allowed into the bay."

"He's a problem if he's headed this way," somebody else responded.

"How? Are we going to make him a problem before he is one? I say he's not a problem until he's inside the bay, within our jurisdiction, or until he's broken reserve regulations."

Kate said, "My concern is the lawsuit, the very real possibility that Pac-Alaska will capitalize on this 'Old Man and the Bay' story no matter what we do. We could lose this case in the Ninth Circuit, and lose a national marine reserve. We could have gold and copper mining in Crystal Bay. Let's keep our eye on the big picture and handle this smart from the beginning."

Anne listened to the opinions fly back and forth.

"If we let Keb Wisting into the bay, or keep him out; if we search for him now, or not at all, there are no easy answers."

"We know that," Kate said. "I don't want platitudes. I want concrete ideas."

"Strategy and tactics," a ranger said.

Taylor leaned over to Anne and whispered, "What are platitudes?"

"If we don't stop him," somebody said, "and he goes up the bay and dies, it will look really bad."

"Are we making too much of all this? He's a hundred years old and sleeping in a canoe. He could get hungry and sore and be back in his soft bed in Jinkaat in two days."

"He doesn't have a soft bed. He sleeps on a cot in his carving shed. But the shed burned down. So he doesn't have a cot and he doesn't have a shed."

"Maybe he wants to die."

"Wanting to die is one thing. Dying is another."

"The public is going to see this whole thing through whatever lens the media puts on it. I was in Yellowstone during the '88 fires and the '95 wolf reintroduction. What we've experienced with this 'Old Man and the Bay' thing is nothing compared to what's coming if it doesn't end quickly and quietly. Ron's right. We need to contain it with strong public affairs and law enforcement, put an end to it before it begins. Find Keb Wisting and escort him home."

"Crystal Bay is his home."

"Yes," Kate said, through the speakerphone. "We know that. He knows that. But the world-at-large doesn't know that. It's his home only if we allow events and the media to make it his home."

"How do we stop him?"

"Safety. We make it a safety issue. We rescue him."

Anne heard herself groan. She pulled back from the open door and whispered to Taylor, "You're right, this is ridiculous."

Taylor showed Anne a picture of her boyfriend on Facebook.

"Nice," Anne said.

Taylor asked, "Why is it sexy men have a 'cute butt,' but sexy women have a 'nice ass'?" She Googled Crystal Bay. "Whoa, look at this." A story from the *Seattle Times*:

Over the past half century, Keb Wisting has become the best—and last—canoe carver in the Tlingit Indian village of Jinkaat, on the north shore of Chichagof Island, nine hundred miles north of Seattle, across Icy Strait from the entrance to Crystal Bay National Marine Reserve, the only marine reserve in Alaska. He alone represents a dying art, for he himself is dying, friends say.

He gave away every canoe he ever carved. Gave them to friends, loved ones, and the sons of powerful clan leaders. But not this one. Beginning Tuesday night, this canoe he paddles himself, headed north for Crystal Bay, a home he hasn't known for a long time. This will be his final journey, some believe. "We don't expect to see Old Keb again," said Dag Nystad, a friend who watched him paddle away with his grandson and two other traveling companions. "We hope he finds what he's looking for."

TWENTY-TWO YEARS AGO this old man—white-haired even then, yet capable and strong—pulled Anne from the sea. Like an angel, traveling alone by skiff from Jinkaat to Juneau, he came upon her and Nancy and their overturned boat. He later visited in the hospital and embraced Anne's mother. Kneeling before Anne, he said, "I'm sorry about your sister." Anne said nothing, words stuck in her throat.

And now? *Say something, do something. . . .*

She heard a division chief say, "It's blowing in Icy Strait. They're probably hunkered down on shore, wet and cold in the forest."

"I feel sorry for the old guy."

"That's how PacAlaska might want everybody to feel: sorry for the old man who can no longer hunt and fish in Crystal Bay."

"From everything I've heard, I don't think Keb Wisting is pro-PacAlaska or pro-corporation of any kind. He's doing this for his own reasons."

"Have you ever seen him? He's barely five feet tall. I saw him at a basketball game a few years back, in Jinkaat. Everybody was screaming and pounding the bleachers and I swear the old guy was sound asleep, sitting there with his chin on his chest. I can't imagine him out in weather like this."

"I can. He's a tough old Tlingit Norwegian who fought in World War II, in Sicily and Italy. You know, there are only about eighty people left in the whole world who speak Tlingit as a first language, and he's one of them."

"He'll probably sleep better in that canoe than he did on those bleachers."

"How do you hide a twenty-five-foot dugout canoe? It'll be too heavy to haul up the shore and into the forest."

"We should invite the Jinkaat elders to Bartlett Cove and ask their advice."

"Good idea," Paul said.

"We're going to need every set of eyes we have, people working in pairs, mostly in the lower bay. I say we get Simon and Joel up on Feldspar

Peak with spotting scopes."

Kate said, "Put Anne and Taylor in Icy Strait, under the guise of looking for whales." Anne felt a spasm. "Paul, call Ruby Bauer. Tell her we will find her father and nephew and make sure they're safe. Safety, safety, safety. That's your mantra."

Anne closed her eyes and tried to think of whales. Only one image came to her: Old Keb out on the sea, appearing as if by magic; her angel. Timeless, yet out of time. A voice in her head kept saying, *Do something . . . do something . . . do something.*

a kindness never heard

S TEVE THE LIZARD dog scrambled up to the bow as James and Kid Hugh paddled the canoe into Flynn Cove. Keb could hear the dog topside on the small foredeck, feet alight in anticipation of landfall. No doubt his stubby tail wagging too. Pain shot down the old man's spine as he pulled back the heavy blankets and raised himself to look around. "Head for the tender," he heard James say.

Tired but still strong, both paddlers had faces strained in the gray morning light. They wore the weather like a second skin, Keb could see. Flynn Cove made a good lee in a southeast blow. The rain had eased. Sitting amidships, Kid Hugh had stripped down to his Lakers jersey, the short sleeves ripped off at the shoulder, to free his arms. James was in the stern, bare-chested, steering with J strokes, his bad leg wrapped in a blanket.

Keb had hoped to find a good coho stream and set the canoe in high tide sand under good alder cover, as Uncle Austin used to do. Keep the keel moist to prevent cracking. Anchored up ahead, he could see a large fish buyer, a wooden power scow, wide and flat, about one hundred and twenty feet long, forty at the beam, probably built as a floating repair rig in the 1940s. The wheelhouse sat aft of two big booms over an open deck.

Silverbow read the black letters on the rounded bow.

As they drew near, a wide-hipped, buxom fisherwoman stepped out and watched them, her arms across her chest. A fish-cleaning knife hung from her thick waist. A large ball of tobacco rested between her yellow teeth and lip. "Well, don't that beat all," she said as she spit her chew. "I figured you'd get about this far in one night. You must be hungry."

Keb regarded her with one bleary eye. Little Mac stirred under her blankets.

As the canoe drifted in, Kid Hugh raised his paddle while James used his to rudder. James said proudly (a little too proudly, Keb thought), "We hunt and fish for our own food."

"I reckon you do," the fisherwoman said as she waved her hand. "You see this ocean? It was a foot higher yesterday than it is today. Know why? It's got that many fewer fish in it. Know why? I got them all right here, inside. Fish are my business, my flock. I got more fish than Moses had chosen people. I didn't catch them myself, but I know every man who did, half of them scoundrels, half of them saints. I got a good price because I always do. I bought fifty thousand pounds of salmon just yesterday and the day before. I'm taking them to Lisianski, and I can feed you, if that interests you. I got crab cakes on the griddle, cornbread in the oven, and horse-kick-to-the-head coffee that's hot in the pot, and it's doing nobody no good until it warms a belly or two."

"Cornbread?" Keb asked.

"That's right, old man."

"Square or round?"

"Keeeeerist. Square, of course. What do you take me for? I make my pies round and my cornbread square. What more geometry does a woman need to know around these parts? Nobody but a damn hick-town clown makes round cornbread."

"Or square pies," Keb said.

"Never have, never will."

"We appreciate your kindness."

"Come aboard then. It looks to me like you could use some comfort and hot food." She leaned down to hand James two heavy straps connected to one of the large booms. Everything lunged against her open-neck denim shirt. Keb saw James stare into a rounded rift valley, a lusty, busty hiding place. After a delicious moment, James looked away, red-faced. "If you run these straps under your bow and stern," she told him, "I'll swing the boom and hoist up your canoe."

"Our canoe floats just fine," Kid Hugh said.

"I can see that, Long Hair. But let me tell you something. The United States Coast Guard has a region-wide alert out on you guys. They're asking every boat from here to Mozambique to look out for you and report anything we find. You're all over Juneau radio and TV. You're even in the *Seattle Times*. The minute this storm lays down, all manner of search and rescue and law enforcement people are going to come looking for you. Floatplanes, helicopters, hucksters, lots of folks with nothing better to do. The whole US

Air Force might come after you, with Yoda and Luke Skywalker and a bloody armada too—boats from Jinkaat, Elfin Cove, Strawberry Flats, Lisianski, Juneau, even Japan. You hearing me? Once this storm is over, Icy Strait and the north shore of Chichagof is going to be a Monty Python Flying Fuckhead Circus, and Flynn Cove might be the first place they come looking. It's the first place I looked."

"You came looking for us?" James asked.

"In a manner of speaking."

"Why?"

"I heard about you on the radio. I got a big boat; figured you could use a lift, maybe a place to hide for a day or two. Am I wrong?" Keb could see James sizing her up. She was a bunker, a battleship when you crossed her, but otherwise honest, maybe even honorable. She said, "If we put your canoe up here on deck, I could cover it with a tarp and nobody would know what it was, except you and me."

"How do we know you won't turn us in?" Kid Hugh asked her.

"You don't. I offer no guarantees. Now I have a question for you? What makes you a Lakers fan?"

"Phil Jackson."

"Not Kobe Bryant?"

"Nope, Phil Jackson."

"You ever heard of John Wooden?"

Kid Hugh grinned. "UCLA, ten NCAA national championships in twelve years, including eighty-eight consecutive wins."

"Damn straight."

James said, "You can't be alone on this boat. It's too much work."

"Me and my two boys run this boat. Morgan and Quinton. They're good boys, strong as oaks and deaf as posts, and trustworthy in all things except poker, which I take full responsibility for. We could take you to Graves Harbor, where nobody will look for you, if that's what you want."

Graves Harbor, far to the west, beyond Icy Strait—past the entrances to Crystal Bay, Dundas Bay, and Taylor Bay—all the way to Cape Spencer and beyond. Oyyee . . . north into big water, the Gulf of Alaska, another world, stormier and wilder than this one, where mountains cut holes in the sky. Old Keb hadn't been there in a long time. He'd spoken to James about it, and told him stories, many stories, about wolf and wolverine, *gooch* and *nóoskw*, and brown bear tracks the size of pie plates. He could see James chewing on the fisherwoman's offer, her words tasting better the more he chewed. He wore a look of deep satisfaction, the paddle in his hands, power-ful arms, bare chest, a young man unmindful of the wind and rain, no longer the basketball gazelle he used to be, the indoor boy, more like a seal or a sea lion, *tsaa, taan*, half-man, half-water, leaving behind the lacquered court and screaming fans.

The fisherwoman lowered down the straps.

Old Keb remembered something Truman once told him: Suicide, sugar, whiskey, television, Twitter, incest, drugs, boredom, and beer. For a lot of Native kids in village Alaska, the tragedies of Hamlet would be an improvement.

James was looking at Keb, the straps within reach. Fisherwoman wait-ing for a decision. "Take the straps," Keb told James as Little Mac climbed up from the fo'c'sle, ready for hot food.

THE CORNBREAD WAS the best Old Keb had ever had. He ate two corner pieces lathered in butter, and gave the other two to Little Mac. Steve the Lizard Dog fared well, wolfing down three crab cakes courtesy of the fisherwoman.

"I like your dog," she said.

She might have been pretty once, on the other side of hard experience and poor men's promises, before her red hair turned platinum and her smile died. Before too much tobacco and booze. She'd fed a lot of loggers, she said, cleaned a lot of fish, washed a lot of dishes. Keb looked close and found a his-tory of heartbreak and lowered expectations in her gray-green eyes, a reminder that we can only get so far away from ourselves. She said she'd cooked in log-ging camps on Prince of Wales and Kuiu Islands, run a tavern in Lisianski, prospected for gold up the Taku, and finally bought the *Silverbow*. She said she knew Galley Sally; everybody knew Galley Sally, the woman whose cook-ies made good roofing tiles. Fisherwoman told stories, and Keb was struck by how every one was funny and sad. "I've known about you for a long time," she said to Keb. "You and I know a lot of the same people."

"Are you Marge Farley?"

"That I am. Large Marge, people call me, and that's fine by me."

"I've known about you for a long time, too."

"Well, there you go. You and me, we should start a club or some damn thing."

"Thank you for the food, it's good."

James and Kid Hugh nodded in agreement, their mouths full, while Little Mac fed morsels to Steve.

Morgan and Quinton paid little attention to Keb and his party, though James caught them sneaking furtive appraisals of Little Mac. Red-haired boys with crooked teeth and freckles gone to peach-soft facial hair, they spoke with fingers blackened by bilge grease; they wheezed, grunted, screeched, laughed, and whistled in response to one another. Marge signed with them, though not as fast, and seemed disinterested in their lower-deck humor.

They didn't wait for the storm to break. The *Silverbow* weighed anchor and headed west toward Point Adolphus and beyond, down to Lisianski to off-load fish and refuel, then northwest toward Cape Spencer and the Gulf of Alaska, birthplace of storms. A long journey, to Graves Harbor. The last place anybody would search for a canoe from Jinkaat. The only other people Marge expected to see out there were salmon trollers and salt-bitten longliners fishing for black cod on the Fairweather Grounds.

Keb stretched out on the long padded bench next to the galley table, and must have fallen asleep. He awoke with no idea who he was, where he was, or how much time had passed. He had seen Bessie dancing. Bessie his love, his wife in another life, long ago—in a dream, a memory? A memory of a dream? Did he remember that he had a memory problem? Or did he forget that he forgot? He heard the distant thump and knock of twin Detroit diesels. He watched lamplight play on the galley ceiling. He felt the roll of the storm, the scow being pushed by her port quarter. No longer in the protection of Flynn Cove. Headed west? Yes, west. James and Little Mac and Kid Hugh and me, yes, and Steve. If the storm is a southeaster, then we're headed west, still in Icy Strait. He smelled coffee and cigarette smoke, and heard voices, those of James and Marge. James said something that Keb missed. Marge laughed a throaty tar-in-the-lungs laugh that turned to a cough, salted with contempt, as if James wasn't funny, but naïve. She blew a train of blue smoke, and got up and asked him if he wanted coffee.

"Got any Coke?"

"Nope."

"Root beer?"

"Nope."

"Coffee will do then."

"So where you headed in that canoe of yours?"

"Away."

"Running then?"

"No."

"Sure you are. Every young man runs at your age. If he doesn't, he's a fool."

"I got a girlfriend."

"All the more reason to run."

"She's pretty, don't you think?"

"Having a girl because she's pretty is like eating a bird because it sings."

"I saw your sons looking at her."

"And they saw you looking at me."

Keb could feel James thrumming his good leg.

Marge said, "This coffee's bitter. I'll make a fresh pot."

James said nothing. Keb could see him thinking things so hard that you could almost see his thoughts.

Marge left the galley and returned with two large cohos and slapped them down on the counter. She began cutting up fillets. She said to James, "So tell me, what are you going to do now that you can't play basketball anymore?"

"I could have played for the NBA."

"Oh shush. I didn't ask you what you could have done. I'm asking what you're going to do."

"I could go to school. My Aunt Ruby went to Princeton."

"Keeeeerist." Marge shook her head and left the galley again.

Did Keb fall asleep? He saw Bessie dancing in her bare feet, a flowered dress around her legs, her smile filling the room. Nathan Red Otter was there, and Father Mikal standing in a circle with Keb. Bessie had a toddler, a little girl she wheeled about the room. Was it Gracie? Like her mom, she tossed her head back and laughed. Keb said to Nathan, "We need to bless the canoe." The three men looked at him. "Bless the canoe," Keb said, "I forgot to bless the canoe. It's not running true. It pulls to the left. It doesn't move right. Maybe it's a crack? Not good. Uncle Austin, he mended his canoe by pulling the crack together with roots and tightening the stitches with a wedge." While on shore you had to keep the keel moist. Haul the canoe up the beach and sink it deep in the wet sand. The glaciers . . . the glaciers are going away, the ice is melting all over. . . .

"Gramps?"

Keb gasped awake.

"Gramps, you're dreaming and kicking the table."

"What?"

"Can you sit up, and join us?"

He was back in the galley, on the *Silverbow*. His dreams hadn't been this vivid since—when? Since he had last been on the water a thousand years ago.

James pulled him up gently.

Marge said, "Look who's decided to join us. You want something to eat?"

"Got any more cornbread?"

"Hell, yes. I got cornbread I haven't even eaten yet. How about some garlic-pesto salmon? Or halibut caddy ganty with cashews and red peppers?"

"Sounds good."

Keb realized that Little Mac and Kid Hugh were at the table, too. When did they show up? How does this happen? How does an old man fall out of time? Little Mac was picking a melody on her guitar. She had her head down as her fingers worked the frets. Keb tried to remember his dream of Bessie and Gracie. Bessie had always been good at remembering. She had a Rolodex of her dreams. Keb's friend Truman kept his memories on Post-it Notes, a million of them all over the place, on his computer, desk, refrigerator, stove. He wrote everything down on little scraps of paper, and once told Keb that the strongest memory is weaker than the palest ink. Maybe it was a hallucination, a crazy fantasy, him seeing Bessie and Gracie dancing. "Gracie's not well," Keb said softly, almost to himself. They were all talking and didn't hear him.

"Gracie's not well," he said, louder this time.

They stopped.

"Your mom," Keb said to James. "She's not well. We need to call her."

They were looking at each other, not knowing what to say. Keb had seen people respond to him like this before. *They think I'm crazy.* "I'm not crazy," he said.

"No, Gramps, you're not crazy."

"She might have to go to the hospital, very expensive." These days only doctors could afford doctors. "We forgot to bless the canoe. Nathan Red Otter was going to be there, at the steaming, but he . . . but he . . . we have to bless the canoe."

The cornbread arrived and just as quickly Keb forgot his concerns. Little Mac cut him a corner piece and added butter. Keb was about to take a bite when his chest seized and his arms froze and he couldn't breathe. A searing pain buckled him. He dropped the cornbread and Steve got it.

"Gramps?" Little Mac and Kid Hugh were on their feet in seconds, holding him while James supported the other side. Keb gasped as pain shot from his chest to his hip and back. *Yéil Yeik.* Jesus, Mary, Mother of God.

Marge got him a cup of water. James whipped off his shirt and carefully removed the necklace with the raven feather. He held it against Keb's chest. Keb said, "I need . . . to . . . lie . . . down . . . now." He did, and soon said, "I think I feel better."

"You do, really?" James asked.

Keb nodded.

Marge said, "That's the black feather, the one they talked about on the radio, on the news. They said it gives him special powers, that he can see things that others can't see, and he knows things others don't know."

"It's mostly black," James said. "But it's also blue, if you look at it right."

"I must be looking wrong then." Marge turned away to check the oven. Little Mac comforted Keb with her delicate fingers. When Marge turned back, she directed herself to James. "I wish I were you, any of you. You're free. You have the whole world in front of you. I'm not talking about the world we've made for ourselves. I'm talking about the world that's always been here."

James handed her the feather. She took it tentatively. "Do you see the blue?" he asked. He spoke with a kindness Keb had never heard from him. Marge wiped away tears and looked hard, as if imploring the feather to show her its secrets. "Turn it in the light," James said, "like this, slowly, at an angle."

She did, and handed it back to him, saying, "It's not for me to see; it's for you. This is your journey, not mine."

resentment eating her alive

Y OU REALLY THINK he wants to die?" Taylor de la Croix
asked Gracie Wisting.
Anne winced at Taylor's straightforwardness as she
checked the twin outboards and greased the steering cables on the *Firn*. They
were adrift off the north shore of Pleasant Island, near Strawberry Flats, in
the lee of the storm, which wasn't as stormy as predicted—so far. Leave it to
Taylor to go right to the heart of things, to ask the question about Old Keb
that nobody else dared ask—of his daughter, no less. Taylor was acting frisky
these days, capable of anything, getting laid every night in Strawberry Flats.
Anne wondered: How long has it been for me? Who was president of the
United States the last time I got laid? Nixon? Hoover? Grant?

Gracie responded to Taylor's question with a wry smile. She looked
out over Icy Strait as if drinking it up, and finally said, "I think my dad
thinks he wants to die. That's why he's on this journey, to find out. Death
takes us all, you know. Some quicker than others."

Taylor said, "My first boyfriend was a star quarterback in high school.
He was a lot of fun until he freaked out about that fact that he would die
someday. So he bought the big insurance package in the sky; he signed up for
heaven and the Bible and all that, in his junior year, and got down on his
knees and brought Jesus into his life."

"How'd that go?" Gracie asked her.

"Good for him, bad for me. His mom never liked me; she was super
religious. They celebrated by going to Disney, in Florida."

"How American," Gracie said.

Anne liked this woman better than she liked Gracie's hard-edged sister
who sat forward in the wheelhouse, deep in conversation with Superintendent

Paul Beals, the two of them folded over maps and documents, with Ruby doing most of the talking. Paul had an easy manner, a voice that made you listen, but with Ruby he never got the chance. Near as Anne could tell, Ruby would have it no other way. On those rare occasions when Paul did speak, Anne could see Ruby sit rigid-backed and defiant. Gracie must have caught Anne watching them. She said, "My sister always gets what she wants."

Taylor asked Gracie, "Are you worried about your father and son, about them being out in a canoe in weather like this?"

"No."

"You think we'll find them?"

"No." Gracie answered with such calm conviction, it surprised Anne. She could see it surprised Taylor too. How could this woman be so certain?

For the tenth time Anne climbed topside, above the wheelhouse, and glassed the waters. She could see sport charter fishing boats at anchor off the Strawberry Flats Public Dock, and a salmon troller to the west headed their way, beating into the waves, and farther still, a tugboat pulling a barge loaded with containers, westbound toward Cape Spencer and beyond, north to Seward perhaps, or Anchorage. No other vessels. Modest whitecaps across Icy Strait. A fifteen-knot wind blowing from the southeast, not as fierce as predicted, the seas much calmer in a good lee. Gulls everywhere, a few alcids, pigeon guillemots mostly, and now and then a Steller sea lion.

"Anything?" Taylor asked when Anne returned.

"Nope. Anything on the VHF?"

"Nope."

"They've gotten a ride," Gracie said, again with calm assurance, almost pleasure.

Anne felt it too. The thrill of Keb out there in his canoe, befriending strangers, winning hearts, outwitting anybody who sought to find him and bring him in.

"A ride?" Taylor said.

"Just a guess," Gracie said. "A ride from a sympathetic skipper, or they've hauled their canoe onto a beach under cover of alder and spruce and made camp. My James can set up a tent blindfolded in a rainstorm and a wind tunnel. Either way—on a big boat or in the forest—they're fine."

WHAT TO MAKE of these Wisting women? Anne studied them: two sisters, one the mother of the runaway James, the other his aunt, filling the *Firn* with the measured spaces between them. Ruby, the small one with the fine-featured face, fashionable in her black pantsuit and lavender scarf, wearing the sad eyes and hard beauty of a woman who long ago learned to use that beauty to test for faithfulness and deceit. And Gracie, the big one who didn't look well, the mother in cheap jeans and a baggy sweater who seemed to take nourishment from gratitude while her sister took hers from pride. She devoted long minutes to looking out over the water. Anne thought: We could use some whales now, mountains moving through the sea. But of course they weren't looking for whales.

Earlier that day Ruby had arrived in Bartlett Cove and requested that since the federal government had closed Crystal Bay to traditional Tlingit activities like hunting and fishing—first as a national monument, then a national park, and finally as a national marine reserve—would the federal government please find her father and nephew and escort them home before somebody died. Her father was a frail old man; he didn't always know where he was or what he was doing. And the kids, while capable in the wilderness, would defer to him and make poor decisions. Paul could have offered a rebuttal and reminded Ruby that no canoe was prohibited from entering Crystal Bay. He could have told her that the limits on vessels applied to motorized craft only; that while people belonged in a national marine reserve, hunting and fishing did not. Neither did corporate mining. He could have sounded as intelligent as Ruby, and used lots of big words. But, by golly, he invited her on a boat ride instead . . . with her sister.

"My sister?" Ruby had said. "What's she doing here?"

Earlier that day, upon hearing that Ruby was coming, Paul had sent the NMRS plane into Juneau to bring Gracie to Bartlett Cove, before Ruby arrived.

"He's my father, too," Gracie said, weakly.

All this according to Ranger Ron, who had told Anne that when Tall Paul got up from his chair that morning to greet Gracie, and later Ruby, you got the feeling he kept standing and standing until he towered over those women like Honest Abe or Old King Lear. He had welcomed the two sisters, saying, "It's always an honor to have Jinkaat Tlingits in Bartlett Cove." And he meant it. Paul was always sincere. He then invited them onto the *Firn* to brief them on the NMRS search: the boats and planes and "all-points bulletin" sent via VHF channel sixteen to vessels all over Icy Strait. The report sounded official and heartless, which Anne supposed was necessary. She preferred the rendition she'd heard passed around by fishermen, picked up on her own radio: Be on the lookout for a twenty-five-foot-long dugout canoe carrying a nine-toed, barefoot old man who's half seal, awkward on land but clever and elusive at sea. With him are two long-haired boys, a Chinese girl with a classical guitar, and a mongrel dog that thinks he's a big lizard of some kind—maybe a dinosaur.

The search consisted of rangers, field biologists (Anne and Taylor among them), a public affairs officer, a task force commander from Washington (assigned by Kate Johnson), a high-tech headquarters with state-of-the-art, top-of-the-line stuff, and a can't-go-wrong strategy that so far hadn't gone right. Paul promised the sisters they'd find Old Keb. Maybe not today, maybe not tomorrow. But soon.

Anne got the feeling that despite Gracie's obvious ill health, nothing would keep her from derailing her sister's corporate agenda in Crystal Bay. Paul had said that when PacAlaska was stripping Chichagof Island of old-growth trees years ago, Gracie Wisting emerged as a folksy but powerful voice in opposition. She had her health back then. She wrote for the newspaper and got herself on radio, and testified in Washington, and never backed down. When a Yale-trained forester once proclaimed—as Yale-trained foresters had proclaimed for decades—that the oldest, largest trees in Southeast Alaska should be cut down and processed into wood pulp because their rates of rot had exceeded their rates of growth, making them "overmature," Gracie famously asked the forester if he too one day, in his old age, should be measured so crudely. And processed into pulp, rayon, and throwaway cellophane. More recently, she coordinated with NMRS educators to have the Jinkaat School kids visit Crystal Bay every summer to hike and camp. It's a national marine reserve, she told them, not a mall, not a chemical plant, not a damn gold mine. Embrace it. You are welcome here. Go sleep on the ground. Wake up to bear tracks and wolf howls. Let whales swim into your dreams. Gracie didn't oppose having Tlingits in Crystal Bay. She did everything she could to bring them here. What she opposed, she said, was industrial enterprise in Crystal Bay; corporate suit-and-tie types with their hearts in briefcases and their heads in computers, thinking numbers. Always numbers.

"I'm here with the best of intentions," Ruby had said to Paul. As if Gracie were not.

So Paul sent the NMRS plane to get Gracie and bring her to Bartlett Cove before her sister arrived. The whole thing gave Anne dreams of insurrection, of finding Old Keb and taking him wherever he wanted to go, wherever he could be who he'd once been.

Boldness, Anne thought. Was I ever, truly ever bold? Maybe now, somehow. Maybe here.

LIVE IN HAWAII, as Anne had, and you learn about the revenge of good intentions; how Captain James Cook died at the hands of Hawaiians in Kealakekua Bay, his blood—the blood of the greatest explorer of his time—the same color as any other man. Not a god at all. You learn about his brilliant but flawed midshipmen, George Vancouver and William Bligh, incapable from that day forward of speaking of the great man's death. You learn about Columbus and Magellan, all the places they discovered and opened up to destruction and disease. Dig a little deeper, as Anne had, and you learn about Parry and Ross, fifty years after Cook, the Englishmen standing in the snow of Greenland and speaking through a translator to the Inuit, small squat men dressed in seal skins who stared back at the tall white strangers in their cocked hats and black boots—the same uniforms the British wore at Trafalgar—and asked, "From where do you come, the sun or the moon?"

Growing up in Juneau, it was Nancy who first put dreams of Hawaii in Anne's head. Everybody in Alaska thinks about Hawaii, the warmth and sun and gentle breezes, the fresh fruit, perfect beaches, and Aloha spirit. We Americans took the islands from them, Nancy once said, and still the Hawaiian Natives treat us kindly.

"You must love each other a great deal," Anne's mother once told her. "To needle each other as you do, you must love each other very much." They only had one bad fight, Anne and Nancy, a screaming match to take out on each other what they couldn't on their stepfather. After that, they discovered boats and whales.

At the university many years after Nancy died, Anne heard a professor say there was no underestimating the potential for variation within a population. It struck her that the same could be said of families, all those differences tied tightly together like a knot. The harder you pull, the tighter it gets.

In bed one night, in their small, dark room, with their mother watching TV and their stepfather out drinking in a Juneau bar, Nancy said, "I think Captain Cook was a great man."

"So do I," Anne replied.

"They couldn't swim, you know."

"Who?"

"Cook's men, sailors from England. They couldn't swim. It's weird, don't you think? They sailed around the world, and they couldn't swim."

The same with whalers. Men who couldn't swim killed the greatest swimmers on earth. The two girls were still awake when their stepfather came home and began yelling at their mother for all the things she was and was not. "Cover your ears," Nancy said to Anne. "That way he won't be so bad." Soon after, Anne got her first journal:

You said we should forgive him

His love would see us through
I didn't reply
Cold heart, empty sky
And you?
You said we should forgive him.

ABOARD THE *FIRN*, Anne watched Ruby interrupt her discussion with Paul to flip through the VHF radio dial, searching for chatter about the canoeists among the Icy Strait fishing fleet. *Now that's bold*, Anne thought, *and rude*. She and Taylor stepped forward to listen with Paul and Ruby. Gracie remained seated aft, near the transom, looking out over the sea.

Voices crackled over the radio:

"There's no easy way they could have crossed Icy Strait in that storm," said one skipper. "With the weather on their beam, even with good freeboard, they'd have shipped a lot of water, don't you think?"

"They probably hugged Chichagof and headed west toward Adolphus, or they found a good place to camp and hide, maybe in Flynn Cove or Pinta Cove."

"With a strong southeaster and them having good canvas, they could clip along and cover a lot of water; it would take some fancy ruddering though, with their paddles."

"You mean use the sail as a spinnaker? You can only run fast under sail with a narrow-beamed, flat-bottomed boat if you've got a deep keel, otherwise you're gonna corkscrew."

"Unless you got outriggers. What do you think, Deke? Did you talk to Oddmund? Do they have outriggers?"

"I don't think so. I've never heard of a canoe with outriggers and a deep keel like you're talking about. Somebody could have given them a lift, you know."

"Fred said that some guy said that a buddy of his talked to some guy who said they saw the *Silverbow* making her way west past Adolphus early this morning."

"The *Silverbow*? What's Marge doing at Adolphus when the Lisianski fleet's working the Fairweather Grounds?"

"Hey, does anybody know what Marge is doing half the time?"

"Kenny Marston knows what she's doing at least some of the time because he's doing it with her."

That brought a tide of cheap replies. Paul switched the radio back to channel sixteen as Ruby sat down. Anne watched her write *Silverbow* in her iPhone, then begin texting. Paul stepped onto the aftdeck and Anne heard him say, "How are you doing, Gracie? Can I get you anything?"

Anne watched Ruby answer her cell phone. Soon Paul and Taylor were on their cell phones. Only Gracie remained, still facing the sea. "It's beautiful, isn't it?" she said softly as Anne joined her. "The sea, how it picks up the clearing storm, the sky blue and black. See the way the light moves through the clouds this time of year? It's beautiful."

"Yes, it is."

The last day of August. Cottonwoods beginning to turn gold. Geese kettling their way home. Phalaropes spinning about. Young gulls diving for fish, feasting on the final bounty of summer. Somewhere below, a whale. Somewhere above, a raven.

Anne heard Paul talking about a possible aerial hunt for the canoe . . . a dragnet across the entrance into Crystal Bay . . . spotters on Feldspar Peak . . . nothing so far. . . .

Anne smiled to herself. All these rangers searching for the boy Ron predicted would end up flipping burgers at McDonald's, out there with his grandfather. What must it be like for a mother with an overstuffed heart to look into her son's eyes and see the universe, all that light and possibility, all the darkness and room for things to go wrong? Anne asked Gracie, "Are you scared?"

"No."

"When was the last time a Tlingit from Jinkaat paddled a canoe into Crystal Bay?"

"Oh my . . . a long time ago."

It wasn't Gracie's voice that Anne heard just then, it was Nancy's, soft in the bedroom late at night, speaking low as sisters do when they're supposed to be asleep. Nancy, three years older than Anne, had written a school report on Captain Cook, and told Anne that when the great explorer first arrived on the Big Island, he sighted a hill the Hawaiians called Mauna Loa. That's what it looked like, a hill. Cook ordered a company of men to go climb it. The men returned days later, footsore and weary, and reported that after all that travel on black volcanic rock, the hill appeared no closer than it had before. It wasn't a hill. It was a mountain, a great shield volcano ten times taller and farther away than Cook had assumed. The geography was so new to him, the land and distances so difficult to comprehend that he gave goofy orders. Anne and Nancy laughed about that. Captain Cook. Goofy orders. They giggled themselves silly. All these years later, Anne wondered if the great captain held out his hand at arm's length, and measured it. Did he cover the trickster hill with his finger, as a space-walking astronaut might one day cover Africa? Are we any wiser today than we were two centuries ago?

It isn't the object that deceives. It's the eye.

Paul was still on his cell phone, talking about the search, when Anne said to Gracie, "I met your father once."

Gracie stared at her.

"I was eight. My sister and I were in a skiff off Shelter Island and got caught in a storm and –"

"Oh, my gosh, that was you? You were the little girl he saved?"

"Yes."

"And your sister—she died?"

"Yes. Nancy."

"I remember that. Oh, my gosh. Pops was written up in the papers for that."

"Was he? I don't remember."

"You were probably in shock, you poor thing, losing your sister like that."

Ruby stepped from the wheelhouse. "I just got off the phone with Channel Four in Juneau. They're flying out to Strawberry Flats and will be here in two hours. Gracie, you and I are scheduled to give a press conference. Paul, I'd appreciate it if you could drop us at the dock and help us arrange transportation to the city library, that's where we'll be interviewed."

"A press conference," Gracie said, "about what?"

"About the safe return of our father and your son. We need to ask local communities to help us find and return the people we love. It's nasty weather out there, they have no protection. And somebody needs to apprehend the Gant brothers, or give us a tip about where they are, where they're headed. They're wanted for arson. They could be dangerous."

Gracie took a deep breath, as if what she was about to say would take everything she had. "Dad spent hundreds of hours in open boats when he was a kid, Ruby. You know that. It made him who he is today. He's fine."

Ruby didn't protest, as Anne thought she would. Instead, she hung her head.

Gracie said, "Remember all his stories about time in a wooden boat with Uncle Austin? I'll bet he's more alive right now than he's been in a long time."

"He's not a kid anymore, Gracie. He's an old man. He gets cold and confused and he's always in pain, sometimes acute pain with his arthritis, especially when he's cold."

"It's August, not January."

"And blowing a gale, and almost September."

"He's a tough old man, tougher than you think."

"And if he dies?"

"Then he'll die doing what he loves."

"And his death will be on our hands, Gracie. Please, do this with me. Help me find him." Tears welled up in Ruby's eyes.

Gracie said softly, "Isn't this what you want? An old Tlingit headed home in the old way, with his grandson and his favorite dog?"

"Not like this."

"He is going to die one day. You know that, right? He can't live forever, none of us can."

Ruby rocked back. Paul reached out, but she recovered and said, "Gracie, I'm going to do this press conference, and I'd . . . I'd like to have you with me, okay? Please, do this with me." She stepped back into the wheelhouse to make another call. Paul joined her.

Taylor fired up the *Firn* and began to motor toward the Strawberry Flats Public Dock, less than a mile away.

Gracie stood and faced the sea, her hands on the gunwale, fingers strangely purple and swollen, face drawn, eyes sad. "It's crazy, isn't it?" she said. "This journey, this life."

"Yes," Anne said.

"I told my sister once that she's just an angry Indian, beneath all her bluster, so high and mighty, that's all she is, an angry Indian. She's much more accomplished than me. She has a good husband, a strong marriage, lots of fancy titles and degrees. I guess I'm a little jealous. Maybe a lot jealous. I don't know. But she's at war with herself, and it's sad, it breaks my heart. You know what I told her once? I told her that she lives in resentment, and it's eating her alive, it makes her bitter and blind. She's so resentful."

"What'd she say?"

"She resented it."

They laughed. The next thing Anne knew, Gracie was leaning into her.

"You're lucky, you really are," Anne told her, "to have such a good father."

"I know . . . I just wish they'd let him go wherever it is he feels he needs to go, in his canoe, his last canoe. I just wish they'd let him go."

"So do I."

"Then do it," Gracie said, suddenly facing Anne. "You have a boat. You have authority. You have free will. Help him."

"I have something else, too."

"What?"

"A debt to repay."

jimmy bluefeather

D
AWN WAS HOURS away when a seine skiff throttled deep
and low through the darkness toward the *Silverbow*. James
told Keb to get his things together. They might have to move
soon, push off in the canoe. Keb tried to think: *Get things together? Dry
socks? Do I have my dry socks?*

Marge signaled Morgan and Quinton to kill the running lights as she
monitored her VHF radios. Several times other vessels had hailed her and
she refused to respond. When the skiff came alongside, she said, "Wait here,"
and went out on deck to have her rendezvous.

Keb could hear the shadows of things said between her and the man in
the seine skiff, but not the things themselves. From the expressions of James
and Kid Hugh, they didn't get the words either, and this made them nervous.
Was the *Silverbow* adrift? Keb tried to remember the anchor chain going
down. He stepped outside and approached Marge.

James reached for him, "Gramps, don't—"

"Hey, Keb, is that you?" a voice called from down in the skiff. Keb
stopped. "It's me, Cobb. Cobb Reed." The man climbed up the metal ladder
and shook Keb's hand. Keb wondered: Do I know Cobb Reed? As they
stepped into the galley, Cobb said, "We have to talk. We don't have much
time. It's good to see you, Keb. Everybody's talking and taking bets."

"Taking bets?" Little Mac asked.

"On you, Keb. Where you are, where you're headed in your canoe, if
you're okay—you know, still alive."

"He's alive," James said.

"I can see that. Damn, it's good to see you. So, if you don't mind me
asking, what's your destination?"

Keb didn't like this Cobb man. His eyes were too close together, his teeth too far apart. He smelled like fish, and bobbed his greasy head when he spoke. He had a voice like a forklift, a prying mind.

Nobody answered him.

"No matter," Cobb said. "They're onto you. They know you're on this fishing tender."

Kid Hugh stepped outside to stand guard.

"How?" Marge asked. "How could they know that?"

"Somebody saw you yesterday morning cruising west past Adolphus. It seemed weird, so they called it in. Now everybody's talking on the VHF, channels sixty-eight, sixty-nine, and seventy-two, mostly."

"I monitor those channels and have heard nothing. What's so weird about me steaming west past Adolphus?"

"Shit, Marge, everything. You bought fish three days ago and haven't bought or sold any since. You gotta be low on ice and maybe low on fuel."

"I've got lots of ice and fuel."

"Well, you're thirty miles from the Lisianski fleet and missing the biggest coho opening in weeks. That's weird, and you know it." Cobb turned to Keb. "Everybody's on high alert looking for you, Keb. You're like a hero, you know, like a cult hero or a folk hero or some damn thing."

"I don't want to be a hero."

"Too late. You already are."

"Why?"

"I don't know. I guess because you carved a canoe and got everybody involved, and pushed off like Tlingits used to do a thousand years ago, before the world got crazy with television and Twinkies."

Keb shrugged.

"They're worried about you, that you might freeze or drown or fall off a cliff. Your daughter Ruby is all over radio and TV, asking for your safe return. The Crystal Bay rangers want to catch you and make sure you're okay. But I have to tell you, a lot of people, folks like me, we want to help you. We really do. We want to help you get wherever it is you want to go."

"We don't need any help," James said.

Cobb shrugged. Little Mac sidled up to Keb and put her withered hand into hers.

"Why?" Keb asked. "Why do people want to help me?"

"I don't know," Cobb said. "You're the little guy, I guess, and people want to help the little guy. But you're also a big guy, the old man whose house got burned down but he doesn't sit around and mope about it. I mean, everybody talks about Crystal Bay being a traditional homeland, but nobody— nobody—gets in a canoe and goes back there in the traditional way. You see? You're like a blast from the past. That's why you got everybody stirred up; a lot of people want to help you. Me too. I thought you could use my help, is all. If I'm wrong, I apologize and I wish you luck. I hope you get back to wherever it is you want to go." He turned to leave.

"Back," Keb said.

Cobb spun around. "Back, really?"

"Yes, back."

"Back to where, Keb?"

"Back . . . back to the way it used to be." Keb could feel himself standing taller.

"That's where you want to go?"

"Yes."

"That could be a long journey, you know? You don't remember me, do you?"

Keb did remember him a little, maybe. Was he related to Father Mikal? The friend of a cousin? The cousin of a friend?

"You and Bess took my brother and me berry picking when we was kids."

"Nagoons?"

"Wild strawberries."

"Oyyee . . . shákw . . . put up with salmon eggs, kanéegwál."

"What about the Gants?" James asked Cobb. "Has anybody seen Tommy or Charlie Gant?"

"I don't think so."

"Have they been arrested or anything?"

"I don't think so."

Marge said, "We have to go. It'll be daylight in a couple hours, and we have some distance to cover."

Cobb said, "Keb, if there's anything I can do, any way that I can help, you tell me right now."

"Gracie," Keb said to Cobb. "My girl, Gracie. I need you to tell her not to worry about me, not to worry about James, any of us. She's sick. I don't want her to worry. Tell her not to worry. We are fine. We are good. Can you tell her that?"

"I'll tell her," Marge said, "after I drop you off. I'll reach her by marine dispatch."

Little Mac squeezed Keb's hand.

Cobb said, "I have to go." He disappeared into the liquid night, only after Kid Hugh made him promise to keep his mouth shut. Marge banged on a pipe and Quinton came into the galley. Or maybe it was Morgan. She flashed her fingers and the boy bounded into the wheelhouse. A minute later the *Silverbow* was underway, twin diesels pumping big pistons. Graves Harbor was out of the question now. Too far.

Marge began packing food into a tote. "I'm making you a care package." Her other son came into the galley, moving fast. He smiled at Little Mac, grabbed a bag of tortilla chips, and was gone.

"Was their father deaf?" Little Mac asked Marge.

"No. He heard everything just fine, except me."

"So your boys, do you know why—"

"Why they're deaf? No. Their father said the devil made them that way. I sometimes envy them their silence, you know, how peaceful it must be in there, not having to hear all the crap we have to hear. I can't see either of them ever finding a woman or having kids. But you never know. They might surprise me one day. I'd like that." She paused as chatter spilled across the VHF radio.

Keb was still thinking about wild strawberries.

Marge looked at him with such sadness that everything vague a minute ago came into sharp focus. What a powerful, sorry thing she was, this woman, fallen on a thousand thorns, picked up, and fallen again.

James said to her, "You've been good to us. We'll get off now, with our canoe. We can paddle hard and put good water between you and us before dawn."

"No need," Marge said. "I've got a plan."

AN HOUR LATER, as soft light broke to the east, they made landfall at a place called George Island, between Cross Sound and the small fishing town of Elfin Cove. While Morgan used one skiff to take Keb, James, Little Mac, and Steve the Lizard Dog ashore, Quinton used the other skiff to pull the canoe into a deep cleft in a nearby cliff, where he and Kid Hugh buoyed it out of sight, impossible to see from the air. From the water, too. Marge gave them the tote with three days of food. She told James to take care of his grandpa. She told Little Mac, "I'm sorry. I wanted to help you, all of you."

"You have."

James said to Little Mac, "If you want to stay on the *Silverbow*, you can. We've talked about it."

Little Mac was taken aback by this, Keb could see. Steve wagged his tail as if he'd been in on the discussion too, and was prepared to man a paddle—the canoeing dog. Little Mac appraised James. "You don't want me along?"

"I do. I just don't want you to be wet and cold and frightened."

"I'm not."

"You might be, in the days to come. We plan to paddle at night."

"That's fine. I'm strong. I can paddle. I want to go, James."

"Okay, you go."

"James?" Marge said abruptly. "Is that your real name?"

"It's my dad's name. He wanted me to have his name."

"He's Apache," Keb said.

"Arapaho," James corrected him.

"This might offend you," Marge said, "but James is the kind of name a shithead English king would have, don't you think? Have you got a Tlingit name?"

"Yeah."

"Why not use it."

"I did, for a while. The missionaries took our language away."

"Keeeeerist, you can't blame the missionaries no more. They bully-ragged your people a hundred years ago, but no more."

"I'm not blaming the missionaries, I'm just—"

"You're just ready for a new name. Look, I believe in you. Your life excites me, with all its possibilities. It excites other people too. Go out there. Move at night, like you said. Paddle far. Be sneaky. Use every advantage you can; don't let the rangers find you. Go where you need to go. Listen to your grandfather. Go where he needs to go. Take this beautiful girl and get your language back. Maybe use your Tlingit name on this journey. Have you thought about that?"

"I used to use my Tlingit name when I was a little kid."

"Then use it again, if that's what you're trying to be, a real Tlingit."

"That's what Gramps is trying to be."

"Well, he's not alone. Would either one of you be on this journey without the other? Did he carve the canoe, or did you?"

"He did. I did. Everybody in Jinkaat did. Lots of people."

"Well there you go. Your entire town is with you. I'll tell you what, James Whoever-You-Really-Are, the whole world is out there pulling for you. Well, not the whole world, but some of it, the best of it. Have you thought about that?"

"Yes."

"Where's your father?"

"Denver. I don't see him anymore."

"Do you miss him?"

"No—well, some. Him and my mom, they loved each other a lot, I think, once, when I was little."

Keb said to James, "I remember the day you were born. Your mother cried with joy. After three daughters she finally had a son. She and your father performed magic on you: They buried your umbilical cord at the foot of an eagle's tree."

"They did?"

"Yes."

"Tlingit magic or Arapaho magic?"

"Does it matter?" Marge asked.

James stared at her.

"Look," Marge said, her voice quivering, "you need to go. Go find a fish or a flower or the great bird that gave you that feather. Get to know it and I promise you that fish, that flower, that bird, it'll never lie to you." Keb could see Marge crying. "Nature never lies, is all I'm saying. Your grandfather is old and you learn from him and he learns a little from you. You grow from each other. Even with your bum leg, you're new, you're a teacher, a carver. That's what it comes down to, you and your grandfather and your friends, how you learn from each other; that's a beautiful thing. You're out there in a canoe in wild Alaska while the rest of America coddles and sanitizes its children. Live every moment, James What's-Your-Name. Let nothing go unnoticed. Basketball is just another court in another kingdom filled with indoor people addicted to a box called television and a mythology called winning. You don't need it. You're the feather whisperer or some damn thing. . . . I don't know. Maybe this is all bullshit. You're the sports star who's not who he used to be. You see beyond the obvious. Where others see black, you see blue."

James turned the feather in his hand.

"Jimmy Bluefeather," Little Mac said. "That's you, James. You're Jimmy Bluefeather."

MARGE HUGGED OLD Keb and didn't let him go. She pulled him to her with such ferocity that she nearly suffocated him—bosomed him to death. Not a bad way to die. Keb wanted to tell her stories about his carvings. About his travels and favorite boats and books, the ones Uncle Austin used to read. He wanted to tell her to go deep into her life, what remained of it; a fish cannot drown in water. But words failed him. He said nothing.

She let him go and walked away and didn't look back. In minutes she was in the skiff with her sons, going full throttle beyond the headland and out of sight, out to where the sea writes eulogies and takes us away.

a place of safekeeping

BY MIDMORNING SWORDS of sunlight cut through the clouds and a plane flew low overhead, a Cessna 206 on floats, according to Kid Hugh. Might be a search plane, or a charter on its way to a fancy sportfishing lodge in Elfin Cove. Either way, Kid Hugh didn't like it. Keb half expected him to shoot it out of the sky.

Back in the deep forest, Keb found the terrain such rough going—muddy and root-infested—that he sat down, his heart pounding. He tried to open his pills. Little Mac helped him and put each one in a spoonful of yogurt to make it go down better. James set up a tent near a game trail, and with Little Mac's help put down a thick pad and a sleeping bag for the old man.

Keb had wanted to pick berries as he did with Bessie, years ago, deep in the forest and low to the ground where green was a texture, not just a color. Where moss made the best beds for naps, and you awoke beneath great trees that passed no judgment, and the woman you loved was perfect in how she loved you back and put her head on your shoulder and loved all the things you loved, and you knew without saying that every day was a gift, that you have to go hungry to become real. That's what Milo Chen used to say. Truman too, writing his books. You have to suffer and come out the other side, find compassion in the emptiness. Respond by not filling it up. It's no easy thing. It's not what we build, Uncle Austin used to say. It's what we leave alone that makes us who we are. Look around. We cannot improve this place. We can only honor it by receiving its bounty with wisdom and thanks. Go into the woods when your kids are young and gather devil's club to make tea. "Alaska ginseng," he called it. S'áxt'. Good for fatigue. Keeps you fit and able to split wood into old age. Bessie always made it just right. Remember how she let the kids run wild? Up the slopes and along the beach in bare feet, their prints so small next to the tracks of brown bear. When they and Keb said they were hungry, Bessie replied, "We don't feed them when they fuss, we feed them when it's time." What feisty little things they became, Ruby and Gracie more than the boys. Bessie said those girls were born with their hands on their hips, saying no. After she died, the days were dimmer, the stars brighter. Keb never dated again. It felt better to live with the memory of Bessie than to find another woman. He still drank Alaska ginseng, when Gracie made it for him. He had some with him on this journey, in a Mason jar. The boys might need it, with so much paddling ahead. Crazy kids these days, going to the drugstore to buy cough syrup. "It's all in the forest," Bessie used to say. All you need is caribou leaf salve, devil's club, and yarrow. Yarrow will cure anything. Uncle Austin used to say the best devil's club grew on islands, with the leaves facing west.

Was it September? First day or two anyway. Keb could smell it blowing off the ocean. The taste of winter coming, change and darkness and storms. He could see it in the margins of *yaana.eit*, smell it in the tangy odor of beach grass and meadow sedges. Everything burnished. Cranes and geese and swans going south. Young gulls painted by an artist's brush, testing their wings. Keb's favorite month. It should have cheered him up. But he felt poorly. Even with Little Mac comforting him with her guitar. He missed cornbread and hot coffee; Marge's lively banter. Bedded down, socked deep into a sleeping bag with his nose cold but his bones warm, he could hear James and Kid Hugh setting up a second tent. Talking. Arguing about where to go, how to proceed, how to avoid getting found, arguing about how to argue.

Then what? He must have fallen asleep.

He dreamed that he grew so old people saw right through him. Then he was young again, a thousand years ago, dreaming in a way that dreams make you new. He saw Uncle Austin on a pier, and a missionary telling him that if he didn't follow Christ he'd burn in Hell for eternity. "Burn in Hell?" Uncle Austin said. "How hot could it be? And eternity—how long could it be?" The missionary quoted Luke, John, Matthew, Michael, Meatballs until Uncle Austin pushed him off the pier. The missionary windmilled his arms. The Bible sailed from his hands. No angel caught him. He made a big splash and came up swearing. "You want to test a Christian?" Uncle Austin said to young Keb. "Push him off a pier and see what he calls you." As he said this, his nose became a beak. His eyes grew beady and black. Feathers covered his face. He wasn't Uncle Austin, he was Raven, the trickster, his great wings flexing against the sky. "I have this relationship with change," he said. "It keeps changing." He laughed a back-of-the-throat chortle that rose into a full-bodied croak.

"I forgot to bless the canoe," Keb said.

"You want to be like me?" Raven said.

"I should have blessed the canoe."

"You worry too much."

"When you die, do you see everybody you loved and everybody who loved you?"

"Love, love, love."

"I should have blessed the canoe."

"Worry, worry, worry. You simplify your life, Tlingit man, Norwegian man, German, Portuguese, hound dog man. You simplify, but it's complicated, no?"

"So many people in pain. They need help. Father Mikal says Jesus healed the leopards. Why the leopards?"

"The lepers, he healed the lepers, sick people."

"Them too. The sick, the meek, the weak. Is there a devil?"

"Only in those people who believe in him."

"I can't pee like I used to. When I was young, I could pee my name in the snow. And Yevgeny Restin Gorborukov, oyyee. He could write his name and just keep going, write all of *War and Peace*. He had a bladder the size of Siberia. A good-sized pecker, too."

"Pecker, pecker, pecker. Feather, feather, feather."

"Do you want your feather back?"

"What feather?"

"I can't believe I'm talking to a raven."

"Believe it."

"Am I dreaming?"

"Yes, but that doesn't mean it's not real."

"The pain was real, so much pain; they gave me morphine, in Italy."

"You make no sense; I like you."

"In the war, we slept on rocks because the rocks were dry and everything else was mud."

"Mud, mud, mud."

"There was no meat . . . the people in Italy, they ate pasta, no meat; they were all veggietarries . . . the word you call people who don't eat meat."

"Vegetarian. Old Indian word meaning, 'bad fisherman.'"

"All the children were starving, in the war."

"War, war, war."

"Nothing's the way it's supposed to be anymore."

"Wake up."

"The whites came. They said nobody owned the land unless we had a piece of paper to prove it. The missionaries built six churches in our town. They thought we really needed help."

"Wake up, wake up, waaaake uuuup." Raven gave a loud croak and jumped up and down, and flew away.

Keb awoke with a start, confused, heart pounding, hands clasped over his chest, the light low and dusky, the air, cool. He took a moment to remember where he was . . . *who* he was. An old man with all his accomplishments behind him, until now. *Have I slept all day?* He fumbled for a light and flicked it on. Another sleeping bag was next to his, empty, and next to it, Little Mac's daypack and guitar case. He struggled with the tent zipper until he got himself outside wearing only boxer shorts, bare feet gripping the wet mossy earth beneath tall, silent trees, his mind slowly retelling what it was like, long ago, to be a young Norwegian Tlingit, living by wits and balance and poise. And toughness, always toughness. Bathing in the sea, fishing waist deep in rivers, spearing salmon, rubbing your skin with rocks, pushing through the cold. Was the other tent nearby? And Little Mac, James, Kid Hugh? Steve the Lizard Dog? Had they left him? *Have they left me?*

Is this my place?

He gave himself a moment to let his one good eye adjust. He pulled on some clothes and found the game trail and hobbled his way down to the beach, feeling his way with nine toes. A campfire came into view, the sounds of chatter. Steve barked when Keb smacked his shin into a beach log. Pain shot up his leg, but Keb made no sound, as Uncle Austin had taught him when hunting deer. Swallow your pain. Even when the bear took his toe, Keb didn't yell. A flashlight beamed onto him. He heard James tell Steve to shut up. James got to his feet. "Hey, Gramps, we thought you were asleep."

"I'm awake."

"You hungry?"

"Hungry? Yes, maybe. You never knew your Grandma Bess. She died when your mom was just a teenager, the age you are now."

"I know. Come on, Gramps, have something to eat. We've got lots of food."

"Now your mom is sick."

"I know, Gramps. She'll be okay."

"I forgot to bless the canoe."

"Come on down to the fire, have something to eat."

What they were eating was cigarettes and wine from a box. Seeing Steve sitting there with his lips peeled back, teeth folded into a stupid grin, Keb got the idea he'd been smoking and drinking too. Most dogs curl up by a fire and fall asleep. Not Steve. He sat with the boys and laughed at their jokes, might have told a few himself. Kid Hugh sat next to him, oiling a Colt .44, spinning the chamber, checking the trigger and action. Little Mac fingered her guitar.

"I'm dreaming a lot," Keb said. "Dreaming in Tlingit, seeing things, hearing things—xóots shakdéi sa_xwaa.áx—maybe I heard a bear's voice."

"Not on this island, Gramps. There are no bears on this island."

Kid Hugh said something about them not being very smart, having a fire on the beach with everybody in Icy Strait looking for them, and Elfin Cove not far away, and the troller fleet just out around the corner. Planes coming, going.

"We're forty miles from Jinkaat," James said. "Lots of people build fires on beaches. Fishermen do it all the time." Kid Hugh shrugged and filled a paper cup and offered Keb some wine. "You see the stars?" James said, pointing to the inky sky. Keb looked up and gave his grandson the satisfaction of nodding. The watery stars had winked out on him years ago. Nothing was as bright as it used to be.

"Clearing storm," Kid Hugh said.

Little Mac put a heavy shirt over Keb's shoulders. She gave him a squeeze when she did, and resumed strumming the guitar.

"I like it here," Keb said.

"Me, too," James said. "It's peaceful."

Did Keb hear a longing between his words, mixed with satisfaction? A blue flame of desire? All his life Keb had known men unconcerned with their own improvement, or with anyone else's. Lately he'd seen in James a desire to learn and care for others that warmed the old man. Warmed him deeper than any fire. Small gestures, but also big. Remember Jasper Jakes? He never went into the woods or slept on the ground or learned the songs of birds, or received mentorship of any kind. Nobody had high opinions of him so he compensated by having high opinions of himself. Drank himself to death. Remember Conner Young? His style was not to have one, to be invisible, vaporous, scented to persuasion. He stood for nothing and in the end stood not at all. And Todd Bankovich? Hated his job and complained about it up until the day it killed him; got very quiet after that. Never took a canoe journey. And Carla Howe?

So sad and precious and all the more precious in her sadness. Such wreckage. So many crushed spirits. How to make a meaningful life? "Get back," Keb said. *Back, back, back . . . to the land, the sea, the great glacier that shapes everything . . . even you and me.*

"What's that, Gramps?"

"Get back."

Little Mac began to strum the guitar with greater force, and the three kids sang words to a song written when their parents were young.

Sitting on a log, Keb wrapped his arms around his knees and pulled them to his chest and rocked to the beat as Little Mac's voice floated over James's and Kid Hugh's, searching for the harmony. Bessie could always sing harmony. Soon James and Kid Hugh were on their feet, wine cups in their hands, dancing in and out of the fire, laughing and leaping over the flames. Not to be left out, Steve ran around the fire and barked as if he too were a rock star.

"It's the Beatles, Gramps. You like the Beatles, right?"

"The Beatles, yes." *Bessie liked the Beatles.*

"You hungry, Gramps? I'll make you something to eat."

"Tell a story, Keb," Kid Hugh said.

A story?

The stories that brought greatest satisfaction were the ones Keb had learned from Uncle Austin. "These are not my stories . . . " Uncle Austin would begin. He had learned from his elders, and they from theirs, that story was a place of safekeeping, a bloodline, a tree. Taken together, they were the library of your people. A history. You learned them and preserved them by telling them well. So it was that Old Keb began, "These are not my stories," and Kid Hugh refilled his cup and the wine made him warm and the night scrolled back on itself and the stars shone brighter than before, entangled in the tops of trees.

WHEN KEB AWOKE, Steve was barking. James and Kid Hugh stood on shore facing the sea, Kid Hugh with the Colt jammed in his belt. The fire was out, the sun up. On the water, not far away, a white yacht lay at anchor, and nearer, two strangers approached in a small inflatable boat, one with his back to the beach, pulling on plastic oars, the other waving. Everything made close—too close—by the clarity of the day.

a discovery of your deepest knowing

THE TIDE HAD climbed to within a few feet of the cold-coals campfire. Did the stars still shine overhead, beyond the brilliant blue? Keb rubbed his eyes. He saw James focus binoculars on the lettering on the yacht. "*Etude*," James said to Kid Hugh. "What's an etude?" Kid Hugh had the good sense to pull his shirt over the Colt and throw a blanket over the deer rifle.

The two strangers wore red French berets and wide collared shirts, and belts made of hippie ties looped through khaki shorts. "Bonjour," one called as he stepped ashore.

Little Mac sat next to Keb and said, "*Etude* means 'study.'"

"Gud murneeng," the other stranger said. If what he said after that was English, Keb got none of it. Words spilled from his mouth in soft vowels, wet with dew, a birdsong language. When he got no response from James or Kid Hugh, the first stranger walked up the beach to Old Keb, and reached down to give his greeting. Such an angular face: sun-browned, deep-eyed, thick wavy hair, a chin five days from the last shave. Sandal-footed, Mediterranean, halfway around the world. He looked like a prophet forty days into the desert, the kind of man who eats books, not food, his elbows so loose they could bend both ways, his legs like cooked pasta, knobby knees. He seemed engaged with everything around him. He walked farther up the beach, dropped to one knee, held a rock aloft and called to his friend.

The second stranger wheezed by on his own pasta legs, heavier than the first, more fettuccini than spaghetti. The kind of fettuccini Galley Sally used to make. Soon the two Frenchmen had a dozen rocks in their hands, and were chattering like small birds. Out came a hand lens, and a small hammer.

Keb's head hurt. He regretted sleeping on the beach, and drinking crappy wine. He asked Little Mac for water. As he drank, a troller plied its way west toward Cross Sound, the mast rolling on a gentle swell. "We need to be more careful," he said. "Hide better, and bless the canoe. We need Nathan Red Otter to—"

Little Mac left him. Just like that, she got up and walked to the strangers and spoke French. They responded in a waterfall of words. It didn't slow her down. Keb remembered now. She had spent time in France awhile back, on a school exchange program for maybe half a year, and often wore headphones and listened to language tapes, and sang European songs. After a minute she came back and said to Old Keb, "They're geologists from Paris. They say they're here to trace the route of the French explorer LaPerouse, and to study isostatic rebound. They've invited us onto their yacht for a shower and something to eat, if we'd like."

Keb could see James and Kid Hugh packing up from last night, watching the Frenchmen. It was time to get off this bonfire island, get far away. Get the canoe from its mooring inside the sea cave, below the cliff. Kid Hugh had spoken of swimming out to it, or better, working his way along the cliff to reach it by diving into the sea, what he called "a Mexican Margarita Acapulco Loco Dive," whatever that meant. The kid would strap the Colt to his chest and take the plunge. It might not be necessary now, with help from these pasta-legged Frenchmen, a disappointment to the kid, who itched for action. Keb could see that a large part of the kid wanted to sail off those high rocks to see if he could do it, and if not, to die better than most people died, dying as they did when their clocks ran out, and they ticked their last tock. Or worse, dying before they were dead.

TIME ON THE yacht might not have been the best thing to do, but they did it anyway, riding the hours up the blue water coast, beyond Cape Spencer and Graves Harbor, north to Boussole and Astrolabe Bays. Another world, with big swells coming off the Gulf of Alaska and the *Etude* handling them with ease.

"The canoe's fine," Kid Hugh told Keb and James in a manner that didn't invite discussion. He'd buoyed it deep in the sea cave, and said it was secure. The rifle and totes were back in the tents, hidden deep in the forest, safe on the island.

They had only one gun now, the Colt.

Why do we need a gun? Keb worried, and said to James, "We have to bless the canoe."

"We will, Gramps. I promise, we will."

The rock-hounding Frenchmen had a fancy science lab on board, and hundreds of geology books and journals. Local news held no appeal to them, near as Old Keb could tell. They never turned on FM or AM radio, and seemed unaware of the minor news story about four canoeists in the Icy Strait region doing their best to avoid capture by well-meaning, safety-minded bureaucrats. Five canoeists if you counted Steve, his run of the yacht limited only by the ship's cat, a spoiled tom named Voltaire that sat on the bow and licked his yellow fur, his big tongue like a mop. Voltaire belonged to the skipper, a quiet French-Canadian named Rene, who hailed from Rivière-du-Loup on the St. Lawrence River.

Afternoon softened into evening that first day. Not until dusk did the *Etude* motor into Boussole Bay. Everybody stood on deck while Rene worked the wheel and the sea pushed from behind. The sun fell back a notch. Bold peaks stood against a salmon-colored sky, and beneath them, cradled in high contours, blue-white glaciers gleamed. Keb fidgeted. It wasn't supposed to be this way. They were on the wrong side of the mountains. They were sup-posed to be in the canoe, in Crystal Bay. Patience and openheartedness, Father Mikal would say. Never become so old you cannot make new friends, hard as it may be.

Was Little Mac saying the same thing now, the way she held his hand?

Keb remembered when she was born, how she made her father dance and her mother cry. Keb had hoped to be her godfather, but the Chen family chose an uncle in Seattle. Old Keb still looked out for her. The only Asian girl in Jinkaat, she made a fine target for a thousand small discriminations, big ones, too. If his head was working right, Keb could see a light coming on in her these last few days. In James and Kid Hugh, too.

Time on the *Etude* was easier to accept after a hot shower and cheese crepes with blueberry sauce. Add to that Cajun-blackened salmon and fine conversation courtesy of the black chef, his name a mishmash of syllables that Old Keb could never repeat. "Just call me Angola," the black man said in his deep voice, white teeth flashing, square nails on his long fingers and vein-rippled hands that put out plate after plate of delicacies, a feast for Old Keb, James, Little Mac, and Kid Hugh. Steve did well, too, with a couple rounds of minced beef.

The French geologists had funny names, Shock and Pee Air, as Old Keb heard them. Little Mac spelled them out: "J-a-c-q-u-e-s" and "P-i-e-r-r-e."

It reminded Keb of when two Japanese photographers arrived in

Jinkaat years ago, a husband and wife team who summered at Point Adol-phus to take pictures of humpback whales. They got so close to the whales, they said, that they saw them swim right under their kayaks and roll onto their sides for a better view, eyeball to eyeball. All summerlong the Japanese visited town and bowed before everybody they met, and came into Odd-mund and Dag's store every couple weeks for supplies. They taught Keb how to eat steamed white rice with chopsticks, back when his hands worked bet-ter, and Gracie and Galley Sally how to make good sushi. At the end of sum-mer they gave a slide show in the high school gym that was so popular they had to give it twice in one night. Truman told the newspaper they were more popular than basketball, which was heresy, and he got in trouble for it. Their names, as Keb heard them, were Oreo and Cheetah, the cookie and the cat. That's what he called them. Only after they returned to Tokyo did Oddmund tell Keb their real names: Norio and Chika. Well, what do you expect from a candle-headed old man, his ears filled with hairs and wax?

THE WIND FORGOT to blow. Storms may have descended over the Aleu-tians or Russia's Kamchatka Peninsula, or raked across Arctic Alaska or the Canadian Yukon. They might have hit farther south, the Queen Charlottes, Vancouver Island, or all the way down to Puget Sound. But in Boussole Bay the wind held its breath and that was fine. Keb knew they'd pay later.

He stayed on the yacht to nap while James, Little Mac, and Kid Hugh rowed the inflatable to shore, and Jacques and Pierre ran their skiff all over the place to poke around with rock hammers, maps, magnifying glasses, and big instruments balanced on tripods. The days were so kind, the sun so warm, the light so luminous and rich, the air so still, the mountains so alive, that Old Keb nearly forgot he wanted to die. It's funny how dying is regarded in bad taste, despite the fact that ten out of ten people do it. After Bessie and his sons died, part of Keb died, too. Happy songs made him sad back then. Sad songs made him happy. All back then, when he lost his way and forgot to carve and watched too much TV and rotted his brain.

"The garbage can in the living room," Bessie used to call television.

"Don't go away," the TV announcer would say. "We'll be right back." And back he came every time, the faithful garbage can man, back to tell them all the things they needed to buy. "You deserve it," he would say. And Keb would sit there with Mitch, Vic, Oddmund, Dag, Daisy, Carmen, and Truman, and think about it.

"It makes a man feel mighty good to deserve something," Mitch would say.

"Another round of beers," Vic would say.

"Consumption," Truman would say, his mouth full of popcorn. "People died of it long ago and still do today, only it's different."

Keb had no idea what he was talking about.

Now on the yacht, he kept thinking about his friends, some of them alive, most of them dead, not here, but not absent either. He kept thinking about Uncle Austin, how he taught him to build a fire in the rain, to sharpen a knife, to regard ten cords of wood as money in the bank, to read the wind and tides with intention, to catch a fish, to build a snare, to live off the land and sea and not just survive, but thrive; to know a thousand things with animal senses—to be smart, strong, sensual, alive, more alive than you'll ever be indoors. "You can learn to read words on paper," Uncle Austin would say, "but first learn to read the colors of the wind: k'eeljáa, óoxjaa, sáanáx̱, x̱óon. Storm wind, strong wind, south wind, north wind. Yánde át, dákde át: onshore wind, offshore wind." Keb remembered the first fish he ever caught, how Uncle Austin cleaned it and put the fish heart in Keb's hand, still beating. Some ninety years later he could feel it, the sensation that came over him as a young boy in Crystal Bay. He thought: it's an ocean of beating hearts, a living sea. Is that when awareness begins? Uncle Austin, Milo Chen, Nathan Red Otter, Father Mikal. Each said it in his way. Bessie, too. The more centered you are, the less you occupy the center. That's when awareness begins.

One day many years ago Uncle Austin came to take Keb out of school. "You need a written excuse," the principal said. "Spiritual," Uncle Austin wrote. "That's not a valid excuse," the principal said. "Medicinal," Uncle Austin wrote. "You're making this up. Which is it, spiritual or medicinal?"

"Both," Uncle Austin said. He was taking his nephew out into the woods, to "the temple of tall trees." "There's no such place," the principal said. "Come with us," Uncle Austin said. The principal did. In his starched white shirt and tie, he left the school and walked into the rain forest with Uncle Austin and young Keb, and stretched out on the moss to watch the tops of the trees swaying in crazy patterns high overhead. "Which way is the wind blowing?" Uncle Austin asked him.

"I can't tell," the principal said.

"Stay awhile and watch," Uncle Austin told him. "You'll figure it out."

PALMA BAY WAS another temple, not of tall trees, but of bold geography.

That evening, everybody sat in big soft sofas around a teak table in the

Etude's fancy lounge, drinking red wine and Moroccan liquor. Never mind sipping, Jacques and Pierre knocked back wine like water and sailed through three bottles with help from Captain Rene, Angola the chef, and the final member of the crew, a petite, ropy-haired, green-eyed woman from Montreal named Monique, a crossover first mate and chief engineer whose main duty, near as Keb could tell, was keeping Captain Rene's bed warm. She flirted with Jacques and Pierre, sang with Angola—her voice surprisingly husky, her smile just shy of a smirk—and fondled Voltaire the arrogant cat. She took a turn on Little Mac's guitar and handed it back, saying the neck was out of alignment. She and Rene had been to Alaska before, she said. They spent a summer in Sitka working the sport charter fishing fleet. Kid Hugh had worked the same fleet, and turned sour on what he called the "bubba meathead fishing crowd."

Keb watched Monique regard him from the sharp end of her chin.

Pierre spread a dozen maps across the table, some topographical, one nautical, the rest geological, rich with primary colors showing rock types and faults. Jacques traced his finger along a major fault that ran the full length of the Fairweather Range into Palma Bay at Icy Point. He said two tectonic plates skidded along one another there to create a feature called Earthquake Valley. Yes, Keb knew of a traveler or two who'd gone in there and come out, and others who'd gone in and never come out.

These Frenchmen had a grasp of the past that went back to when Great Raven was an egg. They spoke of millions of years ago when parts of Alaska skidded into other parts and stuck there to make it what it is today. Add to that the cutting and carving by glaciers that a few hundred years ago were much bigger than they were today, the weight of all that ice so great that it depressed the crust of the earth throughout the entire region. Now, with the big glaciers gone, the land was rising, rebounding. That's what they meant by isostatic rebound. Keb knew of it, but by other names. He knew of piers and canneries built one hundred years ago that now stood rotting and moss-covered back in the forest, fifty feet from the highest high tide. The Dundas Bay cannery where he was born was like this, though he hadn't been there in a long time. The land had risen tens of feet. As it did, shorelines changed. Islands once near the mainland, separated by shallow water at high tide, were now part of the mainland, as peninsulas. Was the land rising still? Could people rebound, too? Entire ways of life? The only rebound talked about in Jinkaat these days was the basketball rebound, the tangle of elbows and legs beneath the net, and people screaming from the bleachers as if they were in the game too.

Monique went topside and called down, "You might want to come up and see this." Everybody climbed up and said nothing as Palma Bay filled with weightless, September light. The peaks of the Fairweather Range turned crimson, then pink. Keb found himself gripping the rail, his eyes cast not north-east toward the mountains, but west over the wet curve of ocean where longliners fished for black cod, and skippers played loud rock and roll, and sperm whales cherry-picked the fish off the hooks as the winches hauled them up. That's how the whales worked. They heard the winches and came to feast on the cod. East over the Fairweather Range was Crystal Bay, cast in shadow, as Keb imagined, blue light filling deep valleys where wolves put on their winter coats, and bears worked the last salmon streams before denning up. The taste of winter coming. Lean times, rich times, when you paddled behind the mirror and found the identity you would one day like to be, a discovery of your deepest knowing.

a shadow in black

SEVENTY NAUTICAL MILES east-southeast of Palma Bay, Anne listened. Not so easy to do. You had to slow down and open up to what early mariners called "the trick of the quiet." She'd read about it in books. But books only get you so far. After that, you need time.

No hint of dawn. An hour away, maybe two. Not much time to explore the charred ruins of Keb Wisting's home and carving shed, to learn what she could before the people of his little town were on their feet nursing hot coffee, looking out their windows, and wondering what a fancy-pants federal government boat was doing in their harbor.

Five days since the old man and the canoe had left Jinkaat, and not a word, not a sign. Newspeople encamped in Strawberry Flats asking the same questions all day, every day. Boats from everywhere poking around Icy Strait, as if whoever found Keb Wisting would win a prize. "The old man must be drowned or dead or some damn thing to have disappeared this long," Ranger Ron said yesterday, as if you could drown but not die.

Anne considered the possibilities. Maybe Old Keb was the raven out the window. Maybe the bear up the bay, the whale deep below, the wren on the woodpile. Maybe the game belongs to Keb Zen Raven and always has. So what the hell? Forget the safety system. Get away. Go alone. Leave Taylor in bed with her delicious boyfriend; run your boat south from Strawberry Flats to Jinkaat in the middle of the night, across Icy Strait before the next big storm. Hit no rocks. Make no waves. Slide in behind the breakwater. Take an empty slip. Walk the hog-backed road up to where they say the old man used to live, where you'll maybe find clues about who he is or used to be and wants to be again. Not a bad idea if it weren't so stupid to begin with. A good idea if getting fired was high priority. Anne had no jurisdiction here, tempting the dogs of the night. She wasn't a ranger, soldier, sharpshooter, or shape-shifter. She wasn't Catwoman or James Bond, nothing so cunning or sly. She was a whale biologist who had a federal law enforcement commission in one pocket and a marijuana joint in the other. Maui Wowie. Oh baby. A whale biologist inducted into the SAR. That's what Ron called it: "SAR, Search and Rescue." Everything was an acronym these days.

Thirty years old. She still had time to have a family. One child. Just one. She'd need a man for that, right? She'd never done well in the Man Department. Maybe Taylor could give her lessons. Could she make a career in Alaska? Crystal Bay? Working for the US National Marine Reserve Service looked good on paper. But you'll never get a warm hug from a piece of paper. Many of Anne's coworkers struggled through a layered bureaucracy made worse by too many meetings and never enough creativity. Like Anne, they'd done what they were supposed to: brushed their teeth, cleaned their rooms, set the table, gone to school, gotten good grades, attended the best universities, and scored prestigious jobs in science and conservation only to be frustrated. Even dispirited. And the alternative? Capitalism and the cult of money? The mythology of happiness through more possessions and endless growth? Not that Anne idealized poverty. She had homeless friends in Honolulu whose plight broke her heart. Only a fool idealizes poverty. But to think we can grow our economy forever, always on the back of nature. Madness.

What to do?

Rob a bank? Storm a palace? Grow a garden? Plant a tree? The irony and mystery of it all, this journey called life, this practice of being human. Is home where we begin or where we end up? Is it where we long to be or where we make use of our best gifts?

Minutes ago, as Anne began walking up the road, she'd seen a bumper sticker on an old rusty truck: "I'd rather be here than have a career."

Again, she listened.

A dog barked in the distance.

She continued up the road, moving by the modest light of her small flashlight. She wore a drab raincoat over her uniform.

She entered a clearing and there it was: yellow crime-scene tape surrounding a blackened home and carving shed. Such rebellion filled her as she stepped around it, her rascal side wanting to break every rule, to pull out her joint and smoke it down to nothing. Write her best poem and burn it. Pitch her identity into the ashes. Call Director Kate Johnson, the grandmother astronaut in Washington, and tell her, I'm sorry. I resign.

THE SKY WAS starless, growing lighter by the minute. No wind or rain, yet. Anne could smell it coming, the big storm, a tremor on the tracks. Would she get back to Strawberry Flats before it hit? Her boat had become her home this past summer, its size and shape just right for a woman who curled into herself when she slept. So why leave it? What was she doing here, in Jinkaat? *What am I doing here?*

She had great clarity on how cloudy her life was just then.

Cold ashes stuck to her wet boots. She walked through what must have been the kitchen, found a sink and a small refrigerator, black with soot. Opposite that, the remains of a carving bench, a dozen metal brackets that must have supported shelves. No melted television or radio or computer that she could see. Only the blackened husk of lean living. The roof had collapsed, yet one corner still stood, partially burned, where two walls leaned against each other, held up by large timbers cut into dovetail joints. She found evidence of mortise and tenon carpentry, excellent craftsmanship, not a single nail. What a heartbreak, to see the oldest man in town lose his home this way, not just his home, his carving shed, his art studio, the place where he expressed himself.

Somebody should rebuild this someday.

It began to rain. Anne turned to leave when a strong light struck her in the face.

"Stay where you are," spoke a voice. She brought her hand to her eyes. "Keep your hands down. What are you doing here?"

"Nothing."

"Who are you?"

"Anne Bellestraude."

"Is that your NMRS boat down in the harbor?"

"Yes."

"You armed or carrying a weapon of any kind?"

"No."

"You alone?"

"I was until you got here. Do you mind shining that light somewhere else?"

The light didn't move. "You got identification of some sort?"

She dug into her pocket and almost handed him the Maui Wowie.

"I could arrest you, you know?"

"Arrest me then."

"For entering a crime scene."

"I wanted to learn more about Old Keb, to help find him. I'm worried about him."

The light dropped. "You and everybody else." The cop looked at her ID, handed it back and said, "Some folks around here say they can't believe nobody's found him yet. Others say he's a wise old raven, and he'll never be found."

He was white, this cop, not Tlingit. Anne could tell from his voice. Many Tlingits spoke softly and musically, as Gracie Wisting did, with a rhythm a thousand years deep, sentences like waves. Can you put it on paper, a voice like that, a voice from the sea? This cop had a nametag, *Stuart Ewing*. He introduced himself as "Stu." Deputy Sheriff Stuart Ewing, to be exact. Acting Sheriff Ewing until his boss got back. A big job, Anne imagined, with crime-scene tampering, crowd control, mayhem, arson. And that was the easy stuff. Try breaking up a broken-beer-bottle fight behind Shelikof's Pizza. Anne had heard stories.

"Glad to meet you, Anne," Stu said.

Anne said, "You think we could get out of this rain?"

BACK AT HIS office, Stu turned on the television for Anchorage morning news, and the FM radio out of Juneau. Anne watched as he checked his voice mail, messages from Ruby Bauer and her son, Robert, "a Coca-Cola man from Atlanta," Stu said, plus Harald Halmerjan and a mile-a-minute-talker named Truman. Nothing that offered any new information as to Old Keb's whereabouts. Just inquiries. "Ruby and Harald call every day," Stuart said. "This whole search is because of Ruby, you know. She has a lot of power and influence." He turned on his computer and poured two cups of last night's coffee. He warmed them in the microwave, added cream and sugar, and handed one to Anne. He took the other himself, and faced the moral dilemma of what to do with her.

She sat opposite him and pulled the coffee to her lips. She could see him thinking, sizing her up. It surprised her how much she enjoyed it, having a man look her over.

Stu entered his password, checked e-mails, stole a couple more glances at Anne, ran his hand through his wheat-colored hair. He sat amid stacks of paperwork, his file cabinets ready to burst. "Coffee okay?" he asked.

"It's good." It was horrible.

"You want anything to eat? I got bran muffins in a drawer."

"I'm fine."

"That's a bathroom over there, if you need it."

"Thanks. You going to arrest me?"

"I don't know."

"Detain me, report me?"

"Maybe."

"Or just let me go?"

"Probably." He grinned.

"I could be dangerous, you know. A bank robber, a serial killer. You got any banks in this town?"

"No."

"You got a jail?"

"A little one, in the back. You want more coffee?"

"No."

The phone rang and Stuart answered, "Yeah, Dag . . . Uh huh, I know all about it . . . Yeah, he told me . . . No, he's probably fine. Hey, I have to run."

"Busy, busy," Anne said.

Stuart shrugged. "Not really. Dag's a goofball."

"Why's he a goofball?"

"He eats ice cream with a fork, he takes one shower a month, his favorite Beatle is Ringo."

"I sometimes eat ice cream with a fork."

"Everybody eats ice cream with a fork when they eat ice cream with birthday cake. Dag eats ice cream with a fork all the time."

"Is that a felony or a misdemeanor in this town, eating ice cream with a fork?"

"A felony."

"And one shower a month?"

"Felony."

"And having Ringo as your favorite—"

"Felony."

"Tough town."

"Yep, you'd better watch yourself."

Anne laughed and watched Stuart appraise her, poorly masking his mild infatuation, if masking it at all. "You're a firecracker," he said.

"Is that a felony?"

"No."

"A compliment?"

"Take it as you wish."

"I'll take it as a compliment."

"See, you prove my point. Boating alone into this town under the cover of darkness, a federal officer illegally entering a crime scene. You're a firecracker."

"Somebody told me that the name of this town means 'ten' in Tlingit."

"Jinkaat? Yes, it does."

"What's the significance in that?"

"Long ago, maybe three hundred years ago, when a glacier advanced quickly over their home in Crystal Bay, and the Tlingit people had to leave, they came here in their canoes, and that first winter was really hard. They had no year-round village, no good shelter. It was bitter cold. They had little food, and many people died. Only ten children survived. Those kids were their future. The next winter wasn't so bad, or the one after that, and soon they built a strong village and made a good life here, all because those ten kids survived. They were their future."

Anne could see Stuart get emotional as he told this.

He elaborated, "Most Tlingit place-names come from the natural world, and translate into English names like 'Sea Otter Creek,' or 'Grouse Hen Fort,' or 'Stream at the Mouth.' That's what makes Jinkaat special. It speaks to a profound moment in Tlingit history, a time of survival and hope."

"You're not Tlingit, though, are you?"

His smile reached for his ears. "No, but many of my friends are."

"Remember the night Old Keb and the others took off in the canoe? You were the only person who made any sense. Do you remember what you said?"

"No."

"You said, 'Keb Wisting is a good man, the media is making too much of this whole thing, and people need to calm down and take it easy.'"

"I meant it."

"*Take It Easy*, it's a Jackson Browne song."

"That's right. It's one of his early songs. He actually wrote it with Glenn Frey, from the Eagles."

"Are you sure? I know the Eagles recorded it first and made it a big hit, and I know Jackson Browne and Glenn Frey are friends, but I didn't know Glenn Frey cowrote that song."

"He did. Jackson Browne started it, Glenn Frey finished it."

"Wow, I didn't know that."

"See, you have to come to this podunk little town on the edge of nowhere and drink my really bad coffee and be polite and tell me it's good, all to get educated in American rock music."

Anne smiled, and let her hair fall over her shoulders.

MORE PHONE CALLS. Stuart fielded them while Anne surveyed his office. He hung up and she asked, "What do you hear about Keb's daughter, Gracie?"

"She flew down to Seattle yesterday. She's got big problems, bad kidneys, related to her diabetes. She probably needs to go on dialysis. It's sad." Stuart turned his attention toward the television, then turned back to Anne and jerked his thumb over his shoulder. "Hear that? It's not on the news anymore. Too much murder and robbery in the big city to have time to talk about an old man and his canoe in Crystal Bay."

"You think he's in the bay?"

Stuart sat back and pulled a strange expression over his face, as if hiding something. "A lot of people would like to see him make it, go all the way to the glaciers or wherever he wants to go. They're taking bets in Juneau and Strawberry Flats to see how long he can last, how far he gets. Pedr Clements thinks he went up Excursion Inlet and is hiking into Crystal Bay through Adams Inlet, or maybe he went up Lynn Canal and is hiking in through the Davidson Glacier, or through Endicott Gap. Dag thinks he's hunkered down in a backcountry cabin somewhere. Mitch thinks he hitched a ride on a big boat and went to Lisianski, or Elfin Cove, and is lying low until the whole thing blows over. Vic Lehan, he's the town barber, he thinks Old Keb jumped a luxury cruise ship and is eating like a king and dancing the cha-cha and telling stories and sailing to San Francisco. Hey, you sure you're not hungry? You don't want something to eat?"

"I'm fine," Anne was looking into Stuart's dusty blue eyes, the way they shone, bringing up the dawn.

"You need to make a telephone call or anything?"

"I'm supposed to report into Bartlett Cove every morning at eight."

"It's ten after eight now."

Anne shrugged.

"What are you going to tell them?"

"I don't know. It depends."

"On what?"

"If you arrest me or not."

Stuart laughed, and for a moment Anne felt her summer self again, the happy person she used to be. *Is this the Man Department?*

The phone rang. Stuart picked it up and fielded a question about the federal government boat down in the harbor. Got it handled, he said. Another call came in, same thing. Got it handled. He hung up. "People are talking about your boat. A bunch of them are probably down there right now looking it over. I could run you down there if you'd like; tell them you're here to talk with me about the search for Old Keb. It's up to you. I mean, you're always welcome to stay here if you can't make it back to Bartlett Cove, with the weather. It's supposed to get bad."

"So I've heard."

"There's an apartment behind this office where the troopers stay when they're in town."

"Is anybody going to rebuild Keb Wisting's shed?"

"Hard to say."

"I think they should."

"So do I."

Suddenly the television had something to say: "We take you now to our Channel Two affiliate in Sitka for a report on the search for Keb Wisting, the 'Old Man and the Canoe.'" Stuart jumped to his feet and cranked up the volume. "Yes, Lisa, this is Lynn Mills reporting from Sitka, where early this morning Alaska State Troopers boarded a fish buyer named the *Silverbow*. The skipper may have given Keb Wisting and his party a lift in Icy Strait shortly after they left Jinkaat, five days ago."

A trooper said the *Silverbow* was not under investigation. Then a full-faced, platinum-haired woman filled the screen. "You go up against the world and the world's going to win every time," she said. "We each have to die of something. Why not let Old Keb Wisting die his own way? Is that asking too much? Whose life is it anyway?"

"Did you give Keb Wisting a ride?" the reporter asked.

"Maybe I did, and maybe I didn't. Maybe I picked him up and took him into Crystal Bay in the middle of the night, and maybe I didn't."

"Where in Crystal Bay?"

"I'm not admitting anything."

"He could be wet and cold up there right now, and suffering, an old man in weather like this."

"Oh shush. He's tougher than you and me put together. He's clever; he's wise. His traveling companions are strong and determined. With a light wind and good tides they can cover thirty nautical miles in a night. They'll never be found. My guess is he misses the way things used to be. So what if he's a little hungry and cold. Remember what Dostoevsky said, 'Suffering is the sole origin of consciousness.'"

Stuart turned off the TV and said, "If you really want to make the run back to Bartlett Cove, you need to leave now, to beat the storm." His eyes said: Stay. Don't go.

Anne hesitated. Duty. Conscience. *Arrrggh.*

"Okay, let's go."

BACK IN HIS Jeep, Stuart and Anne rumbled down the road to the harbor. He asked, "Are the Crystal Bay rangers looking for the Gant brothers?"

"No. Should we be? Did they burn down Keb's shed?"

"The fire marshal hasn't finished his report. There's one eyewitness, Kevin Pallen, and he doesn't talk. But he wrote out a statement that said it was Tommy Gant and Pete Brickman."

"Why would they burn down Keb's shed?"

"They were drunk. Drunk guys don't think straight."

"Tell me about it. My stepdad was a drunk."

"There's tension between Tommy and James; jealousy over Little Mac. She used to be Tommy's girl, you know, and Tommy is still obsessed with knowing where she is and what she's doing. As for James, he's just trying to find his way after the accident, or whatever it was that happened on Pepper Mountain. It really made him angry and scared."

"Scared of what?"

"Himself. The difficult choices he needs to make." Stuart said this with such tenderness that it made Anne's heart swell.

She asked him, "Do you speak Tlingit?"

"No. Why?"

"I guess if I find the old guy, I'd like to be able to say something to him in his own language. It seems the right thing to do."

"You got any lemonade on your boat?"

"No."

"Get some. He loves lemonade . . . and moose stew, nagoonberry pie, and cornbread."

"Thank you for not arresting me."

"You're welcome."

"Are you this nice to all the women you meet?" *Please say no.*

"No . . . I don't meet that many women. This is a small town."

"I like it here, the lay of the land, the harbor—" *You, everything.*

"Don't go."

"I have to."

"Come back then."

"Okay."

The steady rain didn't dissuade a dozen townspeople from milling about the dock to look over the *Firn*. A nice boat, if you liked government boats. Stuart parted the crowd and ushered Anne aboard. She collected their silent appraisals, and heard one Tlingit say to another, "Is she going to leave now?

With the storm coming?"

"Yeah, I guess."

"Stupid white woman."

"Yeah."

AN HOUR LATER she was in the thick of it, the *Firn* beating north-north-west where Port Thomas opened into Icy Strait, a crazy swell quartering off her starboard. Strong currents in a cross-grained sea. Windshield wipers working hard to stay ahead of the rain and sea spray. Damn. It had been only a light breeze when she left Jinkaat. She should have listened to Stuart, the marine forecast, the chatter on the dock.

Anne set a GPS heading for Strawberry Flats. Forget Bartlett Cove, too far away. Fierce winds whipped water off the tops of big waves, the biggest waves eating away at her transom, the gale building beneath a dour, undertaker sea. Dryness gripped her throat. She saw Nancy's pale face, a ghost, a raven's wing, an old photograph of two sisters laughing at the camera. She saw her mom coming home from work after midnight, beat on her feet, a shadow after Nancy's death, a silhouette, arranging things already twice arranged, cleaning the floor as if she could scrub it all away.

Anne had a nautical chart but could hardly look at it for the concentration she needed to steer. The GPS said she was moving due north. Again and again she bucked big sets and shipped water, too much water. Sheets of sea washed over the stern and across her decks as the scuppers struggled to keep up. Something broke loose and slammed into something else. The engine sputtered, stalled, coughed back to life. She thought about Taylor in bed with her boyfriend. The *Firn* lurched, corkscrewed, and began to list. No longer buoyant, it felt ponderous, slow. She fought to right it as another big wave hit, and another, and another.

Shit.

She wanted to call Stuart and ask for help, hear his voice. Had she seen a marine VHF radio in his office? His Jeep? He had to have one somewhere. If she called, everybody would hear a federal government NMRS boat calling the Jinkaat Police Station in distress. Not good. What to do? Take it easy . . . take it easy.

That's it. Fake names. Use names only he will understand. *Make it sound like I'm calling another vessel.*

She grabbed the radio mic, took a deep breath, and in the most casual voice she could muster, she said, "Calling the Take It Easy, the Take It Easy, the Take It Easy, this is the Firecracker on channel sixteen, over." She waited.

She couldn't see a thing. Gray-green seawater slammed into her. No horizon. It felt like the end of the world. "Calling the Take It Easy, the Take It Easy . . . this is the Firecracker on channel sixteen, over."

A pause, then: "This is the Take It Easy."

Anne almost burst out crying. "Take It Easy," she said, "you want to meet me on channel seventy-four?"

"Seventy-four . . ." Seconds passed, it seemed like forever. "Anne, you there?"

"I'm here. I'm in a jam, in really big seas. I'm shipping water and cavitating. I'm losing control and I'm scared."

"Okay, stay cool. Make sure your scuppers are clear. Do you have an ELT?"

"Yes, they're clear, and it's on."

"How about a survival suit?"

"Yes, but I'm not wearing it and I don't think I could get it on without losing my boat. I'm about three miles into Icy Strait. The farther north I go, the more fetch I'm exposed to and the bigger the seas get. I'd like to turn around and get back to you, but I'm afraid to make the turn, of taking big waves on my beam."

"Are they coming in sets? Typically the waves come in sets, and if you can time your turn, that would be good . . . go when the waves are at their lowest. And when you do turn, have the throttle full open to make it as fast as possible."

"I know. I'll do that."

"How's your fuel?"

"Good."

"Have you got a kicker?"

"Yes, but I don't know if I could get it started or even hold into the weather if I did."

"Anne, listen . . . you're not far from a small group of islands called the Sisters, due east of you. You could gain their lee after you make the turn."

"Okay. Stay with me on this channel. I won't be able to talk to you while I make the turn. Everything's getting worse."

"I'm here. I'm with you."

She dropped the radio mic and tried to focus, tried to be smart, tried not to panic. Everything was gray except for the nightmare before her, the shrieking wind and pounding seas and a shadow in black pointing a long accusing finger and shaking its head. Stupid white woman.

standing in his own surprise

OLD KEB HAD met a philosopher or two in his life, but none like the black Cajun chef, Angola, a big man, half-African conga, half-Canadian bacon, all Louisiana soul kitchen. How authentic he seemed with his callused hands and clear eyes, his every move balanced against the pitch and roll of whatever life might throw at him.

"Me, a philosopher?" Angola laughed, as the *Etude* rested on her anchor in Graves Harbor, in the middle of the night, with everyone else asleep. "I don't think so. I'm better at defining problems than at solving them. Maybe that doesn't make me a philosopher. I don't know. How about you?"

"My Uncle Austin was a philosopher. He read books."

"You know what appeals to me about philosophy? Nobody wins."

"Half of philosophy is about death, I think. Does it seem that way to you?"

"It might someday, when I get as old as you."

"You don't want to get as old as me. You'll hurt everywhere and eat pills and bury everybody you love, and get lonely, and get the willies."

"The willies? You mean the heebie-jeebies?"

"No, the willies are worse than the heebie-jeebies."

"Not in Louisiana, where I come from. Nothing's worse than the heebie-jeebies."

"How about the wangdoodles?"

"The wangdoodles? What are they?"

"They're bad, but they're not as bad as the willies."

"You're telling me that the wangdoodles aren't as bad as the willies, and the heebie-jeebies aren't as bad as the wangdoodles?"

"Oyyee . . ." Keb was getting confused.

"Man, you people up here got everything upside down, that's all I'm saying. I've seen death, too, old man. It makes being alive look pretty good, that's all I'm saying. How's the cornbread?"

"Good."

"Not too spicy?"

"A little. What's in it?"

"Jalapeños, Tabasco. Cajun love spices."

Cajun love spices? Keb had downed a quart of water. He needed to pee. He needed to take his pills. One for his heart, one for his blood. Others for his thyroid, liver, stomach, bladder, colon, semi-colon, appendix, semi-appendix, muscles, nerves, joints, you name it. Some weren't pills at all, they were capsules the size of small bullets. He took those with yogurt. The cornbread wasn't round. It wasn't square either. Angola made it rectangular, the size of Montana, with four perfect corners cooked to the color of Navajo sandstone. He served up another plate for Old Keb, and a cup of yogurt, key lime pie flavor.

Angola was talking to himself in cryptic Cajun phrases as he made croissants, a baker's tall white hat sitting on his balding head, his elegant long fingers twisting the dough.

"You're from Louisiana then?" Keb asked him.

"That's right."

"Descended from slaves."

"Yep."

"How's that make you feel?"

"I don't feel like I used to feel. Most of my nerves went dead after Katrina."

"Katrina, a woman?"

"No man, the big-ass storm."

Just then Monique breezed into the galley wearing a man's large button-up shirt and nothing else. Without a word, she opened the fridge, pulled out half a gallon of milk and drank from the carton. Keb watched a bead of milk roll down her chin and neck and under her shirt. Everything about her was forbidden: the hard, self-satisfied smile, the hips and spine, the stab of shoulder blade and perfect vixen lines. Looking at her, Keb felt a distant stirring and remembered women as beautiful as her when he was young and strong. Stronger than he'd ever be again. More than a hundred times he had had his entire life ahead of him. Did he realize it then? Even once? Monique finished, wiped her mouth, and said something to Angola in French. Voltaire jumped onto the table and swished his tail past Keb's nose.

"Chat folle." Angola swiped and missed, but sent the cat flying. Monique picked it up with a scowl and disappeared down the passageway toward Rene's cabin.

Keb finished his pills. He watched Angola put croissants on a cookie sheet, slip them into the oven, and brew up a fresh pot of coffee, what he called "Gaspay couffay," a special blend from Quebec's Gaspe Peninsula. Jacques and Pierre would be up soon, eager to push back south after the storm, back to George Island to collect more rocks. Keb was eager to get back too, back to the canoe. Was it still on its buoy, out of sight in the sea cave under the cliff? Kid Hugh might have to do his big dive after all, a Mexican Margarita Acapulco Loco Dive. For a strange moment—one more unsettling than any before—Keb thought about dying, the notion that he'd die soon, probably in the canoe, but where in the canoe? Not where in the canoe itself, but where at sea in the canoe? Trying to decide was no easy thing. Maybe he'd die of indecision.

What was it now that Angola was saying? Keb had no idea, but he had to agree with him. "You've lived through dark times, then?" Angola asked him.

Keb nodded. Dark times, yes, when one more hour was all he could see of the future. Angola jabbered in French, as if speaking in tongues, then flipped into English and said, "That's why I found Buddhism. You ever wonder why people who want to share their religion with you almost never want you to share your religion with them?"

Keb shook his head. He didn't know. Maybe all he believed in, in that regard, was what he told Angola. "My friend Father Mikal says that anything can be made holy, if it's deeply worshiped."

"You have to be careful with that," Angola said. "If people believe something enough, that doesn't make it fact. If they shout it loud enough, that doesn't make it true." The coffee pot began to perk. "It's crazy stuff, the whole story of who we are and where we came from, how we got here. It's all locked up in one big hiding place, a vault, you know, a steel safe with all the answers inside, and a combination. But get this: the combination is locked up inside the safe, too. It's been going on for ten thousand years, that's all I'm saying. It started a long time ago. I wouldn't worry about it."

Keb was thinking how everything was a long time ago.

Angola handed him a croissant dripping with butter. Keb took a bite and heard himself say thank you. He barely got the words out. Such a rag and bone man he'd become. It was time to get back into the canoe and get this dying thing over with before it was too late. Too late to die. It was time to go beyond the cold and indecision, go until nature does it for you, sand in the wind, a wind made of sand, the earth made of air, each of us a cloud, a seed, an angel. Lie down now, in your final garments, made without pockets, and never get up. No more possessions or obsessions. Why is it that death for each of us comes either too early or too late? Keb ate the buttered croissant and ran his tongue over his lips. "You ever had nagoonberry pie?" he asked Angola.

"Nope." The Cajun was making soup over the oven, dicing an onion.

"Ever make kelp salsa?"

"Nope."

"How about beer batter halibut?"

"Nope." Angola laughed. "How about bang butter? You ever had bang butter?"

Bang butter? Great Raven. Did it explode in your mouth? Shoot off your lips?

"Marijuana, my friend. Bang butter has marijuana in it. It makes one hell of a brownie. You should try it sometime."

"The Tlingit people had slaves, taken during wars."

"I didn't know that."

"Maybe I shouldn't have told you."

"Keb, my friend, you can tell me anything."

Jacques came into the galley, rubbing sleep from his eyes. Or was it Pierre? He wore only boxer shorts and asked for coffee, in French. Angola handed him a large cup. Near as Keb could tell, Jacques and Angola were talking about the storm, wondering if it had exhausted itself enough to weigh anchor.

Like every other morning, Jacques had with him a news clipping he'd printed off the Internet in the pilothouse. The clipping came from *Le Monde*. Little Mac had told Old Keb it was French for "The World." Good thing these guys were more interested in the world than they were in Alaska, where local news might tell them their guests were elusive, runaway canoeists.

Jacques and Pierre came from a Paris university, though Angola said Pierre had married the daughter of a billionaire industrialist. Hence the yacht. They spent hours each day and night folded over rocks and maps. One night in the lab, they told Keb, James, and Little Mac about extrusive and intrusive igneous rocks, minerals and glaciers, fault lines and tectonics. They passed around garnet granites that had formed sixty thousand feet under the surface of the earth, millions of years ago. Keb tried to wrap his head around it. He asked about Crystal Bay. "Did it have that name because of the rocks there? Rocks with crystals?"

"Ice has crystals, too," Pierre said, speaking through Little Mac. "Crystal Bay takes its name from the great glacier that carved it and shaped it. A glacier is made of ice, right? Well, glacial ice is a kind of rock. It has crystals."

"How can ice be a rock?" James asked.

Little Mac listened to Pierre; she had to get this right. She spoke to Keb and James, "He said ice has many of the same properties of a rock."

"But it's not a rock," James insisted.

"James, listen. Rocks are made of crystals, or at least some rocks are, okay? Glacial ice is also made of crystals. It begins with snow that changes under pressure and becomes dense and forms crystals."

"And that makes it a rock?"

"Yes, in a way."

James asked, "How can ice carve rock?"

Pierre spoke rapidly and Little Mac listened, her face furrowed in concentration. After a moment she said, "Ice is too soft to carve rock. But what the ice does, what the glacier does, I mean, is it picks up rocks as it moves along and embeds them in its flank, okay? Now the glacier has a sharp tool, doesn't it? It has the rocks embedded in it. As it moves along, it grinds those embedded rocks against the bedrock, and slowly reshapes the land, over a zillion years. It pulverizes rock against rock. That's how glaciers sculpt, see?" Little Mac's eyes were shining. "Pierre says it's like an axe. The ice isn't the blade of the axe; it's the handle. The rocks it carries embedded in the glacier, that's the blade, a million little blades cutting into the bedrock, grinding it down as the glacier moves. That's how your bay was born, Keb. That's how ice shaped Crystal Bay."

Keb understood. He looked at James and could see he understood, too. This was good stuff, Keb thought, another kind of learning, one he could enjoy. Maybe it was too early to die.

BY MIDMORNING, CAPTAIN Rene had eased the *Etude* out of Graves Harbor and into the Gulf of Alaska, southbound. A large swell lifted her but otherwise let her run true. Keb visited the pilothouse, though Rene called it the "wheelhouse," which seemed odd to Old Keb, since it had no wheel. No compass either. Only a vast bank of computer screens with colorful numbers, graphs, and maps. Rene seemed to steer by little buttons, levers, and dials, nothing more. Push this, go here. Push that, go there. But who really ran things on the yacht? Near as Old Keb could tell, Jacques and Pierre told

Rene where to go, but Rene chose the running speeds, times, and anchorages, and doubled as a mechanic while Monique stood by in tight pants and gave him what he needed: hammer, socket, Excedrin, kiss, screwdriver, screw. The yacht must have cost a hundred bazillion dollars. Kid Hugh said more like twenty million. He'd seen similar big-shot boats during the summer he'd spent in Sitka. That's what he called them, "big-shot boats." Granite countertops; Jacuzzi baths; teak tables, counters and trim; showers with twin heads; pool table; piano; and four sofas so deep and soft they swallowed you whole. Eight sleeping cabins in all, three aft, five forward. The *Etude* was a floating five-star hotel. The whole place gave Keb the creeps. He sat up on deck where he could watch the round earth roll. Kid Hugh liked it up there too, and Steve, curled against Keb's leg. James and Little Mac had their own cabin and made good use of it.

By early afternoon the *Etude* had rounded Cape Spencer before a pale, rinsed-out sun. A gray sky threw its dour expression into the sea and the sea threw it back. Half a dozen trollers worked Cross Sound, bringing in the last big salmon run of summer. George Island was still there. And the canoe? As they pulled into Granite Cove, Kid Hugh glassed the sea cave at the base of the cliff but offered no confirmation to Old Keb. They had to be careful; give no hint of their plans, only a casual desire to get off the *Etude* and back on the island.

Jacques and Pierre must have assumed that Old Keb and his party, once back on the island, had no way off. They offered to run them into the little town of Elfin Cove. James countered—too harshly, Keb thought—that they'd be fine left on the island where friends would come and get them in a day or two. That's how it is in Alaska. Friends come and get you. This prompted a big discussion between the two Frenchmen who wanted to make another trip ashore to collect rocks.

Angola announced lunchtime.

They ate on deck as a troller pulled into the cove and dropped anchor a couple hundred yards away. James and Kid Hugh exchanged furtive glances, plotting with their eyes. The net was tightening. How to get off the *Etude*, get their canoe, and get away? The cliff appeared daunting from this angle, an Acapulco Loco Dive and more. How drunk would a guy have to be before it looked like a good idea? Maybe Kid Hugh could use the *Etude*'s skiff to retrieve the canoe, under cover of darkness, while James got the tents and totes that were still on the island, back in the woods.

Rene made no offers, so James asked that they be taken to shore.

"Later," Rene said.

Green-eyed Monique had her own reasons for getting back to George Island. According to Angola, she and Rene had fishing friends flying up from Sitka in a floatplane. "They should arrive anytime," Angola said to Old Keb, as he gathered up the empty plates and made his way down to the galley.

Without a word, Rene moved to the davit, swung it to port, and lowered the skiff. Monique boarded it from the aft swim step, and with one pull started the outboard. Jacques and Pierre got in, and she ran them to shore. Further ignoring his guests, Rene went into the wheelhouse and got on the marine VHF radio.

Keb didn't like it. He struggled to his feet and followed Angola down to the galley. The black man was washing dishes when Keb stood beside him, grabbed a plate, and began to rinse. Uncle Austin used to say that at the moment of self-absorption, when nothing seems more important than your own affairs, that's when you go help somebody else. Remove yourself from the middle. "That's okay," Angola said to Keb. "I don't need any help."

"But I do."

Angola stared at him.

"You said I could tell you anything."

"Absolutely."

For the next ten minutes Keb set his tongue loose about his childhood with Uncle Austin, his dreams to get back to Crystal Bay, his time to die, a complicated story. He talked about the canoe, and James and Little Mac and their journey too, his shed burned to the ground, and his daughter Gracie, sick with something bad, and his other daughter Ruby, sick in her own way, poisoned by power. He spoke about Great Raven while Angola listened, his face pure and uncomplicated.

Keb was telling more about the canoe when James, Kid Hugh, and Little Mac entered the galley. The look on James's face was one Keb had never seen. Standing in his own surprise, James said, "Gramps, what are you doing?"

to save a life is no easy thing

THEN THEY HEARD the plane.

The sun wobbled a degree as Keb went topside and stood on deck with the others, his hand a visor at his forehead. Monique came ripping by in the skiff, heading out to where the plane touched down at the entrance to the cove. She waved vigorously. Whatever this rendezvous was about, Keb and his companions were in the middle of it, trapped. Jacques and Pierre might stay on the island for hours, rockhounding.

Angola was still in the galley.

From the wheelhouse, Rene worked the engines to gently swing the yacht on its anchor for the approaching plane. Monique returned, tied off the skiff, and jumped aboard the *Etude*. From the stern she operated a hand crank that extended the swim step three times its normal width. As the plane approached, the pilot killed the engine, worked the float rudders, turned to starboard, and glided up to the float. Out he jumped and in one swift motion whipped a line around a cleat.

The plane was a beauty, a white and blue Cessna 207 with a turbocharged engine.

"I don't like this," Kid Hugh said. He pointed out that the extended swim step allowed the plane to tie off without the wing hitting the yacht. Monique motioned the passengers out to hugs and greetings of warm exultation. Five visitors in all, four men and a woman, the woman so deeply tanned she looked sautéed. Monique greeted her in French, as if she were a sorority sister. Aside from a glance or two, the five newcomers ignored Keb and his companions. Rene and Monique didn't bother with introductions. The four men were two older guys and two younger, all American. The older ones had the dress and posture of golf course regulars who knew the price of everything and the value of nothing. Keb had seen their kind before. The younger two had the cut and swagger of construction workers who built big homes, caught big fish, and walked through life as damaged goods, courtesy of their parents. They pulled out photos of yesterday's sportfishing escapade to show Rene and Monique. "Meatheads," Kid Hugh muttered, the rage restrained in his throat. Guys who fished the sea as if every day were derby day. He said it didn't require much imagination to complete the photos: sportsmen with horse-toothed grins, big bellies over their belts as they held the salmon, those wondrous fish shaped by the sea, caught by these bozos who'd probably paid a guide and talked boastfully. If left to their own devices as hunter-gatherers, they would be dead in a week. What always struck Keb about a photo of a fat man holding a fish was the beauty and intelligence of the fish.

Rene and Monique ushered the fivesome down the steps to the passageway and into the spacious lounge, next to the galley.

"We have to get out of here," James said.

"Tonight," Kid Hugh said.

But how? How to get the canoe? Three days ago Kid Hugh and Quinton, Marge's son, had anchored it out of sight in a small sea cave at the base of a cliff several hundred yards away. Could Kid Hugh swim to it from the yacht? Keb didn't think so. It wasn't the distance that would defeat him, it was the cold water. They stayed topside, talking. Voltaire the cat walked the rail with his ears up, as if eavesdropping. Steve snarled and sent him scurrying below.

Kid Hugh said, "The Cessna pilot is looking at us funny."

Keb focused his one good eye. Sure enough, the pilot stood forward on the plane float with his head in the engine, doing repairs, partly obscured by the cowling that was hinged back. It was easy to see his head pop out now and then to look their way, his manner more distracted by things around him than focused on a problem at hand.

"He's onto us," Kid Hugh said. "He knows who we are. We might have to take him out."

Take him out? Keb wondered. *Out to where?*

DARKNESS CAME RELUCTANTLY. At twilight Jacques and Pierre, still on George Island collecting rocks, called by radio for a ride back to the yacht. Monique bounded topside to hop into the skiff, and ran into James, who offered to do her a favor and run the boat to shore himself to pick up the Frenchmen. That would give Monique more time with her friends down below. She smelled of cigarettes, garlic, and wine.

"No," she said to James.

Just then Angola emerged. "Jambalaya's on," he announced. "There's plenty for everyone." He spoke in French to Monique, and added, "Go on down and eat. I'll go get Jacques and Pierre. I could use the air."

Monique weighed the offer with her serpent eyes. Somebody laughed from down below. A flood of French phrases sailed up the passageway. More laughter. The pilot had gone below half an hour ago, followed minutes later by Little Mac, who had listened from out of view to hear what he might say about the old man and the canoe. He had said nothing, so far. Maybe he was just a shifty guy who looked at them suspiciously but in truth suspected nothing. Keb had stayed topside to welcome the darkness, and now coughed, sitting in his cold, aching bones. Little Mac wrapped him in a blanket. They listened to Monique speak French with Angola, and watched her point to the skiff, perhaps to tell him something about the outboard.

More laughter from below.

Monique headed down.

"Time to move fast," Angola said. He told Kid Hugh to take the small inflatable and get the canoe. Angola and James would take the skiff to get Jacques and Pierre. Angola would bring the Frenchmen back and leave James on shore to get the tents. Kid Hugh would pick up James in the canoe, pulling the inflatable behind, and return to the *Etude* to get Keb, Little Mac, and Steve. So many instructions. Keb's head was spinning. He reached for the raven feather on his chest and found no feather, no chest either, not like it used to be, barrel-full, when his arms were like fulcrums, swinging the adz.

He had to lie down.

Remember Barney What's-His-Name? He had had big arms, too. Barney the electrician who fell off a rafter and landed on his head and became a half-wit. Went from 220 to 110 just like that. He got in the army, though, a true patriot. When his sergeant ordered him to paint a jeep and Barney asked how much of the jeep he should paint and the sergeant said the whole damn jeep, you idiot, that's what Barney did, he painted the *whole damn jeep*, the idiot. Seats, tires, steering wheel, headlights, gearshift, windows, dash, everything. He painted everything and never got promoted. Went to 'Nam just in time to get shot and killed. It didn't seem much different these days, kids going off to fight in places with names only the politicians could pronounce. Why does an old man remember the dying of the young? The returning of the wounded? Why the rocks . . . why remember sleeping on the rocks to avoid sleeping in the mud? Some men look only at their feet after that, one after another, taking them home.

SOMETIME LATER, LITTLE Mac shook Old Keb by the shoulder and told him she had to go below to get her guitar and daypack, and Keb's belongings. They'd be leaving soon. Angola and the Frenchmen had returned, but not James and Hugh. Soon, hopefully.

Lying there half-frozen, Keb raised himself. Had he fallen asleep? Right on the deck? It was dark, but the yacht was brightly lit. Little Mac told him to stay, but he followed her down the stairs, hands shaky on the rail. Twice he nearly fell. In the passageway he saw her pressed against the wall, listening to the lounge chatter. She was in a place that allowed her to see Angola in the galley, and for him to see her. Could the others see her? Keb didn't think so. It felt like espionage. He heard men and women talking, drinking, eating. He smelled Angola's jambalaya, a rich aroma that made his legs weak. The lights of the lounge threw bold shadows against the rose-painted bulkheads and teak trim. Little Mac turned to see Keb behind her. She motioned him to stay still, stay quiet. Somebody was playing her guitar. Keb heard Rene say, "They were here when we got here, on the island, three days ago."

Another man said, "Maybe it's not them, but it sure could be."

"It's them."

"You got cell phone coverage out here?"

"Off and on. It's better near Elfin Cove."

"How about a satellite phone?"

"I got one in the plane. We could call and find out if he is who we think he is."

"Just use the VHF. Call Bartlett Cove or Jinkaat. Or ask the commercial fishing fleet."

"Their pictures are probably on the Internet."

Monique said, "They're topside right now. Go ask them."

"The old white-haired guy, I mean, you have to wonder what he's thinking, right?"

"If he's thinking at all."

"He really did carve a dugout cedar canoe?"

"Yep, with help from others."

"So . . . where is it? Where's the canoe?"

Other voices moved over words Keb couldn't understand, followed by laughter and the sound of somebody opening a bottle of champagne. A cork bounced off a wall. More laughter.

Little Mac had crawled behind a sofa all the way into the galley, where Keb could see her hunkered down as she dismantled a radio, with Angola's help. Yes, he thought, *get the radios.*

The dinner party was a party all right, with everybody laughing and slamming down jambalaya. At one point Jacques—or was it Pierre?—got up and came around the corner and stood before Old Keb, pasta-legged, moon-eyed, shit-faced. Without a word, he turned and walked back. Had Keb seen something in his eyes, a conspiratorial wink?

Minutes later Keb and Little Mac were topside in the wheelhouse where Little Mac took all the radios and two small computers. They worked their way into the science lab and Rene's cabin, where they found three more handheld VHFs, two cell phones, two iPhones, an iPad, a handheld GPS, and two computers. "Take it all," Keb said. He had never made a habit of stealing. Seemed like a good time to begin. They had to render the *Etude* incapable of outside communication . . . for a while at least. One phone call could bring a team of troopers and federal rangers who would pamper Keb, speak of safety, and end his journey.

Back on deck, Keb and Little Mac found James and Kid Hugh off the port stern, under one wing of the plane, in the canoe, talking quietly and organizing gear, securing lines, arranging totes. Steve was already aboard, ready to go, up on the foredeck in his position as scout. Keb's heart jumped. "How is it?" he asked quietly.

"How's what, Gramps?"

"The canoe?"

"It's good, Gramps. Hurry, we have to go."

Little Mac handed down her pack, then Keb's pack, and a small duffel filled with their loot. She climbed in and helped the old man do the same. Her guitar would have to stay. Just touching the canoe made Keb feel better, stronger, his hands on familiar wood, an old friend. Angola was on deck, watching. That's when Voltaire appeared, his back arched and tail high, amber eyes gleaming. As if to foil the escape, he meowed. Not an ordinary meow, but a bleating, deep-throated, fat cat cry, one to wake up all of Alaska.

In one swift motion Angola grabbed the cat by the nape of the neck, dropped it into a compartment box, and latched the lid.

"I've wanted to do that for a long time," he said with a smile. He reached down and handed Little Mac a container of jambalaya. "You'd better get going. This jambalaya is clean, not the same stuff that I spiked with bang butter and fed to the others."

Keb found one of the yellow cedar paddles carved by Kevin Pallen, and handed it to him. "This is for you."

Angola got down on his knees. He kissed the paddle, put it aside, and clasped his hands together in prayerful thanks. He reached two-handed for Old Keb, who reached back from the canoe. "Both hands," Angola said to him. "You hold a true friend with both your hands. Go now, old man. You have important work to do." The last Old Keb saw of him, Angola was descending back down into the passageway.

HOW GOOD TO be back in the canoe, to smell the cedar and feel the rhythm of the paddles. All the same, the canoe seemed sluggish, burdened by a great weight. Even with three paddlers—James, Kid Hugh and Little Mac—digging in hard, the canoe was fighting them. Something's wrong. Why? Not until he looked aft did Keb see a great winged shadow following them, darkening all things already dark. Moving through the night. Great Raven. They were pulling the plane. "We're pulling the plane," Keb said. It sounded ridiculous. Nobody replied. They just kept paddling, stroking hard and building momentum. If they stopped the plane would run them down, hit them like a harrier on a vole. "We're pulling the plane," Keb said again. He couldn't believe his own words.

"That's right, Gramps." The plane was about thirty feet behind, affixed by triangulated lines running to cleats on the plane's floats, with a single line running to the canoe. A good job, Keb had to admit; the lines and knots arranged to keep the plane on track directly aft, not drifting side to side. A gentle swell made the plane rise while the canoe dropped, and the canoe rise while the plane dropped, further creating an image of the plane as a living thing, a great night bird flexing its wings.

"Why?" Keb heard himself ask. "Why bring the plane?"

"We had to get the satellite phone."

Keb shook his head. He didn't understand.

"In the plane, Gramps. The satellite phone and the radio. The plane's locked. If we left the plane at the yacht, the pilot would make one satellite phone call and we'd be found. So we took it. We took all the radios and all the phones. We need to get you to where you need to go. Get back, remember? Get back to where you once belonged."

"We took the whole plane?"

"Yeah, the whole plane. It was either take it or break into it."

So there it was. James's voice was low and certain, the kind you don't question. They took the whole plane, the floats and wings and tail and all, like a great prehistoric bird, something from the past and future both. Not half the plane. They took the whole plane. If only Uncle Austin could see them now. Oyyee . . . Maybe he could.

After awhile the kids began to laugh about it, laugh with crazy abandon, and Keb laughed too, at the idea of a canoe pulling a fancy Cessna with the pilot back on a French yacht, stoned on jambalaya.

Somewhere deep into the night they let it go, many hours after they'd worked their way north to the Inian Islands, riding the currents. A soft wind whispered from the west, off Cape Spencer, running with the swell and the flooding tide that would carry the plane to—where? They didn't know. They didn't care. They put the radios, phones, and computers in a sealed plastic bag inside a watertight tote, lashed the tote to one of the plane's floats, and let it go.

Now they made good time, keening the night, northbound, then east. They set both masts and raised sail. "Haa gooxlas'ées," James said. We're going to sail.

Keb was too exultant to sleep. He could sleep when he was dead. He gave Little Mac a break, took her paddle and began digging in as they clipped along in a light rain.

Back on the *Etude*, Keb had asked Angola if he thought the world would ever be without poverty and war. No, Angola said. But it was important to *imagine* a world without poverty and war. Imagination is a powerful thing. Angola then asked the old man whose life he expected to save on this canoe journey. It caught Keb off guard. To save a life is no easy thing. It's hard to measure. Whose life did he expect to save?

nobody went home

WHAT IS THIS place?

A place of water, with illusions of land.

Anne awoke fully dressed, her mouth dry, her hair knotted and disheveled over her face. Her mind, blistered from the day before, was gathering now, a little. Gathering in the chill-making dawn, the gray sky and spitting rain. Hardly a postcard picture of Alaska. But a day nonetheless, filling its lungs. She'd take it.

And her boat? Still afloat? Apparently so, on its anchor in the Sisters Islands. The Sisters. Four small islands, according to the Icy Strait topographic map and nautical chart. Did all blessings come with such names?

Thrashed badly in yesterday's storm, all Anne could do was throttle into her turn and beat the swell as Stuart recommended. Take it on the nose. Taste her own fear, the bile in her stomach. So much of her had wanted to get back to Jinkaat, to follow her senses and animal dreams and see Stuart again, sit in his office and drink bad coffee; banter and laugh and see in his eyes a good man who regarded her as pretty. As much as she didn't want to turn off her animal self, she did. She put her trust in digital maps that took instructions from satellites high in the thinness of space. Her GPS didn't lie. It was technology Cook and Vancouver never dreamed of, and it saved her. Together with Stuart's steady voice.

Like angels, the islands appeared and she gained their lee. What hour was it when she finally dropped anchor? Exhausted, she had radioed Stuart, "I'm okay," and collapsed into a dreamless, leaden sleep, too hungry to make dinner, too tired to undress. Ranger Ron, the safety fanatic, had warned her about Alaska storms. Yes, well, it wasn't the storm that got her. It was her carelessness. Same as when Nancy died.

If only our hurt helped us heal. She found her journal and found that finding it, touching it, holding it to her chest, made her whole.

If only
I would
be myself again
and awaken from a dream
I just missed remembering
to be myself again
if only.

SHE HAD BURNED through a lot of fuel. What to do? Icy Strait was settling down. She could make the run to Bartlett Cove. Or head back to Jinkaat. Face a rebuke from Ranger Ron? Or a smile from Deputy Stu?

Easy, Taylor would tell her. Forget the head; follow the heart.

Follow the magic, Nancy would say.

When Captain Cook returned to the Big Island after breaking a mast, the Hawaiians, who had earlier welcomed him as a god, saw him for what he was, a man. Nancy said he changed the world. He made it smaller and bigger at the same time. He and his men practiced science, but also left enough room in themselves to believe in mermaids and unicorns, and best of all, magic.

Nancy loved magic. Nancy *was* magic.

Anne was thinking too many things as she slipped into the Jinkaat Boat Harbor. Stuart was on the upper pier. He waved.

She had expected it to be quiet. It was not. At least forty people moved about the floating dock loading gear and all kinds of boats: trollers, seiners, skiffs, runabouts, gillnetters, go-getters, rust buckets, Nordic Tugs, fancy Bertrams, big Bayliners, sloops, ketches, and funky old Boston Whalers. All kinds of people too: Tlingit and Norwegian, German and Latvian, dark and white, men and women, rich and poor, old and young, some dressed in cotton as if going on a Sunday picnic, others dressed in camo as if headed out on a hunt. Animated people with coolers and totes, dogs and cats, grandparents and kids, barbecues and baby seats, all calling back and forth: "Hey, are you taking this? Don't forget that."

They all stopped to watch Anne approach. The rain fell soft and steady, counting time. A teenager with a ball of tobacco under his lip manned the fuel pump, eyes big with surprise. "Fill her up?" he asked as Anne eased in and put her fenders out. She killed her engine and stepped onto the dock to cleat off her stern line while he held the bow.

"Please," Anne said as she thanked him and handled the beam line.

"Credit card or cash?"

"Credit card." She handed him her federal government card.

"We all thought you was dead, going out in a storm like that."

Stuart walked down the ramp and gave her a hug. Anne was overcome with a desire to kiss him. "It's nice to see you," he said, playing it cool.

"It's nice to see you, too. What's going on?"

"People are crazy excited. There's been a sighting of Old Keb and the canoe."

"Really?"

Stuart pulled her aside. "Things are out of control. It's been a week since any report of him, and now the town is coming undone with everybody loading up their boats and wanting to go help him get to wherever he wants to go."

"Thank you for answering my radio call, for your calm voice and advice."

"Oh, you're welcome. It's nice to see you."

"You told me that already."

"I did? Yeah, I guess I did. Still, it's nice to see you."

Anne smiled. "As you were saying—"

"I was saying?"

"About everybody loading up."

"Oh, right. Everybody's loading up their boats and taking off and it's all coming apart and I can't control—"

"Stuart, it's not coming apart. Look. It's beautiful. It's people coming together, see? They're excited and talking and packing and bringing food to share like one big potluck. It's a celebration. Here's this old man at the end of his life going back to his ancient homeland in the old way. Not in a modern way or a corporate way but in the ancient way, the traditional way, the right way, in a canoe he carved himself with help from loved ones and friends. People want to be involved. Can you blame them?"

"No but—"

"No 'no buts.' Let them go."

"It's risky for some of them."

"Fine."

"Some of their boats aren't seaworthy."

"Ask them to travel in tandem."

"Ranger Ron Ambrose has been calling and looking for you. And this morning the woman from Washington called."

"The woman from Washington?"

"Kate Johnson, director of the Marine Reserve Service."

Uh oh. Paul had given Anne a satellite phone that she put—where? In the bottom of her daypack or duffel. She'd stuffed it down there days ago with her smelly socks and long johns and forgotten about it.

"I don't see that you got an account here or nothing," the teenager said as he thumbed through a notebook in the small shed on the fuel dock. "This credit card doesn't work."

"Put it on the city account," Stuart told him.

"I don't know, because—"

"Just do it, Corey. We have to get going before everybody else does, to make sure Keb's okay, that he gets back to . . . wherever."

Anne stared at him.

"I'm coming with you, if that's okay, in your boat." Stuart smiled at her.

Just then a big Bayliner came by, the *No Way*, riding low, which made no sense to Anne, given the appearance of its two skinny occupants, one at the wheel, the other on the stern, brothers built like fence posts with hawk noses and ponderous eyes loose in dark sockets. She recognized the man on the stern from the television report the night Old Keb left Portage Cove. "We're leaving," the man shouted to Stuart.

"For where, Oddmund? Where you going?"

"North."

"North to where?"

"Crystal Bay, I guess . . . Keb's boyhood home."

"Wait for the others. Everybody should travel together and—"

"You the ranger lady?" Oddmund asked Anne. "We were worried about you, especially Stuart here. He didn't sleep all night."

"Hey, Stuart," said Dag, a cell phone stuck to his ear. "You got your phone on? Mitch is trying to reach you. He's in his truck with Irene and Vic and heading this way and says it's important. He says it's about Old Keb and a plane out near Cross Sound."

Sure enough, Mitch roared up in his Chevy one-ton. He climbed out and stormed down the ramp, a bowling ball of a man accompanied by a guy whose eyes devoured the scene. Stuart told Anne it was Vic Lehan, the town barber, a real talker. Behind them came Irene, her hair in curlers, in the rain. Plume-faced and breathless, Mitch didn't stop until he got nose-to-nose with Stuart. "Have you heard?"

"What?"

"Keb and the others stole a plane, a Cessna 207 on floats."

"A plane? What are they doing with a plane?"

"Not much, because they let it go."

"Let it go? Where?"

"Out in Cross Sound, near the Inians. They were on a yacht for three days, and when they left they took the yacht's plane."

"The yacht has a plane?"

"It did."

"This doesn't make sense."

"I'm just telling you what Harald told me and Ruby told him. It's on the news in Juneau. Stealing a plane is a serious offense. You need to get a handle on what's going on around here, Stu. The whole damn town is packing up to leave, some in vessels that hardly float and can't make it across Port Thomas let alone Icy Strait. Most of these people don't even know where they're going. Somebody's going to get halfway across Icy Strait and drown."

"I'm working on it."

"Work on it harder," said Irene, her voice as charming as a chop saw.

"You want a receipt?" the teenager asked Anne.

Mitch's cell phone rang. He whipped it out, spoke for a minute, and passed it on to Stuart with a roll of his eyes. "It's Ruby."

Anne heard Stuart's end: "Hello Ruby . . . Yep, you bet . . . yep, of course, the rangers are aware. Nope . . . yep, for his own safety. I'm on my way now, by boat, with the NMRS here in Jinkaat . . . Yep, that's her. Nope. They can't travel that far in one night and they can't haul it up a beach either. It's too heavy. I expect there's a fixed-wing aircraft out there already . . . Fog? I don't think so. Yep, okay then . . . yep, you bet. Thanks Ruby, you bet . . . yep, bye." He hung up looking exhausted, and handed the phone back to Mitch.

"I guess Gracie's real sick and close to dying," Mitch said.

"Close to dying?" Stuart said. "How can she be close to dying?"

"Because she's real sick," Irene said, her eyes filling with tears. "She's in the hospital in Seattle and wants to see James and Old Keb."

Anne watched Stuart take the news hard, his face drawn and gray. She liked the depth of his sympathy, the rhythm of his kindness.

More people filled the dock, double the number that had been there twenty minutes before. Everybody loading up. So much chatter and excitement. They wanted to help Old Keb, yes, if he needed it. Mostly they wanted to be witnesses to his dream, participants in some way to how it used to be, when everybody traveled by tides and winds, one paddle stroke at a time, sharing, caring, warring, raiding, trading, fishing and hunting as Eagle and Raven, a proud and paradoxical people who faced danger and in so doing were robustly alive, alert, aware. Anne could see it, feel it. It wasn't the soulless chaos of modern living. It was something simple yet profound, a million little acts of affirmation, an awakening, an endless dance of creation.

A line of boats idled off the fuel station, waiting for service, each filled with anxious skippers and their crews of family and friends, eager to do something, to be part of something larger than themselves—a real community.

Is this why we're here, to come together like this, separate yet one?

It made Anne smile, though she could see the pressure on Stuart was immense. She longed to whisk him away.

Mitch yelled at a heavy-set man skippering a twenty-foot Lund. "For crying out loud, Parker. What are you gonna do with that shotgun?"

"Go fishing."

The others laughed.

A woman shouted, "C'mon, Mitch. You can't miss this. Keb's your best friend."

"Do you have any idea where you're going, Carmen?" Mitch called back.

"No, but we'll talk by radio, we'll listen and camp out and figure it out."

"Keb's going to the glacier," shouted a man with a black goatee, ponytail, and wire-rim glasses. "The glacier that shaped Crystal Bay."

"You're probably right," Mitch said. Anne could see the conflict on his face; he wanted to go but Irene wanted him to stay.

"Hey, Truman, you got a camera?"

"Yep."

"C'mon, Mitch," Carmen said. "It's gonna be a big party."

"The rangers will stop you, you know?" Irene said. "Only so many boats are allowed into Crystal Bay each day."

"They can't stop us all," Truman said.

"We'll sneak in at night."

"Break the blockade."

"Storm the Alamo."

"Go home, all of you," Irene said. "Before somebody gets hurt."

Nobody went home.

the reefs of right and wrong

THE SEPTEMBER SUN offered little warmth as dozens of boats made their way across Icy Strait toward Crystal Bay, many in good repair, others barely afloat. And more yet to leave Jinkaat. Such a flotilla. It reminded Anne of the makeshift boats she'd read about—laundry tubs, fruit boxes, old Buicks—used by people setting off from Cuba to reach freedom in Florida. Most sinking without a trace. Three Jinkaat kids were crossing Icy Strait on jet skis, riding the gentle swell in the aftermath of the storm. Did they wear life vests? Stuart said they were basketball kids who'd played with James. They probably had deer rifles over their shoulders and pockets filled with Snickers bars. "Cheating death," Stuart said. "It's a pastime in Alaska."

Anne suppressed those images and ran the *Firn* a little off open throttle to leave the flotilla behind. Only a couple fast skiffs were up ahead. Where to go? West of Point Carolus, probably. She didn't know. Did anybody? She was supposed to radio into Bartlett Cove every morning and evening. She'd missed three calls now. Soon they'd be searching for *her*.

By late afternoon, she was near the entrance to Crystal Bay, off Point Carolus. Stuart had climbed onto Anne's bunk and fallen asleep. She looked at him constantly: the shape of his nose, the texture of his hair; his delicate fingers and beautiful hands. Adrift now, a great fatigue came over her. She killed the engine, turned down the radio, and quietly climbed onto the bunk next to him, curling her body into his.

Some minutes later—hours later?—she awoke with a start and bounded to her feet to check her drift. Stuart stirred awake. "Everything okay?" he asked.

"Yes, fine." Anne struggled to gather her bearings. "I fell asleep."

"So did I, apparently, in your bunk. Sorry about that."

"No need to apologize." *You can sleep in my bed anytime.* "You hungry?"

"I think I probably am. Where are we?"

"Off Carolus, about a mile, drifting west on an ebbing tide."

Anne found a mother humpback whale and her calf and followed them at a distance while Stuart sifted through papers and checked his handheld GPS. The soft light of dusk leaked through bruised clouds stacked against hard mountains. The sea mimicked the sky, dressed in gray. Anne heard gulls chattering up the last act of summer, diving for small fish, and beyond that, a small search plane beating a path between Bartlett Cove and George Island, scouring Icy Strait for Old Keb. Poor guy. She remembered Gracie's bent frame and musical voice: "Why can't they just let him go?"

Anne killed the engine again and drifted. For how long she couldn't say. Stuart had fallen asleep again, this time sitting up, his chin on his chest. Time passed strangely. Then a presence arrived. Before she turned, she knew it. Bird and shadow in one, a spirit, a moment. Raven. Corvus the Contrarian, black talons tapping the white deck. Practically strutting. Anne looked right at it and could see the bird disliked this, so she lowered her eyes. The raven paced, then flew away, circled back and flew away again in the same direction, west. Around its neck, Anne could see a faint collar of white, the feathers of old age.

"Did you see that?" she asked Stuart.

"What?" He snapped awake.

"That raven?"

"No."

"I think it was leading us in the direction of Old Keb, crazy as that sounds."

Stuart wore an inscrutable smile.

"What?" Anne said. "What's up?"

"I know where he is. I know where the canoe is."

"You do?"

He held up the direction finder. It wasn't a GPS, it was an ELT, an emergency location transmitter. "The night they left Portage Cove, I was there. I walked down and touched the canoe as they were preparing to leave."

"And you put a silent beacon on it?"

"Under the thwart, the middle seat, a small one."

"You've known this entire time?"

"Yes and no. For days it gave me no signal. I don't know why. But now the signal is strong. I'm thinking the canoe must have been in a sea cave, or under a cliff."

Anne stared at him, then threw her head back and laughed harder than she'd laughed in a long time. It felt sensational, like great sex. "That's brilliant," she said. "You've known this whole time and told nobody?"

"Yep."

"You want him to be free, don't you? You want him to die wild?"

"I don't know about that. Part of me never wants him to die. I just want him to get to wherever it is he wants to go."

"So do I, Stuart. So do I. Is that wrong?"

"It's complicated."

"Yes . . . like everything else."

"I think you were right, what you said back in Jinkaat, about Keb's journey bringing people together. People deserve to be a part of this."

"The Marine Reserve Service task force won't allow it. They won't allow all these boats into Crystal Bay."

Stuart shrugged. "What can they do? I've heard there are boats headed this way from Juneau, Haines, and Sitka. What can the Marine Reserve Service do? Arrest everybody? Stop everybody? Impossible."

Anne laughed again.

"I put one of these on Charlie Gant's boat, too, before it disappeared from Jinkaat, but it's given me no signal. It makes me think he and Tommy found it, or it fell off, or the battery died. I was in a hurry and probably didn't attach it as well as I should have."

"Do you know where Old Keb is now?"

"I think so. But I need to tell you, there's a downside. What I've done is illegal. Affixing a tracker of any kind to a car or a boat or a plane without a warrant is a violation of the Fourth Amendment guarantee against unreasonable search and seizure."

Anne found herself biting her lip. Stuart added, "I wanted to be able to find him in case he ended up cold and starving. I didn't want him to die slowly, and in pain, that's all. Sometimes you have to break the rules. You know . . . for the greater good."

That was it. Anne dug out the satellite phone from deep in her duffel, and dialed Paul Beals. According to her message log, he'd called her three times in the last two days. After several rings it beeped. "Hi, Paul, this is Anne. It's Monday, late afternoon, almost evening. I'm on the *Firn* with Deputy Ewing from the Jinkaat Sheriff's office. We're in Icy Strait looking for Keb Wisting, like everybody else. We'll probably stay out and anchor up somewhere. I'll call in the morning, if I can."

If I feel like it.

She hung up and imagined Paul taking the news poorly. And Ranger Ron? He too would not be happy, pacing in his Kevlar vest. She called Director Kate Johnson. What time was it back in Washington? After several rings a woman said, "Hello."

"Kate Johnson?"

"Yes."

"This is Anne Bellestraude, in Alaska. I'm the whale biologist you visited in Crystal Bay in June."

"Yes, Anne. Paul's been trying to reach you. Where have you been?"

"I'm on my boat in Icy Strait. If you recall, you said I could call you anytime if I had any information, or needed anything."

"Yes, of course. What is it?"

"I'm part of the task force searching for—"

"Keb Wisting, yes. He was up the outer coast on a French yacht and is now suspected of being somewhere near Dundas Bay in his canoe, probably traveling at night. I speak with Paul daily. Have you found him, found Keb?"

"No, but I know where he is."

"You do?"

"It's a little complicated. What I want to tell you so that you know before anybody else is that I'm going to help him, if I can."

"Help him?"

"Yes, Old Keb. I'm going to help him."

"In what way? What do you mean? What are you talking about?"

"I don't know, exactly. I'm figuring this out as I go. I think I'm going to help him go wherever he needs to."

"And where's that?"

"I don't know, but he will. He'll know. He's an old man who knows these waters better than anybody. All he wants is to be left alone so he can travel the way he used to through wild country when he was a boy, and things were quieter and less complicated."

"Anne, I know you've got good intentions. So does Paul and his task force. Have you spoken to Paul?"

"I left him a message."

"He wants to do the right thing too; he needs your help. You're a smart woman and this is a sensitive matter that needs to be stopped before it gets out of hand. You can stop it, and give it a happy ending. You can bring Keb Wisting home safely. If he enters Crystal Bay and goes up to the glacier, PacAlaska will use the stunt to its advantage."

"And if I stop him, PacAlaska will use that too, as an example of a heavy-handed federal government interfering with the dreams of an old Tlingit."

"But think about this: if he goes up to that glacier and makes a political statement, we could lose in the Ninth Circuit."

"He's not political."

"His daughter Ruby is. One perfect sound bite could sway the court, believe me."

Anne said nothing.

"Do you want corporate development inside Crystal Bay?"

"No."

"Exactly. Neither do I. I want you to do the right thing."

"That's what I'm trying to do—the right thing. I enjoyed meeting you in June. I admire you. That's why I'm calling. I want you to understand that for me the right thing isn't always the easy thing, or the obvious thing."

"Then find Keb Wisting and his companions and bring them back to safety."

Safety, another form of authority.

"Anne, did you hear me?"

"Yes, I heard you."

"I don't want you to do anything wrong."

"Wrong? Sometimes being overcautious and obedient is wrong."

"The task force risk management team has determined there's no room to think outside the box on this, okay?"

"The task force has a risk management team? No wonder Old Keb feels lost in today's world."

"Don't jeopardize your career."

"My career? I'm a seasonal employee with no retirement or health benefits. You told me that yourself. I have skills. I have good friends. I have a sweet man on my boat right now who talks me through storms and makes me laugh and makes me feel good about myself in ways I haven't felt in a long time. But I don't have a career."

"You can. And you will, if you're careful."

"If I'm obedient, you mean."

"Listen to reason, Anne."

"Reason? With all due respect, Director Johnson, you don't know what you're talking about. You told me that Icy Strait is federal waters under the jurisdiction of the National Marine Fisheries Service, a sister agency of the NMRS."

"That's right."

"That's wrong. Icy Strait is under State of Alaska jurisdiction, and I'm in Icy Strait right now, not Crystal Bay. Federal laws apply here only if there's a federal offense against the Marine Mammal Protection Act, or something like that."

"You're trying my patience. Stay on target. If you escort this old man into Crystal Bay without a permit—"

"He doesn't need a permit. His canoe has no motor. Only motorized vessels need permits. And about this being a stunt: it's not a stunt."

"You know, whenever we argue with reality, we lose. But we only lose one hundred percent of the time."

"Very funny."

"Very true. All the vessels now looking for Keb Wisting, the people who want to find him and accompany him, they have motors on their boats. Do you want them all in Crystal Bay creating a huge scene? If you do what I think you're thinking of doing, it could be a citable offense and a public relations disaster. You'll never work for the federal government again. So here's what I want you to do. I want you—"

Anne hung up. Simple as that. She hung up on the grandmother astronaut who walked in space and covered Africa with her finger.

"Whoa," Stuart said. "How'd that feel?"

"Reckless and sensible, stupid and smart, condemning and liberating. No big deal." Anne felt her stomach turn over.

"'A sweet man who makes you feel in a way you haven't in a long time.' Wow. Sounds like a catch."

"We'll see."

"I'd like to meet him."

"I'll make arrangements."

"You're blushing."

"So are you."

THE HUMPBACK WHALE mother and calf disappeared. Funny how whales do that, Anne thought. You follow them for hours and then, poof, they're gone.

Everything stilled. Even the gulls. Anne sat at the wheel and touched the Maui Wowie through her shirt pocket. She thought about her mother, dressed in black and mourning Nancy; about her stepfather who missed the funeral and a few days later left the house and never came back. She could still feel the weight of it lodged in her heart, the ferocious grief. Was she going crazy?

Am I going crazy?

Stuart stood next to her, his arm gently brushing hers, a thousand volts surging through her. He said gravely, "I need to tell you that there's another reason I put the ELT on the canoe."

Anne looked at him.

"I think Charlie and Tommy are looking for the canoe too."

Anne swallowed hard. Something about this scared her.

"The investigation on Pepper Mountain turned up evidence that Tommy found the choker-setter D-ring that broke that day."

"So?"

"Tommy and Charlie might want to show it to James and Keb as proof of their innocence. Charlie admires Old Keb. Tommy too, in his own way."

"I've heard they're dangerous."

Stuart shook his head. "Those brothers have had a hard run. Their father was wrongfully accused of robbery, and spent three years in jail. They were just kids, but I think it screwed them up. It's a fate they didn't deserve."

"You have a kind heart."

Stuart shrugged. "I'm just me."

"Don't change."

"Okay. Anyway, I've been investigating the burning of Keb's shed. At the big celebration the night before, a few people saw Tommy emerge from the forest in a sneaky manner, grab Little Mac's pack, and put something in it."

"Really? What?"

"A beacon, I'll bet. Tommy's always been obsessed with knowing Little Mac's whereabouts. A canoe journey felt imminent that night, at least for Old Keb and James. And who would James want to bring along?"

"Little Mac."

"Exactly. Tommy's not stupid."

"You think the Gants have the same advantage we have; you think they know where the canoe is?"

"I do."

"Oh—this isn't good, Stuart. You should have stopped Charlie and Tommy."

Stuart lowered his head; hair askew, badge heavy on his chest. Anne regretted her sharp words. After so many wrong men she needed to find the right wrong man. He could do with a comb and a bath. So could she. She watched him sit on the transom where the raven had been.

"I'm sorry, Stuart. I'm just tired and a little scared."

"Me too." That smile. *Dear God.*

Anne got to her feet. "Where to, then?"

"Lemesurier Island, north shore, toward Dundas Bay."

"You hungry?"

"No."

"You sure? Because I know I am."

"Okay, I'm hungry." That smile again.

Anne motored west while Stuart made burritos. At one point he handed her an olive and she took it with her mouth. His fingers brushed her lips and she felt faint with desire, so free she could fly. Who needs magic when life itself is magical? Whales, burritos, bears, birds, butterflies, and newborn babies, this wet, spinning blue-green earth, a grand design of land and love and sea and sky, not a bad place to be.

Ahead lay dark water under the deepening night, full tides moving over the reefs of right and wrong.

"There's beer in the cooler," Anne said.

She took the badge off her shirt and felt better. If Stuart had put his hands on her just then, she would have taken her shirt off, too.

PART THREE

áx' awé koowdzitèe

FALLING ASLEEP WAS an effort. Old Keb had lain down to let the long night take him, deep in his canoe, but the air was high-voltage. The sea, fragrant. And the motion, what a sensation, almost sensual. James and Kid Hugh and Little Mac had put their backs into it until their arms and paddles were extensions of the sea. They paddled for hours and more, sometimes on their knees, other times sitting on the thwarts. "The tide's against us now," James said at one point.

"Hug the shore," Keb told him. "You'll find a countercurrent there, better going." And they did. "Listen for rocks," Keb said. "A light swell heaves waves against exposed rocks." And it did. Something growled and splashed in the night, very near. "Taan," Keb said. "Sea lions." Behind the canoe, they stirred up a trail of phosphorescence, lighting the inky sea. Little Mac said they were a comet now. Nothing was going to stop them.

Keb remembered how he and Bessie would lie on the forest floor, under great trees with outstretched arms, her body tandem with his; she of the soft skin and artful hands, her warmth like the sun. Her cleansing laugh. All the rough edges of his mind made smooth. That's how he felt now in the canoe, if only a little. For an old man, a little is a lot.

"The feather!" he said in the middle of the night, waking up so restless it failed to convince him he'd been sleeping at all, "T'aaw. The feather?"

"I've got it, Gramps," James said. "You want it?"

"Yes. No—you keep it." The pain moved, undecided about where to lodge. First his hips ached, then his legs, neck, stomach, groin, head, hands, feet, all pulled into one long moment. His pills were on the *Etude*. Pills prescribed by doctors who died too. The sea would be his medicine now.

All that night—the night they left the *Etude*—they had paddled until an hour before dawn when they off-loaded on a small island and covered the canoe in a bed of kelp, just offshore. That day, yesterday, they slept all day under watchful trees as planes sliced the sky and busy boats moved back and forth, some very near. Keb's bones seemed to grow more brittle by the hour. His heart acted funny. He felt a throbbing in his neck.

Now again, for an entire night, they paddled ten hours and more with Little Mac digging in as hard as James and Kid Hugh, her jaw set. A crazy east wind beat them back and forced them to find a lee, where they rested. At one point Keb caught Kid Hugh napping. How tenacious he appeared, even when asleep, illuminated by a small flashlight, his body a pretzel; legs over the side of the canoe, his head against the hull, long hair over his face. Angola had said that most people who protest against authority take it only so far, until they find out prisons have no pillows. Not this kid. He'd never break. Never be for sale. That same resistance was in James, too. It might take more time. What had the dark-faced Latvian told Keb the night of the steaming? *If a thousand beliefs are destroyed in our march to the truth, we must still march on.* Paddle on. Nature will tell you who you need to be. Keb knew. It was time to move by memory, the smells of things you cannot find in books. Stay low. Move with the water when no one is looking; go in the middle of the night, like a bat, or *tlénx' shx'aneit*, a small owl. If the authorities find you they might take you to Juneau, put you in a hospital, or worse, down to coffee-drunk Seattle for packaged blood, green Jell-O, and purple potato salad, the nearest nagoonberry pie a thousand miles away.

At one point Kid Hugh caught Keb looking at him and said, "You're not afraid of dying then, old man?"

"No."

"Me neither." He cleaned his teeth with a broken piece of deer bone.

"I've been dying for twenty years," Keb said. "I'm taking my time so I don't miss anything." He thought this was funny. Kid Hugh stared at him with his cold arctic eyes.

"My dad almost died a few years back," Kid Hugh said. "They had to cut off his leg. Too much whiskey and fat." He shrugged. "I don't care."

Keb thought: If only he could sing, this kid. It's not a luxury; it's a necessity, like good food and water, an unfolding, the wind blowing from the beginning. Uncle Austin used to say that all of our joy and suffering comes from the same single sacred utterance; that we live by being wounded and healed and wounded again, and healed, one day at a time. Angola said something similar, during one of his philosophy talks. He said you have to meet the outer world with your inner world to keep your soul anchored. If not, existence will crush you. He talked about a Nigerian man who traveled for many years until one day he sat down and didn't move. That was it. He was staying put. Days later, when another traveler came by and asked why he sat so still, the Nigerian said he'd been moving too long. It was time to sit and wait for his soul to catch up.

THAT NIGHT, THE darkness made itself more oppressive with weasel winds and strange liquid voices even Keb didn't know. He held his hand at arm's length and saw nothing. He heard James and Kid Hugh arguing in low voices over what to do, where to head. They paddled for hours and huddled over a map, then paddled more. They refrained from using bright flashlights that might shine over dark water and give them away.

A light did come at them, though. Not a red or green running light, as you see on boats underway, but a single white light. Despite every effort they made to evade it, paddling this way and that, the light grew nearer. "It's the tide rip," James said. "It's pulling us toward it."

The sound of a diesel engine bore down. Keb could see the vessel now, an old rumrunner from the Stikine River, re-outfitted in a familiar way, working hard, coming at them. "Li-gaaw," he mumbled. It's loud. A boy stood on the bow with the powerful light, near tall white lettering: *Terry Mae.* Keb felt his heart jump. It was Torp Dezkorski, the mill operator from Strawberry Flats who had more yellow cedar logs than any one man in Alaska. He must be pulling a large raft of them, the cable low in the water. On the bow must be Torp's son. Oyyee . . . he's grown. Keb raised a hand.

"Gramps, what are you doing?"

The powerful bow light hit them with fierce inquisition. The engine throttled back. A man in a sou'wester stepped out from the pilothouse and waved. "Keb, is that you?" Ten minutes later they were alongside. Keb made introductions.

Kid Hugh asked the skipper, "What kind of name is Torp?"

He had arms like thighs, and bootlegger's eyes from the Russian steppe. He gave Kid Hugh a hard look, almost severe, as though the softest thing about him were his teeth. A boreal man, his features were invested in the northern forest. He spoke through a bird's nest beard and a boxer's nose that occupied three-fourths of his face. "When I move slow," he said, his voice high-timbered, "they call me Torpid. But when I move fast, they call me Torpedo. Nowadays I'm mostly torpid. But I had my torpedo years, didn't

I, Keb? I didn't sink any ships, but I decked some cocky sailors." Keb nodded with difficulty. The left side of his body had gone numb. Torp said, "Galley Sally told me they'd never find you. Looks like they haven't yet. I suppose you'll be wanting a ride?"

"We're fine," James said.

"You have any idea where you're at?"

"Northwest of Lemesurier, off Dundas Bay."

"Yep. You've crossed the reserve boundary now, if that means anything to you."

"A little," James said.

"Where's the boundary?" Little Mac asked, looking around at the darkness.

Torp laughed. "You can't see it, honey, like most of what the government does around here. The reserve boundary runs over the mountains far to the north, where nobody goes, then turns south and runs right through the water here in Icy Strait, where everybody goes. It's a straight line in most places, an imaginary line that separates the imaginary rights of one kind of people from the imaginary rights of another kind of people. We cross it all the time out here. Crystal Bay National Marine Reserve. Sounds like a military outpost, don't it, since the feds and everybody else is looking for you."

"Have you heard anything about the Gant brothers?" James asked.

"Nope. But that don't mean nothin'. I make myself aware of as little as possible. Wood and women is about all I know about. Old wood, young women. Your canoe looks like red cedar. Does it have a name?"

"*Óoxjaa Yaadéi*," James said. "*Against the Wind.*"

"Against the Wind? That's a Bob Seger song. Him and the Silver Bullet Band. Takes me back to the woods and a girl named Candy who was just that sweet." Torp threw his head back and let the music fly, and nearly fell over from excitement, or from last night's vodka. "Damn," he added, "that's a good song. A good name for a canoe, too."

If what Keb heard just then was supposed to be singing, Torp had a ways to go. The crazy Russian had lost some marbles since Keb saw him last. His son said nothing. A handsome, almost delicate boy, eleven or twelve, he appeared to have gotten his looks from his mother, and showed a fair improvement over his father. Thirty years of hard living would change that. Torp told Keb that his daughter Ruby was in Strawberry Flats with radio and TV people from Juneau. He said it with such venom that it stung Keb. Torp and Ruby had a nasty history over Alaska timber sales. Ruby's vision of high-volume, high-profit corporate harvests had sent thousands of round logs directly to Japan, while Torp ran his own mill and fought to keep the wood—and the jobs—local.

"Have you heard any news about my mom?" James asked him.

"Afraid not. Word's around that you hitched a ride on the *Silverbow*. You're some kind of folk hero, Keb. Ernie Banksly said you were on *360 North* the other day."

"Where?"

"*360 North,* the Alaskan TV show."

"How could I be there when I was here?"

"You weren't. It was other people who were on there talking about you, experts, you know? City people who know everything and nothing. Strawberry Flats is crawling with them, all those media types. Bartlett Cove, too. There are boats from everywhere in Bartlett Cove and Icy Strait. They say you're like Chief Joseph, you know, the Shoshone dude that the US Cavalry chased and never caught because he ate and slept on his horse and led his people into Canada so he wouldn't have to live on a damn reservation."

"Nez Perce," James said.

"What?"

"Chief Joseph was Nez Perce."

"And they caught him," Kid Hugh said. "They're not going to catch us."

"Hey, whatever." Torp laughed. "You didn't play poker with Quinton or Morgan, did you? They cheat like hell. You must be cold. Climb on up here and hand me a line. I'll give you a tow and some hot food." He barked at the boy, "Luke, grab that line."

"YOU EVER SEEN one of these thingamajigs?" Torp put a small tracking device on the yellow cedar logs. Keb and the others watched. Keb wondered if a thingamajig was more complicated than a gadgetgizmo.

Little Mac said in an unsettling tone, "I have seen one of those."

Torp unhooked the cables to free-float his logs, then tied the canoe off the stern of the *Terry Mae*. He may have been quick years ago, but he was slow now. Daylight was coming and Keb could see that James wanted to go. "It's like one of them ELTs," Torp explained, "those emergency locator transmitters they got in airplanes so they can find the plane if it goes down. It beams a signal up to a satellite. This one is programmed to find it with this." He showed them another thingamajig that gave electronic readings when he flipped it on. "I'll be able to leave my raft of cedar logs drifting here, and find it after I drop you off. I'll put a standing light on it too, so no other boat hits it."

"We need to get going," James said.

Torp nodded. "Luke, get these people something to eat."

The *Terry Mae* thugged and chugged but appeared to make no better speed than when it had fifty logs cabled behind it. Luke offered them no food. He took the wheel while Torp made fresh coffee. James made several trips aft to check on the canoe, and said, "We're only making about five knots."

Kid Hugh and Steve curled up in the corner, sleep-starved. The accommodations were dirty at best. Grit and grime everywhere, old bits of food, patches of mold, diesel fumes rising from below. The coffee tasked like tar. Keb screwed his face into a squint.

"It's better with sugar in it," Torp said.

"We're not going to make it," James said after awhile. They all looked at him. All but Little Mac, who was digging in her duffel and daypack with great concern. "We have to turn around and make for Lemesurier or Dundas. Crystal Bay is too far. There's no good landfall between here and there; the seas will be too rough off Carolus to launch the canoe with tides like this. Daylight will be here in another hour."

Continents moved and species evolved in the time it took Torp to respond. Keb glared at him, inasmuch as a man with one good eye can glare. Torp finally yelled to Luke to bring the *Terry Mae* about. "Where to then?" he asked, his eyes cold and flat. "Lemesurier Island or Dundas Bay?"

"Dundas," the old man said.

"Áx' awé ḵoowdzitèe," James added. "He was born there."

eyes she trusted

THE OLD CANNERY made a strong temptation but was too far away on the west shore of Dundas Bay. It had collapsed long ago and was little more than rusted iron and rotting timbers, where it once stood on legs as stout as a bear's. Little Mac had been there a few years back, to see where her great-grandfather Milo worked the slime line and delivered little Keb when he was born. But now with daylight coming, she showed no interest in returning. Like James and Kid Hugh, she wanted to get ashore fast. Keb could see that a cloud of worry had come over her.

"Sorry not to be more help," Torp said as Keb and his companions climbed down into the canoe, off the east shore of Dundas Bay. Keb offered his thanks. Torp flashed a smile and said, "You know, I could turn you in and get myself on TV."

James and Kid Hugh glared at him.

"Hey, just kidding. You guys need to lighten up."

With that, they paddled away as the *Terry Mae* turned south. Torp had cost them time, poisoned them with bad coffee, told crude jokes, given them no food, and eaten the last of their jambalaya.

Never trust a Russian.

In the charcoal light of dawn they glided their canoe onto a large tide flat that tapered up to a cobble beach. Steve was first ashore. To their left, an abandoned fox farm stood back from a large meadow. Straight ahead, across fifty feet of tide flat and up the beach, a fringe of alder fronted a forest of spruce and hemlock, good cover. They had to move quickly and hide the canoe. James said rangers could be camped on Feldspar Peak with spotting scopes, a good place to view the entrance to both Crystal Bay and its little cousin to the west, Dundas Bay. Aircraft would be up soon. Men with search-pattern eyes talking by radio.

What to do? No kelp beds in sight. No cleft or cave in a nearby cliff. No high profile piece of shore where they could gain closer access to cover. The canoe was too heavy to pull across the tide flat and into the forest.

"Sink it," Keb said, "ka-si-yeek."

The tide was slack low. By the time it was that low again, in twelve or thirteen hours, nightfall would be on their side. All day long the canoe would be under water.

"All right," James said. "We'll sink it. Good thinking, Gramps."

Good thinking? Has my grandson ever said that to me? Have I ever said it to him?

They carried their gear across the tide flat and into the forest, making many trips. Each time they returned they hefted down heavy rocks and loaded them into the canoe. Keb's heart jackhammered. He hurt everywhere. "Gramps, give me that rock. Go up into the forest and stay there, okay? We'll get this done."

"Put the canoe . . . on its . . . left side," Keb said, breathless, "with the keel facing . . . seaward so it's easy to re-float. Wedge the . . . the rocks under the seats and into the . . . into the thwarts so—"

"Okay, Gramps. I got it. Now go. Hurry, go."

"Tired, ka-ya-saak . . . no more wind in me."

"Yes, Gramps."

"I dream in Tlingit now. Norwegian too. Viking dreams."

"Yes, Gramps, that's good."

"There's a problem . . . with . . . Little Mac. Something's wrong in her . . . her pack. You need to—"

"Okay, I know, Gramps. I'll talk to her. Now go."

Old Keb grabbed a final load and was making his way across the tide flat when he seized up and fell hard. *Something's wrong.* The world was catty-wampus, everything upright was on its side and everything level was running up and down. And the pain, oh God, beyond anything from before, a terrible tightening in his chest, his lungs clawing for air. He lay there for—how long? Paralyzed. Mud on his face. Legs and arms twitching. *Bessie? Oyyee . . . I miss you.* So much music, light, and love. Time had no passage and somehow he was above himself, floating without pain or the ability to speak, watching as the others ran to him and lifted him and carried him up the beach into the forest. Bless their hearts. They carried him so gently. He was no sack of potatoes, but precious cargo as they lowered him onto a bed of moss under an ancient *seet*, a Sitka spruce large enough to make a canoe. Little Mac put his head in her lap and stroked his white hair with tears in her eyes, a loveliness about her. The same loveliness Ruby and Gracie had long ago in another life, almost.

"Come back," Little Mac was saying. "Don't die, Keb. Please don't die."

Am I dying? Dei xat googanáa. . . . I'm going to die.

He saw Kid Hugh reach over and touch James, a gesture he would have thought beyond him. James knelt and put the raven feather on Keb's chest. He held his hand. "We're here, Gramps. We're all here."

But many are there. I have to go. How strange to feel nothing and feel all things at once, to feel aglow, radiant, free, so present at the moment of absence, a time of loss. *Their loss. Of me?* Was he breathing? *Am I breathing?* Floating higher, he could see himself attached to the Old Keb below. Attached by hundreds of thin strings, some broken, others breaking, many yet to break. Strings made of memories? Regrets? He didn't know. Strings made of all the important events in his life—stories, promises, prayers. "He's still breathing," he heard Little Mac say.

No more pain. This was better than the morphine the army gave him.

Uncle Austin appeared in some vague way and said, "If this is your land, tell me your stories."

And Keb was descending now. *No. Yes. No.* Pulling him back into himself as more strings reattached. Such pain. Great Raven. He saw himself move, heard himself moan as he slipped back into what he had been, a calcified old man. No words. *Oyyee . . . such a mighty hurt.* He felt very small, pinned to the ground by the knowledge of it all. He opened his eyes and took a sharp intake of sea and sky. Little Mac was crying. James held his hand, fiercely. "Gramps, it's okay, we're here."

HOW MUCH TIME? He couldn't say. Spokes of light fell through the *seet.* The earth smelled rich, moist. Whatever vitality Old Keb had before was gone, though something else was there, something beyond defining. He was a bag of bones, more husk than human, his mouth open, finding no words. Part of him heard *Yéil* make its liquid call, as though Raven were dropping a pebble into a pool. How much time? Part of him heard the gentle birth and death of clouds. Another part heard Little Mac tell James and Kid Hugh about—what? About a thingamajig in her daypack like the one Torp had on the *Terry Mae.* She had seen it days before and thought nothing of it, until now. Until she saw Torp's. How had it gotten there, in her pack? "I didn't put it there," she said. "If Tommy put it there before we left Jinkaat, then he'd know where we've been all this time, wouldn't he? He'd be tracking us. He'd know where we are."

James and Kid Hugh looked at her, their eyes holding stones.

"Turn it off," James said.

"I did."

Raven called, insistent now. It called from the tops of the trees. Kid Hugh said to James, "You stay here with Little Mac and Keb. I'll go check the beach."

"Take Steve," James said. "Check the meadow and the old fox farm too, from a distance. Stay in the forest, for good cover."

Kid Hugh nodded and was gone.

LITTLE MAC MADE soup over their small stove. James brought a bowlful to Old Keb who sat with some effort against the great tree. "You need help with this, Gramps?"

An hour ago, yes, but not now. Things were beginning to work again. Keb got the soup down one spoonful at a time. "The canoe," he said. "Where's the canoe?"

"It's fine, Gramps. It's okay. Just rest now." James sat next to him, the rifle by his side as he sharpened a hunting knife.

"You've changed," Keb said to him.

James looked up,

"Your eyes," Keb said. "They're older."

They shone as the forest settled in around them. When James spoke, his words didn't hit Keb as much as their tone. He set the knife aside and pulled out a small rounded rock, egg-shaped, salt and pepper in composition. "Granite," he said, "from George Island. Little Mac gave it to me after Pierre gave it to her." A keepsake. Geology is more than the study of rocks, Pierre had said. It's the study of time. Keb had listened as best he could. James said the rock was made of crystals. "See? Some are black and some are white and others are orange-ish and silver. It used to be molten, this rock. It used to be magma deep in the earth. But it never burst out like lava in a volcano. That's what Pierre said. It cooled deep down, slowly, so slowly that the minerals had time to move through the magma and find each other before it hardened. They made crystals, see?" He turned the rock in his hands. "The minerals made crystals and the crystals made the rock hard."

"Crystals?" Keb heard himself say.

James nodded.

Was that it, then? We find each other, but it takes time. Things have to happen slowly, and deep down. Keb could see himself in that rock, his entire family, the light crystals, Norwegian; the dark, Tlingit. "I can't be like you," James said, as if confessing. "I can't be everything you want me to be, Gramps. I can't live your life."

Keb shook his head. He remembered a winter hunting trip with Uncle Austin when he was a small boy doing his best to follow in deep snow. "I can't walk as big as you," he complained. "You don't have to walk as big as me," Uncle Austin told him. "You just need to walk quiet." Had Keb told James that story? He needed to say so much right now, and nothing at all. Kids these days, you can't talk them into change; you have to *listen* them into change.

"You thinking about your mother?" Keb asked him.

"Yeah."

"Your Aunt Ruby, you know, she tells you what you want to hear. But your mom, she tells you what you *need* to hear. She's a good mom."

"I know."

Keb could see him thinking hard on something. "What is it?"

"My name . . . you know, my new name, Jimmy Bluefeather. It's not really a Tlingit name, is it?"

"It depends." To bestow a name was a serious matter.

"Did Mom tell you? After my accident my dad wrote me a letter, from Denver? He said he was sorry. He has a new job and a new son. He got remarried. And he hasn't touched alcohol in two years."

"That's good."

"He wants me to meet my little brother someday."

"That's good too."

"You know . . . maybe my new name is Arapaho, Jimmy Bluefeather, from my dad. Or maybe it's from my mom and dad both, part Tlingit and part Arapaho."

"And part Norwegian."

James smiled.

After a minute, Keb said, "My shoes . . . off."

James helped him take off his shoes and socks, and said, "Barefoot, eh? It's good."

"Oyyee . . . " *Barefoot. Bearfoot.*

THE HOT CHOCOLATE was ready.

Little Mac poured it into an insulated mug and was walking it over to Old Keb when she stopped, stricken. Not fifty feet away stood Charlie Gant, and behind him his brother Tommy and their sidekick, Pete Brickman, dressed in camo. Keb felt James go stiff at his side, ready to spring. He was not as quick as he used to be, with his bad leg. Keb held him back.

"Hey, Keb," Charlie said, "it's good to see you."

Keb tried to get his tongue to work.

Nobody said a thing.

"We don't mean to frighten you," Charlie added, his words measured. "We just want to show you something . . . something important." He motioned to his brother who stepped forward with a mangled piece of light metal in his hand.

"What's that?" Keb heard himself ask.

"I know what it is," James said as he climbed to his feet and hobbled forward to take the piece of metal from Tommy. "It's a D-ring used by choker-setters. This is what broke, isn't it?"

Tommy nodded and looked forlornly at Little Mac.

"You got any more hot chocolate?" Charlie asked her.

"This thing's not even steel or cast iron," James said. "It's not even titanium. It's heavy aluminum."

"Tell him, Pete," Charlie said.

"It wasn't my doing."

"Tell him, Pete."

Only then did Keb see that Pete had that stupid baseball bat, the Louisville Slugger. What'd he expect to do? Hit a homer?

Charlie said, "Pete has a confession to make, an apology. Go ahead, Pete."

Pete fired back, "You and Tommy were the ones who yanked the cable from up on the yarder."

James hobbled over to Pete and stood before him. With no apparent fear he said, "But you were the choker-setter. You weren't cutting that day, were you? You weren't down the line with a saw. You were right in front of me. You were the choker-setter and you used only one stupid aluminum D-ring to cable the logs. You should have used three at least, all of them steel or cast iron, but you only used one."

Pete froze.

Again, for a long moment nobody spoke. James turned the D-ring in his hands.

Keb was trying to get to his feet. No easy task.

Little Mac said, "Tommy, you want some hot chocolate too?"

Tommy flashed with anger. "You almost shot me with a pellet gun."

"I missed you on purpose."

"Not by much."

"By enough. I could have hit you easy."

"You hate me."

"I don't hate you, Tommy. I don't hate anybody. You taught me to play the guitar and to sing. I'll always be grateful to you for that."

Tommy's face twisted with confusion. Keb could see that he seldom heard such kind words.

Little Mac said to him, "I learned that Paul McCartney song you told me about, the reverse 'Blackbird' song."

"'Jenny Wren'? Was I right? Does he tune his guitar down a half step?"

"A full step. Some of the chords are real dissonant, but beautiful. Do you want hot chocolate?" This time Tommy nodded and mustered a small smile.

"There's more," Charlie said. "Pete and Tommy burned down your shed, Keb. They didn't mean to, but they did. They were drunk and picking up pieces of burning wood from the campfire after everybody left that night, and throwing them around like goofballs, and one broke through your window, and with all the shavings on the floor, it just exploded and really took off. They're sorry."

"I am sorry, Keb," Tommy said as he scuffed the ground with his boot, his head down.

"It was Tommy who done it," Pete said, defiantly.

"Was not."

"Was too."

Pete raised the bat and James took a step back, the mangled D-ring still in his hand. He caught his leg on a root and fell. It happened so fast, Old Keb felt himself pass through a single drop of water and into the black eye of *Yéil*.

Raven.

ANNE WAS IN the woods, forty feet away, when she saw the wolf—no, a coyote—no, a crazy stub-tailed dog charging straight at a man who raised a big baseball bat, a dog coming in from behind with blistering speed.

Pete turned but was too late. Steve hit him like a falcon and in seconds had him pinned to the ground, a mouthful of sharp teeth around his neck. Pete went pale as a mushroom.

Stuart walked into camp, picked up the bat, and helped James to his feet.

Keb blinked, and *Yéil* was gone. He heard Pete taking small rapid gulps of air, fighting back pain.

"Call off your dog," Stuart said to Kid Hugh.

Anne walked directly to Old Keb, where the Chinese girl was already kneeling at his side, holding his hand in an obvious expression of love. "Keb Wisting," Anne said, also kneeling beside him. "Stuart told me I should greet you in Tlingit, but I haven't had time to learn a greeting, or even common names, I'm sorry."

"Lyee sakoowoo saawx' ch'a tleix ee jeedax goox la hash ee koosteeyi," Keb said.

James spoke: "Gramps says 'Language is everything. If you don't know the names of things, your Tlingit way of life will drift away forever.'"

"Forever is a long time," Anne said. "I don't have any cornbread either."

Keb brightened. "Cornbread?"

"Stuart recommended that I have some cornbread for you, and venison stew, but I don't. Maybe another time. I do have a fast boat, though."

"You're the ranger . . . in the plane."

"Yes, in May, when we flew from Jinkaat to Juneau, I was the ranger in the plane, sitting next to you. I'm really not a ranger, though."

"You had sad eyes then. They aren't so sad now, that's good."

"Yes," Anne glanced at Stuart, "there's a reason for that."

"You gave me my feather," Keb told her, "after I dropped it."

"Yes."

"I still have it."

"I know. I'm glad. We don't have much time. The Marine Reserve Service has spotters on Feldspar Peak. They've probably already seen us, or our boats. Your canoe, I know you tried to sink it until tonight's low tide, but it's floating on the tide flat."

"The canoe?"

"Yes, it refuses to sink."

"Laax," Keb said. "Red cedar, from Nathan Red Otter."

"The rangers will be here soon. I have a fast boat and can take you wherever it is you want to go."

"No canoe?"

"Later, Keb. We'll take good care of your canoe. But if you want to get someplace before the authorities arrive and overmanage you, your best bet is with me."

He looked at her with eyes that had seen both sides of ninety-five years. Eyes she knew from twenty-two years ago, the most traumatic moment of her life. Eyes she trusted.

"Who are you?" the Chinese girl asked her.

"She's a whale biologist," James said, "and a good boat handler."

bring the children

"C AN'T THIS THING go any faster?" James said with a mischievous grin.

"It's a whale research boat," Anne told him. "Whales go five knots or so. We're doing twenty-four. You ever seen a whale go twenty-four knots?"

"Orcas, maybe."

"They're big dolphins, not whales."

"They're killer whales."

"They're big dolphins."

"They have the wrong name, then."

"Lots of things have the wrong name."

"He's teasing you," Little Mac said to Anne. "It's really good of you to give us this ride. Thank you." She elbowed James in the ribs.

"Yeah, thanks," James said, as he pushed Little Mac back affectionately.

Anne smiled, thinking: this Mackenzie Chen, alluring but not fragile, her long hair beneath a black beret. No wonder James fell for her, the way she leans into the morning and attends to Old Keb. *Was I ever so confident, beautiful, and kind?*

They were headed east in Icy Strait, between Lemesurier Island and Point Carolus. The entire world would soon be on them: rangers, newspeople, boats from all over, people wanting to help but getting in the way. Anne knew that wherever they were going—wherever Keb decided to go—they needed to get ahead of everybody. In a few minutes they would make the turn north into Crystal Bay, if that's what Keb wanted. Anne watched the old man sit low in a chair on the aft deck.

"Where to, Gramps?" James asked again.

The wind whipped Keb's white hair. He put his face into it and let his one good eye drink in the dawn. He had his shoes off, toes pointed to the sky, the feather in one hand, three yellow cedar paddles across his lap. "Sít'," he said. Anne watched Mackenzie sit beside the old man. Keb gestured with the feather, "Sít' . . . sít'."

"I am sitting, Keb," Little Mac said.

"No, sít', sít'."

"The glacier," James said. "That's it, isn't it, Gramps? *Sít'* is Tlingit for glacier?"

Keb nodded. *The glacier, yes, the ice of my youth.*

"North," James said to Anne. "He wants to go up the bay."

They passed Point Carolus and began a long turn into Crystal Bay. Anne could see boats at a distance, many others on her radar. Dozens. Maybe fifty to a hundred boats clustered around the entrance to the bay, and in Bartlett Cove. Any moving to intercept her? But how could they? She'd just go around them. It's a big ocean, a wide bay, a free country. Stuart had said he would give her an hour before he called into Bartlett Cove about apprehending Tommy Gant and Pete Brickman, wanted for arson; one hour before the task force would know what happened in Dundas Bay. Kid Hugh had stayed behind to offer assistance. Steve, too, Deputy Dog.

"Go," Stuart had said to Anne and Keb. "Go do what you have to do."

It pained Anne to leave him behind.

As they moved north past Point Carolus, she could see boats heading out from Bartlett Cove, five miles or so to the east, and more boats behind those. She checked her radar. "They can follow us and even flank us," she said, "but they can't stop us."

"We got enough fuel?" James asked.

"To get us to the glacier, yes, but back? I'm not sure."

James pointed toward Point Carolus, now off their port quarter. "That's where I heard the whales sing."

"We're going to have to talk about that someday," Anne said, thinking, when I'm unemployed, next week, maybe tomorrow. She looked at Old Keb, who kept his face into the wind. He seemed both far away and present, deep in the moment. Mackenzie held his hand. The sea was flat calm over a flooding tide, the entire bay, a painting, a watercolor. A low September sunrise hit golden cottonwoods that shone like candles. Distant peaks stood at ease with new snow below a rosy glow. Seabirds busied themselves everywhere—murrelets, scoters, phalaropes, guillemots, gulls.

"How'd you know how to find us?" James asked Anne. "Back there in the woods, in Dundas Bay?"

"If I told you it was a raven would you believe me?"

"Yes."

"It wasn't. It was an emergency location transmitter in your canoe."

James stared at her, his mouth open in surprise.

"Stuart put it there before you left Jinkaat."

"Are you serious?"

"Yep."

"That Stuart," James said in wonder. "He's full of surprises."

"Yes, he is."

ANNE TURNED ON the VHF radio and got a barrage of hails. First from Ron, then Paul, then a voice she didn't recognize, each calling the *Firn* on channel sixteen. She turned it off. She had to think. She could call Taylor on Taylor's cell; hear a friendly voice, find out what's going on. But that could get Taylor in trouble for conspiring with a rogue ranger, a runaway biologist. Anne throttled back.

"What are you doing?" James asked.

"Slowing down."

"Why?"

Anne turned on the radio, channel sixteen, and announced, "All vessels in Crystal Bay, this is the NMRS research vessel *Firn*. You're now in 'whale waters' and are required to travel mid-channel and no faster than thirteen knots. Please slow down."

A spotter plane flew by at five hundred feet, circled, and passed over again. A helicopter ripped in from the east, probably from Strawberry Flats. It hovered off Anne's starboard bow, pacing her, a TV cameraman shooting out the open door. Anne saw Old Keb put his hands to his ears. Off her stern, an armada followed. Maybe it was time to smoke the joint. She asked James, "Are the other boats gaining on us?"

"No, I don't think so."

"So they're pacing us?"

"Yeah."

The NMRS patrol vessel *Esker II* hailed her on channel sixteen. She answered, and Ron requested that she switch to her satellite phone. She did. "Anne, what are you doing? Where are you going?"

"I'm taking Keb Wisting up the bay."

"Up the bay? Where up the bay?"

"Up the bay, Ron. Just up the bay. I need to talk to Paul."

"Stand by."

Ten seconds later. "Anne, this is Paul. Are you okay?"

"I'm fine."

"Look, we just spoke to Deputy Stuart Ewing. We're glad you're safe. We need you to stop so we can make sure Keb is okay, medically. He doesn't have his pills for his heart and other things. He hasn't had them for days. He could be in danger. We have EMS here on the *Esker II* to take care of him." Paul paused, to allow Anne time to respond. She made no reply. "Anne, a lot of people here are concerned. We know Keb was involved in stealing a plane and some radios and other electronics. We also know the plane was found undamaged, and the owners of the yacht are not interested in pressing any charges. We know about the apprehended arson suspects in Dundas Bay. We've sent personnel over there. We know you're just trying to help Old Keb. We want to help him too, make sure he's safe and well. We'll put him on the *Esker II*, give him his medicine, make sure he's okay, and run him up the bay if he's well enough, if that's what he wants. We've got his daughter Ruby here on board. She needs to see him. She needs to talk to him."

Anne looked at James and Keb. The old man was rocking with his head down, his hands over his ears as the media chopper paced them, making a racket. James shook his head and motioned Anne forward, onward, north to the glacier. "I'm continuing on this course and speed, Paul. Keb Wisting is fine. He's with his grandson. I'm asking that you give them a little more time together. Give them some privacy, some space. And get this damn helicopter to back off."

Anne could hear Paul speaking to others, but couldn't get the words. Finally Paul said with exasperation, "Anne, look, you're creating mayhem with all these other boats following you, entering a marine reserve without permits. You have to listen. Stand by. . . ."

"Anne, this is Gary Hoffman, chief ranger of the National Marine Reserve Service in Washington, D.C., and incident commander of this task force. You need to stand down. You're creating a dangerous situation with dozens of boats illegally entering this bay and pursuing you."

"They're not pursuing me."

"Yes they are."

"No they're not. They're following me, maintaining course and speed. I can track them on radar. Are you pursuing me? If you are, you're going too fast. These are whale waters."

"Listen, I'm ordering you to stand down. Put your vessel in neutral and—"

She turned off the satellite phone. A minute later the helicopter retreated. Old Keb lifted his head and opened his ears. Anne said to James, "I think they got the point."

But they didn't. Minutes later the helicopter returned, with the same goofy cameraman hanging out the door, pacing the boat at thirteen knots. Anne unlatched a cabinet next to her, pulled out her NMRS rifle, a 30.06, and handed it to James.

"You want me to shoot them?"

"It's unloaded. You could bolt it back, open the chamber, and stand out on the open deck so they see you. Shoulder the rifle and take aim at them. Mackenzie could use that Lumix camera to photograph you and make sure the picture clearly shows the bolt is back and the chamber open."

"No," Little Mac said. "James could still get in big trouble for that, for aiming any rifle at a helicopter. Have you got a flare gun?"

"Yes."

"Use that."

A minute later James stepped out on deck and took aim. Little Mac got the photo, and the helicopter peeled away. James laughed and said to Anne, "Are all whale biologists as crazy as you?"

"No. I'm the only crazy one." *Stupid white woman, soon to be unemployed.* "Keep that flare gun handy, in case they come back."

"Why the photograph?" Little Mac asked.

"To show it was just a flare gun, at our trial. You know, to keep us out of jail."

THE OTHER BOATS kept their distance, fifty or more from what Anne could tell. Not only were they following; they were forming up in single file, making a boat train. And not just government boats but boats carrying half the townspeople from Jinkaat. Maybe *all* the townspeople from Jinkaat. And from other places too. Anne asked James to take the wheel. "Don't hit anything," she told him.

"Like an iceberg?"

"Or a rock." She told him to put the Marble Islands off his starboard at half a mile, and make a heading up the West Arm. At Geikie Rock, turn ten degrees north, and off Blue Mouse Cove, another ten degrees north. It's all on waypoints entered into the GPS. After that, stay mid-channel up the east side of Russell Island, past Tea Cup Harbor and up Tarr Inlet to the glacier. "You got that?"

"Yep."

"Watch for whales."

"Yep."

"Good man." Anne pulled out the joint and lit it. She took a drag and held it . . . took another drag and was soon stoned. She sat down next to Keb and said, "I think my career with the National Marine Reserve Service just ended. You want a hit?" Keb nodded. She handed him the joint. This startled Mackenzie, Anne could see. A plane flew high overhead, circled to the north, and flew over again.

Keb fumbled the joint in his bent fingers but got it to his lips and took a small puff, thinking about Angola. *Will I ever see him again?* And Marge on the *Silverbow*? He coughed on the joint.

Anne took it back and said, "Maui Wowie. It's the number one cash crop in Hawaii and it's illegal. Men can get fall-down drunk on whiskey and beer and ruin their lives and their families and never get arrested. But I can't smoke this joint." Keb studied her: the burnished hair and long fingers. Somebody told him once that gray eyes meant wisdom. Or was it blue eyes? This woman had both, eyes gray-blue, the color of late winter, early spring, the last patch of snow. "Why are you doing this?" he asked her. "Why are you giving us this ride?"

"I don't know. I never had a real father, or a grandfather."

Mackenzie thanked Anne again for the ride, for helping Keb.

"Everybody else is worried about his heart medicine," Anne said, "and I'm getting him stoned."

"You study whales?" Keb asked her.

"Yes."

"You have stories about whales?"

"Yes, many."

"That's good. Stories are medicine, you know, small doses of good things. When you tell them . . . the stories, they release the medicine."

The next thing Anne knew, she was telling stories. Stories that ran together in no set order, stories of her mom and Nancy, of boats and whales. She told about a humpback that was struck and killed by a cruise ship. "More than one hundred volunteers cleaned the bones and helped to rearticulate the skeleton for a new outdoor pavilion in Bartlett Cove. That's what they call it, you know, when you put a skeleton back together, you 'rearticulate' it. As if it can speak."

Keb had to agree with her, whatever it was she said.

He felt airy, elevated, serene.

"When the pavilion was finished and the whale was mounted," Anne added, "it got a Tlingit blessing that was very powerful. My friend Taylor told me about it."

Yes, Keb knew of this. He had wanted to attend the opening ceremony, but could not, for reasons he couldn't remember. Distant events were more vivid than recent ones. He told Anne that many years ago, after he and Uncle Austin would catch the first salmon of spring, a big king, they would share it with family and friends, mostly elders, and put the bones back on shore in thankfulness, near where the fish had been caught. "That salmon had a story, too. It gave us a lot." Keb spoke about the yellow cedar canoe paddles, how Kevin Pallen made them to go far, so far that the moon exhausted itself and the stars made no sense. "The paddles are perfect, you see, the points and the ribs and the shapes of the blades that make them good to go, good to hunt. Fast and quiet." He handed her one. She admired it and handed it back. "No," he said. "It's for you."

"I can't accept this," Anne said.

"You must," Little Mac told her with an earnest look. "You must, it's a gift."

Keb said, "My people had many names for Crystal Bay. One name reaching back to when Great Raven created it. Another from when the glacier came. Another from when the glacier left and the bay was reborn. Names for rivers and coves, good places to hunt and fish and pick berries. Oyyee—places to fall in love." He pointed to starboard and said, "Over there is Xóots Xh'oosi X'aa, Brown Bear Paw Point. Good memories. Makes me feel at home again." He offered Anne a second paddle and said, "Do you know the fisherwoman?"

"Who?"

"Marge, the fisherwoman who gave us a ride. She was good to us. She made good cornbread. You need to give her this for me, if you can. Can you?"

Little Mac said, "I'll get it to her, Gramps. She told me she often spends her winters in Seattle. I'll find her down there."

"Now you only have one," Anne said to him. "One paddle."

"Yes, one . . ." His voice trailed off as he lost himself in the mountains, their flanks rising higher as the *Firn* approached the glacier.

James said from the helm, "There's a million people following us, Gramps. A line of boats as far as I can see, a bunch of them from Jinkaat, I think."

Keb said, "Tell them to bring the children, at yátx'i."

to die we must forget,
but also be forgotten

ANNE FOUND HERSELF falling through memory to a time when her mother took her and Nancy to a zoo in California to eat ice cream and look at curious creatures and lose themselves in other worlds. She remembered how people said the zoo animals were lucky because they lived longer in cages than they did in the wild, how that was good, as if any price, even captivity, was worth living longer. Is that why she and Nancy grew up to admire whales in the wild, off Auke Bay and Shelter Island, whales dancing in the sea? Living and dying free?

"You rescued me, long ago," Anne said to Keb. "My sister and me, off Shelter Island, in a storm. We capsized and you came along and pulled us out of the water."

Old Keb stared at her.

"Do you remember?"

"Your sister died."

"Yes."

"That was you?"

"Yes."

"Where have you been?"

"Hawaii."

"Oyyee . . . nice place."

"Not as nice as here. Not as wild."

"No glaciers."

"No, no glaciers."

"Your sister . . ."

"Her name was Nancy. She had given me the better life jacket that day. She was older than me. She always wore cotton skirts with bright flowers and believed in everybody. My stepfather left home after she died; he never came back."

"Maybe he was brokenhearted," Little Mac said.

"Maybe." Anne shrugged. "I guess you have to give your family permission to be imperfect, don't you? Otherwise you go insane."

Yes, Keb thought, *imperfect, even terribly flawed.*

"You don't remember me, then?" Anne said to Old Keb.

"I remember you. You were a little girl."

"I was eight."

"You were small."

"Yes."

"You were also big. I knew you'd be okay."

"You did? How?"

"Your mother. She was strong. I remember her. You remind me of her. You're all grown up now."

"In some ways I am. In other ways I'm not."

"My two daughters, my girls, Ruby and Gracie, they're sisters and they're hard on each other."

"Nancy was my only sister."

"She'd be proud of you today," Mackenzie said.

"Would she? I'm not so sure. I'm about to get fired from a really good job. Maybe I could be a poet, or a community activist, or a whale biologist in Kansas. Do they have whale biologists in Kansas?"

THE GLACIER WAS still there, made of crystals, flowing into the sea.

Keb watched Anne take the helm and navigate through thousands of glittering pieces of floating ice—sunlight dancing off each one—until their boat was half a mile from the glacier's massive tidewater face.

"Tsaa," Keb said quietly. Seal.

"I don't see any, Gramps." James scanned the ice for harbor seals. Mother seals gave birth to their pups on the ice, near tidewater glaciers, in early June.

Keb climbed to his feet, with Little Mac's help, and listened.

Anne killed the engine to let everything go quiet. Not silent. Nature is never silent. But without noise, that's the trick, the hunter's way.

"We hunted seal," Keb said. He could see Uncle Austin's features in beautiful detail, the hands and eyes of a hunter, a teacher.

The glacier tumbled down the mountain in deep crevasses and tall towers, now and then giving up parts of itself with cracks and rumbles, calving icy shards into the bay as it did when Keb was a boy. Look how it stands in defiance of a warming world. Keb knew then as he'd always known: *Glaciers give us ice, and ice gives us seal.* Oyyee . . . thinking about seal steaks made his mouth water. Yesterday was every day, not a billion Coca-Colas ago. It was ice and rock, the brisk air of youth, when Keb's mind was sharp as a whetted knife and he felt capable of anything, even greatness. Men talk about change, how everything must change, how it's inevitable, and so they bring about change with their own greed, seeing only what they want to see. But do they themselves ever change? These men? Maybe one day, in the presence of something like this.

Keb watched James and Little Mac sit on the gunwale with their legs over the side, facing the glacier, laughing in the icy air, Anne too, their eyes filled with all things possible. James had his shoes and shirt off, the feather on his bare chest. Seeing it filled Keb with feelings beyond words. He recalled Uncle Austin, shoeless in a bay of new beginnings long ago, how he would bathe in icy water and drink the sky and say to young Keb, "You see, nephew, we leave open space because we are small and not certain. We leave room to learn."

BOATS APPROACHED. KEB saw Ruby and Coach Nicks and other people on the bow of the *Esker II*, and tall Paul Beals, not so tall against the glacier. More boats came near, and more after that, and still more—some government boats that Keb didn't recognize, and others he did, many others: the *No Way*, with Oddmund and Dag and a million friends, and Corey Blaines in his apple crate of a skiff, and many other skiffs, and Mitch and Irene, of all people, on their runabout, *Harrd Tymes*, with the bumper sticker: "Norwejun Speling Champyun," and Truman and Crazy Daisy with her cribbage board and cherry red lipstick, and Carmen Kelly with her horrorscope, and Vic and Galley Sally with her peanut butter cookies, and Trinidad Salazar with his inflatable puffin, and Myrtle the chicken wrangler who boasted that she could win one of every three games of solitaire but only after she'd been struck by lightning. It wasn't easy being a chicken wrangler, she said. You had to wear the right expression; wear it wrong, and the chickens won't lay eggs. And who should be on Reverend Billings's boat but none other than Harald Halmerjan, the great H. H., and next to him the news lady, Tanya-What's-Her-Toes, and her sidekick cameraman. Albert Bestow was there with Brad Freer on the *Call Me Fishmael*. Big Terry McNamee had Father Danes on his boat, the good father with a cross in his hand, and Helen Pasternak, who must have closed things down at the Rumor Mill Café. And there on the stern was the young carver, Keb's friend Kevin Pallen.

"Hey, Keb," Oddmund yelled, "you still alive?"

The boats moved in and circled the *Firn*. And more boats after that, boats from everywhere. Lots of kids. Many of James's basketball teammates. People holding signs: "Paddle On," "Let Him Go," "Keb Ain't Dead," and Keb's favorite: "We Are Still Here." Keb waved. James stood next to him with his hand on Keb's shoulder. People would say later that Keb looked timeless then. People shouted greetings:

"Good to see you, Keb."

"You got your shoes off?"

"We brought nagoonberry pie."

"And cornbread."

"Hey, Keb, you rock."

"We love you, Keb."

"Did you really steal a plane?"

"Where you been?"

"Does the feather really do magic, like brush your teeth and do your taxes?"

"We missed you."

"It's good to see you, Keb."

"Tell a story."

And still more boats arrived, boats from Jinkaat, Haines, Juneau, Sitka, Elfin Cove, Hawk Inlet, and Excursion Inlet. Keb saw Warren Master-carver on a Bayliner pulling a canoe, not any canoe, but a *gudiyé*, a seal hunting canoe from Yakutat designed for moving through ice-choked waters. Hunters of the Kwaaski'kwaan/K'ineixkwaan clan, House of the Owl, sons of the Coho Salmon and Brown Bear clans, they would wear white when they paddled that canoe, to blend in, fool the seals, sneak up close.

Nathan Red Otter? Is he here?

And now Keb could see other canoes tied off the sterns of large boats, people getting into them and waving, holding up adzes, young people and elders wrapped in Chilkat blankets and beating drums, representing maybe a dozen clans. "We are still here," they chanted.

So many canoes of clever design: *jaakúx*, made of caribou skins; *ch'iyaash*, flat-bottomed canoes for traveling upriver; *l'áakw*, old worn-out canoes that needed work but still floated true. How many? How many canoes?

"Gunalchéesh," Keb said as he waved and everybody closed in around him like so many petals of a single flower.

"Gunalchéesh," they replied, waving. Thank you. "Gunalchéesh."

"Nathan Red Otter?" Keb said to James. "Ask Warren if Nathan Red Otter is here?"

James did, and Warren replied that Nathan wasn't well but was expected to get better soon, and would visit Keb then.

The *Esker II* came alongside and Anne threw out lines. Standing on the bow, Ruby put out a hand. Keb didn't take it, but James did. She stepped nimbly over the bow rail and onto the *Firn* and embraced her father and nephew. She looked about and for the first time in sixteen years acknowledged Little Mac. Tears stood in her eyes. "You okay, Pops?"

"I'm good."

"We have an emergency medical technician with us if you need him."

"I'm good."

"We have your medicine."

"I'm good."

"Pops, Gracie's in the hospital. She's really sick. She needs a new kidney."

Keb felt his mouth go dry. *Kidney? Do we have one of those, or two?*

"If she doesn't get one soon, she'll die. She's asking about you. She wants to see you. You, too, James."

"I want to see her," James said.

"Kidney," Keb said, "from where?"

"Well . . ." Ruby lowered her head and seemed to compose herself, then raised her eyes to her father, "from me, Pops."

"You? You would do that for her?"

"She's my sister."

Anne caught her breath.

As more boats circled up, people joined hands and reached out boat-to-boat over open water, thirty, sixty, one hundred, two hundred people, joining hands. Where they couldn't reach hand-to-hand they threw lines and held tight and pulled until every boat was near and connected, and nobody was alone. And still more boats came, and more after that, throwing lines, joining hands, pulling, waving.

"Tell a story, Keb."

"Please, Keb."

The glacier calved no ice and held still, as if to listen. Ruby squeezed her father's hand. "I think it's time for a story, Pops. You okay with that?"

The old man looked at James and said, "Let it go."

Everybody watched as James pulled the necklace off his bare chest, untied the raven feather, held it over the water, and placed it among pieces of floating ice, the children of the glacier.

Uncle Austin used to say the Tlingit sang and danced and dreamed the world into creation. Not long ago, everything was how it ought to be, and could be again, when mighty canoes arrived six abreast at a potlatch, the paddles dipping ever so gently. As they approached, the chiefs, dressed in their wooden helmets and blankets, stood in the sterns to speak about their families. Listening on shore, the host would emerge by hopping out of his house sideways to imitate the motions of an eagle before perching on a high rock and moving his head side to side, his feet bare beneath caribou skin trousers, a white eagle tail feather in each hand.

Keb took a deep breath. All eyes were on him. For the first time in a long time, he didn't feel old. He was young, with everything before him. Mountains, forests, rivers, and the sea. The ongoing creation of the world. Was any part of it—any single moment—ever without wisdom, guardianship, and grace? And always the glaciers, great carvers in their own right, shapers of the land, not as many as before, but . . .

We are still here.

To tell a story was no small thing; you had to have both permission and authority.

And so Keb nodded to his ancestors, and acknowledged the elders around him, and sons and daughters of elders, their clans and houses. He couldn't remember some names, so asked that they announce themselves, which they did, with thanks. Paul Beals assigned one of his rangers to afix a small, portable microphone to Keb, and set two speakers atop the *Firn*. All while other elders paid their respects and gave more thanks.

"Gunalchéesh."

"Go ahead and talk for as long as you'd like, Keb," Paul said. "These are your people. This is your place."

Keb filled his lungs and began, first in Tlingit, then English. "This is not my story . . ." More boats drifted in, engines off, people listening. "It comes from the long ago time, the ice time. It's a story my Uncle Austin used to tell me, and his uncle told him, and his uncle's uncle told him. 'Two hunters were coming home from over the glacier, the glacier that made this bay. . . .'"

KEB FINISHED, BUT his voice still filled Anne's heart. A couple hours passed as others told stories, visited, shared food, and took photos. Soon, more than one hundred boats headed south, again in single file, at thirteen knots. Here and there they doubled up or ran three abreast as people visited boat-to-boat, and laughed, and told more stories. Anne had only one word for it: Magic.

Chief Ranger Gary Hoffman, the task force incident commander from Washington, confiscated her rifle and flare gun, and piloted the *Firn* back to Bartlett Cove. He had nothing to say. It was obvious how he felt: this entire fiasco was her fault, all these non-permitted motorized vessels in the bay, the mayhem and recklessness, the paperwork for weeks, maybe months, explanations on top of excuses on top of apologies. Paul rode with them and told Anne he understood, he truly did; he'd do everything he could to give her a break. His evaluation of her would make interesting reading. Ron gave her a sympathetic nod. Maybe she'd get work in a marine lab somewhere, cleaning petri dishes in Patagonia, testing test tubes in Texas, mopping floors in Florida. Maybe she'd winter in Alaska, teach Stuart how to make good coffee, or better bad coffee.

Off the entrance to Bartlett Cove, the *Esker II* came alongside the *Firn*, escorting Keb, Ruby, James, and Little Mac back to Jinkaat. Keb waved and Anne waved back, knowing she might never see him again, knowing too what it was to be privileged, a witness to what can happen. Not until Keb was out of sight did she reach for her journal.

> To have a father like this
> a daughter could believe
> not in greatness or fate
> for that it's too late
> but simple things
> steady things
> a strength
> in surrender
> a wooden boat
> a photograph
> of you
> in flowers and cotton
> To die we must forget
> but also be forgotten.

PART FOUR

we are each other

WHEN JAMES WHEELED Keb into her room, she was sleeping.

But where? *Where is she?*

Keb was too low in his wheelchair. He couldn't find her. There were too many gadgetgizmos and thingamajigs and plastic tubes and shiny metal rails all around her bed. Too many metal rings and things and soft beeping sounds and nurses moving in and out, friendly in their blue shirts, blue pants, and blue eyes. When Keb finally did find her, her size alarmed him. She was too small, too frail. Her color wasn't right. He reached for her—the only thing he knew how to do—and put his hand on hers. She had never been frail before. Never this small. She had always been feisty and fit.

She was sleeping now. Yes, sleeping. That's good. Everything will be okay.

Robert and Lorraine were there. They announced that they were going out to get Chinese take-out: kung pung shrimp, ping pong pork, hong kong fish, king kong beef, something like that. Keb didn't care. Actually, he did care. Egg rolls would be nice. He liked egg rolls and soy sauce. And "death by chocolate" and "killer vaniller" ice cream. "Get some of that too, if you can, for me and little Christopher."

Christopher was not so little anymore. He played a good game of checkers. In their last game alone he had triple-jumped Keb twice. Lorraine said he would play chess one day, be a champion. Robert's new job at Coca-Cola had him working seventy hours a week, projecting sales, selling projections, something like that. Lorraine said they missed California.

James and Little Mac decided to go with Robert and Lorraine. They had spent all day in the hospital in Ruby and Gracie's rooms, and wanted a break. "Will you be okay here alone, Gramps?"

The old man nodded. He wheeled himself to the window and watched traffic on the big freeway. The window was cracked open. He drank the cool air. He could hear the sour, persistent drone of a siren, and closer, the music of boys playing basketball on a concrete court next to the hospital. They moved like gazelles, like the basketball artists in Jinkaat. Then what? Did he wheel back to Ruby's bed and fall asleep? Yes, he must have, with his head against her bed. When he awoke, golden light was spilling into the room. Keb looked up. His daughter was awake.

"Pops," she said weakly.

"Ruby."

She reached over and touched his arm, her hand not talonlike as before, just a hand. "What are you doing here?"

"Seeing you."

"You don't like Seattle."

Keb said nothing. On the *Etude*, off George Island, Angola had asked him whose life he was going to save. Oyyee . . . *how do you answer a question like that?*

"I'm like you now," Ruby said. "I have only one kidney."

Keb rubbed her arm.

"How's Gracie?" Ruby asked.

"She's good."

"You've seen her?"

"Not yet."

"You came to see me first?" Ruby turned her face away. When she turned back she looked as though she wanted to say something beyond reach. "Is James here?"

"He went with the others to get dinner. He goes by Jimmy now."

"Jimmy?"

A nurse breezed in and out.

Ruby said with some effort, "You know, Pops, you and I could sneak out of here and go eat dinner in the hospital cafeteria. Green Jell-O. Purple potato salad."

They shared a laugh.

"I get to see Christopher again tonight," Keb said. He loved the magical boy who was missing a chromosome or had one chromosome too many, something like that; the boy who smiled as deeply as a smile could go. In Keb's mind, he, Keb, would always be old and Christopher young. Maybe it's not what we have that makes us who we are, it's what we're missing. A chromosome, a kidney, a sister, a feather, a bay.

"You're in a wheelchair," Ruby said.

"For a while, until my legs get better."

"Your legs?" Ruby attempted to shift in her bed.

Keb watched her wince. He wished he could do something for her. "Does it hurt?"

"No," she lied.

Another nurse came in and adjusted her pillows to make her more comfortable.

Ruby closed her eyes and fell asleep.

The others returned with dinner, along with Günter and Josh. Keb let go of Ruby's hand to eat his egg rolls. They all watched *Wheel of Fortune* and *Jeopardy*.

"Gramps, you have to make your answer a question."

Keb asked Little Mac to roll him to the window. The lights of the city were up, and beautiful. Above, Keb could barely make out the brightest stars. Down below, the basketball boys shuffled over their court, shooting through hoops without nets. One boy in particular caught Keb's attention, how he moved with boldness and grace, artfully floating his jump shots.

"He's good," James said, suddenly at Keb's side.

"Yes."

"He moves better to his left than he does to his right."

"Yes, and the others know that."

"I miss it, Gramps."

"Basketball?"

"No, the wind and the sea and the canoe and the whole thing. Being out there, it's so real. I mean, sometimes I didn't even know where we were going."

"Neither did I."

"The nights were amazing."

"Yes, ax tòowoo kligéi ee kàa-x, I'm proud of you."

"Me?"

"You learned the language."

"No, I have a long ways to go."

"Not Tlingit, the other language, older than Tlingit. The oldest language of all."

"I don't understand."

"You will. One day."

"I've been thinking about my name."

"Grandmothers give us our names, but your grandmothers passed on to the great spirits before you were born."

"Do you remember Anne, the whale biologist who gave us the ride to the glacier? She said many things have the wrong names."

"Your mother changed her name back to Wisting after she divorced your father. That was good. She changed your name back to Wisting, too."

"I'm glad she did."

"It's Norwegian."

"I've been thinking that maybe my Tlingit name—"

"Bluefeather," Keb said. "X̱'eishx'w yax T'aaw. That's your new name, your Tlingit name, as of today. I'm giving it to you now. Is that what you want?"

"Yes, Gramps . . . thanks. It's another way of being alive, isn't it? In a canoe. A better way, I think . . . I don't know. Everything made sense out there."

"X'éigaa át," Keb said without explanation.

"The canoe pulled to the left a little, don't you think?"

"Yes."

"I'll bet if we reworked the keel line we could correct it, using small adzes."

"Yes."

"Anyway, Gramps . . . we're going down the hall, Little Mac and me, to see Mom."

"Yes . . . good. Tell her you love her."

"You want to stay here with Aunt Ruby, or come with us?"

"Stay."

WHEN RUBY AWOKE, Keb was at her side. She asked for water and he managed to move the drinking cup close enough for her to reach the straw. "You see those flowers?" she said, motioning toward the largest bouquet on the table. "They're from Paul Beals. Can you believe it?"

Keb believed it.

"Actually, the card is signed by Paul and his entire staff. And that card there, see, the one with the whales on it? It's from the woman who gave you the ride to the glacier."

"Oh?" Keb tried to find the card among all the others. He said, "She isn't a ranger anymore. She's in Jinkaat with Stuart Ewing."

"Stuart and the woman whale ranger? Really? You got any more gossip?"

"Not me, but Helen does." At the Rumor Mill Café.

Ruby grinned. "You used a canoe to steal an airplane. That's funny."

"It is?"

"Yes. It's funny and crazy and brilliant and a whole bunch of other things."

"Stuart and Truman say a judge will probably order the kids to do community service, for stealing the plane and the radios."

"Tell the judge that all those people coming together at the glacier was a pretty good show of community. Thank you for that, Pops . . . Gunalchéesh."

"I wish Gracie could have been there."

"And Mom. She would have hugged you to pieces."

"Ruby, you have to get well and come home. We're going to bless the canoe next week, in Mitch's Garage. Lots of food. Smoked coho, nagoonberry pie. Oddmund and Dag are cleaning it up good, the canoe. We're going to paint it and carve clan crests on the bow. Make it look real nice. Nathan Red Otter will be there this time, and Father Mikal. I want you there, too, for the blessing. I brought you the last paddle. It's for you. The one Kevin made, over there, on the table, by the flowers, see?"

"For me?"

With great effort Keb rolled himself over to the table, put the paddle on his lap, and rolled back. "Yes, for you." He put the paddle on Ruby's bed and gave her his hand, and was surprised by the strength she used to pull him to her, such strength that he rose from his wheelchair and found her, his first child, small in his arms. He cradled her and could hear her breathing, the little girl she used to be. He remembered loving her for her bewilderment, all those years ago, her face wet with tears, her spirit—like the spirits of so many others—caught between two worlds then and still today. "You didn't have to do this, Ruby, for your sister. You didn't have to, but I'm glad you did."

"We are each other, Pops. You told me that once, remember? You, me, Gracie, all of us. We are each other."

"Yes."

"I did it because I wanted to. Do you believe me?"

"I believe you."

"I've always tried to do the right thing."

"I know, Ruby. Don't be angry and resentful, okay? It steals your soul. Everything's not going to be the way you want it to be. It's okay. Give it time. You're too beautiful to be angry."

"Oh, Pops." She held him fiercely and he held her and in the holding Old Keb knew what Angola had meant. It wasn't Ruby's life he had saved. It wasn't James's life, or Gracie's life.

It was his own.

EPILOGUE

Seven years later

a choice nobody gets to make

KID HUGH MOVED the forklift forward with the massive central beam balanced on the wide tines. Mitch directed him with hand motions while everybody moved out of the way. "Higher, okay, higher still . . . good, now a little to your left, more, good . . . good . . . okay, now forward, forward . . . stop . . . now, down . . . slowly, slowly. . . . "

As the central beam eased into place atop the end posts, teams of carpenters, all volunteers, shimmed the joints, set in the wooden plugs, and went to work placing in the mortise-and-tenon hip rafters and jack rafters.

"Once the rafters are in," Jimmy explained to Anne, we can start laying down the two-by-eight, tongue-and-groove red cedar."

"Not a single nail?" Anne asked Jimmy.

"Nope. Canoes don't need nails, neither do carving sheds."

"It's really not a shed, is it? It's more like a shop, or an art studio."

"Hey, Jimmy," Truman yelled, "you got the bevel square?"

"Albert's got it."

"It's next to Vic's chop saw," Albert yelled.

"Look at you, Truman," Vic said. "You've got a real job. You're going to ruin your reputation."

"This isn't a job, Vic. It's a hobby. I'm doing this for fun. So are you."

"Hey, Anne," Dag yelled, "Oddmund and I put a kroner under the end posts, you know, for good luck. Keb would have liked that, don't you think?"

Anne smiled. She did that often these days.

"Where's lunch?"

"It's coming."

Anne was torn. She wanted to be here and watch the shed go up, four walls raised in a single day, forty people working together. She also wanted to be at the airport where Stuart and little Nancy were due after a week away, visiting his family down south. He had called to say that he'd see her at the shed. His sheriff's rig was at the airport; he'd drive straight to the construction site. "You've worked for years on the fund-raising for this," he'd told her. "Stay. Watch it go up."

This was her day, everybody's day, a major construction day of the new "Keb Shed."

"Here comes Ruby," yelled Big Terry McNamee, as he put down his Skilsaw.

The one-ton Dodge rumbled up the hog-backed road and stopped in the clearing, halfway between Ruby's house and the site of the new carving shed, where the old one used to be, its charred remains hauled away years ago. Ruby got out with ten pizzas. Kevin Pallen got out with two cases of root beer. Stiff-legged with arthritis, Steve the Lizard Dog got out and followed the pizza.

Everybody stopped to eat, and to pet Steve.

"Thanks, Ruby," somebody said.

"I didn't pay for these," she said. "Anne did."

They all understood. The money came from the nonprofit Anne had created. Nearly on her own, she'd written a mission statement and business plan, assembled a board, gotten nonprofit status, and raised half a million dollars to rebuild the shed and make it the "Keb Wisting Jinkaat Community Arts Center," where local kids and adults and visiting artists would express themselves through carving, basketry, weaving, music, and who knows what else. Anne might one day rearticulate a humpback whale skeleton, or teach poetry, with help from Truman. PacAlaska had offered fifty thousand dollars; Anne accepted one thousand dollars for the high school shop class to build a mini-canoe for the preschool playground. The rest of the money came mostly from private donations, some anonymous, one from France, another from New Orleans. She'd raised the full amount in ten months.

"Hey, Ruby," Vic said, always pushing buttons, "I just heard that Pac-Alaska considered buying a bird shit fertilizer company in Peru."

"I didn't vote for it."

"But it's true?"

"It's true. Why don't you stuff a little more pizza in that big mouth of yours, Vic."

People laughed.

Gracie drove into the clearing with Helen and Myrtle. They pulled out three large bowls of fresh green salad, all from local gardens, topped with nasturtium flowers. Myrtle had fancied up the salads with strips of Cajun blackened chicken and smoked salmon.

Anne kept checking her watch.

"They'll be here soon, honey," Helen said. "I heard a plane land just minutes ago. I'll bet they're on it."

"Hey, sis," Gracie said to Ruby. "We just heard on the radio that PacAlaska put a bid on a guano factory in Peru."

More laughter.

"I voted against it," Ruby said.

"Good," Truman quipped.

"You realize of course," Ruby said, "that if we can't get into our home-land in Crystal Bay and make a decent profit there, then we have to go somewhere else."

Nobody took the bait, though Anne could see Truman was tempted. PacAlaska lost the Crystal Bay Ninth Circuit case by a 6-3 vote and did not appeal. Ruby had just one kidney and wasn't the tiger she used to be. Her father's death three years ago had hit her harder than anybody else, except maybe Jimmy.

"Whoa," Gracie said, suddenly distracted. She put down her salad and walked into the shed to admire the framework. "You got the central beam in place, and some rafters, oh my . . . oh my. . . . " She noticed the shims and the chisel work. She walked over to the canoe and put her hands on it. It was her touchstone, many people's touchstone, not just in Jinkaat but in Juneau, Haines, Yakutat, Klukwan, Sitka, Angoon, Kake, Saxman, and all the way down to Seattle and beyond. People came to see it, touch it, photograph it, and have their photos taken with "The Canoe That Stole An Airplane," the canoe made famous on television and the Internet. The Burke Museum and the Field Museum had offered to house it and preserve it. Ruby and Gracie said no. It would stay in Jinkaat, in the new Keb Shed, thanks to Anne Bellestraude—wife, mother, biologist, and "kickass community activist," according to Truman.

An activist himself, Truman often talked about taking Stuart and Anne's Little Nancy to New York when she got older, so he might show her the city of his youth, famous for its museums, coffee shops, restaurants, parks and bars, its thinkers, writers, artists, and musicians. He wanted Little Nancy to see it, together with his own remarkable little girl, Rebecca, so bright and earnest, born out of wedlock with Daisy Robinson, a scandal in Jinkaat until people fell in love with Rebecca. Little Nancy and Rebecca were best friends. "Gal pals," Anne called them. Truman wanted them to grow up aware, that's all; he wanted them to see the world.

Forget New York, Oddmund and Dag would say. Keep the girls in Alaska, the last, best place. Teach them to work with their hands, to build boats.

Teach them to be mechanics, Mitch would say. To fix anything.

Teach them basketball and history, Coach Nicks would say.

What kind of history? Truman would ask. History from the bottom up or the top down? You going to teach them about Indians, suffragists, and slaves, or about presidents, generals, and capitalists? Coach Nicks would roll his eyes and say the architects of freedom will always be attacked by people free to do so; that Truman getting his stupid antiwar novel published—*Catch-11, Catch-44, Catch-88*, whatever—was proof that miracles happened.

Helen and Myrtle would teach Little Nancy and Rebecca to cook. Gracie would teach them to pick berries. Jimmy and Kid Hugh would teach them to hunt and fish.

So many teachers, so much to learn.

ANNE ATE A nasturtium flower from the top of Gracie's salad and checked her watch again. Stuart had phoned every day to tell about Little Nancy's happiness with her grandma and grandpa, adding that she missed home terribly. He was a sheriff now, but only after the State of Alaska had put him on probation for a year for tracking two boats with silent beacons without the knowledge and consent of the owners. In the parlance of constitutional law and due process, it was "the fruit of the poisonous tree." Instead of hanging around Jinkaat, Stuart took Anne to Hawaii and proposed marriage atop Mauna Kea, the highest mountain in the world, from base to summit.

"You're standing on top of the world," he told her. "You deserve this."

She cried.

They got married in Jinkaat, with a blessing from Old Keb.

The day his probation ended, Stuart was rehired as the Jinkaat deputy sheriff, and the town threw a big party. Two years later he was promoted to sheriff.

Tommy Gant and Pete Brickman got light sentences, at Stuart's behest, backed by Old Keb who said the best revenge is the one not taken.

Again, Anne checked her watch. *Where are they?*

She watched Gracie run her hands along the posts and beams, the frame-and-panel double doors that opened wide enough to move large carving projects—future dugout canoes—in and out of the shed. "I like the scalloping on these beams," Gracie said.

"Jimmy did that cross-handed with the adz," Ruby said, "same as he did the canoe."

"Pops would love this," Gracie said. "You think so, sis?"

"Absolutely."

OLD KEB HAD lived his final days alone in Ruby's house, on the edge of the clearing, trying his best to beat Daisy at cribbage. He never missed the chance to eat nagoonberry pie. Helen and Galley Sally brought him slices all the time. So while he lived alone, he seldom *was* alone. Visitors were constant. He never locked a door. He died one night in his sleep, the night he managed to get up from his bed, leave the house, walk barefoot to the canoe, climb in, and lie down for the last time under a Chilkat blanket, Keb Zen Raven, Nine and a Half Toes of the Berry Patch.

They found him in the morning. Doctors said he died of no one thing and everything, his entire body worn out by a lifetime of full living. On a small piece of paper found in his hand he had managed to write *kayéil'*, meaning "peace, calm." Anne loved the word because Tlingit for raven was *yéil*; she liked to think that *kayéil'* was Keb's peace raven, the one that lifted him onto its back and took him into another world.

"My grandfather, du daakanóox'u," Jimmy said at his memorial, fighting back tears as he looked out upon an ocean of faces, a sea of beating hearts, hundreds of people, maybe a thousand. "He had no money, but he wasn't poor. He was—" Jimmy choked up.

Ruby was a basket case, and Gracie not much better. Anne was tempted to come to Jimmy's rescue, but it was Little Mac, then a medical student in Los Angeles, who stepped up and took the paper from Jimmy's hand, the eulogy he'd written. "He had no money," she said in a firm voice, "but he wasn't poor. He wasn't poor because he had you and this land, this forest, this sea. He had his home, his friends, and family, his place in this world, this life and beyond. He had stories. He knew who he was and where he belonged, what he stood for. It was everything to him. He was the richest man in Alaska."

Little Nancy was only one year old then. Anne remembered holding her so tight she thought she might crush her. Dear God. On this generous and brilliant home we call earth, we have life and death and the mysterious cycle of things, we have knowing, understanding and comprehension, and a grand design we can simply accept and find in that acceptance not surrender, but achievement. It might quench our thirst for understanding, this acceptance, but does it ever satisfy the desire for *more*? If from death comes new life and rebirths and fresh starts and all that, a linear, circular, triangular, organic whatever, then what does it mean to die? Is Keb the raven in the trees, the eagle on the iceberg, the wolf in the meadow, the bear on the beach, the flower in the forest? If perishing is no more than preservation of some kind, then why is it so hard to say good-bye, to let people and ideas and romance die?

A child of Woodstock, Truman loved to sing the Joni Mitchell song of the same name and put gravel in his voice that he said made him sound like Stephen Stills, though others shook their heads. Still, they sang along, and pounded out a beat. Even Coach Nicks would tap his tool belt.

LUNCH ENDED. EVERYBODY was getting back to work, the Skilsaws and chop saws starting up—Albert cutting compound angles at fifteen and twenty-two and a half degrees—when Stuart drove up. The door flew open and Little Nancy came running. "Mama!" She vaulted off a small wooden box and launched herself at Anne, who caught her like a leaf and spun her around, drawing her near. "Sweetie, you're back."

"I'm back. I've been away with Papa, and now I'm back. I'm home, I'm home." Skinny as a wire, with wheat-colored hair, a sensitive face, dusty blue eyes, and a get-anything-she-wanted smile, Little Nancy looked everything like Stuart and nothing like Anne. Another one of life's mysteries. "I brought you a present. Oops, I forgot, it's supposed to be a surprise."

"Okay, I'll be surprised."

"I missed you."

"I missed you, too." *You are my everything, my world.*

Stuart walked up, a look of deep satisfaction on his face. He kissed Anne.

Little Nancy said, "Is Rebecca here?"

Truman answered, "She's behind Ruby's house, playing. She's expecting you."

"Can I go see Rebecca?" Little Nancy asked her mom.

"You don't want to spend time with me? I haven't seen you in a whole week."

"I know, I will, Mama. I've missed you, but I have to see Rebecca."

"Of course you do."

Anne put her down and watched her run across the clearing to the house.

"She's a firecracker," Vic said.

"She's an only child," Ruby said, and people laughed, Stuart included. He spoiled her and made no apologies for it.

Anne put her arm around his waist; he put his around her shoulder. "C'mon," she said, "let me show you what we're doing here."

USED TO BE it was hard to live and easy to die. Not anymore. Nowadays it was the other way around. Anne smiled in Stuart's embrace, walking through the shed, pointing things out, thinking, yes, there are many questions, some of them aching questions. We really don't have a choice to participate or not, do we? We engage in the mystery and the wonder, the journey and drama, the living, loving, and dying. It's a choice nobody gets to make. It doesn't matter why it works this way. It only matters that it *does* work. If we want to inhabit wonder, we'd better learn as many languages as we can. We'd better meditate on light and leaves and birds and salmon and rain. And whales, of course. Always whales. The world is not ours to be mastered, only cared for. All in all, it's a pretty good deal. This gift of guardianship.

"Hey, Stuart," Jimmy called from atop a ladder, "could you hand me up that four-foot level, and that hammer and chisel?"

Stuart did, and said, "It's looking really good, Bluefeather."

"Oyyee . . . I think Gramps is here with us today, don't you?"

"Yes, he is."

"I have to get these joints just right."

"Yes, you do."

It's all so mysterious, Anne thought. Some days are harder than others; that's just the way it is. But on days like this, it's very clear why we are here, why all of us are here.

TLINGIT GLOSSARY

The following is a list of Tlingit words in addition to
those found in the story.

physical world

áak'w......................pond
at gutú......................woods, wilderness
dleit......................snow
dís......................moon
eech......................rock
éil'......................ocean, salt water
gagaan......................sun
gus'shú......................horizon
héen sháak......................river, head of

héen wantú......................riverbank
héen wát......................river, mouth of
kagán......................light
kagít......................darkness
shaa......................mountain
sít'......................glacier
té......................stone
tl'átk......................land, earth
xáatl......................iceberg

animal world

cháatl......................halibut
dagitgiyáa......................hummingbird
gáax'w......................herring eggs
gooch......................wolf
ishkeen......................black cod (sablefish)
kaashaashxáat'......................dragonfly
kageet......................loon
kaháakw......................fish eggs
kaax......................merganser
kéet......................killer whale (orca)
kichyaat......................tern
k'wát'......................bird's egg
lugán......................tufted puffin
nóoskw......................wolverine
saak......................eulachon (candlefish)

s'aak......................bone
s'áaw......................crab, Dungeness
s'eek......................bear, black
shé......................blood
s'ook......................barnacle
t'á......................king salmon
tayataayí......................sea anemone
ts'ítskw......................songbird
xóots......................bear, brown
yaaw......................herring
yáay......................whale
yáxwch'......................sea otter
yéin......................sea cucumber

people

al'óoni .... hunter
asgeiwú .... seine fisherman
ashalxóot'i .... sport fisherman
ast'eixí .... troller
at layeixí .... carpenter
at kach'áak'u .... wood carver
du dachxán .... his/her grandchild
du éesh .... his/her father
du shagóon .... his/her ancestor
du tláa .... his/her mother
du xux .... her husband
du yéet .... his/her son

káa .... man
kashxeedí .... writer (scribe)
k'idaaká aa .... neighbor
kóo at latéewu .... teacher
sh yáa.awudanéiyi
.... respected person
shaawát .... woman
shaatk'átsk'u .... girl
yaa at naskwéini ... student
yaakw yasatáni ..... captain of a boat
yadak'wátsk'u .... boy
yanwáat .... adult

carpentry/construction

jishagóon .... tools
néegwál' .... paint
shanaxwáayi .... axe
sh daxash washéen
.... chain saw
tákl .... hammer

téeyaa .... chisel
xáshaa .... saw
x'éex'u .... shim
xút 'aa .... adz(e)
yees .... wedge

numbers

tléix' .... one
déix .... two
nás'k .... three
daax'oon .... four
keijín .... five
tleidooshú .... six
daxadooshú .... seven

nas'gadooshú .... eight
gooshúk .... nine
jinkaat .... ten
jinkaat ka tléix' .... eleven
tleikáa .... twenty
tléináx káa .... one person
dáxnáx káa .... two people

ceremony, spirit, life & death

at wuskóowu	witness
at shí	music, singing
gaax	cry
héi**x**waa	magic
íxt'	medicine man
kootéeyaa	totem pole
ku.éex'	potlatch (party)
kusaxán	love
laaxw	famine
latseen	power, strength
lékwaa	spirit (fighting spirit)
naná	death
sagú	joy
tá	sleep
tula.aan	kindness
yéik	spirit (Indian doctor's spirit)

time

kutaan	summer
nisdaat	last night
seigán	tomorrow
táakw	winter
taakw eetí	spring
taat	night
tatgé	yesterday
yakyee	day, afternoon
yeedát	now
yeis	autumn

Author's Note

Certain source materials were invaluable in writing this story: *English/Tlingit Dictionary, Nouns,* printed at Sheldon Jackson College, 1976; *Tlingit Verb Dictionary,* compiled by Gillian L. Story and Constance M. Naish at the Summer Institute of Linguistics, University of Alaska's Alaska Native Language Center, 1973; *Being and Place Among the Tlingit* by Thomas F. Thornton, University of Washington Press, 2008; *The Tlingit, An Introduction to Their Culture and History,* by Wallace M. Olson, Heritage Research, Auke Bay, Juneau, 2004; *The Tlingit Indians* by George Thornton Emmons, American Museum of Natural History (#70 in the Anthropological Papers), 1991; *Cedar: Tree of Life to the Northwest Coast Indians,* by Hilary Stewart, University of Washington Press, 1984; *Qayaks & Canoes: Native Ways of Knowing,* by Jan Steinbright (photography by Clark Mishler), Graphic Arts Center Pub. Co., 2002; *Tlingit Place Names of the Huna Káawu,* a 2006 map by the Hoonah Indian Association with assistance from the U.S. National Park Service; *Tongass Timber, A History of Logging & Timber Utilization in Southeast Alaska,* by James (Jim) Mackovjak, Forest History Society, 2010.

At times I use outdated names. Winter wren versus Pacific wren, for example, given that Keb Wisting, as an old man, would probably be unaware of a new name, or unwilling to accept it. He'd have known the bird by its earlier English name (and of course its Tlingit name) for most of his adult life. While taxonomists often change the common names of species, indigenous peoples do not. For them, names—and the acts of naming and being named—are often sacred. As for the practice of using an adz cross-handed, I've seen it done only once, in Alert Bay, British Columbia. It so impressed me that I integrated it into Old Keb's teachings for James, to set him apart from other carvers. Certain elements in the Pepper Mountain logging accident are contrived to make the plotline work. And certain clans and places within the geography of this novel I leave undiscussed (e.g. Mount Fairweather) as they have great Tlingit cultural and spiritual significance and are best addressed from that point of view exclusively by Tlingits.

Because languages represent the intellectual legacy of humanity, and are disappearing rapidly around the world, a percentage of the royalties from this book are dedicated to an organization devoted to preserving the Tlingit language.

Acknowledgments

It took twelve years and many revisions to write this book. George and Jessie Dalton (in Hoonah and Glacier Bay) introduced me to the power and beauty of the Tlingit canoe culture, and the importance of storytelling, seal hunting, and berry picking. Melanie, my wife, believed in Old Keb from the beginning. Dan Henry (in Haines), Wayne Howell, Greg Streveler and Hank Lentfer (in Gustavus), and Richard Nelson (in Sitka) offered sage and sincere advice. Carvers Nathan Jackson (Saxman), Tommy Joseph (Sitka), and Lou Cacioppo (Gustavus) inspired me with their artistry and skills. An additional nod to Lou for showing me the many exquisite details in a raven's plumage. Ken Grant and Gus Martinez (both with the National Park Service in Glacier Bay) helped me: Ken with Tlingit sensibilities, Gus with law enforcement matters. Ben Stroecker (Gustavus) set me straight on commercial fishing. Dawn Morano, Jane Rosenman, and Nick Jans made valuable suggestions. Elizabeth Kaplan, my wonderful literary agent, read *Jimmy Bluefeather* in three days and embraced it with great love and commitment. After many publishers said no (I've saved their rejections, laminated them, and intend to put them on the walls of my outhouse), Doug Pfeiffer at Alaska Northwest Books rescued this story from the wood-burning stove and gave it a good home, perhaps even a long life. Kathy Howard and Tina Morgan made valuable edits. Vicki Knapton and Angie Zbornik also made strong contributions. The Gustavus City Library provided friendly shelter and good Internet connectivity. Finally, several works of fiction inspired me to write a cross-cultural story with a protagonist whose life experiences and worldview were far different from my own: *Cannery Row* by John Steinbeck, *The Milagro Beanfield War* by John Nichols, *The Confessions of Nat Turner* by William Styron, *The Help* by Kathryn Stockett, *The Century Trilogy* by Ken Follett, *The Adventures of Huckleberry Finn* by Mark Twain, and *Hamlet* by William Shakespeare. Imagine an Englishman writing about a tormented Danish prince. All things considered, he did well. Thank you friends, mentors, and exemplars. In the end, I believe our similiarities far outweigh our differences, and nothing matters more than compassion and love.

Kim Heacox
Gustavus, Alaska
21 December 2014

Jimmy Bluefeather Q&A

Q: Alaska roots this novel and plays a large part in the overall story line. How does the perception of Alaska as a kind of mysterious and remote place play a part in *Jimmy Bluefeather*? Why can't the story have happened anywhere else?

A: This story is an after-image of the ice age. It's set in a wild coastal world of storms, bears, mountains, whales, temperate rain forests, and tidewater glaciers. It's set in Alaska, the America-that-used to-be, where rivers of ice run from the mountains down to the sea, and calve massive pieces of themselves into inlets and fjords, and create icebergs that provide nursery platforms for seals to give birth to their pups. It's a land of eagles and ravens, of rebirth and resilience; a coming-back-to-life place in the wake of a massive glacial retreat. As such, that resilience infuses everybody who lives there, even an old man like Keb Wisting. The land itself, cut and carved by glaciers, is still youthful and wild, patterned by the tracks of wolves and bears. It inspires him to be young again, to finish carving his last canoe and take off, undaunted by the wind or rain. Such a thing could hardly happen in a cornfield or a city, in a shopping mall or a subdivision.

Q: What was your biggest challenge in writing about Keb? Is there another character you enjoyed bringing to life?

A: First, to endear the readers to him; make him likeable, believable. Second, to cross the age and culture barriers with accuracy and respect. I'm not Norwegian, Tlingit, or ninety-five years old. I've spent time with Norwegians (been to Norway several times) and with Tlingit elders (living as I do in Southeast Alaska) and always found them to be engaging, quick-witted (often with great senses of humor), soft-spoken, and wise; rooted in the past, yes, but also much more attuned to modern life than you'd think . . . knowledgeable about things like politics and basketball. I also enjoyed developing Anne as a character, since the novel moves from Keb's point of view to hers. I enjoyed writing about her budding romance with Stuart, something I didn't have in earlier drafts.

Q: What was the genesis of publishing *Jimmy Bluefeather*?

A: I began writing it in September 2002 and finished the first draft in three years, and put it away (thinking: *Yikes, what have I just done?*). Months later I reread it with new eyes, cut it by 20 percent, filled out a few characters and scenes, and tried to sell it. Rejections rolled in, many on beautiful letterhead (all rejections today come by e-mail and make less interesting keepsakes, unless they're brilliantly written—few are). I hired a manuscript doctor, revised it again, tried selling it, hired another manuscript doctor, added a new epilogue, let it sit for another year, then found a literary agent—Elizabeth Kaplan—who read it in three days and loved it. More rejections. I let another year or two go by, and revised it again. Random House and Henry Holt came close to taking it. Then one day, almost as an afterthought, I sent the manuscript to Doug Pfeiffer at Alaska Northwest Books ("Hey, Doug, how are you? Look what I've been working on."). I've known Doug for twenty-five years, but wasn't sure he was interested in publishing fiction. He loved it, made an offer, and here we are. My advice to writers: write for the joy of it, not to be rich or famous (whatever that is). Tell a good story. And never give up.

Q: Could you discuss the transformation of the relationship between Keb and James as the story evolves?

A: Through a profound experience (the canoe journey) they come to understand and trust each other, and develop great respect for each other. It's not an easy transformation, just as travel by canoe is not always easy. It's hard, and it's the "hard" that makes it great. Early on, Keb dislikes much of what he sees in James. James in turn regards his grandfather as a relic waiting to die. They love each other, of course, but they don't easily relate to each other. The canoe—and wild Alaska—changes all that. The story opens in May and closes in September, and a lot happens in that time. Not until a later draft did I land on the epilogue, with the rebuilding of the Keb Shed, and James (Jimmy) using his hands so artfully, beginning to show the mannerisms and speech of his grandfather.

Q: Is there a symbolism between James and the Canoe?

A: Yes, the canoe is James's new legs. It's his new freedom and identity after ruining his leg (and basketball career) in a logging accident. The idea of the canoe floating above all his grief—the ocean of his loss—appeals to me. I've known young athletes who've suddenly faced the end of their careers. It devastates them. They struggle for years, if not entire lifetimes, to find themselves again. The canoe saves James; it gives him new purpose. It allows him to work with his hands, to paddle into his terror and his potential, to become an artist in a new and rewarding way, one that will enrich the rest of his life.

Q: You discuss the struggle between tribal and environmental issues. How does that affect the story? Is this happening in current news?

A: Keb's two daughters, Ruby and Gracie, see things differently. They love each other, but don't always respect each other. This breaks Keb's heart. His three sons are dead. Ruby and Gracie are his only remaining children, and he wants them to get along. He wants peace in his family. But large modern forces get in the way: politics and power, primarily, built on the idolatry of money, which in turn is built on an economic model that's addicted to growth and never full, never satisfied. Ruby is pro-Native corporation while Gracie is not. This goes back to the 1971 Alaska Native Claims Settlement Act that created a dozen regional Native corporations and 200-plus village Native corporations across the state. While Ruby and Gracie both want to return to their ancient homeland, Crystal Bay, Ruby wants to capitalize on its mining and tourism potential, while Gracie wants to take kids and elders there to pick berries and maybe one day hunt and fish (ceremonially) as in the ways of old. Then along comes Keb who goes back in his own way, by canoe, something nobody's done in recent memory. Many Tlingits today talk about going back to their ancient homeland, but nobody does it in the ancient way, by canoe. In fact, the art of canoe carving is largely gone today. So to think of an old man finishing his last canoe and taking off for the glaciers that shaped the geography that shaped him—I found this a powerful story line to explore.

Q: What's up with Steve?

A: Ah, yes, Steve the Lizard Dog. People love dogs. I think a good story can be improved by a quirky, endearing dog. Look at Snoopy in the cartoon strip *Peanuts*. He's comical but also wise. Look at John Muir and Stickeen and their amazing adventure together on the Brady Glacier in 1880. I brought along Steve to help develop all the other characters in the town of Jinkaat, and in the canoe: Old Keb, James, Kid Hugh, and Little Mac. Each has his/her own relationship with Steve, and that's fun. Also, early on we discover that Steve irritates some people, but not Keb. Keb likes him, and sees his goodness. This helps to develop Keb and Steve as characters that benefit from each other's company.

Q: How does *Jimmy Bluefeather* shed light on Alaska Native tradition and perception of family and place? How are they caught between times and places and how are they meshing them together?

A: For thousands of years the Native peoples of the great canoe cultures of the northwest coast of North America lived extraordinary lives, traveling far, living large. They read the tides and stars and storms; they knew every plant, every track in the sand, every salmon stream and red cedar grove. In the novel I describe Keb and his cohort as being "liquid people" who wore the rain like a second skin. In just a couple hundred years (1780s—1980s) all that changed. The canoe culture is largely gone now, and with it some of the wisdom it engendered. Yet Keb still has it in his bones and blood, from his childhood. He was born just in time to live the last vestiges of it. I created Keb to bring the canoe culture back, to represent a piece of that past that lives on, despite all the distractions and trappings of modern civilization and runaway consumerism.

Q: Of all the wisdom Keb shares, which predominant life lesson(s) would you like readers to take away?

A: Don't die before you're dead. Most of your limitations are in your head. Dig deep and live young, even when you're old. Find what you're most passionate about (in Keb's case, carving a canoe and traveling by canoe), and do it. Honor the past and where you came from without being blinded by ideology and too much money; stay open to new ideas and other ways of seeing and being, to what's really true. Honor and caretake the elderly but surround yourself with young people. Be thankful. Live in gratitude. It's seldom too late to be young again, to find the vibrant you that you might have stopped being long ago. Oh yes, and don't let anybody take away your language, force you to wear tight shoes, or put too much sugar in your nagoonberry pie.

Discussion Questions

1. Were you immediately hooked by Keb Wisting and drawn into the story or did it take a while to relate to this unique character? Why?

2. Alaska roots this novel and plays a large part in the overall story line. How does the perception of Alaska as a mysterious and remote place play a part? Could the story have happened anywhere else?

3. Discuss the transformation of the relationship between Keb and James as the story evolves.

4. How does the struggle between tribal and environmental issues affect the story? If similar conflicts are happening where you live, what impacts have they had on you?

5. How does *Jimmy Bluefeather* shed light on Alaska Native tradition and perception of family and place? How are they caught between times and places and how are they meshing them together?

6. Is there a symbolism between James and the canoe?

7. What do you think Steve the dog adds to the story?

8. Can you imagine yourself as a character in *Jimmy Bluefeather*? If so, which one? Or would you be a new character? What role would you play in the story?

9. There are numerous quotes in the book that Kim Heacox has dubbed "Kebisms"—which, if any, resonate for you?

10. If you were to talk with the author, what would you want to know? (Feel free to contact Kim Heacox direct @JimmyBluefeather on Facebook.)

ON HEAVEN'S HILL

If you enjoyed *Jimmy Bluefeather*, consider reading author Kim Heacox's next Alaska novel, *On Heaven's Hill*, named by the *Anchorage Daily News* as "a favorite book of 2023." Kim calls it a "sequel-lite," as it's set in the Icy Strait region of Alaska and reprises several characters from *Jimmy Bluefeather*. See if you can find them.

On Heaven's Hill (its title taken from a Dylan Thomas poem) is also very much a stand-alone story told from three alternating points-of-view: that of a wolf named Silver, a trapper named Salt, and a pre-teen girl named Kes (short for Kestrel). Each character gets his or her own chapter (Silver, Salt, Kes... Silver, Salt, Kes...) throughout the entire novel. As the story progresses, the characters intersect in surprising and exciting ways.

Kim was inspired to construct *On Heaven's Hill* this way by two other novels that use the same literary device: *Cold Mountain* (1997), an American Civil War story by Charles Frazier, and *All the Light We Cannot See* (2014), a World War II story by Anthony Doerr (mostly set in France).

On Heaven's Hill and Kim's other books can be ordered through his website, www.kimheacox.com, or directly from Bookshop, Amazon, and most independent and chain bookstores.

Read on for a sneak peek and critical reviews of the novel.

CHAPTER ONE

Silver

Late again.

The wolf pup, far behind his pack, follows the river through a tangle of young cottonwood, the leaves golden medallions in the September rain. He works the ground with his big paws and keen nose. Wet ears. Searching eyes. Great heart. No stranger to hunger, he moves from one distraction to the next. A dusting of silver-black in the shoulders. A touch of russet in his lower flanks. All black in the legs and feet. "A real beauty," men will say of him. Men with a hunger of their own, their hearts made of light and stone.

He follows the scents of moose and geese, circles, and moves on. Hunting. Listening. Working the air with his nose. Were he among his littermates, born this past spring, he'd play all day. But he's alone now. As such, he must be mature for his age, mindful in a way that doesn't create panic but instead makes him smart. Far ahead somewhere, his family travels in single file, fast and distant with the distance growing. The rain has washed away all but the faintest traces of their passing. Whenever his pack travels like this, Alpha and Mother and the subadults all work together to keep Old One up front so as to not leave him behind. As tough and determined as Old One is, his age slows him down.

Silver hurries on.

Mother must have lost track of him. It's happened before. And she'd always come back for him and grab him by the nape of his neck—he was so little then—and carry him to where they needed to go.

He's bigger now, growing fast. And hungry. Often hungry.

He emerges from a willow thicket and climbs a gentle slope onto a long, flat nothingness that reaches from one horizon to the other, its surface lifeless, hard, and dark. And worse: foreboding somehow, with strange marks down the middle. He holds still for a moment, as if death might speak and tell him what happened here.

How far does the nothingness go? And to where?

He travels upon it a short distance, then drops downslope and rejoins the river—so exuberant and free-flowing by comparison—and heads downstream, unaware that by traveling over the flat nothingness, he's crossed the river where his family did not and is now on the opposite side from them.

He hears a strange sound, and stops. From behind a veil of willow he watches a shiny object cross the river over the flat nothingness, moving fast without wings or legs.

Silver continues on, following the river that's fed by many small tributaries, growing as it goes. Again, he gets distracted as he tests rounded stones underfoot—rolls them back and forth with a nimble paw—and picks up the scent of a bear, then something else. Otter, perhaps. The river bends in a set of rapids, uncoiling over ancient scripts and hidden texts from the Ice Age. This is where his family would chase salmon and pin them in the shallows—and feast. The pup feels an ache in his belly. Hunger.

He thinks all wolves eat salmon.

He thinks with his stomach.

ONWARD. The rain lightens. The sky brightens. A strong smell assaults the young wolf. He pauses as fear rises in his throat, a fear new to him yet somehow familiar from long ago. He's never smelled smoke. Never seen a man. Never tasted human kindness, cruelty, or greed, never mapped the soulful intelligence between their needs and his. That will change.

A raven flies low overhead, circles, and continues on.

The rain stops.

He climbs a cut bank, and sits, and begins to yip, his face turned to the somber clouds. Were he older, he'd howl and sing. Were he older, like his elders, he'd dream of mammoths, and of taking down a moose, and leading his pack through this wet, blue-green world of forests, glaciers, tides, and fish.

For now, though, he yips.

After a minute or so he stops, and listens. Then he yips again.

Soon it will come—the reply.

The chorus of his clan.

CHAPTER TWO

Salt

SALT D'ALENE STEPS back to admire his work.

The Sitka spruce wheelchair ramp climbs at ten degrees, makes a less than elegant 180-degree turn, and continues up to the deck, four feet off the ground, where Salt has yet to finish the handrail. He can hear Hannah already, hours from now, when she returns home with the boys. It's nice, love, she'll say. But won't the boys fall off it? Of course they will, Salt will tell her. They're rowdy and carefree. Have faith. They'll land on their feet. And if they don't, they'll land on their heads. They have hard heads.

The concern, of course, is Solomon in his wheelchair, with his brothers—especially Abraham, the eldest—racing him around, and Solomon laughing and screaming gleefully, asking for more, breathless without ever getting to his feet. Duchenne muscular dystrophy. One chance in thirty-five thousand that a boy his age will get it. And Solomon got it.

Why? Hannah asked one night in bed a couple years ago, not long after the genetic testing, the muscle biopsy, and Solomon's diagnosis. Would he even live to age twenty? Why our son? Our beautiful son. Why... why... why? She began to cry. He's exceptional, Salt told her as he fought back his own tears. That's why. He's one in a million, a gift from God. He's our son—our sun, the brightest star in the sky.

Yes, she said. Our sun. And she cried herself to sleep.

AGAIN, SALT TAKES stock of his carpentry. *Not bad*, he thinks. *Not so good either. Many of the joints could be tighter. But they'll hold. Structural integrity, that's the important thing.*

Later, while making a difficult compound cut with the chop saw and unsure of what he's doing, Salt takes a break. He's tempted to drive over to Willynillyville, the veteran encampment only a couple miles away, founded by the bush pilot Tyler Nash. There, he could ask for help from Nash's buddies, the McCall cousins, Chippy and Cap, former Oklahoma Thunderbirds who served in Afghanistan and are said to be the best carpenters in Strawberry Flats. People say Chippy uses old, gnarled shore pines to make beautiful bannisters and handrails; that he has a fully outfitted carpentry shop and enjoys giving tours. *How good it would be to get some strong advice; to build something beyond functional. To make art.*

Salt has never been to Willynillyville. Never had a good talk with any of the war veterans there. Never apprenticed himself to a true craftsman.

He could be there in ten minutes. Drop by. Give his regards. Ask a question or two. Maybe have a few laughs. Make new friends.

But he talks himself out of it.

"You're shy," his mother used to tell him in Idaho, back when he was a teenager. "And that's fine,' she'd add, "until it keeps you from realizing your potential."

The last time I was an artist, Salt tells himself, *I was a trapper.*

Rumors around town say Tyler Nash is down in Texas with his younger brother, a former singer/songwriter who had his own band and touring bus and recording contract until he joined the National Guard for some crazy reason—extra money, no doubt—and got shipped off to Afghanistan. Three weeks later, he got blown up.

AS HE REACHES to put his earmuffs on to make the compound cut, Salt hears a sound familiar to him from the cabin life he knew on Minto Flats, near Fairbanks. Interior Alaska, another world, where the winters aren't as cold as they used to be, and river ice cannot be trusted, and one wrong step is all it takes—for both wolf and man. Where wild animals know a hundred times more than we ever will. Be careful not to look them in the eye. They'll take your stare and turn it back on you.

Salt listens. Another howl—not distant, not near.

A third.

A fourth.

He smiles. *Now that's something I haven't heard in a while.*

CHAPTER THREE

Kes

"HE'S STILL IN THERE."

Again and again, Papa's doctors say this down in sunny San Antonio, at the Brooke Army Medical Center, as if words themselves were bandages.

Eleven-year-old Kes Nash sits next to her stepmother, Rita, and feels the room begin to spin, her stomach turn. *Where in there?* she wonders. *Is he going to be okay?*

And now in another office, for another consultation, another doctor is talking about "blast concussive trauma" and Papa's "complicated impaired blood flow" and his "clinical picture" and "bilateral involvement." The doctor finally says, "Not to worry, Mrs. Nash. He's still in there. The shattered legs are stable right now, free of infection. We'll deal with them later. Our chief concern is the trauma to his frontal lobe and to his ear and eye, and any stenosis that may have caused anoxia."

"Anoxia?" Rita asks.

"Lack of oxygen to the brain," the doctor explains. "The SCA—the subclavian artery—doesn't directly provide blood to the brain. The left and right carotid vertebral arteries do that. But damage to the SCA can redirect blood from the vertebral arteries, resulting in vertebrobasilar insufficiency. That's why the shoulder wound concerns us. If you're going to have damage to the head, the frontal lobe is the place to have it because of all its redundant systems. In that regard, your husband is lucky."

Lucky? Kes looks out the big windows, hoping to see a butterfly, a bird, a tree.

The doctor adds that the field report from Afghanistan had noted that the first thing an Army medic told Papa as he lay dying on the dusty ground, blown to bits, was this: "Stay with me, soldier. Don't close your eyes. Because if you do, you might never reopen them."

Kes rocks with unease. Rita grabs her hand and says, "He's going to be all right, honey. Your papa… he's going to make it."

Don't lie to me, Kes wants to scream. At Rita. At everybody. At the whole stupid world. *Don't lie to me.*

She gets up and leaves, and joins Uncle Ty, Papa's older brother, out in the waiting lounge. A pilot with his own Cessna down from his homestead in Alaska, Uncle Ty wears a red bandana on his head and has a missing front tooth, like a pirate. She sits next to him, opposite her grandpa. Uncle Ty wraps an arm around her, and asks, "What's the latest?"

"They're worried about his brain."

Uncle Ty nods.

"Please don't tell me he's going to be okay."

Another nod.

"I hate lies," Kes adds.

Uncle Ty gives her a hard look. "People here don't lie, Kes."

She shrugs.

"He's still alive, isn't he?" Uncle Ty says softly, cajolingly. "He has no spinal cord injuries. He has no inner organ injuries… none that we know of, anyway."

But will he ever sing again? Laugh again? Play music again? Write another song? Take me hiking, river rafting, birding?

Grandpa sits opposite Kes and her uncle. He appears stone faced, much older than he was a few days ago. Kes hears herself ask, "Are you okay, Grandpa?" Her own voice sounds distant and weak, as if about to blow away, as if her body and soul were made of ashes.

"I'm fine."

Grandpa doesn't look fine. He looks like he might die of sadness, his face white as chalk. He fought in Vietnam and still thinks the US could have won over there if we'd dropped more bombs. He's the one who convinced Papa to join the Texas National Guard for extra money after little Kipper was born and Papa's music career stalled.

"We're a family of patriots," Grandpa had said one night many months ago in the kitchen, back in Lubbock. Kes had eavesdropped from around the corner, unable to sleep.

Later, Rita begged Papa not to join. The other band members too. Stringer, the bass player, Kes's favorite because of how he would read Dr. Seuss to her on the band bus, using funny voices that made her laugh. He always said Danny and Rita were just one hit song away from big money and fame, and nobody in Texas wrote better songs than Danny Nash. But Stringer had been saying things like that for years as he lived in an old funky trailer outside Lubbock and ate cold refried beans from a can.

Later, Uncle Ty, talking about Grandpa, had told Papa, "The old man is crazy, little brother. We all know that. Too much John Wayne and *Top Gun* and Agent Orange. Don't do it. Come live with me and the other guys in Alaska. Bring Rita and the kids."

"It's the National Guard," Papa replied to Uncle Ty, flashing his trademark Nash smile. "It's only one weekend a month. I'll end up defending Texas from Louisiana. Or piling sand bags on a levee. Or working crowd control at an Aggie-Tech game."

"You'll end up in Afghanistan," Uncle Ty said.

Sure enough.

Beginning in Germany, from what Kes had gathered, a team of Army doctors had worked to save Papa, to relieve the pressure on his brain. Keep him on oxygen. Save his eye. They'd rebuilt his face and ear by grafting in new bone, cartilage, and skin. They'd shaved his head, cut him open, and bandaged him up. More surgeries were yet to come, each one followed by CT scans and more tests. Days. Weeks.

And again, they said Papa was lucky. Others died, all in a single Humvee. He lost three brothers that day, men in the same unit. That's what the military does, Uncle Ty says: it forges men into a band of brothers.

SOMETIME LATER, asleep in a lounge chair, Kes startles awake when Uncle Ty takes a call on his phone. "Hey Chippy," she hears him say as he gets up and walks away, headed down the sterile Brooke corridor past legless men in wheelchairs, his collared shirt untucked, his blue jeans tattered and faded to gray. Flip-flops on his feet.

What time is it? Kes sees Rita thumbing through a magazine. Little Kipper sits on her lap, innocent as a baby bird. Kes rubs her eyes, gets up, and walks to a bathroom where she dabs her face with cool water. She stares into the unforgiving mirror and sees nothing new: burnished red hair knotted behind her neck, a lightly freckled face, sad, gray-green eyes. She wonders if she'll ever be pretty, and happy. From her small purse she pulls out a tattered photo of Papa when he was young, and of Mom—Kes's first mom, her birth mom—sitting in his lap, the two of them laughing. Taken the year before Kes was born, six years before her birth mom died. Long before Papa met Rita and they began writing songs and singing together, and drawing big crowds.

Kes bends down to drink and is startled to see bright drops of blood on the bathroom's white tile floor. She draws back and wills herself to stay calm. *Breathe.* She leans against the wall, closes her eyes, and lightly taps her forehead, temple, chin, and sternum with her middle finger—an exercise Rita taught her to help keep her heart from racing. She hears soft sobbing coming from one of the toilet stalls. Quickly, she leaves the bathroom and returns to the others.

She still hasn't seen Papa. "Is he still in surgery?" she hears herself ask Rita.

Rita strokes little Kipper's hair. Grandpa sleeps sitting up, his chin on his chest.

"Yes," Rita says, her voice thin. "Still in surgery."

Uncle Ty returns with his phone in hand. "I just heard from the guys up in Willynillyville," he says with a twinkle in his eye. "They heard wolves, a whole pack of 'em, howling from across the river. I'm telling you, Rita, wolves make music too. Alaska is the place to be."

"I can't think of that now," she says. "Danny's in surgery. You know that, right?"

"Absolutely," Uncle Ty says. "And I know my brother has a huge spirit, a huge will to live. He'll get better. He will. And Alaska is calling." When Rita raises her weary head and stares at him, Uncle Ty asks, "What's the worst that could happen?"

Rita thinks for a minute. "We could all freeze to death."

"Okay," Uncle Ty says with a grin. "What's the second worst thing that could happen?"

Praise for *On Heaven's Hill*

"The novel's painterly prose evokes Alaska as a place of great beauty and scarcity...a well-plotted tale of frontier utopianism that should appeal to nature lovers." —KIRKUS

"A sprawling novel brimming with suspense, ideas and unforgettable characters, *On Heaven's Hill* paints a captivating group portrait of a rebel alliance discovering their true selves in America's most glorious natural landscape. This book will appeal equally to aging idealists reared on Edward Abbey and adventurous kids hooked on Gary Paulsen. Oh, and it's laugh-out-loud funny, too."
—MARK ADAMS, *New York Times* bestselling author of *Tip of the Iceberg* and *Turn Right at Machu Picchu*

"Kim Heacox poses the age-old question—what price progress?—with new urgency in *On Heaven's Hill*, his compelling novel of an Alaskan hamlet whose remote location is no defense against big-money development. All that stands in its way is a pack of wolves and the twelve-year-old girl determined to save them. Reminiscent of John Nichols' *The Milagro Beanfield War*, Heacox deftly weaves lyrical tributes to the healing power of nature with a fast-paced plot that builds to a heart-pounding conclusion."
—GWEN FLORIO, author of *Silent Hearts* and the Lola Wicks series

"A dazzling tale of a young girl, a desperate father, and a silver wolf caught in the middle of a battle between an Alaskan band of war veterans and corrupt land developers. Another compelling read from the author of *Jimmy Bluefeather* and *The Only Kayak*."
—LYNNE M. SPREEN, author of *Dakota Blues* and *We Did This Once Before*

"Kim Heacox is the bard of Alaska, drawing stories from the power and music of the land itself. His new book, *On Heaven's Hill*, is truly a novel to match Alaska's mountains. The braided plot runs fast. The characters are broken and shining, as if eroded to their cores. The language calls out with rain-carved clarity. And the truth that the novel tells is both eternal and seismic: a girl, a wounded vet, and a hungry wolf all come to know that in our struggle to heal the reeling world, we may find a chance, maybe a last chance, to heal ourselves."
—KATHLEEN DEAN MOORE, author of *Earth's Wild Music*

Printed in the USA
CPSIA information can be obtained
at www.ICGtesting.com
JSHW012022140824
68134JS00033B/2818

9 781943 328710